Beg(ga)(he)r

Beg(ga)(he)r

J.R. Armstrong

Willowrose Publishing
Fowlerville, Michigan

All rights reserved. Published in the United States by Willowrose Publishing

www.jrarmstrong.net

Cataloguing-in-Publication Data

Armstrong, J. R. (Janice R.)
   Beg(ga)(he)r / J.R. Armstrong. — 1st ed. —Fowlerville, Mich. :
Willowrose Pub., c2013.
      p. ; cm.

      ISBN 978-0-9822299-4-1

   1. Female friendship—Fiction. 2. Vacations—Idaho—Fiction.
3. Impersonation—Fiction. 4. Women—Fiction. 5. Mystery fiction. I. Title.
II. Title: Beg ga he r. III. Title: Beggaher.

   PS3601.R5761 B44 2013   2013937439
   813/.6—dc23   1306

Printed in the United States of America

First Edition

COVER DESIGN BY SARAH THOMAS
TEXT DESIGN BY TO THE POINT SOLUTIONS
EDITING BY MARY JO ZAZUETA

Other books by J.R. Armstrong

OWE IT TO THE WIND

TRULY, EVERYTHING

To my "Sisters."
Those I travel with and those who have cheered me on with
e-mails, phone calls, and through Facebook.

'ly,

J.R.

Acknowledgments

My sincere appreciation to the three people—my husband, Will, and friends Julia Kraus and Cathy Skelton—who took the time to read my manuscript and offer comments, thank you.

I want to send out a big thank you to the MSU Womens Rowing and a special thank you to Christiina Donley for answering my many questions.

To Marion Cornett—thanks for the two great ideas!

To my writing group—thanks for being honest and helping me to grow.

To Tom Skelton—I haven't been up in a small airplane since I was a kid and watched my mom turn green. Thank you for answering all my questions and for taking me up on a beautiful fall day.

Beg(ga)(he)r

Other ideas—

Beg Her to Leave

Beg Her to Stay

Beg Her to Die

Beg Her to Marry

Beggar on the Street

The Beggar and the Coach Purse

The Beggar and the Borrower

The Beggar and the Banker

The Beggar in the Dumpster

The Coach Purse Beggar

Prologue

She stared dreamily out the kitchen window while she did the breakfast dishes. She smiled to herself and put her hand on the wall. The kitchen window was, in actuality, a painting her mother and she had done two years ago. In the four panes they painted what they wanted to see if it had been a real window. Her mother had drawn a lilac bush in bloom and a horse she used to ride.

But she had dreamed of faraway places, places she knew she'd never see. One pane was of the ocean and the other was a picture of Italy she had copied out of a book from the library. She still hoped to travel someday . . .

She returned to the dishes, almost done. As she thought about her mom, the depression surrounded her. She was never going to travel. She remembered once seeing a tombstone that had made her laugh: She finally got to go somewhere. *Well, Mom, you finally got to go somewhere and I'm still—*

What in the world? She shut off the water and listened.

"Give it back!" she heard her older brother scream loud and clear from the other room. "It's mine! Give it back!"

She heard their neighbor laugh and then suddenly something—someone?—slammed up against the wall and a cry of pain. *Were they beating each other? Well, this was new. The great friends weren't such great friends today, huh? Still, they could at least behave like the adults they were supposed to be.*

She grabbed the baseball bat she kept nearby whenever their neighbor was over and made her way into her brother's bedroom. The man was no friend of hers. "What are you two idiots—" she stopped in midsentence.

1

Her brother wiped blood from his nose. Their neighbor turned to face her. He didn't look much better.

"Hello," he said quietly as he started towards her. "Don't think I can't get rid of you, too."

"Get out!" yelled her brother. "Get out now!"

She wasn't sure which one of them he meant.

Their neighbor hadn't seen the bat. As he brought his hands up to put around her throat, she jabbed hard, connecting with his ribs. *Oh, I have been waiting so long to do that!*

The man howled as he crumbled. Her brother grabbed him and threw his now former friend against the wall. He had been so betrayed. He then walked over and rummaged around in the man's front pant's pocket and pulled out a small object. Staggering, he walked back to his sister and held up a key.

"Take it and go." His breathing was labored as he pressed a hand against his side.

She simply stood there, her mouth moving with nothing coming out. What was he talking about? He knew how ill-equipped she was to function outside the apartment. Especially with Mom not there to help her. Where did he expect her to go? For how long? What was going on? *What was he thinking?*

Her brother looked back to see their neighbor slowly coming around. He whirled on her. "NOW!"

She dropped the bat, ripped the key out of his hand, ran to her bedroom, and grabbed the only thing remaining that she cared about. It squawked at her, reminding her to grab his food.

"Don't ever come back!" followed her as she fled out the apartment door.

"You'll pay for this!" Did their neighbor mean her, her brother, or both of them?

She hurried as fast as she could, with the additional weight she carried, down the stairs and let out a terrified scream when the door that led outside suddenly opened and she came face to face with—

Chapter One

"If you don't get downstairs this instant, you will be late!" he hollered. He loved how she ignored him. Setting his jaw he hollered once again. "Seriously, we need to leave, *now!*"

Silence.

When he entered the bedroom, she was nowhere in sight.

He heard her swear and followed the direction of her voice. Getting down on his hands and knees, he pulled up the bed skirt. She stared at him.

"I know you're afraid to fly but this is not very adult-like. I would have expected more from a—"

She flipped him the finger. "My grandmother's hatpin rolled under the bed. I'm looking for it, you moron!"

He dropped the bed skirt. The next thing DeMaris knew, two hands were wrapped around her ankles and she was being dragged out from underneath the bed. The shiny wood floor made it too easy for him. He hauled DeMaris to her feet. One hand firmly gripped her arm, the other rested on her shoulder as he forcibly walked her out of the room.

"I can't leave without—"

"I'll find it."

"Do you know how old that hatpin is?" she screamed.

"If it's in the room, I'll find it. But, you have a plane to catch."

He unceremoniously dumped her in the passenger seat and got in behind the wheel. They barely spoke during the forty-five-minute drive to the airport.

As he parked at the curb to let her out, DeMaris looked at him. "You promise you'll find the hatpin?"

"I promise," he smiled. Her stomach always did flip-flops when she saw his straight teeth and twinkling green eyes directed at her. "This way I have a guarantee you're coming back. Promise me you'll give serious thought to our discussion."

"I promise."

He pulled her close and kissed her. She moaned. *God, he has the best kisses.*

He chuckled and leaned back to get a good look at her. "Ya know, if you won't take drugs or drink alcohol maybe you just need to think of my kisses. You look pretty relaxed now."

"Well, there's a thought. I'll try it. See ya." DeMaris got out of the car.

"You sure you don't want me to come in and wait with you?"

"Trust me; I'm not a pretty picture. I would rather you remembered me boldly walking to my death rather than whimpering and screaming."

He shook his head. "See ya. Hey, if you find you're connected out there in the boondocks, call me!"

— — —

DeMaris stared at the plane parked on the tarmac. *When the time comes, just get on it. Don't think about it, just get on.* "I can do this," she said sternly to herself feeling her face drain of all color. *I wish Mother had never broken me of the habit of biting my nails. It would give me something to do. Too bad I don't smoke. Listen to yourself. You don't do drugs, you don't drink, you don't smoke, you don't chew your nails, you don't fly, you don't drive. No wonder your husband agreed to a divorce.*

DeMaris thought about the genealogy she had immersed herself in over the last year. *Your ancestors gave their lives to this country so you had the freedom to fly . . . even though they knew nothing about flying back then. Go! Go do it! You're not going off to battle, you're going to spend time with your sorority sisters—go! GO!*

No. She couldn't do it. *Call Sara? Tell her I'm not coming? Well, not by plane. And since I don't drive, I am coming by . . .? All right, you can do this! Think of your last trip. You survived that, didn't you? God saved you then, he'll save you now. You can do this! No, I can't.*

She turned away from the window, intent on leaving the airport when a blur of arms encircled her neck and she heard a yell of "Surprise!"

She untangled herself to see who it was. "Jacyne! What are you doing here?" DeMaris screamed.

"The Army sent me out west and I ended up being here longer than

4

anticipated; so I decided to start my vacation from here. I called Sara and found out you were here . . . I knew you'd need help getting on the plane—so, here I am. God, you look great! How much weight have you lost?"

"Over fifty pounds," DeMaris said proudly.

"Wow. Well, it shows. Come on."

Relieved, DeMaris followed Jacyne . . . to the bar. They hiked themselves up on barstools, Jacyne only interrupting to order drinks.

"What are you having?" she asked DeMaris after ordering her own.

"Nothing."

"She'll have an amaretto—"

"No!"

"Why not?"

"Religious purposes."

Jacyne stared at her. "You're back on that kick again?"

"I'm asking God to pull out all the stops to fly me there safely. The least I can do is forgo liquor for a few days."

"So, you'll be drinking with us?"

"Well, I'm still debating. After all, I have to fly back."

"But after that you can drink again? Come on, it's not like you're a lush."

DeMaris raised her hands. "I'm not drinking until we land."

The bartender brought Jacyne her drink. "Do you at least want a Coke?"

"No! Then I'll have to go to the bathroom! And you know I'll have to go right when I'm not allowed. When we're landing or experiencing turbulence or crashing or something."

Jacyne looked at DeMaris and then the bartender. "Could you bring her a glass with just a little bit of water in it to make it look like somebody's drinking with me? Please?" The bartender obliged.

The friends caught up with what each had been doing. "Let's go find our plane," DeMaris finally said as Jacyne started to order another drink.

"Relax, we've got time."

DeMaris checked her watch. "Actually, we don't. You've had three drinks inside forty-five minutes—and here I thought it was so great that *you'd* conquered your fear of flying. I thought there was hope for me—and now I discover," she leaned in close and hissed, "you have to get bombed before you can get on a plane!"

"I'm relaxed, aren't I?" Jacyne downed the fourth drink quickly and stood up. "See, I'm fine."

DeMaris caught Jacyne's sleeve and pulled her into a standing position. "Great. You couldn't just pick up a magazine or read a book on the flight?"

"Naw, it's so much easier to sleep."

As they found their seats, DeMaris said, "Since you're going to be passed out, mind if I have the window seat?"

"Have at it."

The first hour of the flight went well. The second hour did not. Jacyne slept while DeMaris hung onto the armrests with white knuckles. *Turbulence happens . . . turbulence happens . . . you know this. Whoa! Oh, Goddamn it! No! God, I didn't mean that. Turbulence hap— Holy shit! Make it stop, God! Make it stop!* "Jacyne, wake up."

"Are we there?"

"No. Wake up. It's turbulence."

"I don't want to be awake for that." She shifted her body to the other side.

"Oh no, you don't. You're going to wake up and go through— shit— this with me. When you wake up from being dead do you really want to realize that you were of no help to anyone in this crisis?""

"Huh?"

"Wake up! So help me—" DeMaris watched a cart whiz down the aisle unattended. "I'll unbuckle you!"

Jacyne roused herself as best she could. "It's just a little— Shit! You woke me up for this?! Shit!"

"That's what I was trying to tell you."

"Listen, I really need to be passed out if you're gonna hold my hand."

"Sorry." DeMaris let go.

Jacyne worked to get the feeling back in her hand. The plane went up and then dropped several feet. DeMaris was fairly sure she wasn't screaming although other passengers were. "Shut those people up!" she ordered Jacyne.

"Unless they're military personnel, I can't do a thing about it. You shouldn't have woken me. I'm not feeling too good."

"What? No! No, you can't!" She watched as Jacyne pawed through the pocket in front of her and pulled out the barf bag. "No! If you throw up, then I'll throw up, and I don't feel like throwing up. If I watch you or if I smell it— No, you just can't. I've got enough to deal with without you doing this."

"It's your own fault. You shouldn't have woken me up." Jacyne snapped open the bag and vomited.

DeMaris clasped her hands over her nose and concentrated out the window. If she didn't get a whiff she'd be okay. At least with all the things flying around, the banging and the screaming, she couldn't hear Jacyne. That was the only plus.

"Hey, I'm keeping you from thinking about crashing, aren't I?" said Jacyne.

"That's your plan?" DeMaris muffled through her hands.

"How did you manage with two kids when they were sick?"

"One, they were rarely sick and two, when they were, I gave them a bowl and told them they were on their own."

"Nice mother."

"Hey, how difficult is it to keep it in a bowl? And, if they were really smart, they'd make it to the bathroom in time. I taught them self-reliance."

Jacyne went for the barf bag again. DeMaris concentrated heavily out the window. The plane leveled out. *Thank you, God. Thank you. Down, down, down. Shit!* "Stewardess, I need a ddddrrrriiiinnnkkkk!" DeMaris screamed.

Jacyne leaned back in her seat and took a few deep breaths. "I think it's politically incorrect to call them stewardesses today."

"You know what? I don't give a flying—I don't care! And I'm not taking that from somebody who's drunk!"

"I'm not drunk!"

"No, just passed out! I need a drinnnnkkkk!"

"Passed out is where you should have left me. We'd both be happier. Besides, if you drink, won't we crash? I mean, aren't we all depending on you to keep us up in the air because you're being pious for a couple hours?"

"You're really starting to piss me off."

"*I'm* starting to piss *you* off?"

"Hey! Hey! What are you doing?" With one hand pinching her nose, DeMaris pushed Jacyne's hand away from the pouch in front of her seat.

"I need another bag."

"You're not taking mine."

"I might need it. This one's full."

"I might need it and it's mine!"

"Do you feel sick? I feel sick. Give it to me!"

"If I smell that—"

"You're gonna smell it if you don't give it to me."

"Oh, I'll give it to ya."

Sara and Caroline watched the plane taxi in. Two sorority sisters ready for a little R & R away from their demanding families and rewarding jobs.

"Wouldn't you know she'd be the last one off?" sighed Caroline, as the area emptied of people. "Was it me or did everybody look a little worse for wear? Are you sure this is her flight?"

Sara got out her note and checked the flight number. "Yes, this is what she gave me."

"I knew it. I knew she wouldn't get on." Caroline stomped her foot and folded her arms across her chest.

"No … she promised me she'd come. Besides," Sara pawed through her purse, pulled out her cell phone, and checked it, "she would have called if she hadn't gotten on. She knew we'd be waiting for her."

"What was she doing in California anyway?"

"Visiting friends. Excuse me," Sara stopped a flight attendant walking by. "Are all of the passengers off?"

The woman turned and glared. "Are you waiting for two women?"

Sara and Caroline glanced at each other. "One, anyway."

"Well, there's a gray-haired lady who once we hit turbulence kept screaming for a drink and there's a dark-haired one who came onboard drunk and insists she's a general."

"Oh! Jacyne's with her! Good, we didn't know if she was coming or not."

"She's not really a general, is she?" asked the flight attendant, reflecting on some of the things she had said. Her Army husband might not be pleased.

"No," said Caroline.

"Yes," said Sara at the same time. They looked at each other. "Well, this week at least …"

"I don't think that's what we're supposed to say. Don't tell her I goofed up the first time I was asked."

"She's— she's in the military. That's all I can say. If we tell you more, she'll have to kill you."

"Yes," said Caroline, "she's in the military. I don't think I can lie the whole time we're all together." She looked at Sara, who tried to ignore her as the flight attendant eyed them suspiciously.

"The captain is dealing with them."

The gals grimaced. "They haven't misbehaved again, have they?"

The flight attendant nodded. "There was a problem during the flight. The one needs a shower."

"No!" yelled Sara. "I told her she absolutely had to take a shower today before she got on the plane!"

8

Caroline gave her a perturbed look while the attendant decided to move on.

"I mean— well— she— you know— It's not what you think," Sara hollered down the hall. "She has always hated taking them and she's always aspired to be a hermit so that she'd never have to shower again. She's divorced now— not because of the non-showering, of course. Her children are grown. She's a hermit—" Sara turned to Caroline who was looking at the ceiling. "When I saw her six months ago she was actually letting the gray come in and telling people she liked it. Shay should already be there. She'll be able to get her to take a shower. Shay— Oh, my God!"

But Caroline had already turned to see where the smell was coming from. Both women clamped their hands over their noses and mouths. "I think I'm going to puke," said Caroline.

"Hi," said DeMaris. The two women raised a hand in greeting. "This is not mine, in case you're wondering," DeMaris said as she pointed to her midriff. "It's my seatmate's." The three turned to watch Jacyne slowly make her way toward them.

"Why don't we clean you up?" offered Caroline.

"I did clean up. Have you got the car rented yet? Let's just get to Viva's so I can take a shower." DeMaris walked off.

"You're willing to take one?" asked Sara as she followed far behind.

DeMaris turned back around. "Yes, I'm willing to take one! I've been taking showers for fifty years!" For someone who didn't know where she was going, DeMaris certainly took off at a fast pace.

"What's wrong with your eye?" asked Caroline as she walked beside Jacyne.

Jacyne steamed. "Let's just say she's not fun to fly with and leave it at that."

"Me?" DeMaris whirled around. "At least I didn't get drunk and pretend that I don't mind flying."

"I didn't mind, until you woke me up!"

"And, just for the record, the black eye was an accident. Just like I told the captain."

"Yeah, so was my hand letting go of my full barf bag."

"*That* was done on purpose!"

"Come on, we're not starting our vacation like—" said Caroline.

"I admit my hand was in a fist, but the plane hitting turbulence once again was what put it in your face. But you—"

"And when you hit me, I was startled and let go!"

"You guys had turbulence? Gosh, we had a beautiful flight, didn't we, Caroline? Smooth sailing the entire—"

"Do you want an eye to match hers? Because I'm feeling turbulence again."

Pouting, Sara walked on ahead. The girls picked up the rest of their luggage and made their way to the van. Sara unlocked it and poked her head inside, rummaging around in the back. DeMaris tried pushing past her but Jacyne and Caroline each took an arm.

"You're not getting in the van. You reek. Here's a plastic bag, a top and shorts. Go back inside, find a bathroom, and change."

DeMaris stood still. She looked from one to the other. "Fine."

"What are you doing?" said Sara.

"Let her go," said Jacyne, throwing her hands up in the air.

"No! No! You can't do that! Stop!" both Sara and Caroline were yelling as DeMaris stripped down to her underwear.

"I am *not* walking all the way back inside and looking for a damn bathroom. Quite frankly, I don't think I could find the van again; which might be the whole point. However, I've lost weight, I work out nearly every day, and I have on Victoria's Secret's finest. I've got nothing to be ashamed of." From the car ramp above they heard a wolf whistle. "Thank you," she hollered. "At least somebody appreciates me."

———

Viva met them at the door. She hugged each one as they passed, DeMaris was last. "Shay!" Viva hollered. "They're here. DeMaris hasn't showered!"

"I have to!"

"Listen, we're all going to be living in close proximity to each other. You've got to shower—or bathe."

"I did," growled DeMaris.

"She's much cleaner than she was," Sara said.

"What is with you people thinking I don't shower?"

"Um, your e-mail stating you hadn't showered in a week and how great it was to be a hermit," offered Shay coming into the room and hugging everyone.

"Okay. Well, right after that, a really good-looking salesman came to the door and after I opened it and he got a whiff of me he realized he didn't have anything to sell me. I was embarrassed enough to immediately take a shower. On the other hand, I didn't have to listen to a sales pitch," DeMaris stopped talking as she re-thought the situation.

"Let me show you your rooms," said Viva. The girls oohed and ahhed at the luxuriousness of Viva's newest acquisition. Being in real estate, she always had an eye out for a new home.

Caroline and Sara, who had been roommates in college, would share a room. Shay and DeMaris would have a room together "with your very own shower," Viva made a point of turning to DeMaris as she said this.

DeMaris looked at Shay. "Guess you're out of luck."

Viva and Jacyne would sleep in the master bedroom with the swimming pool off the deck.

"And, here's the kitchen, which comes complete with a live-in cook." There were screams all around when the girls saw Liset whipping up a batter.

"You made it!" Excited chattering and hugs followed. "Melissa comes in tomorrow, and then we'll all be here."

"You're not cooking for us the whole time, are you?" Caroline asked Liset.

"No, I'm sure we'll go out to eat. But when we're in, I'm the cook." Liset turned to DeMaris. "That's the identity I choose."

"Oh, great!"

"Ah, yeah, we wanted to talk to you about this changing our identity thing," said Shay.

"We can discuss that over dinner. You've got just enough time to take a shower," Liset pointed to DeMaris.

"I did! I took one this morning! I scrubbed up in the women's bathroom at the airport! They made me!"

"We can still smell ya," they all yelled.

DeMaris threw up her hands and took off down the hall. "I take one week off in my whole entire life and now I've got to take two showers in one day. Not how I wanted to start my vacation."

Chapter Two

Seven women who had known each other for over thirty years, sat around the dining room table, enjoying the fabulous dinner Liset had prepared. Conversation flowed freely and photographs were passed around, including those of the first grandchild. Every year when they got together, it was like they were back at college. They knew each other's favorite foods, who was a night owl, and who would turn in early. They knew secrets about each other that their husbands and the world would never know.

"So, where's Harlan?" asked Sara. "I thought he was going to be around."

"Oh, sweetie cheeks."

Forks halted in midair; conversation stopped. Not because of what was said but because the voice clearly came from Viva's garage, the screen door allowing for a breeze.

"Who's sweetie cheeks?" asked Jacyne, laughing.

"Well, obviously my husband!" said Viva as her face turned scarlet.

"I didn't think Harlan came up here that often," said Caroline.

"He's here all the time. Why would I be up here without him?"

"Because—"

"Don't answer that!"

"You picked ventriloquism for your be-somebody-else change?" asked DeMaris. "And why say *that* to us?"

"God, you're really good," said Shay. They were all impressed.

"No, no," Viva shook her head. "Follow me." They went into the garage where they could hear the toilet running.

"You have a bathroom in the garage? Well, that's handy if you lock yourself out of the house."

Viva laughed. "No. Meet Sophocles."

There was the exact same laugh and then Viva's cell phone began to ring. Viva pulled her phone out, looked at it, and rolled her eyes. "You got me again, Sophocles." She showed her friends her cell phone which had no calls showing.

"That ringing was the bird?"

The girls stared. "So, you've got yourself a parrot," offered Caroline.

"This is an African gray. He can imitate anything. The toilet running, that was him."

"He can flush a toilet too? That must come in handy."

"No. He was just making the sound. You couldn't tell it from the real thing, could you?"

"That was the bird?"

"Oh, shut up Harlan." It sounded just like Viva.

"I don't think Harlan is 'sweetie cheeks,'" DeMaris mumbled to Shay, who nodded.

Viva colored. "You really have to watch what you say. He's worse than a kid—"

"Harlan, he's worse than a kid."

"That's not what I said!" Viva yelled at the bird.

"Oh. This could be fun."

"DeMaris," warned Viva.

"DeMaris," Sophocles mimicked.

"Ooh, two of you. That's not fun."

"He mimics *everything*. Please watch what you say when you're in the house and out by the pool. He came in swearing and I've really tried hard to get him to stop."

"Yeah, shut up is a good substitute," pointed out Shay.

"Shut up, Blanche."

"Who's Blanche, and whose voice is that?" asked Liset.

"I have no idea. He came with some key phrases. He loves to talk."

"He loves to talk," Sophocles said in Viva's voice. "He loves to talk, damn bird," Sophocles continued in a man's voice, before he cleared his throat.

"He loves to talk," this in a nasal-sounding female voice.

"That must be Blanche," offered Jacyne.

"Where'd you get him?" asked DeMaris.

"It was the damn— darndest thing. I drove to Walmart and ended up circling around the store because the place was an absolute mess, and there in the back was this bird. Honest to God. He was just sitting in his cage, with food and a sign that said 'Take Me.'"

"Oh, come on!"

"I know. I know how unbelievable that sounds, but it's the truth. Do you know how expensive these birds are?" Several nodded. "Hundreds. And he was just sitting there near the trash. I took him to the vet's. He has an identification number on him that lets us find out who he's registered to, but we can't find the owners. So, until somebody comes along to claim him, he's mine. I have always wanted one of these." She looked to see if he needed food, pulled his birdseed bag out, and reached her hand in.

"Never lose this key!" Sophocles said in a high-pitched woman's voice.

"What key?"

Viva shrugged. "Who knows?"

"Why is he in the garage?" DeMaris put her face near the cage.

"I figure it's cooler for him out here."

"I thought parrots came from the tropics." DeMaris and Viva stared at each other. "Besides, you could always turn the air-condi—"

"What do you know about birds?" asked Viva defensively.

"That parrots come from the tropics."

"He is not a parrot. I told you, he's an African gray."

"But isn't that part of the parrot family?" DeMaris gave Viva a quizzical look.

"Let it go," Viva said quietly.

⌐ ═ ⌐

They retired to the living room with their drinks—except for DeMaris who was abstaining. Three had margaritas, the others had strawberry daiquiris.

"We're on the ground now," Jacyne said to DeMaris.

"I have to get home, don't I?"

Caroline rolled her eyes.

"Okay, De," said Liset. "Why are we changing our identities?"

"I thought it would be fun." They stared at DeMaris. "Look, every year we get together, and we've been to some great places. This year let's add a little twist. I read about a family who did this for every one of their vacations. It sounded like fun."

"But, what are we going to do with it?" Jacyne persisted.

"We're going to go around the room and find out what each of us has been studying for a year and then when we're out in public that's who we're going to be. We're not housewives or teachers or," she turned to

Viva, "real estate agents. We're astronauts, DNA research scientists, forensic scientists, something exciting." Each one exchanged glances. They looked surprised at the lofty suggestions.

Sara cleared her throat. "Why don't you start us out? What exciting occupation did you pick?"

"Okay." DeMaris grinned. "What's the last thing you'd think I would be in this life?"

"A flight attendant," said Jacyne; they all laughed.

"No. For the week that we are together," DeMaris struck a grand pose, "I am going to be DeMaris Azaygo."

There was silence for a few seconds and then Liset softly said, "The famous writer?"

"Yeah."

"International, *New York Times* best-selling author DeMaris Azaygo?" She nodded.

"DeMaris, you can't go around impersonating a real person. I don't know. I think you can get sued for that," said Shay.

"Look, I did my homework. The woman is a recluse. That's me! She's a writer. That's me. We have the same first name. She's never going to find out about me, and if she should hear about this, I'll be long gone by then. It's not like I'm going to give an interview to the local newspaper or do a book signing. Just for this week you are to introduce me as her and we'll see where it goes."

"Ugh...I think, somehow, we're all going to wind up in jail," said Jacyne.

"Again," mumbled Viva.

"How?"

"I don't know. But we all asked the same question in Cancun. Look what happened there," said Sara.

"A little miscommunication. Come on, I gave you people something to talk about! I gave you an adventure." DeMaris was on the defensive now. "You're all telling me I should publish what I write. For this week, I have published twenty-five books, had five of them made into movies, well, six with a new one coming out, am internationally known because they have all been translated into foreign languages, and I'm wealthy. I've read all her books, so I won't be stumped on anything. Oh! Wait, wait, wait! Here's the best part!" she exclaimed excitedly. "The woman has a series called the *Traveling Sorority Sisters*! Doesn't that sound like us? It's actually another reason why I picked her. It all works out beautifully. Let me live this life for the time that we're here together. That's all I'm asking. Since we all know I'm never going to get published beyond my magazine articles, let me be somebody."

Silence.

"It's just while we're here," she reiterated slowly.

They glanced at each other. DeMaris always sounded rational. It was *after* they got into trouble and were explaining what happened to friends, business owners, cops, clergy—whoever—then it never sounded rational. The inevitable reaction was: You are grown women and you bought into that? What were you thinking? And right now, they all heard those two questions in their heads. And yet . . .

DeMaris wasn't going to *do* anything, so what was the harm? Face it, they all knew, at some point, DeMaris *would* do something. They also knew there was no way to stop her.

"Okay, Shay. You're next."

"Have any of you heard of Zelma Huff?" They shook their heads. "Well, she's an up-and-coming female race car driver and she just happens to be my neighbor. She invited me to some of the races and . . . I'm part of her pit crew." The girls hooted.

"Gosh, I didn't pick out anything glamorous," sulked Sara.

"What'd ya choose?"

"It seems like I've been at the dentist all year, what with the kids getting their cleanings and my root canals and crowns. I hadn't gotten around to studying anything; so I asked questions while I was there."

"So, you're a dental hygienist?"

"No, I'm a dentist!"

They laughed.

"That's fine," said DeMaris. "But, if somebody asks you a question, are you going to be able to answer it?"

"Well, I'm not going to do any dental work on them. Besides, who are we going to be telling this to?"

"People we run into. We've got to remember each other's new identities. You're not a teacher this week."

"Well, crap," said Caroline. "I didn't think about anybody asking me questions!"

"What did you pick?"

"Doctor. When Bob had his stroke, I learned a lot. I was always asking the doctors questions. I didn't have time to study . . . actually with all that was going on, I forgot DeMaris asked us to do this, until Sara mentioned it on our flight out. Sorry," she glanced at DeMaris. "But, it works. I can at least answer questions about strokes." She sat up straight and with both hands grabbed hold of her open cardigan. "I'm Dr. Caroline Snyder for a week."

"How is Bob?" Shay asked quietly.

"He's progressing. The nurse that's staying with him right now is excellent and the kids have promised to help out. God, I needed this vacation." It was silent for a minute. "Liset," Caroline said, "what about you?"

"I'm the live-in chef. While hubby and the kids and I were living in Hong Kong, I took cooking classes all the time. Loved it. Now that I'm back in the States, I've taken a few more."

"Ya know what?" said DeMaris. "You're still the only person I know who burned a hardboiled egg."

"That stunk up the house," they all remembered.

"It was the seventies! I forgot about it, okay? This," she pointed to DeMaris, "from the person who makes grilled cheese sandwiches by hovering over the toaster so that as soon as the toast pops up she puts cheese between them and mashes them together."

"Hey! Isn't that how it looks? Toast with cheese in the middle?"

"So, Jacyne," said Viva. "How's the government been treating you?"

"Fine," she looked around at her friends. "For this week, I'm a general." This was funnier than Sara being a dentist. "I figured, why not go big? I know the military so there was nothing to study."

"You were supposed to do something different though," said DeMaris. "Not give yourself a promotion."

Jacyne shrugged. "Somebody had to. Okay, Viva, your turn."

"Well, I actually took some lessons. It's something I've been interested in and I thought why not do this for DeMaris? Hit two birds with one stone, ya know? For the time we're together, I am a hot air balloonist."

"You're kidding?" three yelled in unison.

"You wouldn't get me up in one of those!"

"It's really a lot of fun. I thought maybe we could all go. I know someone who owns a balloon and—"

"Not me!" two said.

"Great, I've always wanted to go," said Jacyne.

"Me too!" They all turned to look at DeMaris.

"You won't get in a plane, but you'll go hot air ballooning?"

"That doesn't bother me." A few rolled their eyes. "Hey, I did get on the plane today, didn't I?"

Talk shifted to work-related problems and funny things that had happened in their lives over the last year. "I've got one for ya," offered DeMaris. "I did a stint at a children's clothing store. One day, one of the gals comes in twenty minutes late to work. She doesn't say she had to go to the doctor's, or she was waiting for her work clothes to dry, or that her kids were sick—no, she goes with the truth. Now, keep in mind, the manager has to write down what her excuse is for corporate to read. So, the gal blurts out, 'I'm sorry I'm late. My husband is stuck at home with the kids and he wouldn't let me leave until I gave him a blow job.'"

"No!" They all laughed.

"I swear to God. I was standing there with the manager yelling, 'flat tire, I'm writing down flat tire, not flat— Oh, never mind!'"

The girls laughed; then Shay asked, "De, you've lost a lot of weight. What's your secret?"

"Well," she sat forward in her seat, "I finally did it. You all know how much I love to row. I finally joined a rowing club."

"You're kidding!"

"No, and I'm having a blast. We're even going to do a couple of competitions this year. I'm really psyched."

"God, you've talked about that for years. Good for you."

"We have a rowing club here," said Viva. "I'll have to introduce you to the girls. They're friends of mine. I told them I had a friend who always wanted to row."

"Oh, I'd love to meet them."

They talked into the night, until one by one they went to bed.

⌒ ⤙ ⌒

DeMaris and Caroline were the only night owls but Caroline had jet lag whereas DeMaris did not. Consequently DeMaris was the only one who stayed up late and slept in. She was sound asleep when someone jumped on her bed.

"Wake up, sleepy head. I'm here!" shrieked Melissa. Her pilot boyfriend had flown her up first thing in the morning.

DeMaris was lying flat on her stomach. Without warning her hand complete with pillow came flying out catching Melissa's legs, knocking them out from under her. Melissa nearly fell off the bed.

"Pillow fight!" yelled DeMaris.

"No! No! Wait!" said Melissa as they both heard the other girls running to their bedrooms and then rushing in with their pillows. Melissa reached out to grab Shay's but was too late. "No! Stop!" This ritual had started when they lived in the sorority house together. The gal who came dragging home in the morning after a night of being out with someone always got pummeled by those who had slept in the house. Alone.

Liset stood in the doorway for a few minutes laughing. She did not have a pillow. "Hey! Breakfast is ready!"

Pillows were quickly dropped and six left the room, leaving behind Melissa who had been beaten to the floor. She sat up, brushed her medium blonde hair back, and looked up at DeMaris.

"That's the thanks I get for all I've done for you?"

"I don't think you were beat enough as a college student. Oh, wait a minute. Yes, you were."

As they sat around the breakfast table, DeMaris asked Melissa, "What are you?"

"Excuse me?"

"Last night we discussed what everybody picked for their new identities. What'd you pick?" asked DeMaris.

Melissa sat with a frozen look on her face. "You were serious about that?" DeMaris gritted her teeth. "De, you always have these fantasy ideas and then you forget about them. I really thought you'd forgotten. Let's see . . . something different that I can answer questions about if asked . . . I'm living with an airline pilot. I'll be a pilot. I've learned a lot from him and I can call him if I get stuck."

"Yeah, that looks professional." DeMaris still looked disgusted. "Somebody is going to believe you're a pilot for an airline?"

"Yeah, oh Ron," Jacyne pretended she was on a phone, "could you tell me how to start up this 747, please?"

"I'm not going to be flying anything!"

"Pick something else."

"Fine . . . um, okay, I'm an aircraft instructor . . . a small aircraft instructor. I have seen Ron start one of those." Melissa glared at Jacyne.

DeMaris nodded. "Yeah, okay."

After breakfast they trekked outside and jumped in the van. Viva looked at them, and shook her head. "Girls, the easiest way to town is by boat." She pointed to the lake behind her house.

The motor boat was beautiful but DeMaris looked wistfully at the row-boat. "Can I take your rowboat out later?"

"You can take it out all you want. The oars are in the garage." DeMaris had grown up on a lake and loved rowing.

They spent the day shopping and visiting a few antique haunts. DeMaris, not interested in antiques, took off across the street to the quilt shop. Shortly thereafter Viva entered.

"What?" DeMaris eyed her warily. Viva was not interested in quilts, she was interested in antiques. What was she doing in here?

"I don't want the other girls to know this, but I'm having a heck of a time selling my house."

"Which one?" Viva owned several.

"The one I've got us all in. Nobody will tell me what's wrong with it. I thought after living in it one of you could tell me."

"You think it's haunted?"

"Only you'd come up with that. No. It's less than five years old. I think it needs some pizzazz. It looks like every other house on the market," she sighed. "It's not my favorite house but still I think it's nice—plus we're in a slump at the moment. I wondered if you'd have any suggestions."

DeMaris put the bolt of fabric back on the shelf and looked squarely at Viva. "We both know I'm the last person you'd ask decorating tips from. What's the favor?"

"That's not . . . exactly true. Oh fine. I thought, maybe if I stenciled in some of the rooms that it would perk it up a bit. I hate stenciling and I'm not good at it."

DeMaris chuckled. "Was that your stencil job in the bedroom Shay and I are staying in?" Viva nodded. "I'll be happy to show you what you're doing wrong and—"

"No," Viva hesitated. "I'd like you to . . . just do it." DeMaris stared at her. "Shay said you were really good. God, I hate doing it. Please?"

"So, while you guys are out having a good time I get to work?"

"We've been friends for thirty years. We all know, including you, that in a few days you're going to tell us you're sick of shopping, you're sick of us, and you want to be alone. You can do it then."

"It's nothing personal—it's just the creative spirit in me, it takes over."

"I know. *We all know.* Take the rowboat out, I don't care. But please, take over the stenciling."

"How many rooms are we talking?"

"Just the kitchen and the bedroom you're in."

"Liset will love that. Okay, but I'm not painting and that job you did in the bedroom has to go."

"I'll ask Caroline if she'll repaint it. And hey, while you're here, we have a great hair stylist in town. Before you leave, I'll take you there and pay to have your hair done."

"What's wrong with my hair?"

"It's a dingy brown with . . . gray."

"It's natural. I don't see you picking on Caroline."

"Hers is silver. Hers looks good, yours does not."

DeMaris stared at her. She was not put out that Viva spoke freely: friends should always be honest with one another. "I actually like my natural color, now that I've let it grow out. I've colored it for years, and for what?"

"You've lost all that weight. Get a better hair color and you'll look ten years younger. Catch yourself a young guy."

DeMaris nodded and smiled. "Maybe you're right."

Chapter Three

"You're lucky I like the smell of paint," growled DeMaris in the morning.

Caroline ran the brush over the stenciling. "Time to get up and take a shower. We're going out on the lake today."

"Oh, I did want to get up for that," DeMaris agreed and rolled out of bed. "And, by the way, I don't need to be told to take a shower every morning. Cripe, I'm jumping in the lake. What difference does it make?"

"Sorry. You have . . . shaved recently . . . haven't you?"

DeMaris slowly turned and glared at her.

"Sorry, stupid question. Of course, you have. Liset made you chocolate chip muffins," she offered by way of an apology.

They spent several hours on the lake. A few of them water-skied, some jumped in and swam. Sunscreen lotion and advice were shared liberally.

They went out for a late lunch and shopped for a couple hours before finally making their way home. Viva went into the garage and brought Sophocles and his cage into the house. "You moron, Fox," he greeted them in a shrill voice.

"What woman's voice is that?" asked DeMaris. "Blanche's?"

"How would I know?" answered Viva. "He does a running commentary with a man and a woman. I presume his former owners. "

"Shut up, Blanche," Sophocles said in a man's voice.

Viva went back into the garage to get his food. "Never lose this key!" said a refined woman's voice.

"I won't," said Viva.

"Again with the key," mused DeMaris. "Hey, I'm getting an idea for a book here."

"How's the writing coming?" asked Sara.

"Fine."

"Why don't you try to get published?" asked Jacyne. DeMaris waved a hand at her.

"Ya know, we'd like to read something besides a letter before we all bite the dust," injected Caroline. "Why do you continue to write and not publish?"

DeMaris looked around the group and sighed. How many times had she answered this question? Why did they keep bugging her about it? Obviously, after all these years, she didn't *want* to publish. "Do you know what one has to do to get published? It's hard work . . . and boring. And, I don't care to have the world know how I think. Writing is fun. I love to write. I don't need to be published to write. Do you actually read my letters and e-mails?"

"Yes!" they all said.

"You have a real talent," offered Shay. "Get published. Lord knows, you could use the money." It suddenly went quiet. They looked in every direction except at DeMaris.

"Fine," DeMaris said. "Who wants to ask me about my divorce?"

"That's okay."

"Whenever you want to talk about it."

"It's none of our business."

"I don't care to talk about it," DeMaris spit out. "I'm on vacation."

"Fine."

"I understand."

"That's okay."

"We understand . . . we're just curious as hell."

"Did you ever tell the police about this bird?"

"No, why should I? He was just sitting behind Walmart. I didn't steal him. What would I possibly tell the police?"

"You don't think maybe there was some foul play? I mean, who leaves an expensive bird behind Walmart unattended? And with food."

"Why would there be foul play?" Viva talked quickly, her words tumbling out in a jumble. "I mean, there's foul play every place—but why here? Somebody wanted to get rid of him is all. Look, if I took him to the police, they'd confiscate him. It's not like he can tell them anything

23

and I wouldn't have this really neat bird. The police wouldn't take care of Sophocles properly and then he'd die. Do you want that on your conscious? Huh?" Viva folded her arms across her chest. "We . . . listen to me De, we, you, I, are *not* taking Sophocles to the police."

"No need to get worked up. I'm not going to do anything. But what an idea for a book," said DeMaris with a dreamy look in her eyes.

"Like what?"

"A bird that holds the key to . . . murder . . . a missing person . . . oh! National security! 'Never lose this key.' It doesn't even have to be a physical key."

"That's a great idea," said Shay. "Why don't you do that? Better yet—publish your books."

DeMaris picked up a notepad and pencil that were sitting nearby and started to write. "Ya know what? I do all right with the magazine articles and short stories that I sell."

"You're telling us you can make a living that way?"

"I do okay. Being a freelance writer, I can write what I want and most of the time I don't have to adhere to a timetable, although some publications give me a deadline. I don't want that pressure."

"What pressure? You've written how many novels? Sell those."

DeMaris went back to writing.

"All right," said Jacyne, "let me just say what we've all been discussing. You need to get your novels published, DeMaris. You're fifty, you're not getting any younger, and you need the money now that you're divorced. Plus, we all think you are really good. We want to be able to say yes, we know her. We're her personal friends."

DeMaris looked around the room. "You're all afraid you're going to be stuck with me; that I won't become self-sufficient."

"How many novels have you written so far?"

"I don't know. I've tried to get published, but you know what? It's tremendously competitive and it's really no fun. Rejection after rejection which just drains on your creativity. I'd rather be writing. It will be my legacy to my kids when I'm gone. They can get my stories published and live off of them. They are good," she admitted.

There was momentary silence; then Shay said, "But you need something to live on now."

"I'm doing okay."

"De," said Melissa. "We know the strain you've been under. Getting a divorce, losing the house you were in for twenty years—"

"It's not like Kirk and I don't talk," said DeMaris. "We get along just fine. I'm having fun traveling. Somebody needs to take care of the house and Kirk is definitely a homebody."

"So are you. You put a lot into that house and now, you don't have it."

"So? I'll get another one. Really, I'm doing fine. If you must know, I have someone new in my life."

"You do? Who?" asked Shay suspiciously.

DeMaris smiled. "You'll be seeing him tomorrow."

"He's coming here?"

"You'll just have to wait and see." They could get nothing more out of her. "Liset, tell us about dinner. Are you cooking tonight?"

"Yes." Liset realized DeMaris wanted to change the subject, so she launched into a lengthy description.

"Are you describing hamburgers with French fries?" asked Melissa.

"Exactly."

"Is that what your cooking classes in Hong Kong taught you?"

"No, we ate stuff like snake and—"

"God, you're kidding!" yelled DeMaris.

"It's really quite good."

"Don't you even dare to think about feeding snake to us!"

They all laughed picturing tall, petite, city-born-and-bred Liset stomping around the woods looking for snakes to feed them.

"It might do you all some good to have a change of taste," said Liset as she stood up and walked into the kitchen.

—◆— —◆— —◆—

"What are you doing?" Viva found DeMaris in the garage by Sophocles.

DeMaris was having a staring contest with the African gray. "How can he make so many sounds? All of our different cell phone rings, the toilet flushing, motorboats going by . . ."

"I don't know." Viva shrugged her shoulders.

"How do you get him to say something?"

"I don't teach him anything. Besides, I haven't had him that long. He just says what he wants." Viva suddenly grew suspicious. "Why?"

DeMaris smiled. "Just trying to teach him something."

"DeMaris," Viva warned. DeMaris raised an eyebrow at her. "Please."

"Please," said Sophocles.

"There, he learned something nice," said DeMaris.

"Blanche, feed your damn bird," said a man's voice.

"Shut up, Fox!" said a nasal-sounding woman's voice.

The bird cleared his throat and in a different masculine voice said, "Damn bird talks too much."

"Wow. Blanche and Fox. They make quite a pair, don't they? They must be married. Fox is probably a last name, don't you think? But then again, I wonder who the third person is who keeps cropping up along with the other woman. Do you think there were two couples living together?" DeMaris pondered this for a moment.

Viva grabbed the bird food and shook the bag in front of Sophocles to see if he wanted any. "Never lose this key," Sophocles said in a refined female voice.

"Tell us about the key, Sophocles."

"He's not going to tell you a story," said Viva.

"Give him a chance."

The two of them stared at the bird, which stared straight back at them.

— —— —

The talk and laughter continued into the night. DeMaris shook her head no when asked if she was drinking yet.

Late in the evening, Sara went outside on the deck for some fresh air. She was gazing at the stars when she heard someone behind her softly say, "Look at me. I can fly! I can fly!"

Sara smiled. "You are never going to let me forget that, are you?"

"I thought it was cute, that's all," said DeMaris as she stood next to her friend. "While you are all discussing me, I just want to go on record as saying I'm not the only one who tried to kill myself back in college."

"No. You tried to commit suicide, my thinking I was Wendy from *Peter Pan* would have been ruled an accident. I learned my lesson though: never take a joint from a stranger. I have always been very grateful that you were there that night . . . and sober."

"Yeah, somehow I couldn't see how jumping off the sorority house four stories up was going to come out all right. Although the people on the ground who were as high as you, thought you could do it."

"I cried at Rick's wedding," stated Sara.

DeMaris nodded. "He's your son."

"Yeah. I'm sure everyone thought I was crying because it was my first child getting married, but I was crying because if you hadn't been there

26

that night, and if you hadn't been sober . . . well, I think how often we've bugged you to drink or smoke with us . . . I'd be dead or paralyzed. And I'd have never had my three kids. That's what I was thinking about when Rick got married. I would have never had that moment if you hadn't rescued me."

"Oh, it's a two-way street," said DeMaris. "You all rescued me."

"Yes, but the difference is, you never thanked us."

It was silent for what seemed like a long time. DeMaris finally said, "No, I never did." Her voice was hard.

"So, you haven't forgiven us?"

"I wouldn't say that," DeMaris softened. "I really have had a great life. But when I think back to that time . . . God, I just get depressed again. But," she smiled, "thank you. I am glad to be here."

Sara smiled. "Rick—all of us—were unhappy you didn't come to his wedding."

"I sent a present."

"Yes, and while we're on the subject—when the kids picked out their dishes, they weren't expecting to receive a serving for eight. One place setting would have been enough. My God De, I know how much that set you back. I really wish you hadn't done it; although Rick and Becky were thrilled. DeMaris, you've got to hang on to your money."

"I don't care about money, never have. Probably why I don't have any," she laughed and then grew serious. "I was happy to do it for Rick and Becky."

They stood quietly for several minutes; then DeMaris offered, "I really thought when I told you all to think of a new identity that you would pick astronaut or NASA scientist or something along that line."

Sara shook her head. "I've been too busy with . . . things. You know, my classroom . . . my parents decline . . . just . . . things I don't want to talk about. It's been a trying year."

"I understand."

"You and Kirk . . . Was there . . . somebody else?"

"No, we just grew apart. We each had our own agenda. We still have an amiable relationship. Actually, not a whole lot has changed except . . ." Sara turned and looked at DeMaris when she didn't continue.

The two of them studied each other. DeMaris smiled. "I just travel a lot, that's all."

"You? The homebody?"

"Well, I decided there were places to see and things that I needed to experience. I suppose some would call it a midlife crisis. I call it living."

"You're right. Could I change my identity?" asked Sara. "I could pull off being an astronaut."

"You could?"

"I've always been interested in outer space, you know that. I've read a lot and I'm teaching astronomy to gifted seventh and eighth graders. Living near Chicago I've even taken the kids to the Yerkes Observatory to look through the telescopes. Einstein's actually walked the halls there. I'll just be an astronaut who never made it into space. I was ready to go but the budget was cancelled. Let me be an astronaut for a week!"

DeMaris laughed. "I don't care. Be an astronaut. This is your week." She turned and grabbed the oars she had brought down from the garage. "Let's go for a ride in the rowboat."

"In the dark?" Sara stood still as DeMaris walked down the ramp toward the lake.

"The moon's out, come on."

"Hey!" There was a shout from one of the windows. "You're not going in the boat! At least not without us!" There was yelling and scrambling and Sara was nearly trampled on when she didn't move fast enough.

Jacyne, Shay and Melissa jumped in the boat and Sara slowly got in. DeMaris looked towards the house. "They went to bed," offered Jacyne.

"Oh, so they think," DeMaris smiled as she pushed them away from the dock.

The girls chuckled knowing exactly what she meant.

They sang sorority and college songs at the top of their lungs for the whole lake to hear.

Chapter Four

"This isn't snake, is it?" asked DeMaris, playing with her breakfast.

"Honestly, the things you think of," mumbled Shay.

"I don't hear Liset denying it." Five forks stopped in midair.

"It's sausage!" Liset yelled. "I didn't think I had to justify that with an answer."

"Never lose this key!" Sophocles demanded as Viva fed him in the garage.

"You are my favorite bird," Viva cooed.

"He's your *only* bird," yelled Jacyne.

"Shut up, Fox."

"Ah, the elusive Blanche again, I presume."

"What are you thinking about?" asked Melissa. "De? DeMaris!"

DeMaris turned and looked at her. "The newspaper. Viva, do you get the paper?"

Viva walked into the dining room. "Yeah. Why?"

"Where do you keep it?" DeMaris got up and dumped her plate and glass in the sink.

"Since when do you read a newspaper?" three of them asked.

"Out on the back porch, getting ready to go to recycle."

"Hey, don't disappear," hollered Caroline. "It's yours and Melissa's turn to do the dishes."

"Yeah, yeah."

Shay came out on the porch. "What are you looking for?" She watched as DeMaris rifled through a stack of newspapers.

"Looking for last month's newspaper." She pulled one out and started to scan it.

"Why?"

"Viva said she hasn't had the bird for very long. It obviously lived with people named Blanche and Fox. I want to see if there are any missing persons or murders that have those names."

"Viva's got her fingers in a bunch of community projects," pointed out Shay. "Just ask her. She knows everybody here."

DeMaris shook her head. "I've asked enough questions. She would have told me if she knew them. Besides, I'm getting an idea for my next book."

"How about trying to sell this one?"

"Yeah, great idea," DeMaris said absently getting to the end of the stack. "Nothing. Viva! Have you had any murders or robberies in the last month or two?"

"DeMaris," Viva came onto the porch. "This is a nice town. The crime rate is very low. Any ideas that you have about the bird, Blanche, and Fox are all in your head."

"All right, what's your explanation as to why someone would put an expensive bird behind a store? If they wanted to give him away, wouldn't you think they'd have given him to a friend, or a neighbor, or even the vet? You wouldn't just dump him."

"You are letting your imagination run away with you—*again.* Put it in a story."

"That's what I'm trying to do."

"But leave *my* bird alone."

"Hey, we're heading out to go shopping and then see a matinee before we come back here, change, and then go out to a nice place for dinner," announced Melissa, sticking her head around the corner. "The majority has decided."

She and DeMaris quickly cleaned the kitchen.

"I'm out," said Shay. "I've got a migraine. I'm gonna take one of my pills and lie down. Hopefully I can make dinner."

"Should somebody stay with you?" Caroline looked concerned.

"No, I'll be all right."

"I'll stay," offered DeMaris. "I'll start on the stenciling."

"You sure?" asked Sara.

"Yeah."

"She's sick of us already," Jacyne was heard saying as the rest of them went out the door.

DeMaris chuckled and turned to see Shay staring at her. "I've already seen the movie."

"Okay, but that paint isn't going to stink, is it? My head's killing me."

"I'll do the kitchen. Since we're going out tonight for dinner, I won't be bothering either you or Liset." Shay disappeared to the bedroom while DeMaris went and got out the stencils, brushes, and paints that Viva had shown her. Viva had told her expressly what she wanted done but as DeMaris studied the stencils she decided on her own course of action. For company she got Sophocles and brought him into the kitchen with her.

Several hours later, she had finished two walls and was humming to herself. "Hey, Sophocles, like my song?"

"Blanche, feed that damn bird," Sophocles said in a male voice. He cleared his throat and in a different male voice added, "Damn bird talks too much."

DeMaris chuckled, put down the paint brush, and walked over to the birdcage. "You're hungry, huh? I don't think Viva feeds you. All I ever see her do is shake the bag in front of you."

"Blanche, feed that damn bird."

"Okay, okay, hold your horses." DeMaris disappeared into the garage and came back with the bag of feed she had seen Viva use.

"Never lose this key!" the refined woman's voice scolded.

"I won't." DeMaris frowned. Why did the bird say that every time he got fed? She dumped food in his cage. "What key, Sophocles?"

The bird seemed to study her. "Never lose this key." She shook the bird-seed. Sophocles opened up his feathers. "Never lose this key."

DeMaris looked inside the bag. *Birdseed.* She reached her hand inside and felt around. *Noth—wait a minute.* Her fingers had hit something hard. *What was that? Here it is.* She pulled out a key—a safe deposit key. She turned it around in her hand. The number 1501 was pressed into the metal.

Story lines whirled inside her head. What would a safe deposit box hold that would make an interesting story? You would have to have a murder. Have to be a bank robbery. But in the box itself . . . Map of buried treasure? Gold doubloons? – what was that place her friend in high school always talked about, said her Dad was big into hunting for it? *Make note to look up old high school chum.* Jewelry? Hope diamond? What kind of valuable art could you fit in a safe deposit box? Guess it depended on the size of the box.

She twisted the key back and forth, staring at it. Sophocles squawked and brought her back to reality. Where was her notepad and pencil? She had to write down all of her ideas before she forgot them.

⚬   ⚬   ⚬

Shay had drifted off to sleep but somewhere in the back of her mind little flashes were telling her to wake up. Disaster, wake up! She could feel herself coming around to quiet noises. She rolled over. "What are you doing?"

"I'm trying not to disturb you," whispered DeMaris. "Go back to sleep."

"Well, I am disturbed. What are you doing with my bra?"

"I need it."

"Do laundry."

"No, I don't need *a* bra, I need *your* bra."

"DeMaris," Shay swung around and put her feet on the floor. She looked closely at her friend. "Have you suddenly gained weight?"

"Oh good, it shows," DeMaris said delightedly. "I'm headed into town, do you need anything?" She started for the bathroom.

"Stop!" Shay put up a hand. "What are you doing? Why are you dressed like that?"

"I've got a great idea for a story," DeMaris said excitedly. "I need to go into town and try something out but I think it is best if I'm not noticed as Viva's friend. You know . . . in case I do something stupid. She knows everybody here. I don't want to embarrass her. So, I need to look different . . . just in case."

"DeMaris! What are you going to do in town? Why do you need my bra? How have you gained weight so fast and why? What great idea have you—" she pressed a hand to her head as the throbbing started up again. She glanced at DeMaris. She needed to concentrate on one question at a time. "What do you need with my bra?"

"I need a larger look, so I've been ransacking everybody's clothes and layering myself. Look at me," she ran both hands down her sides, "I'm out of proportion."

"Huh?"

"When you hear the name Blanche, doesn't that conjure up a picture of an old lady?"

"No, I think of a *Streetcar Named Desire*. Are you talking about the Blanche the bird keeps mentioning?" Shay was getting a bad taste in her mouth. She had had her share of DeMaris's exploits.

32

"Isn't this kind of what Blanche sounds like?" DeMaris said in a shrill tone.

"Not even close. And, I hate to break it to you, but you *are* an old lady."

DeMaris made a face at Shay. "Anyway, Blanche is an old lady's name so . . . I have to look like an old lady. But, there's a problem," she brought her hands up and pointed at her chest. "I'm perky."

"Excuse me?"

"I pay big bucks to have my boobs stay on my chest—I'm talking *bras* here—unlike you, who goes for the boobs-on-the-waist look. That's why I need your cheap bra."

Shay's mouth dropped. She suddenly stood up, reached over, and ripped her bra out of De's hand. "Go braless!"

"Oh," DeMaris snapped her fingers. "What an idea." She ran into the bathroom and peeled off several tops to get to her own bra. "Ya know what?" she hollered. "I've lost so much weight I got into everybody else's clothes by layering them, except for Caroline and Liset. Actually, I could get into Liset's skirt but she's so tall it just dragged on the ground."

"Everything drags on you!" yelled Shay. DeMaris was the shortest in the group.

"Not my boobs!" She stepped out of the bathroom and headed for the bedroom door.

Still keeping her hands on her head because of the throbbing headache, Shay came out after her. "Let's wait 'til the rest of the girls get back."

"I'm not waiting. I won't be gone an hour."

"How are you going to get there? They took the speed boat and you don't drive."

"Rowboat."

"You don't want to row all that way—" forget that tactic. DeMaris loved to row.

"You want anything while I'm in town?"

"Well, yeah," Shay said slowly. "I need something stronger for this migraine."

"What do you want?" DeMaris grabbed a sweater in case it was cold on the lake.

Shay told her and then asked, "Where did you get that sweater?" It was knit in various colors and also had flowers appliquéd on top.

"It's Jacyne's."

"I can't imagine her wearing something like that."

She could see DeMaris doing a slow burn. "I made this for her, for her birthday."

"It's gorgeous but—it's more you. It's bright and bold and . . . a little on the wild side. She's in the military—"

"I know! I thought she needed some color. She's not in costume 24/7."

"Uniform!"

"Whatever. I purposely used pink, purple, and orange because that's the way she and Viva painted their room our senior year."

"I can hardly forget," stated Shay. Later, she would say it was the pounding in her head that kept her from stopping DeMaris. She just wanted to lie down again. "Wait, let me get you some money."

"I've got it!" hollered DeMaris. She went out the garage door; found the oars; and on a sudden inspiration grabbed Viva's big, floppy gardening hat that was hanging on a hook. *My gosh, does she really wear this?*

I shouldn't let her go, thought Shay as she rummaged through her purse. *Think of the other disasters when DeMaris has gone off by herself. I just want to lie down. She's an adult. Oh, how many times have we said that?* "Here, De! Here's a ten! DeMar—" Shay walked around the corner and into the kitchen. She stopped dead in her tracks when she saw the two stenciled walls. "Oh . . . my . . . God."

Chapter Five

DeMaris moored the rowboat at the marina Viva had gone to the day before. She wondered if it mattered where she docked. She just knew she didn't want to be near Viva's speedboat; so she tied the rowboat at the other end.

How would an old woman walk? How would a Blanche talk? She pulled the floppy hat down around her face and tried out a nasally voice. "Could you direct me to the nearest bank, please?" The man she stopped gave her directions.

She walked flat-footed and slow. She hoped the girls didn't run into her. *Naw, they wouldn't recognize me anyway. Well, Viva would probably recognize her hat, and Jacyne would undoubtedly recognize the sweater and the fact that the two pieces don't go together . . . especially with the long, flared skirt. Hmm, maybe I made myself too noticeable.* She'd have to write that down on her notepad when she got back to the house: have character dress in regular, non-descript clothes.

DeMaris entered the small bank and looked around. It appeared to be fairly new. She stopped a woman who looked like she worked there. She had several papers in her hand. "Excuse me, dear . . ." *Nasal, think nasal.* "I'm Blanche . . . ah, Fox." *No, I shouldn't be using that name! Why can I never think things through? Just because those two names are stuck in my head! Honestly! Think ahead! Then again, what difference does it make? Nobody knows me here.* "Could you direct me to your safe deposit boxes?"

"Why, yes—" Suddenly there was a man standing at DeMaris's elbow.

"I'll be happy to assist you. Marilyn needs to get her papers delivered." The gal stared at him for a second and then walked off. "I'm the manager here, Brian."

"Brian? Oh my." *Do some fluttering with your hands, that's what an old woman would do.* "How nice."

"Yes," said Brian. "And Blanche is such an attractive name. I've always liked it." *You've got to be kidding me!*

He smiled. He was actually good-looking: tall, trimmed brown hair, and blue eyes—yet something about him put her off. "Do you have your key with you?"

"Yes." But she made no move to get it.

"Well, if you give it to me," he held out his hand, "I'll be happy to get your box for you and bring it to you. You can sit in my office." He motioned behind her. "I'll have one of the girls bring you some coffee."

She stood there. Were things different in this state? "Where I come from, we have someone with a second key who helps unlock the box and then I go in a private room, by myself."

He motioned again to his office. "You will have a private room all to yourself."

"Brian," they heard someone call. He raised a hand indicating not now while he kept his eyes on DeMaris.

"I'm not . . . comfortable doing that," she said. *Something is not right here. He hasn't even asked me for identification.* "I just want you to take me to my box." *And then what am I going to do if he takes me there?*

"Brian!" The voice was more insistent now.

"Where are you from?" he asked pleasantly.

"I live mostly in Michigan."

"And you have a safe deposit box here? In Idaho?"

"Ahhh . . ." *Shit! I was just curious about what was in the box. I wasn't going to take anything. Yeah, like I was going to get that far. I just need this for my new book. I was only going to walk in, look, and leave! Why didn't I stick with that plan? Oh, yeah, because there's no fun in that. What is with this guy? You're a writer. You live on imagination, think of something!* "My friend did . . . died and . . . mailed the key to me. She wanted me to have the contents."

"Oh, so your friend died here? What's her name? I probably knew her." *None of your beeswax! This story would work if only Viva were dead. Has Viva mentioned any friends of hers that recently croaked?*

"Brian!"

"Then we definitely have some paperwork to fill out. Please step into my office and I'll be right with you." His hand gripped her elbow and he forcibly pushed her into his office; then he left to address the matter up at the front.

Shit. This was not going to work. He would undoubtedly ask for ID at some point. All right, she couldn't prove she was Blanche; in fact, she couldn't even prove she was herself. She'd brought nothing with her except the various clothes she wore and some money. *I need to leave now!* She turned to see Brian with his back to her. Quietly she walked out of his office and headed toward the side door. She glanced over to see row upon row of boxes. *People get their mail here too?* She turned to see Marilyn in her office staring at her. DeMaris pointed. "That's sure nice." *Talk slow, remember nasal.* "Getting your money and mail all at the same time."

Marilyn smiled at her. *Poor old, dotty woman.* "No, those are safe deposit boxes, dear."

DeMaris swung back around and looked at them. "You've got them out in the open—" *No!* She was talking quickly in her own voice, she was so startled. She cleared her throat. "Mine back home are all locked up. You need a bank employee to get to your box."

Marilyn nodded. "Yes. I remember those days. This bank is only five years old. When we knocked down the old building and built this one they went with user-friendly boxes. This way you don't have to wait for one of us. You're the only one with a key."

"I don't have to wait for someone with a second key?"

"No, ma'am. You just go to whatever box is yours and get it out yourself."

So why didn't Brian, the manager tell me that? "Where would I find number 1501?"

Marilyn frowned and shook her head. "You won't find that number here."

"Oh." DeMaris was stumped. *Why had Brian wanted her key so badly that he hadn't even asked her what number she had? Why hadn't he pointed out the boxes only ten feet from where they had been standing?* "Is there another bank in town?"

"Yes." Marilyn gave DeMaris directions.

"Thank you," DeMaris headed for the door.

"Brian!"

DeMaris turned and saw him walking her way. *Dang it! Give it up, Brian.* Behind him she could see a young girl of about nineteen who looked flustered. "Mr. Fox!" she called out.

DeMaris saw Brian stop. His eyes met hers and they were anything but pleasant. The young girl was at his side now talking to him; he could go no farther.

DeMaris quickly flat-footed herself out the door. She made her way down the sidewalk, turned, and as soon as she felt she was out of eyesight from the bank, she put one hand on her hat, the other gathered up her long skirt, and she ran.

She made it through the first light and to the middle of the next block before she got to laughing at herself and went back to a flat-footed walk. She must be a sight in her get-up and running for all she was worth. Did she really think a bank manager was going to leave his job just to chase her? Not really, but maybe in her book . . . DeMaris glanced over her shoulder.

Holy crap! What's he doing outside the bank? Brian had gotten stopped at the traffic light but was now making his way across the street. *I don't believe him!* She ducked down an alley. She needed both hands to hold up the skirt so she could run. For the last few months, she had been jogging with a friend three times a week—and she'd hated it. Now she was thankful. DeMaris glanced back and the hat flew off. *Sorry Viva! Hope it wasn't your favorite one.* For a long-haired lady with a lot of gray, she was putting distance between herself and Brian—but where should she go? *Mom! Dad! Somebody up there help me! God, this braless bit is not for running. Boobs on the chin, boobs on the waist, boobs on the chin, boobs on the waist . . . Yes, Mom, I know that was not smart of me but I was only after information. I swear, that was all I was doing! The courthouse? Dad your attorney days are over—people. There will be people there. Thanks, Dad.*

The big impressive building stood in the middle of town. She dashed up the steps, barely breathing hard; Brian was obviously out of shape. She flung the door open, ran up the flight of stairs in front of her, and then looked for a courtroom.

One was in session; she quietly let herself in. Although there were seats near the back, she didn't want Brian to see her so she went three rows up and pushed herself past several people. "Excuse me," she whispered. She plopped herself down between two men. One looked to be in his twenties, the other in his fifties. Good, to anybody glancing inside the room it would look like two parents sitting with their delinquent son.

She needed to do something with her hair. Undoubtedly Brian had gotten a look at it. She removed the very noticeable purple, pink, and orange sweater and fished around in Melissa's skirt pocket. She had noticed the hair tie when she'd put it on. She dropped her head between her knees, combed her fingers through her hair, wrapped the hair tie once, and pulled her hair through. She wrapped it a second time, but this time only pulled her hair halfway so that the bottom half was caught in the tie. That way nobody could tell how long her hair really was.

She glanced around. *Good, nobody seems to be looking.* Carefully she pulled her top off and folded it neatly. Very slowly she unzipped the side zipper to the skirt and slid it off. She sat quietly as the two men beside her watched. She got the second layer peeled off. The older of the two men leaned over and whispered, "How far you goin' with this?"

"Not much further," she whispered back. She was squirming out of the third layer when she was hit in the head with a purse. She turned around to see an elderly woman glaring at her.

"This is a court of law, show some respect!" she hissed.

"I'm terribly sorry. I'm . . . hot." Carefully DeMaris stripped off one more layer. She could see both men eyeing her now and why not? She was down to her own thin tank top, braless, and it showed. She grabbed one of the t-shirts and put it back on. She had a pile of clothes, which if they'd been hers she'd have left behind, but they weren't so she couldn't. *What to do with them?* She turned the sweater inside out. The purl side looked slightly different and you could no longer see the appliqué flowers. She placed the other clothes inside and tied the arms together.

Then she sat. For two hours. *This is a great idea Dad. Why didn't I just go into the women's restroom? By now Brian should have left the building. Surely he could not stay away from the bank for this length of time. What was that all about?* DeMaris wondered now that she had time to kill sitting there.

He had latched onto Blanche's name immediately but had said nothing about having the same last name. He didn't sound like anyone Sophocles imitated. Was Brian a relative? Son? Nephew? Grandson? But if he did know a Blanche Fox (and she'd just thrown those two names together at the last minute) then he would know she was lying. So, why hadn't he called her bluff?

He wanted that key.

Chapter Six

She filed out of the courtroom with the rest of the people, looked quickly around for Brian, did not see him, and headed for the front door. She decided against returning to the alley to look for Viva's gardening hat. It wasn't worth the risk. Instead she walked down Main Street.

She also decided against going to the other bank. DeMaris had had enough excitement for one day and needed to come up with a better explanation as to why she was looking for a safe deposit box that she couldn't get into plus she needed to get back to Viva's.

For some reason the drugstore caught her eye. Was she supposed to be doing something there? No, but a candy bar would sure taste good. She walked out of the drugstore chewing her Milky Way bar. To get to the marina, she would have to walk several blocks to avoid the bank; and hauling the bundle of clothes was a real pain. She ate the Milky Way while she studied a bag lady sitting on the sidewalk. DeMaris walked up to her. "Hey, do you have a clean bag that can hold this stuff?" She held up the stuffed sweater. "I'll buy you a meal for it."

"Want money," barked the bag lady.

"No money," countered DeMaris. "You'll just use it for booze or drugs. What would you like? Hamburger? Meatloaf? Spaghetti?"

"Steak."

"Steak? Have you got the teeth for it?"

The woman showed her yellow teeth, but a solid set all the same. "Money."

"No money. I'll get you a steak, but let's see the bag." The woman eyed DeMaris for a moment then rummaged around in her grocery cart. The bag she produced was big enough but it was filthy. Everything would be protected by the sweater though and it was all washable. DeMaris debated with herself. She could always knit Jacyne another sweater if she had to.

"Hold clothes while ya get meal." The woman stuck out her hand.

"No," said DeMaris, seeing the headline: Woman Fights with Bag Lady for New Wardrobe. She could envision the woman claiming that the clothes were hers all along.

DeMaris ducked inside the family-style restaurant. Twenty minutes later she came out with a Styrofoam takeout box and silverware. "The people inside are trusting you to give these back, so please do. I just couldn't see you cutting this with plastic."

"Cheap stuff." The woman sniffed her disdain at the thin silverware.

"Yeah, well, they still want it back." DeMaris handed her the box. The bag lady opened it and stared. There was steak, green beans, and mashed potatoes with gravy. "They seemed to know you inside. Said you liked coffee, so here." She handed her a Styrofoam cup. "And I bought you a water." She shook the bottle before handing it to her. "You know what this is?" DeMaris held up an envelope. "It's a gift certificate for one hundred dollars. This way you can go inside and order yourself some food when you're hungry."

"Why?" she demanded.

"So you don't starve!"

She shook her head. "Why ya doin' this?" She eyed DeMaris suspiciously as she ate.

"Because, I've seen the rich walk by with their heads held high and I've seen people who had nothing share what they could. Now, it's my turn to share."

The woman stared at DeMaris while she chewed her steak. "Need different bag." She shoved the Styrofoam box at DeMaris and started to go back through her grocery cart.

"That's really not necessary."

"Here," the woman thrust a different bag at her while grabbing the box of food back as if she thought DeMaris might finish it off. She had pulled it up from the very bottom of the cart. The bag was semi-clean except for one big stain. *Hmm, not a bad looking bag.* The clothes wouldn't all fit. Deciding that the sweater stood out the most, she put that inside, got Melissa's gypsy skirt in, and carried the rest of the clothing in her arms. DeMaris thanked the woman and then asked, "Where's the Walmart store?"

"Don't got one. Spokane."

"Spokane?" *Hmm, something to ask Viva about.* "Hey, if you come across a large brimmed hat with flowers on it, it belongs to a friend of mine. Pick it up for me, would you? I'll check in on you before I go."

She suddenly saw the time. *Great!* The girls would be home by now. She had hoped to return their clothes before they arrived. Maybe they were still shopping. She hurried to the marina, threw the bag and clothes in the rowboat, and took off.

DeMaris rowed as quickly as she could, pulled up to Viva's dock in record time, and threw the rope around a post. To hell with the oars, she'd come back later for them. She grabbed the bag and clothes and ran for the house. *Gosh, I can write about everything that happened today in my new novel.*

"Shay! Shay! You are never going to believe this!" she yelled excitedly as she entered the house. "I am living one of my own mys—" DeMaris came to an abrupt halt. *Uh-oh.* "—teries." She was face to face with her sorority sisters. They were all in the room. None of them looked happy.

"Where have you been?"

"I took the boat out for a ride."

"Where are my pills?" asked Shay. "Remember, migraine?"

"Oh! I knew there was something—"

"You didn't get them?"

"No, sorry. I have chocolate—no, I ate that."

"Of course you would remember chocolate!" yelled Shay.

"And of course you ate it," said Jacyne.

"Let me see if I have something," Melissa disappeared down the hallway.

"I got caught up in something and I forgot. I'm sorry, Shay," said DeMaris.

Melissa was soon back with an aspirin bottle in hand. "Which one of you went through my clothes?" Shay immediately pointed at DeMaris.

"I've got your stuff right here," she set the bag and clothes down on the table.

"That's mine!"

"That's mine!"

"That's mine!"

"So, how was the movie? Did you girls buy anything? Find any exciting shops?" DeMaris asked, hoping to distract them.

"Hey, Viva!" hollered Sara into the next room, "Don't forget to tell DeMaris that you ran into Gloria."

"Who's Gloria?" asked DeMaris.

"DeMaris," Caroline was swinging her top back and forth.

"I borrowed it. I gave it back. What? You want me to wash it?"

"No. Well, I guess that depends on where it's been. I want an explanation."

"I . . . needed it."

She could see Caroline about to blow when Sara stepped forward. "Do you . . . not have any clothes of your own?"

"Oh, God." DeMaris looked skyward.

"Why didn't you say something?"

"We'll take you shopping."

"We're your sisters!"

"Don't look at me like I'm destitute! I have clothes! I have money!"

"She needed to fatten herself up." They turned to Shay. "What were you talking about when you came in: living one of your own mysteries?"

She looked from one to the other. Clearly they were not going to let her leave the room quietly. "I got an idea for a book and I've been taking notes."

"You've written ten or more books and done nothing with them—yet you continue to write?"

DeMaris nodded. "I love writing, hate getting rejection letters."

"So, you *have* tried to get published."

"Yes, I have and what it boils down to is that you basically have to know somebody in the field. I write for the enjoyment of it. I don't need a lot of money or recognition. It's the actual writing that fulfills me. I do all right with my freelance stuff."

"De, you need to come down to earth," said Jacyne. "Find a job that pays decently, maybe with some benefits, and write in your spare time. You are such a dreamer."

"And don't sell yourself short. Maybe you will get rejected but maybe somebody will buy your books. You have to at least try!" This from Sara.

DeMaris glanced at her. "Has anybody seen the kitchen?"

"Oh, yeah. Gorgeous."

"It's beautiful."

"You have a talent. Why not start up a business doing that?" They all walked into the kitchen to look at it again.

"What'd ya think?" DeMaris asked Viva as she entered the kitchen carrying Sophocles in his cage.

"Wow! That's all I can say. Shay told me you were good but . . . it's incredible what you did with a few stencils and paint, De."

DeMaris looked at her handiwork. "I don't think the other two walls need anything. It would just overwhelm. I thought I'd leave it like this."

"I agree," said Viva.

"It really livened up the room," said Liset. "It inspires me to be creative with food."

"Oh, good. I'm glad I was able to do one thing right."

Viva had picked out stencils of vines and birds; she had imagined the vines going across the room like a border, with a few birds in it. DeMaris, however, looked at the vines and on one wall had them pointing down and overlapping each other with birds flitting here and there. It gave it a jungle appearance rather than a plain everyday border. On the second wall, which also held cupboards, she only painted a few vines and birds giving the feeling of just leaving or entering "the jungle" depending on your point of view or entry.

"You are so creative—and always have been. Why don't you harness that—"

"*I write!*"

"—and start your own business?"

While they were discussing what DeMaris should be doing about her future, she did a slow burn.

"—sell your quilts, sew for people—"

"Who's Gloria?"

"Oh! I nearly forgot!" said Viva.

"Yes, tell her about Gloria," said Liset.

"You're going to be so excited," this from Caroline.

"Gloria is one of my friends who is on the rowing team in town. We bumped into her today and she told me that Paula—one of the other gals—had to fly to Florida because of an emergency with her daughter. She's going to be gone indefinitely and now they're short one person to practice with."

DeMaris's face lit up, "And you told her about me?!"

"We sure did. Do you want to row tomorrow?"

"Yes! Oh, thank you!" And then it suddenly struck DeMaris. She couldn't be seen looking like this. At least not by anyone who lived or worked in town. Not after Brian, the restaurant people, and the bag lady had seen her.

"Can your stylist do my hair today?"

They all stopped talking and stared at DeMaris. "Today? Like *now*?"

"Now would be great. You should take advantage of this while I'm in the mood. I'll let you do whatever you want—cut, color."

"I'll give the boat keys to Jacyne and you can row the two of us into town. That way we can all meet for dinner."

"Deal."

After putting on a scarf, a bra and a different blouse, DeMaris was ready to leave. The other gals would follow in two hours.

"What Walmart store did you get that bird from?"

"I didn't get him— Spokane."

"I need to check those papers."

"What papers? He didn't come with any."

"Newspapers. Do you bank here, in town?"

"We have a small account here. Our main one is back home, in Nevada. Why?"

"Which bank?"

Viva eyed DeMaris suspiciously but told her.

"Is that the new bank or the old one?"

"The old one. How do you know—"

"Oh, good. I need to go there. What's their safe deposit box setup?"

"You don't want to get one here. You want—"

"I know that. Are the boxes locked up? I mean, in a vault? Do you need a bank employee for a second key?"

"Yes. Why?"

"Can we stop there?"

"No. Not until you tell me—"

"How do you think I should get my hair done?"

"De," Viva started; then stopped. DeMaris had always jumped from one subject to the other. It was just easier to go with her flow.

Two hours later they entered the restaurant. "You look great!"

"You look ten years younger!"

"I really like it."

The only thing DeMaris had insisted on at the salon was change. "I want something totally different." Viva and her hair stylist had done the rest. Her hair was now blonde with highlights and cut extremely short. *Greg is going to kill me,* was her only thought.

But she had to admit she liked it.

Over dessert, the conversation turned to finding someone for DeMaris.

"I don't need anybody!" she insisted.

"I know a nice banker," said Liset. "Nice-looking, money, intelligent—"

"What's wrong with him that nobody has snagged him yet?"

"Oh, no. He's been snagged three times."

"I know someone," said Sara. "He's been widowed for over a year. Still can't get over losing his wife. Maybe you could help him get on with his life."

"Just what I want to do."

"Somehow I don't see DeMaris as the sympathetic type," offered Jacyne.

The rest of them talked about men they knew—as if DeMaris wasn't there. "Honestly," she finally said, "I told you I have someone."

Silence. Stares.

"You were serious?" asked Shay.

"Yes. I told you, you'll see him tonight."

"If that were true, wouldn't we be sitting at home waiting for him?" asked Jacyne.

"No." DeMaris smiled. "You'll see . . . tonight." They couldn't get any more out of her.

"Fine," said Melissa. "Keep your secret. Right now, what I want to know is what you were doing with our clothes."

DeMaris squirmed. "I needed to look different. I got an idea for another book— don't start up about publishing again—and wanted to try something out. I didn't want to go into town looking like me because we're here as Viva's guests and I know everybody in town knows her. I did it so I wouldn't embarrass Viva. Nobody knew who I was."

"Yes, you never embarrass us," Caroline said dryly.

"At least this time I made an attempt not to!" DeMaris shot back. "I didn't know what was going to transpire at the bank and when we went into town later I didn't want anybody pointing me out, okay? I went in disguise for all of your sakes."

"You asked me about banks in the boat," Viva sat up. "Did you already go into one?"

"Maybe."

"What exactly did you do there?"

"I . . . I didn't do anything."

"*DeMaris,*" three of them said.

"I just went to look around. I spoke to some of the employees. Nothing happened."

"I hear an 'I can explain' coming up," muttered Shay.

"Something happened," Melissa sat up. "*That's* why you had your hair done."

Viva glanced at Melissa. "You went to the new one, didn't you?" There were several groans. DeMaris made a face. "You are *not* going to mine."

"Oh, come on!" *No wait. Maybe it would be better if I went by myself.* "Fine, be that way." DeMaris leaned back in her chair as if she were pouting.

"Well, she's not going to tell us anything now," sighed Shay.

The girls went back to the subject of eligible men for DeMaris; but in the end decided none would survive her.

"Here it is! Here it is!" yelled DeMaris excitedly. "Come see!"

"We're not watching TV on vacation."

"Oh, I love this show."

"Let's go sit outside and enjoy our drinks. There's a nice breeze."

"We don't have to watch TV," said DeMaris. "I just want you to see the dreamiest-looking guy."

"I know who you mean," said Sara. "Greg Delray."

"Yes!" DeMaris tapped her finger on the screen to point him out to the gals who didn't watch the popular crime show. "Now, this is top secret—but this is who I'm dating."

Except for the TV there was silence. The girls stood or sat motionless. "Come on! If I were the famous DeMaris Azaygo, this is who I would want to be dating."

"How far were we supposed to take this 'change our identity thing'?" Jacyne whispered to Caroline.

Caroline shrugged.

"Oh, I want a hunky TV star for a boyfriend," said Melissa.

"Yeah, well, let's be realistic," commented Shay. "De, he's young enough to be your son."

"Actually he's thirteen years younger and since I didn't start having sex at that age, he couldn't possibly be my son."

"How do you know he's thirteen years younger?"

"I had to research him too, as long as that's who I'm dating. Come on, ask me a question about him. See if you can stump me."

They all looked at each other. "We don't know anything about him; so we wouldn't know if you were making it up or not."

"Oh. Well, that's good to know. If anybody asks me something I don't know about him, I'll hope they don't know any more than you and then I'll just make up something. Thanks for the tip."

"Great."

"Can you guys keep a secret? Well, of course you can; so here's the secret you need to keep." They sat stone-faced and DeMaris plunged on. "He's asked me to marry him and I'm considering it."

Silence.

Finally Shay got out, "Who?"

DeMaris pointed to the TV screen. "Greg Delray!"

The girls once again glanced at one another.

"I'm DeMaris Azaygo this week. *Hello*, let's keep up with the plot! Honestly, you people have no imagination!"

Chapter Seven

"I wasn't expecting you to be up this early," said Liset as she pulled her bathrobe tighter around her body.

"I see that," said DeMaris, who gave a long look to Liset before glancing at the man hopping into his truck and driving away. "Well, most of the ladies on the rowing team work; so this is the only time they can practice."

"At five-thirty in the morning?"

"Yep! I'm hyped!"

"I can see that . . . Are you going to tell?"

"No. But I should," said DeMaris.

"Thank you. Have fun."

—◦— —◦◦— —◦—

Gloria introduced DeMaris to the other two women. "As you can see, we're rowing straight four."

DeMaris stared at Gloria for a moment when it hit her. "Ah, no coxswain."

"Right."

"That will be a little different for me," said DeMaris. "But I will manage."

—◦— —◦◦— —◦—

By eight o'clock DeMaris was back at Viva's. The house was still quiet. She took her notepad and pen and sat on the far side of the deck. A half hour later, Shay wandered outside and found her.

"What are you doing?"

"Writing. Need to get some ideas down before I forget them."

Shay sat down across from her. "Want to talk about anything?"

"No."

"De, we're worried—" she stopped as DeMaris put up a finger. She continued to write and then stopped. She set the pen down, leaned back in her chair, laced her fingers together, and gave Shay her full attention.

Shay leaned forward. "We're worried about you. You . . . haven't exactly been yourself and you need to think about your future. Now that you're divorced you need to be thinking about how you're going to pay bills, where you're going to live—"

"Are you offering?"

"Well, you're certainly welcome to come and stay with me, with any of us, but . . . you need a plan. You need an income, benefits, things of that nature."

"How old do you think I am? Or how stupid? Don't any of you think I haven't thought of these things? Did you ever think I might be getting alimony?"

"Yes. But . . . Oh, come on. We all know that you and Kirk never lived high on the hog. You can't be getting much."

"Did you ever consider that maybe we liked the simple life?" Shay looked doubtful. "What makes you think we were so bad off?"

"Well, the cars that you drove forever."

"We really liked not having car payments."

"You bought a really old house."

"It's historic."

"Because it was cheap."

"It needed a lot of attention. Any idea how much attention it cost us?"

"Yes, but the two of you did all the work because, well, you couldn't afford to hire anyone."

"We contracted for a couple of things. The kids helped out. It was a learning experience for all of us. We actually enjoyed doing the work. It's called self-reliance, family projects."

"DeMaris," Shay said kindly, "you live on a farm."

They stared at each other. "Let me remind you that it is a nonworking farm. You say that with such distaste. Do you want to venture where your food comes from?"

"I'm just saying that while the rest of us did something with our degrees, actually worked, you and Kirk . . ."

"Went a different route," finished DeMaris. "Kirk taught for awhile. We enjoyed our life. We knew and liked our neighbors—unlike those of you who have a fancy address in Washington DC, Chicago, Santa Barbara, or Bloomfield Hills and don't know your neighbors. We led the life we wanted. None of you seemed to mind visiting us. You never heard Kirk and me complain, did you?" DeMaris was starting to fume. "You guys all went after material things. Kirk and I didn't. We raised our kids simply and they have a childhood to remember instead of just sitting in front of the TV. We camped out to be with nature. Yes, it was a cheap way to go, but we met some interesting people along the way. I never had a problem with the way we lived—and I don't think Kirk did either. And, quite frankly, it's none of anybody's business how we lived."

"I didn't mean to upset you." Shay raised a hand. "But, the two of you always lived for today. There was no planning for the future. We're worried, DeMaris."

"None of you are going to have to support me."

"Why not?"

"Why not?" DeMaris stared at Shay in disbelief. "Because I'm perfectly capable of taking care of myself."

"Are you gonna make me say it?"

"What?"

Shay sighed and said softly, "We don't want you to, you know . . ."

"Commit suicide?"

"Yeah."

"I wish you girls could let that go. That was a low point in my life. I am past that—*way* past that. I am not going to do anything stupid. I promise."

"You promised me that before and then we all found out about you being in a body cast because you—"

"And I told you, I was researching an idea I had for a story. It went horribly wrong I admit—"

"No, it didn't go horribly wrong! Fortunately you are still with us," said Shay. "We really, really wish you'd seek help for your depression. Do it for your family, for us. Please."

"What? I'm *not* depressed. I wasn't depressed then."

"Then, why can't you tell us how you came to be in a body cast?"

DeMaris sighed. "I did something *really* stupid. I know. You girls think I've done a lot of stupid things . . . but this . . . kind of topped it. If I tell you, do you promise not to tell the others? I mean, I am really embarrassed. As I was flying through the air, I thought: this is really stupid."

"Flying through the air?"

"I was Velcro woman." Shay stared at her. "You see them at fairs. They

51

put you in this suit with Velcro all over it and then they shoot you toward . . . you stick . . . I thought of something else to do . . . Ya know what? If you're that curious, they had a big write up in the paper about it. The fortunate thing about being in the body cast was that the fairgrounds and the Velcro people agreed not to sue me. They figured I'd gotten my punishment. But the point I'm trying to make is that I wasn't *trying* to kill myself. It was just an unfortunate accident."

Shay studied DeMaris for several seconds, shook her head, and said, "You and Kirk were always so blasé about the future and this is the result. Liset's husband has talked to you about investing, all of us have made suggestions—but to no avail. You always sounded like Scarlett O'Hara: 'I'll think about that tomorrow.'"

"Don't worry, I have a plan."

"Where are you going when you leave here?" asked Shay.

"To a friend's house."

"May I ask who?"

"I'd rather not say."

"Okay, this is not like you," said Shay. "You've been cagey, evasive . . . you've always had a wonderful imagination but . . . you're beginning . . . to not see the difference . . . between . . . fact and fantasy."

"I see," said DeMaris as her lips curled.

"God, DeMaris!" Shay slammed her hands on the table. "You are *so* exasperating! We are trying to help you and the whole reason you're in the spot you're in is because of your live-for-today-never-think-about-tomorrow attitude. It's not fair that we ALL have to suffer for it."

"Do you honestly think," DeMaris's voice was so low Shay, at the risk of being hit, leaned in closer to hear, "I haven't thought about the future? Don't forget—oh, that's right, none of you ever let me—that I always have suicide as a choice. I'm always thinking about the future. So, don't worry about having to take care of me! I can take care of myself." She snapped her notepad shut, got up, and walked into the house.

—◆— —◆·◆— —◆—

"Where's DeMaris?" asked Liset when Shay walked into the kitchen. They were on their own for breakfast. Various fruit and cereals were sitting out. It was easier this way since everybody was getting up whenever they felt like it.

"Taking a shower."

Liset was waiting for DeMaris when she came through the kitchen door. Liset placed a green-and-white bag on the counter. "Do you know what this is?" she demanded.

"Yeah, it's the bag I had some of your clothes in— Oh, my gosh! That's a Coach purse, isn't it?" Liset had cleaned it, had even removed the huge stain. It looked as good as new.

"This is a Coach pur— how do you know what it is?"

"Yeah, living down on the farm, I wouldn't know of such things."

"Well, no. I just meant . . . I mean, you're not into purses, accessories, or that sort of stuff. Do you know how much this is worth?"

"I'd say about four or five hundred dollars."

"This is worth—" Liset started to shake the bag. "Yeah. How did you— Where did you get this?"

"I paid for it in town."

"You paid four or five hundred dollars for a purse? When you don't have a job?" *She's just getting more irresponsible with age!*

"Would you people stop harping? No, I did not pay anywhere near that. Truth be told, I bought it off a bag lady for a whole lot less."

Liset leaned across the counter. "De, it's just you and me here. Tell me where you got the purse."

DeMaris looked at her then bit her lip and cast her eyes downward. Tears started to fill her eyes. "Oh, God. Liset, if I tell you, you have to promise not to tell anyone."

"Of course, of course." Liset leaned in closer.

"Well," DeMaris sniffed, "things have been really rough since the divorce. I . . . oh, this is so embarrassing."

"It's all right. You can tell me."

"Well, I ended up on welfare. In my community, they have a program where they give out coupons to the Salvation Army and . . . I went there . . ." DeMaris blew her nose and sniffled. "Somebody must have died because there were a bunch of clothes just brought in that were my size. New, can you believe? It really was most fortuitous. Anyway, someone had also donated the purse. You saw the big stain. I didn't care. I just liked it . . . Oh, what you must think. I mean, at last, I could actually *own* a Coach purse."

"Oh, DeMaris. I'm so sorry. What you've had to go through. Here," Liset picked up her own purse and pulled out a wad of cash.

"What are you doing?" demanded DeMaris.

"I really like the purse. Let me pay you what it's worth."

"No!"

"Here's three hundred. I can get more for you at the ATM when we go into town. This way you'll have a little spending cash while here."

"Liset, no! If you want the purse, just take it. I don't need your money."

"This isn't charity. I'm paying you for the purse."

"I don't want you to pay me. Just take it!"

"Forget it." Liset shoved the bills into DeMaris's hand.

"No! Take the money, Liset."

"No!"

"What's going on in here?" asked Sara. She had decided to investigate the shouting.

Liset had a ready explanation. "DeMaris is trying to pay for everybody's meals. Look at this. Three hundred dollars." She shook the money and threw it on the counter.

DeMaris's mouth dropped as she stared at Liset, who wouldn't look at her. It dropped more when Sara said, "Honestly, De. What are you thinking? We've already covered your share. You need to hang on to your money. However, if you're going to be that way about it, we each chipped in fifty." Sara counted out fifty dollars and slid it across to Liset and then handed the rest to DeMaris. "There, happy?"

DeMaris looked from one to the other. "Are you telling me you gals paid for the groceries upfront and that you never told me what my share was?" She was yelling now. Liset was quite taken with her new bag.

"This is not a time to be proud," continued Sara. "You have helped us all out at one time or another."

"I have always paid my own way!"

"And now it's our time to help you out. Let us do this for you." She shook her head. "Come on, we're all out by the pool." Liset walked outside with Sara.

DeMaris sat with two hundred fifty dollars in her hand and did a very rapid burn.

———   —◆—   ———

"You're not teaching him any dirty words, are you?" asked Viva, who heard DeMaris talking to the African gray as she walked into the house.

"No, I'm saving that for my last day here. I'm trying to get him to tell me about the key."

"Never lose this key!" warned Sophocles in a woman's high-pitched voice.

"I haven't lost the key. Where does the key go?" DeMaris didn't want to name any banks in case the bird just picked one and repeated it. She wanted him to answer without any guidance.

"There is no key, DeMaris. Give it up. Come on out to the pool."

DeMaris kept her back to Viva and bobbed her head up and down with the bird. "I need more information for my book. I'm doing research here."

"Just make something up."

She heard Viva leave the room. Carefully DeMaris pulled out her gold chain from beneath her blouse. She wiggled the key dangling at the end of it in front of Sophocles. The bird eyed her but said nothing.

"You know what this goes to," she whispered. "Playing hard to get, huh? Maybe I'll go ask Liset if she knows how to fix roast parrot—or whatever it is Viva calls you. What do you say to that?"

Sophocles remained silent and eventually DeMaris made her way to the pool.

Chapter Eight

"I really need to go to the bathroom," said DeMaris. "Is there a public restroom around here?" One of the women on the rowing team pointed. "I am not using a Porta-John. Where's there a real bathroom?"

"There isn't one."

DeMaris looked down at the water. *I think I'll use the lake before I get inside one of those smelly, nauseating things.*

"If you want to walk three blocks," offered Gloria, "you can use the shop bathroom."

"The shop bathroom?"

"Yeah. I own a small store: The Nasty Habit. The bathroom's not open to the public but Rachel's there. Tell her I sent you, and hurry." The rowers weren't happy. Nobody had to work early today so they were meeting at nine. Now they had to wait on a bathroom break.

"I have to go! Of course, I'll hurry! Thank you." DeMaris took off. Always a fast walker (being short she always had to keep up with her long-legged friends) she was there in no time. It was a shop full of vintage wear and knick knacks. DeMaris recognized things she'd grown up with in the sixties, and seventies. *Neat store,* she thought as she gazed around.

DeMaris's ears suddenly perked up. "Tim, stop. Someone might see us."

"There's nobody around."

"Tim, really." This was followed by giggling. There was more conversation she couldn't distinguish, giggling, the sound of items being moved . . . *Great, what have I walked into?* DeMaris sighed and came around the corner. "Hi," she yelled.

She heard a scream and saw a man with his hand way up on the woman's thigh. He had her pinned down on top of the counter. He immediately stood up, letting the woman right herself.

"You must be Rachel," DeMaris smiled.

The woman got her feet on the ground and pulled down on her skirt as well she should. Next, her hands flew to her hair and she tried to do the best she could without a mirror. "Yes, can I help you?" The woman was as red as anybody DeMaris had ever seen.

"Now I know why Gloria has the cleanest counters in town."

The man had not turned around. The young woman turned purple.

"Okay . . . I'm with the rowing team. Gloria said I could use the bathroom."

"Yes, well, fine." Her hands were back to straightening her skirt.

"And it would be where?"

Rachel pointed. As DeMaris walked toward the bathroom, a thought suddenly came to her. She snapped her fingers and yelled over her shoulder, "The Nasty Habit! I get it!"

DeMaris hurried to relieve herself. *Ahhhh, there are times this feels better than sex.* She was washing her hands when she heard a commotion. She turned the water off. Yes, there was definitely shouting. A holdup or were the lovey-dovey couple arguing already?

DeMaris opened the door a crack. "Joe, for God's sake," said Rachel. *I thought his name was Tim. Maybe that's why they're arguing. She's mixed him up with somebody else.* "You can't come in here and talk to the customers like that."

"He's not a customer!"

"I am too a customer." *Ah, that must be Tim.* "I came in to buy this."

Oh. This is just great. How do I stumble in on stuff like this? DeMaris rolled her eyes. *People always think it's me! Honestly, things just happen that I have no control over. Mom, Dad, I'm trapped in the bathroom. Any ideas?*

"I've been watching and this isn't the first time you've been here."

"Joe, please."

"Have you ever heard of a repeat customer?"

DeMaris whipped open the door. "Tim. Honey? Are you ready to go? Thank you for letting me use—" She came down the aisle and stopped. All three stared at her. "Is there a problem?" DeMaris asked innocently.

Joe had the startled look of someone who realized he'd made a terrible mistake. For the first time, Tim faced her. *Wow, I can see why Rachel is fooling around with him, good-looking.* Rachel stood beyond the two men, her hands to her head. Tim grinned and then his face hardened as he turned to Joe. "I'm not going to stand here and be accused of something I didn't do—and I am definitely not paying for this." He set down the object he held in his hand. "You know," he turned to Rachel who still couldn't look at him, "if he's like this with every male customer who comes in here, you're definitely not going to last long in this business."

"Oh, wait. Wait a minute," said Joe.

Tim turned to DeMaris. "Come on, we're leaving."

The two of them walked out together as Joe tried apologizing. They both ignored him.

They got halfway down the block before DeMaris turned and said, "If you're going to have an affair, for God's sake, don't do it in public."

"I know. I know. Thank you! I owe you."

"Well, you can buy me off with a candy bar." She pointed to the drugstore. "I'm dying for some chocolate and I have no money on me."

"Lady, I'll buy you a five-pound box." He opened the door for her.

"That's not necessary."

"I insist."

The rowing team was getting restless waiting for DeMaris. Finally one of them spotted her. "Here she comes."

With her mouth full, DeMaris offered the chocolate box to each of them. "We've been waiting for you and you stopped off to buy chocolate?" one of the gals accused.

"I had to use the bathroom and then this guy offered to buy me chocolate. I just can't say no to chocolate. Fortunately, no strange men ever approached me as a little kid." She saw the puzzled looks. "I'd be dead! I can't say no to chocolate. I'd have gotten in some strange guy's car and been raped, beaten, and killed."

"But as an adult," Gloria ventured, "you decided it was safe to take candy from a stranger?"

"Well, I'm smarter now. There were people around and then I ditched him."

"Who was this guy?" asked one of the women.

"I don't know, some stranger."

"But *why* would he buy you chocolate?"

"I helped him out of a tight spot. This was his thank-you to me."

The girls stared at DeMaris and then Gloria ventured once again, "Viva says you try out different lines on them all the time for your books. Is this one of them?"

"Yeah. What'd ya think?"

"No stranger is just going to—"

"Can we row?" someone yelled. "Some of us have time constraints."

"Sorry."

The practice went well and with DeMaris rowing they shaved seconds off their best time. "Gosh, I wish you could go to competition with us," one said.

"Don't let Paula find out you said that!"

"We're getting better," offered Gloria to DeMaris. "We've been together for a couple of years now."

"I am really enjoying this. Thank you for inviting me."

"Thanks for helping us out. We really need the practice. So, can you be here at six the rest of the week?"

"Wouldn't miss it. And I won't let Liset force juice and tea down me before I come."

"We'd appreciate that."

DeMaris lingered on the pier until she was sure all the women had left. She hid the box of chocolates under a life jacket in Viva's rowboat to protect it from the sun and then made her way into town. DeMaris didn't see anybody she recognized. Slowly she walked to the second bank in town. It was a small brick building on a side street. DeMaris walked up the steps and pulled on the heavy door. She appeared to be the only customer.

"Can I help you?"

DeMaris turned and saw an older woman sitting in an office. "Yes, I'm going to be moving into the area shortly and am checking out the two banks in town. Can you tell me what you have to offer?"

The woman motioned for her to come in and sit down. She handed DeMaris several pamphlets while explaining their different accounts and CDs. "Thank you," interrupted DeMaris. "What about your safe deposit boxes?"

"Oh, I'm afraid they're all in use," the bank officer said. "I could put you on a waiting list though."

"How many do you have here?"

"Five hundred."

"Oh," clearly DeMaris was disappointed. "I don't suppose you start numbering your boxes at 1500, did you?"

"No," the woman laughed. "Is there a problem?"

"I know how stupid this sounds but . . . I'm into numerology. I have to have a higher number. This bank isn't going to work for me, I'm sorry." The woman stared at her. "Where might one go to . . . get a higher box number?"

"I suppose Spokane," she finally answered.

"Spokane, yes of course. All answers seem to lead there. Thank you." DeMaris promptly got up and left, leaving the pamphlets on the desk.

As she rowed back across the lake, DeMaris found her sisters water-skiing. When Melissa fell, DeMaris rowed over and tied the rowboat to the speed boat. They swam and sunned themselves until lunchtime.

"I'm not all that hungry," said DeMaris as she produced the five-pound box of chocolates.

"Where'd you get that?"

"I met some guy who got caught having an affair; so I pretended to be his wife and we escaped. He paid me off with this."

"Is this a story for your book?"

"Yeah, what do you think?"

"I don't find it very plausible. Come on, a box of chocolates?" Several of them nodded. "Only you would think of that."

"Okay, I'll think of something else. I was in town and picked it up."

They headed back to the house for food and a discussion on what to do next.

"Why don't we drive to Spokane?" asked DeMaris. "Do some shopping?"

"Okay." They nodded and left for their rooms to change clothes.

"We're not going for any ulterior motives, are we?" asked Viva when she got DeMaris alone.

"Yeah, I want to see the back of Walmart where you found the bird."

"You're not serious." The two stared at each other. "What do you hope to accomplish?"

"I've got an idea for a book. I want to get a feel for the place. Maybe I can find something that you overlooked and we can return him to his owner."

"I don't *want* to return him to his owner! He's mine."

"He's mine," squawked Sophocles from the living room.

While the others shopped, Viva begrudgingly took DeMaris behind Walmart. "See, there's nothing here."

"Where exactly did you find him?"

"I don't know. Just out back. Have you got a feel yet? I feel a little funny standing back here."

DeMaris looked at Viva. "What are you hiding?"

"Nothing."

They looked at each other. DeMaris decided to let it go. She wandered around back, taking in the garbage containers, the landscape, and the number of cars parked in the lot. She also observed Viva constantly looking around and checking her watch. "I'm ready."

"Thank God," she heard Viva mutter under her breath.

DeMaris made a beeline for the payphones when they got inside the store. "What are you doing now?"

"Why don't you go see what everybody else is doing?"

"Not until I know what you're doing."

"Honestly. I want to see," DeMaris opened up the phone book, "how many banks there are in Spokane."

"Why?"

DeMaris sighed. "In my story the main character actually finds a safe deposit key and she needs to go to the bank and see what's in the box."

"But why would you need to know that?"

"I want to make it as realistic as possible. If I make the story here, I need to see Spokane so people get a feel for it. We need to wander around town."

"We don't have to go inside banks, do we?" asked Viva.

"Hey! What a great idea," said DeMaris as if the thought had never crossed her mind. "Can we?"

Viva stared. "Sure. Let me get the girls. You're going to . . .?"

"Write down addresses."

Viva left. DeMaris waited until her friend was out of sight before she walked over to the greeter. "Do you have a copier here?"

"Yeah," the older woman pointed to the right.

"Thank you." DeMaris walked back to the phone book that was bolted to the wall. She waited until she was sure nobody was around and carefully ripped out the page she needed and stuffed it in her shorts pocket. She made her way to the copier, made a copy of the page, paid for it, stuffed the copy in her fanny pack, the original in her pocket, and returned to the phone book. She inserted the original page back inside the book. *Never let it be said that I stole anything. This is exciting though, it's just like being in the movies.*

On sudden inspiration she thumbed through to the F's. "Fox, Fox, Fox," she spoke quietly to herself. The only Fox listed was Foxx, Owen and Maureen. *A double x. I like that. 123 Jones St. That's certainly easy to remember.* She was disappointed not to find a Blanche Fox listed. Apparently Fox wasn't Blanche's last name. So that hunch hadn't panned out. *I need a last name to go into banks with—my character does anyway. Well, I guess Fox will work. It got me somewhere at the last bank, maybe it'll get me somewhere here.*

She found the girls arguing in the women's clothing section and stopped behind a rack to listen.

"She's not going to be suicidal this week," Shay said.

"Why? Because she's with us?" asked Caroline.

"No, because she's on the rowing team. That's always been a dream of hers." They all agreed with that.

"You don't think she's actually found a key and is trying to find the box—"

"Don't be ridiculous, Sara. I've had that bird for a while now. If there was a key to be found I'd have found it."

"Let's just humor her. How hard can it be to visit a few banks?" asked Jacyne.

"I agree."

"Yeah."

"I vote no. We've done this kind of stuff before and *nothing* ever goes as planned. Look what happened at the capitol building!" yelled Sara. She looked at Caroline who burst out laughing. "We were just going to look there too!"

"What capitol building?" asked Liset.

"The one in Lansing," Sara's voice was decibels louder than everyone else's.

Caroline laughed some more. "I'm sorry, it wasn't funny. It's *not* funny." She got as straight a face as she could.

The girls went back to staring at Sara. "I was visiting Caroline when DeMaris called and invited us to meet her at the capitol. She had, once again, an idea for a story and wanted to take a tour and look out the window from the top of the building. Did we want to join her? We said sure, and then agreed we would go out to lunch afterward. Tour, look out the window, lunch. Sounds harmless enough, right?"

"Are there windows in the rotunda?" Shay was trying to remember her grade-school excursions to the National Historic Landmark.

"No," said Caroline, "not in the rotunda. The very top, *top* of the building. You know, that small space just below the flag."

It was quiet, until Jacyne said, "And you girls thought it'd be a good idea to break in? You can't just climb up to the very top. That has to be off limits! And once again, nobody tried to stop her." Jacyne threw up her hands.

"No, no," said Sara. "She actually found someone who would give us a tour. An honest-to-God tour. As it turned out, there were ten of us, until Caroline realized how high up we were going and that you had to squeeze through a very tight spot. She begged off, but I went."

"None of this would have happened if DeMaris hadn't lost all that weight," said Caroline. "She'd have never fit."

"Well, the young tour guide was busy hitting on two girls in the group. We got to the top, DeMaris and I got enthralled with staring out the window—it really was neat—and the next thing we knew . . . we'd been forgotten. Really, how hard is it to count to nine to make sure you've got everybody down?" asked Sara. "Stupid guide."

"Weren't you there to ask where they were?" Liset turned to Caroline.

"I didn't know how long they'd be gone; so I went off on my own to look around," said Caroline. "And then, all hell broke loose."

"It's dark up there," continued Sara. "We were fortunate that De had a penlight on her. We made it down the stairs and then realized the door was locked. The door is actually a panel in the wall—it's called a guillotine door. If you saw it you'd know why—well, DeMaris, being DeMaris . . . I mean, ya can't tell it's a door. It looks like a panel. You're basically inside the wall."

Caroline started to laugh again. "I'm standing there when I hear kids screaming and running every which way. They're screaming 'ghost' and 'terrorist!' The security guards are running with their guns drawn and my first thought was, *What's DeMaris done this time?* I followed the guards until they stopped in front of a wall where there was a bunch of banging and yelling coming from behind."

"Yeah, DeMaris thought since we could hear children on the other side she'd give them a history lesson," continued Sara. "So in a deep, spooky voice—which quite frankly, scared the hell out of me—she pounds on the wall and yells, 'Hello, kiddies! Can you guess which governor I am?' Then she turns to me and whispers, 'You're a teacher. Which governor was around when this building was erected?' I can hear the screaming and pandemonium on the other side of the wall and she's worried because she doesn't know the answer to her own question!"

The girls were laughing now—except Sara. "Oh, come on," said Caroline, "I brought you lunch in jail."

No one was surprised by this revelation. They nodded their sympathies.

"For a good part of the day, security couldn't find the gigolo who took us up—seems he did get lucky. So, we were originally charged with breaking in, although we got that charge dropped. But we were charged with causing the Capitol to be shut down for the rest of the day and inciting a riot. Ya know, when you do something at the seat of government there's an overkill mentality," mused Sara.

Caroline looked at Viva who was standing next to her. "The SWAT team wasn't happy. They were pumped for something big to happen."

"And the same could be said for the people with the bomb-sniffing dogs."

"You're kidding!"

"No, the governor was in the building, as were the state legislators. They were getting ready for a big vote. They had no kind words." Caroline stood for a moment lost in thought. "I suppose if you think about it, the whole state wasn't happy since they put off the vote."

"Kirk came and bailed me out," said Sara. "But he was really mad. He made DeMaris spend the night in jail."

"Well, her bail was a lot higher than yours," Caroline pointed out.

"Yes, I did luck out there," agreed Sara. "DeMaris got a hefty fine because the judge said something like, 'She obviously hadn't learned her lesson from being Velcro woman.' What kind of expression is that?" Except for Shay, the girls looked puzzled and shrugged their shoulders. "The judge said he needed to make an impression on her once and for all. He also added to her, apparently lengthy, community service that she already had going on."

After laughing some more they returned to their original discussion about letting DeMaris go into banks.

DeMaris listened to them argue when it hit her. *No! I don't want them coming in the banks with me.*

"How's the shopping going?" asked DeMaris as she walked out from behind the rack of clothes, pretending she hadn't heard anything.

As they wandered through the store, Jacyne said, "De, you've lost a lot of weight. What size are you now?"

"I am down to an eight," she said proudly.

Jacyne held a blouse up against her. "I think this is cute. Why don't you try this on?"

DeMaris stared at her. "Why?"

"Oh, look," said Caroline. "This goes with it. The fitting rooms are right over there."

"Why would I—" they all began talking at once; before DeMaris knew it she was in the fitting room, door closed, with clothes sailing over the top. "Try this, try this." She smoldered.

She came out in an outfit that didn't match: dark-orange blouse with dark polka dots, an aqua vest with multi-colored thread peaking through, and a red skirt. "You're just trying stuff on, right?" asked Melissa. "I mean, you know that . . ."

"I like it," DeMaris said. "What's wrong with it?"

They glanced at each other and Viva cleared her throat. But DeMaris exploded first. "You really think I don't know how to match, don't you? Me, the one who has made you quilts, sewed clothes for you, knit for you—tell me, what hasn't matched?"

"Well, some of it's been pretty wild—" started Sara.

"—but it matches!" yelled DeMaris.

Yes, they agreed, things did match.

DeMaris folded her arms across her chest and glared. "Why am I trying on these clothes?"

"You've lost so much weight," said Liset, "we thought we'd each pitch in and get you a little something."

"Why?"

"We're your sisters. Can't we do something nice?"

"No."

"Don't be so full of pride," said Jacyne.

"You are going to need new clothes for when you go job hunting."

"You lost the house to Kirk," this from Viva. "So, you're obviously not going back there."

"I don't think this is the place to discuss it," Shay warned.

DeMaris was so furious she was shaking. She flew back into the fitting room. Clothes and hangers came flying over the top of the door. They moved out of the way to avoid being hit.

"De!" shouted Jacyne. "Whichever one of us you end up living with while you get back on your feet, you're going to need to work. You need more than the clothes you arrived in. Be sensible—"

They stepped back when DeMaris shot the lock back and came out of the dressing room. She appeared calm as she looked around. "Let me remind you that this week I am DeMaris Azaygo, not DeMaris Pala. I noticed that you think it's okay for *me* to wear clothes from Walmart but not one of you would even *think* to buy a piece of clothing from here.

You all have your noses up in the air. So, if you are truly inclined to buy me clothes, you can buy me stuff that an international best-selling author would wear. I want designer clothes."

DeMaris walked off as they stared after her with their mouths open. Slowly they gathered some snacks and went through the checkout line.

"Did you want to visit some banks?" Viva ventured when they met DeMaris outside, hoping to placate her.

"Yes, I do." DeMaris handed Viva the phone list. "And, I want to go in alone. I just need to look around. I don't need you all in there." Not a word was said as they piled into the van.

By the time they arrived at the first bank, DeMaris had her story ready. She strolled inside, looked around, and headed for a teller.

"Hi," DeMaris smiled at the thirty-something woman. "I just flew in from California to try to settle my aunt's estate and upon reaching my motel room I discovered I left all my papers at home. My husband found them and is mailing them to me overnight. In the meantime, I hate to waste this day, so I'm going from bank to bank to at least track down which bank it was that she banked at. Could you tell me if you have a— had a Blanche Fox as a customer?"

"Well, let me see," the woman began to type on her computer. "Ya know, since your husband found the papers, why don't you have him look at them and tell you which bank it is?"

Silence. "Because . . . by the time I thought of that . . . he wasn't home. Probably at the post office right now." She saw the woman glance at her suspiciously. "I know she had a safe deposit box." DeMaris pulled out her necklace and showed the woman the key to make her story more believable.

The woman continued tapping on the computer. "I'm sorry. There's nothing."

"Well, thank you. One down, several more to go."

"Why not just call them? It would be so much easier."

"Yes, it would, wouldn't it?" DeMaris kept walking. "But I'm so distraught over my aunt's sudden death that I can't just sit in my motel room. I need to be moving. Good exercise. Have nothing else to do with my day." *Shut up, you know talking too much always hangs the talker.*

The woman nodded. "I understand."

Chapter Nine

By the third bank, DeMaris had changed her answer to "it's already in the mail" when asked why her husband didn't just tell her the name of the bank. The fourth bank was closed. She checked her watch. They were probably all closed since it was after five.

No longer mad at her friends, DeMaris went to find them. They were wandering through some of the smaller shops while she checked out the banks. As DeMaris joined them, she heard Viva talking excitedly on her cell phone. She hung up. "I just remembered this great restaurant I was told about. Supposed to be fabulous. I used my friend's name and got us a reservation but we have to go now. I told him we were right down the street. Actually we're about twenty minutes away. Hurry!"

They all jumped in, except for DeMaris who brought up the rear. "Uh, wait a minute." The only seat available was the driver's. "Viva?"

"You're driving."

"No, I'm not."

"Yes, you are," commanded Shay. "You've got to get over your fear of driving in strange places. You're going to have to get a job somewhere and you're going to have to drive to it."

"I've been with you. You do just fine," offered Sara.

"That is in my own comfort zone. I am not driving here."

"We've always let you off the hook—but you've got to get over this. You need to do your share of driving," stated Caroline. "You can thank us later."

Slowly DeMaris got in, slammed the door shut, and started the van. She eased onto the street, staying in the right-hand lane. Viva was up front with her to give directions.

"See, you're doing fine. In the next block you need to get over. You need to make a left."

"I don't do lefts."

"What?"

"Oh, God, I forgot," mumbled Shay. "Three rights make a left."

"Just turn left here. HERE! We're already late."

"Then I guess you should have driven."

They all looked to the left as DeMaris passed it by. She went to the next block and after three right-hand turns they were pointed in the direction Viva wanted.

"Fortunately the expressway is on the right. Get on right up there," said Viva, pointing.

DeMaris turned to her. "We're getting on the expressway?"

"Yeah. Watch the car, don't get over yet!" There was honking and then they merged.

"I haven't driven on the expressway since I was twenty-two."

"You're not serious."

"Yes, she is," hollered Jacyne from the back. "I'd forgotten."

"Anything else you've forgotten? Ya know, you're twenty-five miles *over* the speed limit. Slow down."

"I'm keeping up with traffic."

"No, you're passing everybody. Slow down. You hate driving and you're driving this fast?"

"Yes, the sooner I get there, the sooner this is over."

"In more ways than one, I'm thinking," said Liset.

"I am *not* paying for your speeding ticket!" Viva had her hand through the hand grip and was hanging on for dear life.

DeMaris smiled. "I don't have any money, remember?"

"Slow down!" Several yelled.

"I need to make up time from my left turn."

"Forget I said that!"

"And, you forgot to ask me if I had a driver's license."

"What? Well, of course you . . ." Viva turned around to look at the others. Shay and Jacyne had already dived for DeMaris's fanny pack.

"Yes, she has one."

"Can you get over? Our exit is coming up."

"Ya know, the reason I stay off the freeway is because I don't merge well."

Viva was silent.

"What kind of place is this?" asked DeMaris, staying in her lane.

"You'll like it, I promise."

"Chinese? Mexican?"

"No! It's meat and potatoes. Would you please try to get over? It looks clear."

"I would hate to arrive and find it's not to my liking." DeMaris smiled.

"I promise you—they specialize in ribs, steak, seafood! You're gonna miss—"

At the last second, DeMaris swerved onto the off-ramp. The restaurant was fortunately on the right. It was silent as she pulled into a parking spot.

"This looks good," said DeMaris. "I made up some time too." She turned and looked at her friends. They were all white-faced. She chuckled. "Everybody out!"

DeMaris seemed to be the only one capable of speaking as they crowded around her while she talked with the host about their reservation.

"Madame," the man in the tuxedo glared down at her from the podium. "You are ten minutes late. We did NOT hold your reservation. There is an hour's wait—if you care to sit."

"You couldn't hold it for fifteen minutes?" asked DeMaris. "We told you we were right down the road. Traffic is terrible."

She watched as he looked her up and down and surveyed the rest of her party. They were wearing shorts, t-shirts, and had sandals on. "Perhaps, ladies," implying by tone they were anything but, "this is not your kind of restaurant. May I suggest the fast-food across the way?"

None of them had gotten their voices back, so it was still up to DeMaris. "Excuse me. Do you know who this woman is?" She put her hand out, which only found air. Back a little further, air, further, she glared over her shoulder. They had all moved several feet from her.

"De!" they hissed.

"This is Liset Sumnerfeld as in Frank Sumnerfield's wife." She was forced to point.

"I doubt it," he said as he watched a line of customers gather behind them.

"Do you even know who Frank Sumnerfeld is?"

"De!"

"The Chairman of the Federal Reserve? Yes, Madame, I know of him and I hardly think Mr. Sumnerfeld would want you linking his name with yours."

DeMaris's jaw tightened. As the silence thickened, she turned on Liset. "Say something!"

They all watched as tall Liset became smaller and smaller. With her head down Liset whispered, "I'm terribly sorry."

He waved his hand as if he were batting at flies. "Out, out!"

"Fine," DeMaris plowed on, "I didn't *want* to have to say this—"

"DeMaris!" her friends hissed.

"I am—"

"No!" said four of them.

DeMaris folded her arms across her chest and glared at the man. "—DeMaris Azaygo." *There, take that you miserable piece of—*

"Well, I admit you stumped me on that one. I'll bite—if you leave quietly. *Who* is DeMary whatever you said?"

"What?" yelled DeMaris, her jaw dropped. She turned around, looking for sisterly support, but instead watched as they appeared to all be in a dance routine parting for Liset to lead the way and one by one with their heads down filed in behind her leaving DeMaris to do the finale.

"I see," DeMaris eyed their departing backs and then turned to face the host. "I want to apologize for our tardiness," she said sweetly. He raised an eyebrow. "You see, it was my responsibility to pick up everybody—" She felt two hands pulling her shirt. "—and . . . well, I got a late start—" Two more hands grabbed her. "*DeMaris!*" someone hissed in her ear.

"—because—" the fingers that dug into her scalp and pulled her hair got her attention and she finally began to retreat—but not before shouting, "—my husband insisted on a blow job before I left!"

DeMaris fumed as they walked through the parking lot. "Yeah, let's see how Frank Sumnerfeld likes having his name linked with us now. And thank you, Ms. Graysen, for backing me up," she yelled at Liset.

"I'm sorry, but what proof would I have had if he had asked for it?"

"*Please,*" said Viva, getting into the driver's seat, "when we get back to town, where everybody knows Harlan and me, will you not yell out stuff like that? If you do, I'll never be able to show my face there again. My God! The things you come up with, De. I must say your imagination is really running rampant this week."

"Probably the stencil paint I'm sniffing," DeMaris said dryly staring out the side window. From the exchanged glances one could tell it was a possibility that suddenly crossed their minds.

"Who's DeMaris talking to?" asked Jacyne.

"I don't know," answered Melissa. "She's been rather mysterious since returning from rowing practice this morning."

Having discovered the first day that cell phone coverage was poor DeMaris kept her voice low and stood in the far corner of the room, stretching Viva's house phone cord to its limit. She didn't put it past any of her friends to listen in on her conversation.

Before she dialed the bank's number, she had her story ready. "Yes, I wondered if you had a safe deposit box for a customer named Blanche Fox."

"I can't give out that information," the woman said.

"I'm Blanche Fox's niece. My aunt died and—"

"Oh, no. I'm so sorry. How is Owen doing? He must be devastated."

Owen? Huh. The name in the phone book. Didn't even think about them being related. I guess because I didn't really think Blanche's last name was Fox. Although Brian certainly indicated that it was. But in the phone book it listed a Maureen, not a Blanche. Odd. "Yes, he is. He can't even tell me about this safe deposit key that I've found." DeMaris held her breath.

"Well," the woman hesitated. "I'm not supposed to give out information without proper ID."

"I understand completely; however, I did know what bank to call. . ." *Just because you're near the bottom of my list . . .* "And, I'm sitting here at 123 Jones Street."

"Well . . ." *Yes, yes.* "maybe if I talked with Owen."

"Oh, dear. I gave him a sedative. He's out. I'll just wait and we'll come in—"

"Let me see." DeMaris could hear typing. "I'm afraid I really can't tell you anything but bring him and the key in and I'll help him get in the box."

"That's great. Once we get things settled here, I'll bring him in. Thank you very much. And your name, please?"

"Abigail VanLoon. And yours?"

DeMaris looked outside at the deck and watched her friend spread out her beach towel. "Melissa Hoffman."

⚊⚊⚊ ⚊⚌⚊ ⚊⚊⚊

Viva walked into the kitchen with an odd look on her face.

"What's the matter?" asked Sara.

She shook her head. "Ever since I brought that bird home, whenever I fed him he always said 'Never lose this key.' It dawned on me today that for the last day or two he hasn't said it."

71

"You also said he pretty much stopped swearing too," said Shay.

"Yeah. I guess he doesn't repeat it because I never say it."

DeMaris could feel the key burning a hole in her chest. Should she tell Viva? Naw, right now she was having fun playing detective. She'd give it to Viva as she was getting on the plane. No time for a lengthy explanation then.

DeMaris quietly walked over to Sophocles in the next room. "Owen," she whispered.

The African gray cocked its head and stared at her. "Owen, you horse's ass," the bird said shrilly.

"Blanche?"

"Blanche, you fuddy-duddy bitch."

"Did they do nothing but yell at each other?" DeMaris asked.

"Shut up, Fox," Sophocles said in another man's voice.

DeMaris turned on her heels and walked out of the room. *Okay, I've got two people with deep-seated issues who dumped their expensive bird behind Walmart. Why?* She found her notepad and wrote down her thoughts. *Let's see. The bird is a witness to something diabolical and has to be gotten rid of. Why not just kill it? Family pet? Who would believe him? Neighbors bang on the door right then and the bird somehow escapes when the door is opened? For other reasons the bird is valuable? Holds the key to buried treasure? Swallowed something, waiting for it to pass? Hmm, maybe in my book my main character will find him somewhere other than a parking lot. Oh! He got away before anyone realized he was a witness. Okay, I can do something with that.* The wheels of ideas were rolling faster than she could write.

———— ——•—— ————

After several hours on the lake, they came in for a late lunch. Liset had prepared French dip sandwiches. DeMaris declined and fixed herself a salad. They stared at her.

"Why are you eating just a salad?" Melissa finally asked.

"I'm in training for the rowing team."

"But you love French dip sandwiches. I made them specifically with you in mind."

"Thank you, but I have to sacrifice . . . just not chocolate." Several of them exchanged glances. This was definitely not the sister they knew. "Remember, I lost quite a bit of weight. How do you think I did that?"

"By eating chocolate?"

"That's the diet I want," said Sara.

⚬   ⚬   ⚬

"Never lose this key. Never lose this key," squawked Sophocles. He was in his cage, out on the deck enjoying the sunlight with the girls.

"That's funny. He hasn't said that for the last couple of days and now – DeMaris!" Viva looked across the pool.

"What?"

"What's with the key on your necklace?"

DeMaris gasped, her eyes widened, and she put her hand over the key. Then hoping to recover said, "What key? Oh, you mean this old thing?" DeMaris always left the house early in the morning for rowing dressed in shorts, a top, and bathing suit underneath. She had made the mistake of ripping off her top and shorts to jump into the pool. The necklace with the key dangled for all to see.

"Never lose this key. Never lose this key." Sophocles moved back and forth on his perch.

"Shut up, you stupid bird," yelled DeMaris.

"DeMaris," Viva was up and on the move. For one fleeting moment DeMaris thought about shoving her in the pool and making a run for the rowboat.

Viva grabbed the key and studied it. "This is a safe deposit box key."

"Yes, I have a box in Michigan."

"Okay, but why wear it here?"

"So I don't lose it. Duh."

"You didn't have it on when you arrived."

"Yes, I did."

"No, you didn't," said Jacyne. "You stripped in the airport parking lot. That necklace was just a plain gold strand. I would have noticed a key. Where did you find that?"

All eyes were on DeMaris. "I'm having fun with the key," DeMaris pouted.

"What do you mean you're 'having fun'?"

"Where did you find it?"

"I'm pretending to be DeMaris Azaygo and now she has an idea for her new book. I like acting the part—you should all do it with your characters. Let me just keep the key while I'm here, please? I'm playing detective. I'll give it back before I leave."

"This is why we looked at all those banks, isn't it?"

"Yeah."

"You know, you can't snoop into somebody's box."

"Well, of course I know that! But I have to find a way for my character to!"

"No! This is how it starts out and somehow we all end up in trouble. Give me the key." Viva stuck out her hand.

"You had that bird for how long and didn't find it! I'll give it back before I leave!"

"You weren't going to tell me about it, were you? Where did you find it?"

DeMaris looked at her. "It was in the bird food."

"You're kidding. All this time? What do you *need* it for?"

"I told you: I'm living my own mystery. I need the key for the excitement. It makes me feel . . . special. I just . . ." she put a hand over her face and her voice cracked. It sounded like she was going to cry—none of them had ever heard DeMaris like this. "I guess the divorce has finally hit me. I'm all alone and the key . . . well, it gave me an idea for a story. It's making me productive . . . finally. Maybe I can get this book published . . ."

"Oh, De!"

"We're here for you."

"We're your sisters!"

"Let her keep the key, Viva."

"What can she possibly do with it?"

"You're never going to be alone."

"What do you want the key for?" Viva growled.

DeMaris peeked from behind her fingers. *Okay, Viva's not buying it but the rest of them are. Maybe they'll work on her to lighten up.* "I've just been having fun going to the banks and making inquiries about a Blanche and Owen Foxx."

"Where did you get the name Owen?" Viva screeched.

"From the bird, he's always saying it."

"He never says it! Owen hated that name! He would never allow anybody to use it, let alone the bird repeating it."

"How do you know?" said Jacyne.

Viva glared at DeMaris, and then looked around at all of them. "Okay, in the interest of . . . I'm not being rude, I just don't want to discuss Sophocles or . . . his owners. You're all better off . . ." she stopped and looked at DeMaris, who was trying not to smile. "Fine, keep the key—only while you're here, though. You know you can't get in the safe deposit— You haven't been in their safe deposit box, have you?"

DeMaris gave Viva a disgusted look. "One, I'd have to know where it is and two, how would I get in? My name is certainly not on the list. Do you know Owen Foxx?"

"You're right, you're right," Viva mumbled, running a hand through her hair. She started to walk toward the house. "Of course, you weren't supposed to be able to get inside that cage at the zoo either; we don't know how you got past security that time at the concert—"

"I was doing research for a book. Do you know Blanche Foxx?"

"—we never got a *reasonable* explanation about what you were doing in the Captain's quarters on the cruise. We never—"

"Do you know Sophocles' owners?"

"No," said Caroline, "The question is, *why* did you want to be in *that* Captain's quarters?"

"I was doing one of my travel articles . . ."

The others had already dispersed.

Chapter Ten

"What do you think about getting a job around here?" Viva had the newspaper spread out on the table.

"Ah . . . why?" asked DeMaris.

"Harlan and I need someone to look after this house until it sells while we're back home in Nevada."

DeMaris screwed up her face. "Gosh, I'd like to help you but I'm expected back in California."

"Who are you staying with out there, since you're not staying with Melissa?"

"I have some friends."

"You have a lot of friends. Which ones are these?"

"I'd like to discuss Blanche and Owen Foxx but . . . I need to go rowing." DeMaris put on her baseball cap and left.

Viva stared after her, then turned to Liset who was standing nearby. "When did DeMaris become evasive about her friends and where she's staying?"

Liset shook her head. "Since her divorce."

"How long did she stay with you?" Sara turned to Melissa.

"Little over a month. Then, one day she said she was going to see friends further down the coast. I dropped her off at the train station and that was that. She did call me a couple times but refused to say who she was staying with. I was concerned."

"I'm worried about her mental health. You don't think she's planning to spend all her money and do a lot of fun things here because, well, because she's planning to kill herself, do you?"

The girls looked at each other.

"You know, she's not going to see a shrink," said Jacyne. "We're going to have to get her to talk."

"Yes, but talk in the real world. She's so into this fantasy she's created—"

"But she's happy."

"How happy can she be? She's divorced with no money and no home."

"She has friends back home who I think would help out."

"Yes, but she can't live with them permanently. Where's she going from here? What's to become of her?"

"She has told us nothing about the divorce. Do you think they're in the dark as much as we are?" They looked at each other and shrugged.

"Ron and I told her she could stay with us for as long as she needs," said Melissa. "She has her own room with a private bathroom. Plus a stocked kitchen. I'll take care of her, don't worry."

"Okay, but why did she leave your place—and who is she staying with?" No one had an answer.

———　——　———

They were headed for the lake when the house phone rang. The gals listened when they heard Viva say, "You understand that's a small plane . . . but DeMaris . . . ya know, with gas prices it might be a little expensive . . . you're not writing a check, are you?" Viva made a face. "Hang on." Pressing the phone to her stomach, she faced them. "Gloria's dad is flying DeMaris to Spokane. She can take two other people. Anybody want to go?"

"There was that dress I wish I'd bought," said Melissa.

"If I'm stuck paying for her gas I might as well go," muttered Caroline. "Why is she going?"

"She has a lead on the safe deposit box."

"Why did you let her keep that key?" hissed Liset. Viva waved a hand at her. They had talked long into the night about DeMaris and the key. DeMaris and where she was going to live, DeMaris and how to get her to take a job, DeMaris and how to get her checkbook away from her. In short, DeMaris got a full eight hours sleep while the rest of them were dragging on less than four. Today they would crash in lounge chairs and extra-long towels outside in the sun.

Viva drove Melissa and Caroline to McDonald's to grab DeMaris some lunch (*"Now she wants a hamburger?"*) and then to the tiny airport where DeMaris and Gloria's father, Phil, were waiting.

"You do have the key on you, right?" demanded Caroline as she handed DeMaris the clothes she had requested to change into. DeMaris glared at her and pulled out the chain so they could all see it. "You promise you won't take anything out of the box?"

"Do you actually think I'm going to get that far? Nobody is going to let me in without a death certificate or proper ID."

"So, why are we going?"

"Death certificate? Who died?" asked Melissa.

"It's *my* story. I am going to live *my* mystery—for the adventure. I have no idea why you're going."

"I'm going for jewelry." *Although if I have to pay part of this gas bill, I'm not sure I can afford it.*

"That gaudy necklace?"

"It was not gaudy."

When DeMaris returned from changing out of her rowing clothes, Phil ushered them into his Cessna 182.

"I can't believe you're willing to get into something this small," commented Caroline as she buckled up in the backseat.

"I'm a changed woman," was all DeMaris offered.

They landed in Spokane. A friend of Phil's drove them into town. Phil would lunch and visit with his friend. Melissa and Caroline took off for their shops and DeMaris headed for the bank. They would all meet in two hours.

"Are you sure we shouldn't come with you?" asked Melissa.

"For the hundredth time, no! I have a story ready. It won't work with two people in tow." DeMaris checked to make sure nobody was watching before she ducked into a department store. Had she known she was getting a ride today she would have brought makeup and a hairbrush with her. She hadn't thought about it when asking for her clothes. DeMaris made a mental note: make sure character has makeup and hairbrush.

She made her way to the cosmetics counter and asked for someone to do her face. She wrote a check for a tube of lipstick and asked if they had a hair salon on the premise. The gal pointed the way. DeMaris swung into the salon, bought the smallest bottle of mousse available, and headed to the bathroom where she proceeded to spike her short hair.

She checked her small fanny pack. She had her driver's license, trusty checkbook, and twelve dollars in cash. She zipped it shut and went to ask directions to the bank.

On her way there, DeMaris went through her story once again in her head. As soon as she entered the bank, she found the office door with

Abigail VanLoon's name on it. She knocked on the open door to get the woman's attention.

"Yes?"

"Hi, I'm Melissa Hoffman. I spoke to you on the phone about my aunt, Blanche Foxx."

"Oh yes, come in."

They shook hands and spoke briefly about the gorgeous weather and DeMaris's flight. "It didn't feel like it took me any time at all to get here."

Abigail's fingers flew on the keyboard. "What can I help you with?"

"Well," DeMaris pulled the necklace out to show Abigail the key. "I know I can't get in the box today, but Uncle Owen started talking about another bank. Do you know for sure that this is one of your keys? I mean, if it's not, I have to start inquiring at other banks."

Abigail leaned over and studied it. "Yes, that's ours. 1501." She turned back to the computer screen. "Yes, that's a match. They've closed out the other ones."

The other ones? Hmm, have to think about that. "Oh, thank goodness!" said DeMaris as she fell back in the chair with immense relief. "You don't know what I've been going through with Uncle Owen."

Abigail gave a slight laugh. "Yeah, I can imagine. I thought you'd be bringing him with you to get into the box."

"Well, we've had funeral arrangements to make and . . . he just won't leave the house."

Abigail's eyes narrowed. "The house?"

Crap. I've said too much. What else would they live in? Trailer? Apartment? Boathouse? Their car? DeMaris's eyes lighted on the framed picture Abigail had on her wall. Ten birds sitting on a telephone wire. She motioned to it. "You like birds, huh? You should see my aunt's African gray. Beautiful bird. And the sounds he can make, really unbelievable."

Abigail nodded. "What was his name again?"

"Sophocles."

This apparently satisfied her. "Yes, that bird was the only thing she ever talked about the few times she was in here. I'm sorry, but you do realize I can't let you in the box."

"Oh, I know. Wasn't even going to ask. I just wanted to make sure I had the right bank. My uncle, he's been . . . rather difficult."

Abigail made a noise. *Oh, I'm on the right track there.* "You know, I didn't see an obituary in the paper for your aunt."

Honest to Pete, she's still suspicious of me? The nerve! "I haven't had time. Uncle Owen certainly isn't going to do it."

Abigail drummed her nails on the desk thoughtfully and said, "Do you have some ID that I can see?"

As Melissa Hoffman? No! DeMaris fished around in her fanny pack. "I'm afraid I'm in the middle of moving to California and the computers . . . here's my driver's license." She pulled out her license with a receipt from Walmart folded over her photo. "As you can see, it has no picture. Computer meltdown." DeMaris held the license back and shook it in hopes that Abigail couldn't read it or see that there was a photo.

Abigail sighed. "Well, that won't do us any good."

DeMaris jammed it back in her fanny pack.

"Excuse me, Abigail." A woman stood in the doorway; she had papers in her hand. She glanced over her shoulder and hissed. "Mr. Mason's here."

Abigail sighed and turned to DeMaris. "I'm sorry. Could you excuse me, please? I have to take care of something."

"Oh, sure. It's my own fault for not scheduling an appointment. Take your time," said DeMaris.

"Thank you. I . . . may be a few minutes." She disappeared with the other woman out the door.

DeMaris sat for two seconds and then wondered if anything of interest was on the computer screen. In the movies they would look. But what would she offer as an explanation if she got caught?

Mr. Mason was loud and obviously irate. *I think Abby's going to be awhile.* DeMaris looked out the door and saw no one. She quietly got out of her seat and placed her hand on the monitor. It easily swiveled toward her. *Oh, look at that, Blanche and Owen have two addresses—plus social security numbers. I'm not going to be able to memorize all that. Paper, paper, paper—my checkbook.*

She hauled it out and grabbed a pen off the desk only to drop it on the floor. She cocked an ear toward the door. Okay, the first address she had memorized already: 123 Jones Street, Spokane. She grabbed the pen and on the back of her duplicate check wrote down a Sandy Bottom Cove address. She heard Abigail quietly talking and quickly pushed the monitor back into its original position. She crammed the checkbook into her fanny pack, sat back down, and heart pounding tried to look nonchalant. *Is this how James Bond feels,* she wondered, *when he's sneaking around and poking into places he shouldn't? He's a fictional character, you nincompoop!* she yelled at herself and suddenly got the giggles. *All right, this isn't going to do. Stop being so nervous. You're here to take care of your dear departed, beloved aunt. Think about James Bond. Sean Connery. Bond, James Bond. Double-O-7. Bond, Jane Bond. 34-double-D. Stop it! You can't be laughing!*

"Ms. Hoffman?"

"Oh God! Shit!" yelled DeMaris leaping out of her seat. She was so startled and nervous the words flew out before she could stop them.

"I'm terribly sorry! I didn't mean to scare you." The gal who had announced Mr. Mason was standing in the doorway.

DeMaris, now standing, was breathing shakily with a hand to her chest. "My fault. I was so lost in thought." *Honest to Pete, how would I have reacted if she'd caught me doing something? Get a grip! Certainly not a James Bond response.* "I just lost my aunt," she said in a weepy voice as she brought her hand to her mouth to keep the giggle from escaping.

"I'm so sorry," the gal apologized again. "Abigail is going to be awhile. She sent me to see if you'd like any water or coffee."

"Oh. Oh, no, thank you. I'm fine." The young girl nodded and left while DeMaris crashed back into the chair. *Stupid, stupid. All right, I'm not cut out for this. Maybe I should make an excuse and just leave. I wonder if those social security numbers would come in handy. I really should gather as much information as I can while I'm here. My character certainly would.*

She listened. *Where the heck did Abigail and Mr. Mason disappear to? She said she was going to be awhile. How long will it take to write down eighteen numbers?* She tapped her index finger against her teeth nervously. *I could be done by now. Isn't this part of the excitement of living your own mystery—seeing if you'll get caught?*

Once again she pulled out her checkbook and turned the monitor toward her. She wrote fast and furious, put the monitor back, returned the pen to its holder, and sat back in her chair.

Do I look cool, calm, and collected? Probably not. Okay, focus on something else. Do not scream when she enters the room! Oh, a magazine. She rifled through the selection and found one on the city of Spokane. Not only did it highlight restaurants and shopping, it also included a street map of the city. *Here's the street the Foxx's live on.* Her heart leaped. *It doesn't look like it's that far from here.*

"I'm sorry to keep you waiting," Abigail breezed in.

"That's all right," DeMaris held up the magazine. "I was checking out your city."

"You can take that with you if you want."

"Thank you. I will."

"Now, as I was saying," said Abigail as she sat down in her chair. "I would like to help you but without your uncle . . . or proper identification . . ."

"Um, would having my aunt and uncle's social security numbers help any?"

"Do you have them on you?"

"Yes," DeMaris couldn't let her see she had them written in her check-book so she did her best to hold her wallet where she hoped Abigail couldn't see it over the desk. Abigail moved the mouse around to stop the screen saver so she could see the Foxx's account.

"I have . . ." *Great, I can't even read my own handwriting—and she left me alone for a good half hour.* DeMaris read some numbers off and stopped. "My uncle's handwriting leaves something to be desired. It's either a seven or a nine."

"Nine."

Thank you. DeMaris stumbled through the second set. Abigail looked satisfied.

"I was going to suggest," said DeMaris, "that since I don't have the proper papers, maybe we could just try the key. To make sure I have the right one. I'd hate to travel back here with my uncle only to then find out we had the wrong key. We don't need to open it, just see that the key fits."

Abigail thought about this. "Well, all right. You've been so patient. I do appreciate it."

They walked downstairs to the vault where the safe deposit boxes were located. Abigail pulled out a card. "If you'd sign this, please."

"Oh." DeMaris stared at the card. There was one name consistently on it: M. Bloomgarde. *Shit. The last thing I want is a paper trail leading to me—or rather to Melissa. And who the hell's M. Bloomgarde?* Abigail waited. DeMaris smiled. "Oh, that's great! You are going to let me in. Uncle Owen will be so pleased."

"Oh, no, you're right," DeMaris hoped her sigh wasn't audible as Abigail put the card back.

She felt her heart pounding as they read the numbers, looking for 1501. *Do not start laughing,* DeMaris told herself sternly as she felt her nervousness return. "Here it is," she said. The box was near the floor and was one of the larger ones. *You could hold a lot of stuff in there,* she thought. They both got down on their knees and each inserted a key.

It's going in! It's going in—it clicked! Abigail swung the door open. "Well, now you know it's the right key."

"Yes," DeMaris stood up. "Thank you, um, I was wondering—"

"Abigail," the same gal was standing in the doorway to the vault. "Mr. Mason's found some more problems," she whispered even though there was no one else around.

Abigail gritted her teeth.

"I was just going to ask if we could take a peek in the box together—so

I could tell my uncle what's in there, to relieve his mind, but . . . I've taken up enough of your time. Thank you," DeMaris turned to go when Abigail pulled the box out and shoved it in her arms.

"You can have some privacy in that room over there. Promise me you won't take anything."

"I promise. And thank you. My uncle thanks you too. He's missing some important papers and he's hoping that either he or my aunt put them in here. He's just so befuddled. This way I can tell him or we can keep searching."

"Beth," Abigail turned to her assistant, "will you see Ms. Hoffman out when she's done, please?"

Beth nodded.

"Take your time," Beth offered as DeMaris headed for the private room.

She set the box on the table and shut the door. DeMaris pressed a hand to her mouth. *Unbelievable! I don't believe this!* She felt her adrenalin pumping as she slowly lifted the lid off. All she could do was stare. Money. The box was filled to the brim. "Holy smokes," she chuckled softly. *Well, Owen and Blanche, you are very lucky I'm an honest person. Look at all that cash.* It was not stacked neatly but simply thrown in as if someone had been in a hurry.

She carefully picked through it. All twenties. There was an odor to it. She picked up a bill. *This has been out in the weather . . . and dried out. How odd. Who would do that—and why only twenties? Hmph, some of it looks like it's been chewed on. Some animal? Who would just throw money in here?* She picked up a handful and counted. One thousand dollars. *So a rough estimate would be . . . twenty thousand dollars? Who would leave all this money here? Wait a minute. What was it Abigail had said? 'They closed out the other ones.' Meaning other safe deposit boxes? That had money in them that they spent? Why would you bring money to a bank but not deposit it in said bank? Because you don't want people to see it? Because . . . it's stolen? And you worried about someone breaking into your home and stealing it? Very strange.* She dug her hand down in the bottom of the box. *Oh! Oh! Oh! A key! I can't believe this!* DeMaris was more excited about this discovery than the cash. She hauled it out triumphantly and held it up. She looked around. *Surely there wouldn't be any hidden cameras in here, would there?*

Setting the key on the table she ran her hand around the bottom of the box again. *Another key! Unbelievable! Front door, back door or . . . the first house and the second house? Or something I don't even know about?* She ran her hand around again, took out some of the money, and took

83

her time feeling along the bottom. Nothing. She started to put the bills back in the box when a yellowed folded piece of paper caught her eye. She pulled it out and carefully unfolded it. *Oh my God! This is unreal! A treasure map! An honest to God treasure map with an X and a circle around it! Can my life get any better than this? I'm living my own mystery! I'm living my own mystery!* DeMaris did a happy dance and then stopped. *Really . . . have I dropped into the* Twilight Zone *and not realized it? Or . . . what is it the kids call it? Am I being punked? Hmm.* She looked around the room again for a hidden camera. She hunted around in the box some more but found nothing else of interest. *Come on, after money, keys and a treasure map what more excitement could there be?* She packed the money down, squatted and looked around on the floor to make sure she had not dropped anything.

Would anybody care if I took the keys and the map? Who knows when M. Bloomgarde is going to show again? The signature card indicated no one has come to the box in months. I'm leaving the money, DeMaris reasoned. She dropped the keys in her fanny pack and placed the piece of paper in the Spokane magazine to help flatten it out.

DeMaris looked through the money again. Now that she had calmed down she saw that her hands were covered in dirt. *Strange.* She smiled. *Just like treasure would be—actual* buried *treasure!* She pulled out some of the twenties. Every one of them was printed in 1969 with an L in its serial number. DeMaris had done research for a book dealing with money and how it was numbered and where it was produced. She searched her memory. *Did L stand for San Francisco or Denver? Somewhere out west. So what's up with the twenties all from 1969? Is M. Bloomgarde a collector? Is there something special about twenty dollar bills from 1969? I think I need to do research. Nobody will miss one twenty dollar bill. I could check the serial number on it. Surely as a character in my book I'd take it.* She put one bill in her Capri pants pocket so that it was separated from her money in the fanny pack. That's all she needed to do was to accidentally spend it.

I'm not really stealing, she reasoned. *I have their addresses. When I'm done writing my novel, I'll mail all this stuff back to them.*

She closed the lid on the box, checked the floor again, rolled the magazine up, put it under her arm, and went out. Beth helped her return the box and escorted her to the door where DeMaris thanked Beth for her help and asked her to also thank Abigail.

Once outside, DeMaris smiled. *What a beautiful day. Gosh, this detective gig is fun.* In the past, she had researched her books—but never anything like this. She walked a few blocks, found a park, and sat down at a vacant picnic table. She casually glanced around. Just a bunch of moms with their kids. She opened the magazine to the treasure map. The handwriting was poor but legible. There were a few roads marked; one she recognized as a major highway. She looked at the street map in the magazine to locate the other two streets but they weren't listed. She sat for a moment. *Okay, nothing more I can do with that right now. On to the address here in town.* The street she wanted was only two blocks away. She walked to the street and looked in both directions; only businesses as far as she could see. *Where the heck were the numbers?* DeMaris walked three blocks before she found enough numbers to realize she was walking in the wrong direction.

She walked back the three blocks only to discover that crossing the street brought her to where she needed to be: four apartments above an insurance business. She found Foxx, Apt. #2 printed above a mailbox. She glanced at the names on the other boxes and noted that one was the same last name she had used for one of her characters in a recent book. She tested the outside door; it opened. Ahead was a long flight of stairs: brick on the right wall, wood on the left wall.

Quietly she walked up, leaving the street noises behind realizing that not letting anyone know where she was, especially in this seedy part of town, was a stupid move. She stopped halfway. How many times had she told Allison and Ryan to let somebody know where they were? But she wasn't a mom right now, she was a detective. Detectives never checked in with other people, like they were scared or something. She smiled. *That's right, I'm a detective; not a divorcee with two kids. I am a detective with a purpose.*

She continued walking up the stairs.

Chapter Eleven

Two apartments were on the left, two on the right. On the landing were a coin-operated washer and dryer. One apartment door had plastic plants next to it on the floor, another had a door decoration. The other two doors—one being the Foxx's—had no décor. Apartment #2 was the front one on the right.

DeMaris pressed her ear to the Foxx's door. Nothing. *Okay, if I knock and somebody answers, what will I say? I'll play dumb and ask if this apartment is for rent.*

She knocked on the door so timidly she could barely hear it. *Come on, find out if somebody's here. I really want to see what Blanche and Owen look like.* DeMaris took a deep breath and knocked three good times on the door. Slowly she let her breath out. She waited. Ear back to the door. Silence. She looked around. *Still quiet out here on the landing.* She pulled out both keys and tried the first one. *No dice. It's just as well they don't work. I should not be doing this. But as long as I've come this far . . .* The second key slid in. She glanced around again and pressured the key. It turned and she heard a click. *What the hell am I doing? Have I reached such a low point in my life that I've resorted to breaking into people's homes?*

God, this is exciting.

She pulled out the key and turned the knob. The bad air that hit her nostrils indicated no one had been there for a long time and had obviously left garbage behind to rot. She walked inside and shut the door behind her, holding her jacket sleeve up to her nose, which in reality didn't help much.

The skylight showed a small room with a couch, rocking chair, desk, and TV. She walked to the room on the right. Big bedroom with a high ceiling, windows to the street which were slightly cracked open, a dresser, a bed, and a bunch of boxes. She picked up a bottle of perfume from the dresser. *Cheap. All that money, two pieces of property, and cheap perfume? What do I care?* Noticing a Kleenex box on the dresser, she pulled a couple tissues out and doused them with the perfume to hold up to her nose.

The closet had no door or curtain; only a few items of clothing hung on hangers. She pulled out a blouse. XXX. And pants. XXX. *Apparently Blanche is a big person. This clothing is cheap too.* Hesitantly she looked inside one of the boxes. Clothes. *Is she moving in or moving out? Oh, this is cute.* DeMaris pulled out a multi-colored top and held it up. She read the tag: Medium. She looked at a few more of the items. The clothes were for a medium-sized woman and they were colorful, fun prints with better brand names. DeMaris glanced over at the closet with its few drab pieces. *Blanche has certainly blossomed and apparently is not expecting to slim down any time soon. Come on, you don't have all day, move!*

DeMaris was walking out of the bedroom when a bag in the wastebasket caught her eye. She walked over to it, bent down, and picked it up. *Huh. The bird food Viva feeds Sophocles.* She dropped it back in the trash. She came back through the skylight room and this time looked around. A business card on the desk caught her eye. She walked over and picked it up. *Well, well, well, the plot thickens. Viva's real estate business card.* DeMaris flipped the card over and read **1515 Deacon** written in Viva's neat handwriting. She set it down exactly as she had found it and proceeded on.

The next room could only be seen by the sunshine from the skylight which wasn't much light at all. Dare she turn on a light? With the theme music of *Jaws* in her ears, her hand found the switch and she flipped it. DeMaris was so wired she almost screamed in anticipation.

This was the kitchen and dining room area. She found food in the cupboards and what used to be edible food in the refrigerator. The dishes, pots and pans were clean and put away. On the wall was a hand painted picture of a window. *Interesting, a different picture for each pane.* Nobody had been here for a long time. *Since I'm snooping, I should do these people a favor and take out their garbage. As a thank-you for allowing me to look at their place. Not that they've actually let me inside but . . . Huh? There are only papers in the trash. What the heck smells so bad?*

The bathroom was clean and gosh darn if she didn't have to use it. Although DeMaris was so worried someone would walk in while she was on the toilet she almost couldn't. But finally, relief. She flushed the toilet and washed her hands.

The last room. Carefully she stuck her head in. No windows and it was pitch dark. She flipped the light switch on the wall. And this is where she could have used a really good scream.

The room was a shambles. A chair was overturned, a radio smashed on the floor, along with a lamp. The bed was unmade—but that was the least of her concerns. DeMaris stepped over a baseball bat lying on the floor to examine the stain a little closer. Yes, it was blood, a lot of blood. And now that she looked, there was blood on the floor. *Oh God, oh God! Did I step in any? No. Phew.*

With the Kleenex still pressed to her face, she followed the blood trail with her eyes to the wooden closet door. It was closed.

Get out of here!

She carefully stepped out of the room, double-checked her shoes, and although the blood looked dry she made sure she wasn't leaving any bloody footprints behind. *What did I touch besides the clothes? Light switches. The toilet handle. The doorknob. Think. Anything else?* She found a paper towel in the kitchen and went to work rubbing off her fingerprints. *The box, can you get fingerprints off fabric? And the birdfeed bag! Oh, oh, Viva's business card! Of course, none of this would be a problem if my fingerprints weren't on file.* She berated herself for a few of the stupid things she'd done in the past. Thinking about the girls complaining that they always got dragged along when she did something that they had nothing to do with she grabbed up Viva's business card and put it in her fanny pack. Finally DeMaris looked around, satisfied that she'd removed all of her prints and the lights were turned off. She looked through the peep hole and seeing no one used the paper towel to open the door.

Okay!

She had just closed the door and stuck the paper towel in her pocket when she heard in a commanding tone, "What the devil do you think you're doing?"

Trying to maintain her composure—instead of screaming and running down the stairs like she really wanted to—she slipped the key in and locked the door, turning the handle and pressing against it to make sure the door was secured. She turned around slowly, held up the key, and said in a sarcastic voice, "I was casing the joint."

The man appeared to be in his late thirties or early forties. He had one eye that squinted, a dark mustache and beard, and dark long hair except on top where he only had a few wisps growing. If he decided to wear a baseball cap people would think he had a lot of hair.

He was leaning against the wall, arms folded across his chest. It looked like he had been waiting some time for her. He chuckled, showing bad teeth, then cleared his throat and said in a less-menacing tone, "Okay, what were you really doin'? I live next door. Walls are kinda thin. Had to come check things out once I heard the toilet flush."

Well, wasn't that a bright idea I had. Don't have character do that. Hmm, characters never have to go to the bathroom, do they? Surely in real life one would have to. I mean murderers, rapists, hit men, they're humans too. Don't they ever get diarrhea at some crucial moment? Mental note: find a spy and ask him about bathroom problems while on a case. Why would I have a key to the apartment? A legitimate reason? "I'm thinking of renting the apartment. Came to check it out."

"Really?" He looked her up and down. "Blanche's thinkin' of rentin' it out, huh?"

"Did you know the people who lived here?"

"What'd ya think? I said I lived next door." He looked at her with a 'duh' on his face. "So, what do you think of the place?"

"It's, ah, small." Suddenly remembering her fingers on the outside door-knob she tried to nonchalantly rub her sleeve all over it while carrying on the conversation and thinking about the best way to escape.

She saw his eyes, well, *eye*, suddenly narrow. From opening the door the smell had leaked into the hallway. The man wrinkled his nose, stood up straight, and suddenly gave her a look that warned her she needed to get out of there. "It's not that small. Did you look over the whole place? Why don't you and I go back in—"

"No." She worked up an obvious disgust. "I didn't even bother looking in the last room. I could tell from the smell they owned an animal and never took care of it. I really don't think I want to rent from people like that."

"Oh," he visibly relaxed and cleared his throat. "Oh, yeah. That damn bird."

Well, isn't that interesting; he sounds just like Sophocles or better yet, Sophocles sounds just like him.

"So, what's your name?" he was amiable now.

She thought of the first name that came to mind—the heroine in her last book. "Lisa Caldwell."

"No kidding!" He extended a hand. "Denny Caldwell. Small world, huh?"

Of course. I read the name on the mailbox and thought of my character. What an idiot!

"You're not from Texas, are you?"

"No! Far from it—New Jersey." She started down the stairs and he followed.

"Sure be nice if you moved in." He cleared his throat again.

"Well, I'll see . . . price needs to come down." *Stop talking, you know better! He'll trip you up on something.*

"Hey, I'm sure you can talk her down. Not the smartest bulb, ya know. Um . . . where is Blanche living now?"

Her uneasy feeling increased a notch. "Is that the owner? Cuz I'm working through a real estate agent."

"Really?" He looked off into the distance as he thought about this. A phone rang above them. Denny waved and went back up the stairs.

DeMaris let herself out onto the sun-drenched sidewalk. She realized she was shaking as she walked as fast as she could. She needed to call the police but she wasn't about to use her cell phone. It would easily be traced. She needed to find a pay phone. Did they even have those anymore? They must, somewhere. She found a party store that had one and after she made sure nobody was around, she pulled her jacket sleeve down around her hand and picked up the phone. She wasn't about to leave any fingerprints here either. She lowered her voice and tried her best to sound robotic: "Send police to 123 Jones Street, Apartment 2. Murder suspected." She quickly hung up. Quietly she left the party store and walked back to the park. She sat at the picnic table where she'd begun her journey.

What in the hell was I thinking? What if Owen and/or Blanche had walked in? How would I have explained my being in their apartment (I was looking for a bathroom and gosh, your door was open)? How would I have explained why I had a key to their place? And a map? And one of their dollar bills? What if someone else had walked in and asked me about the blood and the smell? And hey, what's with the dead body in the closet? Could I be arrested for any of this? She saw Denny's face again with the 'duh' written on it.

All right, let's look at this from another angle. I'm helping out here. I reported a crime. A crime that has gone unnoticed until I stepped in. Yes. Feeling righteous makes me feel better.

She looked at the building across the street. The newspaper office. And the question that she had sent through her brain earlier at the bank finally hit upon an answer: *What's with the dirty bills stuffed in a safe deposit box with none of them dated after 1969 and all 'L's?* D. B. Cooper, the skyjacker from years ago. She had been interested in the case, along with everyone else in the country. A man jumped out of a plane in the middle of a rainstorm with money that was never recovered and he was never identified.

And it happened out here some place: Washington? Oregon? Yeah, like I've found the money . . . I have however, found a really good tie-in to my mystery! I need research material.

She checked her watch. Ten minutes left. *Caroline and Melissa are shopping; they aren't going to be on time.* She swung on into the newspaper office. *What story would my heroine use to gain access to files?*

"Hello," she smiled at the gal behind the counter. "I'm DeMaris Pala." *Azaygo! Arrgh. If I can't follow my own rules, how can I expect the girls to? At least none of them are with me.* "My insurance company sent me here to read up on the Cooper case. Do you keep your old papers on microfilm? Microfiche?" DeMaris fished around in her fanny pack. *Oh, look at this! My trusty notepad and pen.* She pulled them out.

The woman smiled. "Depending on how old it is, we keep it on microfilm. Could I see your business card?"

"Yeah, sure," DeMaris pulled one out of her fanny pack, wrote on it, and handed it to the woman.

She looked disappointedly at it, looked at DeMaris who said nothing, and then shrugged. "Thank you. Come on back." *How about my driver's license for ID purposes since I gave you my real name for a change?*

"How far back did you want to look?"

"I can't remember exactly when . . . the late sixties, early seventies . . ."

The woman stopped. "You don't mean D. B. Cooper?"

"Yeah."

"Why would an insurance agency—" They had walked down a hallway and entered a room that held the rows of microfilm when the door opened again. Both women turned to see a man in his fifties.

"Thank you, Doris, I'll take over from here." The woman glanced at DeMaris and then left. DeMaris and the man sized each other up. "What's your name?" he finally asked as he walked toward her.

For an instant Lisa Caldwell came to mind. *Better not, you already struck out once with that. Besides, dummy, you gave Doris your real name and card. Stick with the story. Ah, the truth.* "DeMaris Pala."

Over the years DeMaris had decided that men did not age well, at least not the beer-gutted, balding men she knew. But recently, she'd seen middle-aged men who were in shape; especially those who jogged in the parks. Apparently she'd been hanging out with the wrong crowd. She was sure this man ran. He had wavy salt-and-pepper hair and was trim and fit. His hands rested casually in his pockets.

"You're not an insurance agent," he stated. "So, I'm wondering what you're doing here."

"Well, ya found me out," DeMaris smiled. "Actually, I'm a detective in an agency and I'm new at this. I was sent . . ."

He shook his head. "I'm thinking I should have you thrown out of here."

DeMaris stood straighter, hand on a hip. "Do you have that authority?" she countered.

"Oh, excuse me. I didn't introduce myself, did I?" Not taking his eyes off her, he pulled a hand out of his pocket and handed her a business card.

She took it. "I see. Editor-in-Chief, ah, and owner of this quaint little establishment. Chuck— Charles Dickens—give me a break."

"Sad but true. Which is why I prefer Chuck."

"To distinguish you from that really great writer?"

"I'm still waiting for an explanation." He smiled.

He's toying with me. She glanced around the room. "This is basically your newspaper on film. Everything in here has already been read by hundreds or thousands of people. This is open to the public. I could probably go online and find your archives and look up what I want."

"But you didn't do that," Chuck pointed out. "I'm really interested in the cock-and-bull story. Why say you were from an insurance company? Or a detective? Who exactly are you?"

They stared at each other.

"Okay," DeMaris nodded. "I'm a writer—unpublished as yet except for short stories and magazine articles. I have an idea for a storyline. I'm acting as one of the characters to see if I could get inside here with my insurance-agent story."

"Just telling the truth wouldn't have worked, huh?"

"Well, yeah, but it wouldn't have been nearly so exhilarating. Besides, I'm not sure if my character is a writer. She might not be able to use that story."

"But, even if she wasn't a writer, she could use that as a ruse to come back here."

"That is true. I hadn't thought of that. I'm always looking for the complicated when a simple idea would work."

"Actually . . . you only have to ask to see our archives or you can look it up online."

"Well . . . thank you for that." She checked her watch. "I have run out of time. I will do the online thing, though. Thanks for the tip."

Still not letting her pass he said, "Interested in the Cooper case after all these years?"

"Thought I could use it in my next book."

"Trying to solve the mystery, huh?"

"No, not solve it. Just use it in my book. Oh! Oh!" Another thought came to her. "And, the Lost Dutchman Mine!" *Mental note: No need to look up that old high school chum.*

"I don't think those two stories go together." He looked confused.

"Probably not—still, I need to write that down before I forget." She wrote in her notepad.

"I could tell you everything there is to know about the case say, over dinner?" She made an exaggerated move of looking at his left hand. He pulled his hand out of his pocket and wiggled four bare fingers. "Divorced, five years."

"Ah," she nodded. "I'm new to that title. Almost one year."

"Sorry."

She smiled. "I'd like that, but I'm not staying here. I'm visiting with friends in Sandy Bottom Cove."

He nodded. "I could drive over. Saturday?"

"Oh, I see. You believe the story that I'm a writer."

"Well, you did lie about not being published."

Her jaw started to drop but she quickly regained her composure. "What makes you say that?"

"You're too sure of yourself. You've met with success. I think if I called the police and had you arrested on some trumped-up charge you'd have pulled your ace out and told me who you really are. Maybe I should do that."

She laughed and unzipped her fanny pack. She dropped his card in and pulled out her driver's license. "You know, I'm going to have to accept your dinner invitation because I want you to meet my friends and tell them *exactly* what you told me. I'm not a published book writer. Short stories, travel articles, crafts, cooking, that sort of thing, yes, but neither do I feel that I have failed at life—something my friends say I have done."

"They don't sound like very good friends to me."

She gently pulled her driver's license out of his hand. "Actually, they're the best. I have put them through a lot."

They walked down the hallway together. "DeMaris," he said. "You're not DeMaris Azaygo, are you?"

"The writer?" she chuckled. "Actually, I am . . . for this week. I have seven sorority sisters I've known for more than thirty years—"

He gave a low whistle and shook his head.

"They are all highly successful—and then there's me. Those who are not millionaires are well-to-do and highly respected in their fields. They don't think I've accomplished much with my life. I, who am so creative and imaginative and have a degree—why didn't I ever do anything with it? So, last year, in preparation for this vacation, I e-mailed them and told them they had to pick a new persona and be that for the week that we're together. They're not doing very well at it, by the way, but they at least tried to humor me.

"Well, I picked DeMaris Azaygo, since I already had the first name and I've read all her books—twenty-five—and read everything about her that I could get my hands on. Just so you know, there's not much. I thought, maybe for the week, my friends could be proud of me."

They were by the outside door. DeMaris's hand rested on the bar.

"I don't think I'd be friends with someone for thirty years if I didn't respect them," Chuck said. She studied him. "You must have something to offer."

"You are rather intuitive, I see."

"I've met a lot of people in my day. Street people and millionaires . . . I've had to sort fact from fiction. I'm very good at reading people."

DeMaris nodded. "Well, from one intuitive soul to another, if you want to stay married, next time don't marry someone who's old enough to be your daughter."

Chuck smiled. "Touché."

"Wait a minute," said DeMaris. "If all I had to do was ask to see the archives, why did Doris ask me for a business card?"

He smiled. "She didn't want it, her son does. Doing a school project. The kids are seeing how many business cards they can accumulate, who can get the most, the most-interesting looking ones, who can get the one from farthest away, that sort of thing. She's been asking for them from anyone new who comes in."

"Ah, I see. He'll probably get points for mine being the most unusual one. You'll have to get them from my friends when you meet them. They're from all over the United States."

She was down the street a bit when she heard him yell, "DeMaris!" She turned around. "What time Saturday, and where?"

"Sandy Bottom Cove is having a festival this weekend. I don't know any other place except the docks so, around noon? We'll be in town then. And, if that's too early let's meet around five at the docks?"

He waved. "Okay! See ya Saturday."

While Phil stashed Caroline and Melissa's purchases in the plane's storage area, they asked DeMaris what she had done.

"I went to the bank and we were able to determine that the key I had was for one of their safe deposit boxes. How about that, huh? And, then I looked at an apartment and met this guy—"

"What do you mean you looked at an apartment?"

"In case my character wants to live in downtown Spokane I wanted to see what the view was. Besides, by that time, I needed to use the bathroom."

"You wandered the streets by yourself?" asked Caroline. "Anything could have happened to you!"

"What do I care?" DeMaris yelled back.

"*You* talk to her," Caroline said as she got in the plane.

Melissa looked pleadingly at DeMaris. "De, honey, you know that wasn't the smartest—"

"I have a date for Saturday."

"With the guy you met in the apartment?"

"No! I would not have him! No, with the guy I met in the newspaper office."

"The newspaper office?"

"Yeah."

"What's his name?" hollered Caroline.

"Charles Dickens."

"You had to bite, didn't ya?" asked Melissa as she hefted herself into the plane. She studied DeMaris who had plopped herself in the front seat. Melissa leaned forward. "What did you do to your hair?"

"I brushed it for a change."

Melissa touched it. "No, you've got gel in it. And makeup on. I didn't pack you any makeup." She looked at Caroline, who only shook her head.

"You are not the only two people who know how to shop." DeMaris jammed her headset on and studied the view out her side window while the two gals in back looked at each other.

They had been flying for several minutes when DeMaris felt the plane dip slightly, correct, and dip again. She glanced at Phil. "Hey, Phil, you all right?" she said into the headset. *You sure don't look all right. What on earth did you have for lunch?* He suddenly clutched his chest and slumped over.

"Oh God! Heart attack!" screamed DeMaris at the top of her lungs. "Heart attack! Heart—"

Chapter Twelve

Sara walked out on the porch where the other girls were sitting around talking. She had an outfit in each hand. "What do you think?"

"I like this one." Viva pulled on the one closest to her.

Jacyne was in the military but that didn't stop her from being a clothes horse. She read the tags. "Expensive. You must be doing okay for a teacher."

"They're not mine, they're DeMaris's." They looked at Sara. "I decided that since she went through our clothes, I'd go through hers. Everything she brought with her looks new. And they're all designer labels."

"I . . . wouldn't put . . . too much stock . . . in that." They all turned to Liset. "I think she um, she has that outlet mall near her—"

"I've been there," said Shay. "They're not that big of a discount."

"Don't forget, as an only child DeMaris inherited everything. Her parents had money," said Jacyne.

"And besides, some of the clothes still have the price tags on. They're not cheap," said Sara.

"Still, I think . . . you know DeMaris," said Liset. "She probably got them at some huge sale."

"The prices I looked at weren't discounted. I mean, even if she got these from a fifty percent off rack, they still wouldn't be cheap."

"Maybe somebody donated them to the Salvation Army or Goodwill or something. You know she likes to hit the second-hand places."

"All designer clothes—all in her size?" Sara looked at Liset.

"Yeah. The person didn't like them, they died, whatever—they were donated and DeMaris picked them up. You know how she loves a deal.

Maybe it was somebody's garage sale. She's always hitting those. I'm sure that's what happened."

They were all staring at Liset, so she pulled her sunglasses off the top of her head and put them on. She leaned back in her deck chair and said nothing more.

Melissa whacked DeMaris in the back of the head. "Get control of the plane!" she yelled.

Right. DeMaris grabbed the wheel in front of her and leveled the plane. She pressed the transmit button and started talking with the control tower.

The girls could hear DeMaris. "I have had flying lessons. That baseball course thing. Yeah, yeah, pinch hitter, that's what they told me . . . yes; I have landed before, not well, but . . ." DeMaris glanced behind her. "You're both buckled in, right?" *Are they even breathing?*

"We're gonna die! We're gonna die . . ."

"Caroline, shut up! Melissa, you're a small-airplane instructor for the week, remember? Let's show some confidence and give me some advice!"

"I was just thinking about the last time you tried this . . ."

"I don't see any tower to hit, do you? And remember, in the end, I missed it."

"That's because Ron took over."

DeMaris took both hands off the wheel and turned completely around to glare at her.

"Yes, you can do this." Melissa teared up. "I have . . . confidence?" She sniffed a few times, choked, and then got a hold of herself. "I have confidence in you, DeMaris. You can do this."

DeMaris flexed her fingers and then gripped the wheel tightly.

"Actually," Melissa turned to Caroline, "I have the utmost confidence in De as long as we stay in the air." She gave a timid smile.

"So, how much longer have we got?" asked Caroline.

Melissa checked her watch but before she could answer they both heard DeMaris. "Yes, I see the runway ahead."

"Where did you learn how to fly a plane?" asked Caroline.

They were safely on the ground and Phil had been rushed to the hospital.

"Melissa's boyfriend gave me a few lessons to help me overcome my fear of flying. I actually landed it, didn't I?" Even DeMaris was in awe.

"It was even relatively smooth," said Melissa as she hugged DeMaris.

"Hey!" said Caroline. "We're on the ground! We're all still breathing—including Phil. I'll go with smooth, too."

Liset had dinner ready. DeMaris's emergency landing had already reached their ears.

"I couldn't have done it without Melissa's encouragement," said DeMaris. "She came through as a small-aircraft instructor."

In DeMaris's honor, Liset had made a triple-chocolate cake for dessert.

Jacyne poured wine—DeMaris indulged after the day she'd just experienced. As they sat at the long wood table on the deck, Sara looked over at DeMaris. "You're not eating meat again?"

"I need to watch what I'm eating for the rowing team."

"You had a hamburger for lunch," pointed out Caroline.

"What does the rowing team care? You're not doing any competition with them . . . are you?" They all stopped eating.

"No," DeMaris shrugged. "I allow myself one meat a day. Oh, my diet, that's it." As if the idea had suddenly come to her. The girls looked at one another but said nothing. DeMaris had always been a meat-and-potatoes person.

As the girls were cleaning up, DeMaris pulled Viva into the next room. "I need to use your laptop."

"It doesn't work here."

"You brought it with you."

"Yes. It works in town."

"The cell phones don't work, your computer doesn't work—how are you running your multimillion dollar real estate agency from here?"

"I have a great staff and, if you haven't noticed, the housing market is down at the moment. I need a break. Nobody can reach me here. That's why the laptop stays in the car. Whenever I'm in town I check my e-mail and phone the office."

DeMaris pointed. "What's wrong with your house phone? I just used it the other day."

"Nothing's wrong with it and you're welcome to use it but do you know who has that number? Harlan, our kids, and you girls. Everybody else—including my office—can get me by cell phone or e-mail. Let me repeat, I need a break."

"Okay, on another topic: you need to let the police know you found that bird."

"Why?"

"I discovered something today. As odd as it may sound, I think, possibly, that . . . I know where Sophocles lived before he came here."

Viva's face went through several different expressions before she hissed, "Why do you think I have him in the garage most of the time?"

"You know—"

"A whole lot more than you! Now drop it!"

Viva stomped off leaving DeMaris with her mouth hanging open.

Friday dawned. The festivities in town started with big sales at all the stores, a 5K run, carnival for the kids, and hot air balloons lifted at dawn and would do so again at dusk. The girls were up and out early to mingle with the crowd and to watch DeMaris practice with the rowing team.

DeMaris steered clear of the bag lady when she saw her. She didn't want the woman to recognize her in front of her friends. Wouldn't Liset love to know that's where the Coach purse had come from?

"Brian! Over here!" Gloria yelled and waved.

DeMaris looked up. *Shit! The bank manager!* She pulled her visor down and turned her back while Gloria introduced him as a friend of hers. DeMaris could hear them making small talk with her friends. Her ears perked up and she turned slightly to look when she heard ". . . hat for you."

"Oh, Brian . . . I think that's Viva's." *Double shit! Viva's hat! He must have picked it up in the alley way when it flew off my head. What to do? What to do?*

"Thank God you found that hat," said DeMaris loudly. All eyes in the group shifted to her, particularly Brian's. An outsider would have been able to pick out DeMaris's sisters from the group by the expressions on their faces. Her sisters had the look of "Oh, no! Here we go again." The rowing team just looked puzzled.

DeMaris could see Brian study her. Clearly DeMaris was in good physical shape, thin, and had short blonde cropped hair.

Viva took her hat from Brian as they all stared at DeMaris. "That day you guys left, when I stenciled and Shay had a migraine? She needed me to row into town for something stronger." Years had taught them that no matter what lies a sister told, the rest were there to back her up; so DeMaris had no fear of anyone contradicting or questioning her in front of this group. "The hat was sitting in the boat and it actually kept the sun out of my face . . . I really thought it'd be safe to leave it in the boat, I mean, look at it, who'd want it?" She laughed while Viva glared. "I was only gone a couple minutes and when I came back, it wasn't there. I'm sorry I didn't tell you." DeMaris turned to Viva. "I was so excited when you told me Gloria needed me to row, we ate, and it's just been busy and crazy. I forgot—but I planned on buying you another hat before I left. I'm sorry."

"Well, no harm done." Viva smiled an I'll-kill-you-later smile.

"Did you see a large woman that day, about your height, with gray-brown hair?" asked Brian.

DeMaris knew you should always keep your mouth shut; the less said the better—but living her own mystery was too intoxicating. "Well," she looked thoughtful, "when I came up the ramp, there *was* an older woman standing there similar to what you described. But . . . no, there wasn't anybody else."

"Have you ever seen her before?" Brian asked eagerly.

Oh, what a sucker! "No, but I'm not from around here . . . she was wearing a beautiful hand-knit sweater with a skirt that didn't exactly match." She took the visor off and ran her fingers through her blonde hair to make sure he noticed it.

"Yes!" yelled Brian. "That was her!"

"What was her?" asked Gloria.

"This woman came into the bank the other day pretending to be— she had a safe deposit box key—" he stopped. "Well, it's a private matter—but I would really like to talk to her."

Oh, I bet you would. Hmm, pretending. How does he know I'm not who I said I was? He didn't accuse me of anything while I was there. Was he trying to get me into his office to call the police? And yet, he obviously didn't *call the police.*

DeMaris could feel her sisters' eyes scorching her. "It strikes me, I need some chocolate." She took off for the ice-cream parlor across the street.

They stayed downtown through the afternoon and had an early dinner before returning to Viva's. DeMaris felt she was walking to her doom as she entered the house.

"DeMaris."

"I can explain."

"We haven't asked you anything yet. Feeling guilty about something?"

"No. I don't think guilt's the word."

"Who were you pretending to be at the bank?"

"Why did you show him the key?"

"See, this is where I can explain—"

"Oh, God."

Several rolled their eyes.

"What did you do?"

"No!" All eyes suddenly turned to Jacyne. "You're not going to tell us," she said. "This is how it starts and I'm suddenly remembering a conversation I had with Kirk a few years ago: 'DeMaris does all this stupid stuff and I always end up being an accomplice because I know too much.'

"She does the same thing to us. Look at all the places we've been banned from—and we didn't do anything! I don't want to wake up some day to find out that there is no bank that will ever take me. No. You just keep this little mystery gig to yourself. I want no part of it." Jacyne turned to leave and then stopped. Slowly she turned back to DeMaris. "Is that why Kirk asked for a divorce?"

"Kirk wanted the divorce?" asked Sara.

"Well, it makes sense, doesn't it? I mean, why would she want to get rid of Kirk?"

DeMaris looked at Jacyne. "I see. Well, I could explain, but . . ." She shrugged her shoulders and walked out of the room.

Chapter Thirteen

Saturday everyone was up early. Liset fixed a huge breakfast but the girls felt tension in the kitchen as soon as they entered.

"It's just bacon," Liset declared, shoving the plate at DeMaris and glaring.

"No meat," DeMaris said quietly, putting her hands up in a defensive gesture. The girls didn't even bother to ask.

After cleaning the kitchen, they all jumped into the speedboat and left for town. DeMaris took off to meet the rowing team. Viva and Melissa went to the coffee shop while the others lounged in the boat waiting to see if Charles Dickens would show up.

Viva was on her computer when she felt someone looking over her shoulder. Coffee in hand, Melissa tapped the screen. "What are you doing?"

"Oh, remember De told us we needed to learn all about our identities so that if people asked us questions we could answer them? I thought I'd read up on TV star Greg Delray, so I can ask De some questions and see how well *she* does. She's been screaming at us about how we're not doing well at this . . . it's our turn.

"Humph. I'd forgotten he was in that horrible train wreck several months ago. I knew I'd heard his name someplace, even though I don't watch his show."

"That's probably where DeMaris got the idea to use his name."

"What do you mean?" said Viva.

"Because—" Melissa stopped. Viva looked up at her. Melissa gave a slight laugh. "I have no idea where I was going with that. I'm gonna head back to the dock."

"Melissa," warned Viva.

Melissa stuck her finger in Viva's face. "I did not tell you anything." She almost ran out the door.

Viva sat for a long minute and gave up reading through the article. Her mind was elsewhere. *DeMaris has hated flying for several years. Coming here was the first she's flown in a long time. But, she went to California to stay with Melissa. How long ago was that? She would have gone by car, bus, or her favorite mode of transportation: train.*

—— —•— ——

Melissa made it back to the boat in record time. Viva arrived twenty minutes later. A few minutes after that DeMaris arrived by boat with the rowing team. Jacyne was sitting on the speed boat facing the dock. "De, is that your guy?" she said. "Cuz he's been standing there awhile."

"Chuck!" DeMaris cupped her mouth and yelled.

"Hey, DeMaris!" he yelled happily and waved.

"That's Charles Dickens?" two said in unison.

"She really had a date?"

All of the girls clambered out of the boat to follow DeMaris up the dock. She introduced everyone. "So," said DeMaris, "tell Chuck what you all do for a living."

The girls looked at each other puzzled. "Oh, okay," said Caroline. "I'm a speech pathologist."

"I'm an administrator for a financial invest—"

"I'm a general," Jacyne cut in. She glared and motioned toward DeMaris who was fuming.

"I'm a hot air balloonist," chimed in Viva. "On weekends I pretend I'm a real estate agent."

"I don't remember what I'm supposed to be," said Melissa. "Oh wait! I remember now—"

"You people suck at this game!" DeMaris exploded.

"I can't lie and say I'm a doctor," said Caroline. "What if somebody asks me to do something? Did you ever see the *Seinfeld* episode where George said he was a marine biologist?"

"I can't lie either. I'm the astronaut of the group, but I know nothing about NASA," Sara whispered to Chuck.

"I already told him about our game!" DeMaris was still yelling. "You can practice on him!"

"Yes, imagine my surprise when I found out I was in the presence of DeMaris Azaygo," said Chuck.

A woman walking by suddenly stopped and turned around. "Excuse me, are you DeMaris Azaygo? The writer?"

There were seven soft whispers of "no, no." DeMaris looked at them and mouthed 'watch and learn.'

"Why, yes, I am." She heard a collective moan behind her.

"Oh!" the woman's eyes bugged out. "I am a huge fan. I was so upset when you bumped Nick off. How could you?"

"I know. I cried for days—after all, he'd been with me for five books. But . . . he eventually lipped off to the wrong person—me! That's why he had to go. You know, he was getting mouthy and going off and doing his own thing when he was told to do something else. It was bound to get him in trouble. And it did. It got him killed."

"Stop her," Jacyne hissed to Chuck.

"I just met her. You stop her."

"She doesn't listen to us. You're a man; you've got a 50-50 shot."

The rowing team stood next to Viva. "She's not really . . .?"

Viva looked at them. "How many stories have I told you about her?"

They started to laugh. "My favorite one is when you went on that cruise and the captain was almost arrested when you arrived in port."

"Or when she wanted to re-enact the movie *Seven Brides for Seven Brothers* and found a guy for each of you."

"Yeah, I still don't think our husbands have seen the humor in that one," said Viva.

"Remember her at the zoo?"

"No," said Gloria, "the best one you told me about is when she tried her hand at making a crop circle." Several of them started laughing, "and from the air it looked pornographic."

"Erotic, we use the word, erotic. Oh God," Liset gritted her teeth, "she's signing!"

"See, that wasn't so hard," said DeMaris as the woman walked off. "This is why I told you to do some research so that you could answer questions. If you get stuck, you're old enough to blame it on your poor memory."

"Thanks," said Shay.

"You can't go around signing someone else's name—particularly a famous person," Jacyne pointed out.

"One, DeMaris Azaygo is a recluse; two, it's not like she's even going to find out we're here; and three, even if she should find out, we'll be long gone by then."

"No, no. There is no *we*," said Melissa.

"But I thought you were *all* banned from the San Diego Zoo," said Gloria.

"And the cruise line," added one of the crew members.

"Oh, that reminds me," Viva turned to Jacyne. "I answered your cell phone for you when I saw it was the airlines calling. Sorry."

Jacyne's nostrils flared as she glared at DeMaris. "Don't worry about me," said DeMaris raising her hands, "I am taking the train home."

"Can I kill her *this* time?" asked Jacyne to Viva. "I know several ways. I can make it look like an accident."

"I can explain why she's so upset," DeMaris said to Chuck.

"Please, don't," chorused four.

Chuck smiled. "How about I take you to lunch?" and casting his eyes over her friends added, "This group doesn't appreciate your spontaneity."

"Sounds good to me," DeMaris said as she slipped her hand through the arm he offered.

The girls, mouths open, watched the two mosey down the street. "We've been through plenty of spontaneity!" Shay finally yelled.

"Wait 'til you get a taste," this from Jacyne.

"Her famous *first* words are—" started Caroline.

"'I can explain,'" finished Melissa.

"And her famous *last* words are—" added Sara.

"'I have no idea,'" shouted Liset.

"Or 'I'm doing research for a book!'" Viva fumed.

"I have no idea why they can't see the fun in being someone different for a week or so," DeMaris complained to Chuck.

"You're right," Chuck said, "your friends don't appreciate you."

"Well, in all fairness, I have put them through a lot."

"Hello!"

The two of them glanced over to see an older woman sitting on the sidewalk, her grocery cart next to her. Chuck stared; DeMaris gripped his arm a little tighter.

"Enjoying purse?" the woman asked.

"Ahhh . . . sure," DeMaris hustled them down the street. "I have no idea what that was about."

"You're not even carrying a purse," Chuck pointed out.

"I know," she agreed. They found a restaurant further down the block, ordered, and as soon as the waitress was gone DeMaris said, "Tell me all about D. B. Cooper."

"I can—but right now, I want you to tell me all about you."

They talked nonstop. *Gosh, I have a lot in common with him. He is nice-looking . . . he is my age.*

They ate silently for a few moments. Chuck moved in his chair. "What's your interest in the Cooper case after all these years?"

"I'm trying to get an idea for a book."

"Number twenty-seven?"

She smiled. "I'm not really DeMaris Azaygo. I aspire to be, but believe me, if you saw my house and my car, you'd know I'm not rich. I enjoy writing, can't get an agent but . . . I write just the same. I always tell my kids I'll be famous once I'm dead. I mean, that would be my luck. I'll be discovered after I'm dead and buried."

After lunch, they strolled along the streets, DeMaris darting into shops when she saw something of interest. At one point DeMaris suddenly stopped walking and stared at Chuck.

"What?" he asked.

"It just dawned on me you said *twenty-seven*. DeMaris Azaygo has only written twenty-five books."

"Yes, but my sister works for her publishing house and knows what a huge fan I am of hers. She's assured me there is a twenty-sixth one coming out soon."

"Really?"

"Yes. But I'm sure you already knew that."

"No! No, I didn't. Well, how 'bout that?" she started walking back down the street. "But, thank you for that tip. If somebody asks me, I can use it."

"I think that's why it took you so long. *You* knew—but the general public doesn't." She turned around to retort, but he held a hand up. "Your secret is safe with me. But . . . can you tell me anything about it?"

"I would, except I have no idea."

"Right."

"A bookstore," she pulled on his sleeve. "Come on." She walked over to the classics. "What do you recommend?"

He looked where she pointed. "The only Charles Dickens I have ever read is *A Christmas Carol*."

"You haven't read *Great Expectations*? *The Pickwick Papers*?"

"Like you have?"

"Three months out of the year—summer to be exact—ever since I was in high school, I read the classics. They're great books, hence being called classics." She scanned the titles. "Huh. *Bleak House* is the only one I haven't read." She pulled it out. "If these are all his books, I'll have read the complete works of Charles Dickens. What book would you like? My treat."

"I do not want to read—" he stopped. Slowly he turned and headed for the mystery section. He scanned the titles and pulled out a book and handed it to her. "I actually have the complete works of DeMaris Azaygo; however . . . I kid you not when I say my dog peed on this one."

"Liked it that well, huh?"

"He wanted to make sure he got my attention."

She wrote a check for the two books and they walked out into the sunshine. Chuck pulled the book out of the bag and handing her a pen said, "Sign it, please."

She stared at the pen, mouth slightly open. "What do you want me to say? From the fake DeMaris Azaygo?"

"Is that what you wrote on that woman's scrap piece of paper?"

"Well, no, but what she doesn't know won't hurt her."

Reluctantly she wrote on the title page and slammed it shut before he could read it. Taking the pen back he opened *Bleak House* and wrote his name with a flourish across the title page.

"At least you didn't lie," she pointed out.

"Here," Gloria handed Viva a cell phone. "This is DeMaris's. She forgot it."

"Okay. Thanks." Viva stared at it.

"It's brand-new," said Jacyne. "Look at it. This model just came out last month. They're three to four hundred dollars."

"Where would she get a phone like this?"

"I don't know," said Shay.

Viva jumped when the phone rang. They looked at it and simultaneously said, "Oh my, God. It says Greg."

"Well, don't get excited. It's not the TV star. Obviously she knows somebody named Greg and, like always, just used it," said Jacyne.

"Oh, it's show time!" said Shay as she took the phone from Viva and flipped it open. "Hello?"

Chapter Fourteen

The girls were still up when DeMaris came in just after two o'clock.

"Well, well, well," they hooted at her.

"We were just betting on whether or not there'd be a pillow fight in the morning."

"He's nice looking," offered Shay.

"You can give up that TV star boyfriend now," said Jacyne.

"Ah, Greg; yes, Greg," muttered DeMaris. She made a face. "Well, I didn't do anything I can't tell him about."

"You . . ." they stared at her. "You didn't do anything tonight?"

"He kissed me." She headed for the bedroom with all of them yelling after her. They dragged her back into the living room and handed her a glass of wine.

"What happened?"Jacyne asked when she saw the dejected look on DeMaris's face.

"Well . . ." DeMaris took a sip. "I've been kind of on the fence about Greg."

There was silence for a minute. "Greg? The TV star?" asked Sara.

DeMaris gave a slight laugh. "Okay. I am seeing someone named Greg. He's really nice; he's in good shape; I think he's good-looking; but we have an age difference that bothers me."

"Like, say, twenty-three years?" asked Shay.

"Your senior," ended Liset.

It was quiet while they waited. "What?" DeMaris finally asked.

"You forgot your cell phone. Gloria gave it to me," said Viva.

"And I answered it when Greg called," added Shay. "I thought I should take a message for you."

"Yeah, no sense in letting it go to voice mail," said DeMaris.

"Oh. Do you have voice mail? Because you didn't on your other phones. Remember? You were afraid it'd eat up your minutes."

"Oh, well. I have a new plan. I have voice mail."

"And an expensive phone," commented Caroline.

"I . . . decided to treat myself. I don't have a home but I do have a nifty phone that does everything." They all stared at her. "Are you going to give me the message?"

"Yeah." Shay shifted in her chair. "He said for you to call him no matter how late. He misses you."

DeMaris nodded. "Well, next time we're in town, I'll do that."

"You can use the house phone," offered Viva.

"That's all right. I'll wait."

They sat quietly for several minutes.

"I had a nice chat with Greg," Shay offered.

"I see." DeMaris sat back in her chair and took a long drink of her wine. She set it down. "What did he tell you?" she said in a measured tone.

"Well . . . he is not a thirty-seven-year-old actor and I think he was a little disappointed to learn you hadn't told us the truth about him. That maybe you're embarrassed because he's really a seventy-three-year-old retiree who worked for an insurance company."

"I see." DeMaris was steamed.

"What are you thinking?" asked Jacyne. "Going from Kirk—who's our age—to somebody who is old enough to be your father?"

"That's really my decision."

"Look," said Caroline, "I'm taking care of Bob after twenty-five years of wedded bliss. At least when I'm feeling overwhelmed from taking care of him after his stroke I can fall back on my good memories. If this is a fling, fine—but we hope you're not thinking about anything serious with this guy."

"Yeah, well . . . he's asked me to marry him."

"And you said what?" asked Liset.

"I told him I was going on vacation with my sisters and that I'd give him an answer when I got back."

"Well, obviously you have some . . . doubts then," offered Shay.

"Yes, I do. I admit the age difference has me thinking."

"It should, you're going to end up taking care of him."

"I could be involved in a boating accident the next time I go out on the lake. Or a car accident. There's no guarantee I'll always be in better shape than him. And let me tell you, Greg is in great shape. He makes me jog with him every morning."

"Every— So, you've been living with him?"

"Whoops! Yes, for the last month."

The girls looked at each other.

"Do you feel that strongly about him?" asked Melissa.

"I think he's great. I do though worry about the age difference and the fact that, if I stay with him, there goes my dream of being a hermit."

"You lived with Kirk all those years and were pretty much a hermit."

"Yes, but Greg loves going places. He's got this nervous energy and always wants me to go with him. I mean, it's great for research on a book, but a lot of times I just want to be alone—and he doesn't understand that. Kirk did."

There was silence for several minutes.

"How do you feel about Chuck?" Shay finally asked.

"I just met him and we only had one date!" They stared at her. "Okay. Chuck kissed me and . . . I realized then how much I am really in love with Greg."

"You're in love with a seventy-three-year old?" asked Viva. She made a face.

"He's wonderful. We both enjoy nature. We go cycling and jogging. We hike. I've started kayaking because he loves that and we plan to hit some of the rivers and lakes when I get back."

"It sounds like he's in good shape."

"He's in very good shape. I just don't know if I want to give up my new independence. I'm having a great time being free to do my own thing. I'm having a great time being with Greg. I really wish he'd stop pressuring me though. I like the way things are now. But I did promise to give him my decision when I returned. I just don't know what to do."

"Well, look at it this way," Sara said to the group, "at least now we know she wasn't living on the streets for the month none of us could account for."

"What?" said DeMaris, looking around.

"We've been worried about you; so I called Kirk," said Jacyne. "He wasn't there but Allison was most informative about your life style before you went to California. Living out on the streets? Your daughter is worried sick about you."

"As are we!"

"My God! The streets? Why didn't you come to one of us?"

110

"I was doing research for a book!"

"We're not buying that excuse any longer!"

"How many years have we listened to that?"

"Every time you do something stupid—"

"And living on the streets does qualify as stupid!"

"You always pull out your 'doing research' quote."

"I was still on the phone with Allison when Kirk came home." DeMaris simply stared at Jacyne; so Jacyne plowed on. "He was very evasive, which I found odd. He finally claimed ignorance about your street dwelling and that he didn't find out about it until after you left for California."

"Which brings us to the train wreck," said Viva.

DeMaris jumped to her feet and whipped her head around to look at Melissa who at the same time yelled, "I didn't! It was Viva!"

"Yes," said Viva calmly. "I was on my laptop today. I decided to pull up information on Greg Delray, so I could ask you questions. See how well *you* did. I saw that he was in that horrific train accident. And then, it hit me. You travel by train a lot. And that was the train out of Chicago headed for California. I thought, why did DeMaris use that name? Could it be she met him on the train? So, doing *research*, which I'm sure you'll appreciate, I called up a friend of mine who works for Amtrak. Yes, you were on that train."

DeMaris simply stood there.

"There were more people dead than alive," said Caroline. "Why wouldn't you have told any of us—besides, Melissa?"

DeMaris sunk back into her chair. "That's not anything I want to relive," she said softly.

"You have— You need to talk about it," said Shay.

"Melissa," said Jacyne, "how did you know DeMaris was involved in one of the worst train wrecks in history while the rest of us did *not* know?"

Melissa said nothing and looked down at the floor.

"I told her not to tell," said DeMaris rescuing her. "And Melissa knew because . . . I needed to get away. She was the farthest place I could go. Trust me, after being in a train wreck I had no problems—well, almost no problems—getting on a plane. I ran into some difficulties after getting *on* the plane," she glared for a moment at Jacyne, "but I figured if God wanted me dead he'd have killed me on the train. I just don't want to talk about it. It's over."

"De. You have to. And if not with us, then with a professional."

"You are not serious! Come on! I have always been the odd one in the group."

"In this group, yes. You have always been a little off the wall," offered Jacyne. "But this—us changing our identities, you wearing our clothes and sneaking around, this being in your own mystery—this is not you."

DeMaris was fuming.

"You've always had an imagination," said Sara, "but . . . it seems to be . . . taking over."

"I came here," DeMaris said softly, "to get away for awhile with my best friends. I don't care to talk about my divorce or the accident. I want to think about happy things. I want to leave here with happy thoughts, I want—"

"We want to know about the train wreck," Liset spit out. Clearly they were not going to let it go.

"No."

"What was it like?" persisted Liset.

"It was a lot of fun," said DeMaris sarcastically. "Being sound asleep and then suddenly thrown out of bed in the middle of the night in the pitch dark; rolling over and over again; hearing people scream; the sound of metal twisting; and when you finally come to rest at the bottom of a mountain, wondering if you're alive or dead."

"You've been through something that the rest of us have never experienced, nor will we probably ever."

"That's because you guys don't ride trains."

"What did you do?"

DeMaris looked from one to the other. They were sitting on the edge of their seats. "You were one of just a handful of survivors," said Caroline. "Tell us what it was like. How did you manage to survive that?"

"God," DeMaris said and then sighed. "You know me. I like a lot of weight on me when I sleep. And the train is always so cold. I imagine that helped a great deal. I was cushioned by all the blankets and pillows I had around me.

"I tumbled around in my room with the mattress, sheets, and pillows—it's a tiny room, you know. Then, when things stopped . . . I laid there all sprawled out. The train was on its side . . . and I wondered, was I dead and this is what it feels like or was I still alive? It seemed to me that it was quiet for a while and then I could hear people crying and talking. I crawled around and found my flashlight and I pulled myself out the window. My flashlight showed me dead people, blood and extremities everywhere. I had a child die in my arms; and in the morning light when the sun came up, I could see so much more. I could see how far we had fallen and I wondered how was anybody going to rescue us? I didn't know if anybody even knew where we were. I mean, did we disappear off the radar or would people start wondering when we didn't show up at our destination hours down the road?" DeMaris paused and they all remained quiet. "I helped pull people out and tried to make them comfortable—and then later, when I'd check on them . . . they were dead. Did I kill them by moving them?"

"No."

"Maybe they were better off where they were."

"You couldn't just leave them there. You did the right thing."

"Well, seeing as how it took a rescue team six hours to get to us, that's what I decided too. After that, well, flying wasn't so hard." She got up and walked outside.

DeMaris sat shivering at the end of Viva's pier. The night was chilly for summer and all she had on was a tank top and shorts. Her knees were tucked up under her chin and her arms wrapped around her legs as she hugged them to her body and rocked slightly. She heard someone coming down the pier toward her. DeMaris felt a quilt—one she had made for Viva—fall down around her shoulders. Shay sat down next to her the same way: knees bent and arms wrapped around her legs. Each took an end of the quilt and pulled it around; they sat shoulder to shoulder like they used to do in college.

"Why didn't you want to tell us you were in the train wreck of the century?"

"No reason to."

"No reason to? You don't think any of us would have been concerned?"

"What was there to be concerned about? I pretty much walked away without a scratch."

"You need to talk to us. You need to cry, you need to do something."

"I needed at that point," she said dramatically, "to be gone."

"Please don't. We've been over this, for years—"

"I'm not talking *death*. I'm not suicidal anymore, haven't been in years. Not that any of you noticed. You all still see me as the crazy person. No, what I meant was that I could finally run away. I could finally be free. I could go anywhere in the country—the world—and be a hermit. Change my name. As far as anybody knew, I was dead. I have a sizable life insurance policy. Kirk, Allison, and Ryan would have been happy—"

"They wouldn't have been happy—and neither would we!"

"I left you all something."

"For God's sake, DeMaris!"

"No, for once I was going to accomplish, *really* accomplish, one of my dreams. I've been writing since I was a kid—what do I have to show for it? A lot of paper! A broken family. I'm fifty and I've done *nothing* with my life that I set out to do. Finally I was going to get to run away like I've always dreamed of doing. I was finally going to accomplish one dream! But no, when Melissa heard about the accident and I didn't call, she got worried!" DeMaris spit this out as if it was the ultimate insult. "With Ron being a pilot, they decided to fly over and check on me. Well, Melissa came to find me; Ron came to ID my dead body. I should have walked off into the desert when I had the chance. But no, I stayed to help. That'll teach me! I let the rescue team take me to the trauma unit they had set up and *then* I was going to be free. Here I was, talking to this gorgeous, hunky guy, TV star Greg Delray in the flesh, with his broken arm, when I hear a voice scream, 'I've found her! She's over here! She's alive!' From the moment I heard Melissa, I thought, should I pretend amnesia? That I have no clue who she is? That a stranger was trying to abduct me? As it was, I had to tell Melissa I'd had a blow to the head and I was dazed and confused which is why I hadn't called."

"Well, thank God," said Shay. "I can't imagine what we'd have done without you; let alone Kirk and the kids." After a lengthy silence Shay asked, "Did you *really* talk to Greg Delray?"

"Where do you think I got the idea to use his name?"

"And the Greg that I talked to on the phone . . ."

DeMaris looked at her. "Yeah, right. That was the thirty-something, gorgeous, TV star who dumped his equally gorgeous model girlfriend for me." They both laughed. "DeMaris Pala did actually get to talk to him and DeMaris Azaygo is dating him . . . in her dreams."

They sat for another long minute when Shay asked, "So, your Greg has done well in the stock market, huh? Even for these times?"

"What did you do, pump him for information?"

"He volunteered a lot. I think he thought he was reassuring me by telling me he was a retired insurance salesman and that he had a nest egg that was doing well and that he dabbles in the stock market. In fact, he was quite talkative. He seemed very nice."

"He is very nice . . . sweet. Actually a very good-looking man for his age." Shay nodded. "So, you're thinking marriage with this guy?"

"I am to give him my answer when I get back."

"Promise you'll wait at least a year from when you got your *final* divorce papers before *actually* getting married."

"I can't promise you anything like that."

Shay sighed. They sat on the pier long after the others went to bed.

114

Chapter Fifteen

DeMaris came out onto the porch. Due to bad weather, rowing had been canceled. Her one morning to sleep in found DeMaris still in her pj's and bathrobe while the rest of them were dressed. "Listen, I have to tell you something. I was going to last night and then . . . we talked about other things."

"What's wrong?" Jacyne leaned forward.

"I . . . I . . . I gave Chuck an interview."

"What?" Viva yelled jumping up from her seat.

"For his newspaper."

"What are you thinking? I don't care how much of a recluse DeMaris Azaygo is. When it hits this little newspaper every major newspaper in the country is going to pick it up! Why don't you ever think?"

"I did!"

"You'll be sued for sure!" said Caroline.

"I know," DeMaris said shouting over them. "Which is why I refused to answer any questions concerning the real DeMaris Azaygo and instead talked about the train wreck. So, I was going to tell you all today."

There was a collective sigh of relief.

"But, thank you for thinking I would be that stupid."

"De, you have done some stu— du— idio—"

"Crazy things," Sara rescued Liset.

"Crazy things," Sophocles repeated from the far end of the room.

DeMaris pulled out a chair and sat down. "It just brought back so many memories. Things I'd forgotten . . . things I'm sorry I remembered. The more questions he asked . . . the more I remembered. And, I don't want to remember!" she ended up yelling. They all sat and waited. "I think of the few times I've tried to kill myself, obviously unsuccessfully!" She threw her hands up in the air. "And the numerous times I've contemplated it. But, when I was tumbling around in that little cubicle I suddenly realized I didn't want to die. And then, I didn't . . . and so many did.

"I think of all the research I've done: poisons, guns, hangings, jumping off things, anything in the name of death for my books—and when it came right down to it, I didn't want to die. God," she slapped a hand to her head, "I'm not consistent with *anything* in my life." She stood up and headed for her bedroom.

They sat in silence and finished their breakfasts.

The sun came out and everyone except for Viva and DeMaris took the speedboat to spend the day on the water. Harlan had flown in from Nevada as Viva and he were meeting clients.

DeMaris looked up from her writing. Maybe she could check out another Foxx address. Better catch Viva before she left.

"Where's Deacon Road?"

Viva stared at her. "What?"

"Where's Deacon Road? Street?"

Viva stood there for a long minute. "Why would you ask that?"

"Because I want to look at a house."

"What's the number you're looking for?"

"Fifteen fifteen."

"DeMaris, how do *you* know that address?"

"What? It means something to you? How do *you* know it?" DeMaris tried to look as blank as she could. "I saw a newspaper clipping about the Foxxes," she finally offered.

"The Foxxes? I don't believe this! Because of a stupid bird saying their name?"

"I'm just doing research for a book—maybe I can get this one published."

"You never read it in a newspaper. There is no way— Where did you get that address?"

"How do you know it? What do you know about the Foxxes?"

"Honest to Pete, DeMaris. You know what? I'm not going to tell you what I know." Viva turned on her heels and left the room.

DeMaris sat for a moment. She heard the bedroom door shut and although Viva's voice was muffled it was plain she was complaining to Harlan.

DeMaris strolled over and looked into Viva's purse. Carefully she pulled out her key ring. *My word. How many keys did the woman need?*

Grabbing her own fanny pack she went into the garage. Not a regular driver, she paid scant attention to vehicles. Sara and Caroline had rented a van for the trip and DeMaris should have thought to ask to borrow it; however . . . She looked at the keys in her hand. There were few cars DeMaris could identify—she would have failed any police line-up involving vehicles—but there were some she knew because they were different from the norm. A VW bug for example.

She smiled at the vehicle at the far end of the garage: a Hummer. She walked over, opened the door, and hoisted herself up into the driver's seat. *Oh, nice. And look, a GPS thingy. I can plug in the address.*

She tried several keys before finding the right one. She buckled and looked out the rear window. *Guess I should have put the garage door up first. That's all I need! The girls would have a field day if I asphyxiated myself in Viva's garage! They would never believe I wasn't trying to kill myself.*

She found a remote control device in one of the compartments on the ceiling and pressed it. Voila. The garage door opened. Carefully she backed out.

"What am I gonna do?" hissed Viva.

"I don't know," Harlan shrugged. "Tell her the truth, I guess."

"She'll make me go to the police. She'll take Sophocles there!"

"The police aren't gonna want him. It's not like the bird's done anything and they're not going to get any straight answers out of him."

"Oh, I don't know. Things always turn out differently when DeMaris is involved."

"Ain't that the truth," mumbled Harlan. "She can at least keep secrets— she's kept plenty over the years. Just tell—" They both stopped talking and listened.

"Isn't that the garage door?" asked Harlan.

"Yeah, but it can't be. I mean, DeMaris doesn't really drive."

Harlan scampered out of the bedroom with Viva directly on his heels. He happened to glance out the living room window to see his Hummer rolling down the driveway. "No!" He took off at a dead run through the house, threw open the front door, and ran down the street. "DeMaris! DeMaris!"

"Did she wave or flip us the bird?" asked Viva breathing heavily beside him.

"*What is she doing?*" screamed Harlan. "My baby! Why didn't she take your Porsche or the MINI Cooper? Or the van the girls rented?"

"Have you seen how she drives? She needed protection."

"Where do you think she's going?"

"1515 Deacon."

"Quick! Get in the MINI." Harlan was pulling his keys out.

"No," Viva shook her head and headed toward the house. "I'm never going to that address again . . . not even to sell it."

<hr />

"And so, besides the steak dinner, she buys this street person—bag lady, whatever ya wanna call her—a $100 gift certificate so this woman can come in here and buy a meal whenever she's hungry." The waitress behind the counter was telling her friend sitting on a stool about the strange day she'd had a few days before.

"Well, that was nice of her," said the friend.

"Of course, it was. I'm just saying . . . I thought it was, I don't know, staged. I'd never seen either one of them before and the bag lady is a huge woman, you couldn't miss her. I kept thinking somebody was going to jump out at any minute and say 'Surprise, you're on such and such TV show.' I just didn't buy it."

"Why?"

"The bag lady shows up one day out of the blue, and just plops down in front of the restaurant and then this other lady comes waltzing in with a ton of clothes. Who walks around town like that?"

"Maybe she was headed to the Laundromat."

"No! They fell out of her arms just as she got to the counter. She said she was tired of wearin' all of 'em all day. Wearing all of them all day? Who would do that? Nothing matched. Do you know how fat you'd look if you actually wore everything? Anyway, one of the things she had was a gorgeous sweater. I asked her about it and she said it was hand knit."

"Excuse me."

"Oh, hey Brian. The usual?" asked the waitress as she whipped out her order pad and a pencil.

"Yeah . . . but I couldn't help but overhear you." *A hand-knit sweater. Where else have I heard that? The festival. One of Viva's friends. Yeah, the blonde.* "What color was this sweater?"

The waitress looked at him. *Brian interested in a sweater?* "Bright, multicolored . . . purple, pink . . . orange. Why?"

"I think she was in the bank that day. Have you seen her since?"

She shook her head no.

"I'm not much on knitting. How can you tell if it's hand-knit?"

The waitress looked thoughtful and then shrugged. "I don't know. She said it was."

"And she paid a hundred dollars for you to feed who?"

"Some street woman who showed up here."

"This woman just showed up out of the blue and bought a gift certificate for a stranger?"

"Yeah. Said she'd lived out on the streets herself for a time and was back on her feet. Wanted to help out." The waitress put in Brian's lunch order and went back to her friend.

Brian's head spun. Hadn't Gloria told him in passing that Viva had recently found out a friend of hers had been living on the streets? How mortified she was? *I've got to ask Gloria which gal it was. In the meantime—*

"—figured just handing her money she'd never use it for food," the waitress continued her story to her friend. "Traded her the gift certificate for a purse. You know, one of those purses she held up was a Coach purse. Can you believe someone living on the street—"

"A *Coach* purse?" interrupted Brian.

The waitress looked over, startled. "Yeah. I happened to be looking out the window at the time. It had a stain on it but it was definitely a Coach. Why?"

"What does this street person look like?" Brian asked, ignoring her question.

"Tall and big. Awful looking gray hair. Matted, I guess, would be the word. Why?"

"Where is she now?" He looked outside.

The waitress shrugged. "I don't know. She comes and goes. When she gets hungry, she'll show up. Why?"

"Did this woman take the Coach purse?"

"I don't know. A customer came in right then. Why?"

He jumped off his stool and walked out.

Once DeMaris was sure Harlan and Viva weren't following her, she pulled over to the side of the road and typed the address into the GPS. *Boy, this is nice. So, this is what it's like to drive a car that doesn't already have 30,000 miles on it when you first get it.*

"Turn left," the GPS said.

"Off course, off course," it said as DeMaris did her three right turns.

DeMaris arrived at 1515 Deacon, parked across the street, and looked around. *Okay neighborhood, modest home, tall trees indicating an older subdivision. One woman with a stroller and dog. Looks harmless enough, although in my book maybe her stroller will turn out to have a gun instead of a baby in it. And the dog? Hmm, have to think about that.*

DeMaris got out of the Hummer and crossed the street. She hoped she looked casual—then realized she only saw older homes, old cars, a rundown lawnmower, rusted children's playground equipment—the brand-new Hummer stood out. She returned to the Hummer and parked it two blocks away.

Children were outside playing. They gaped at the large vehicle. *Why didn't I take a different car? They were plain and simple, nobody would have noticed them.*

She got out, made sure it was locked, and walked slowly down the street. *Woman with baby stroller gone. Man about my age mowing. I can take him if I have to—certainly my character can.*

She walked up to 1515 and knocked on the door; then realized she had no story ready for when someone answered. She looked around. Tall grass, weeds in the flower bed, cracks in the driveway with grass coming up, and paint was peeling on the house. Okay, she would say she was from the neighborhood welcoming committee and they had rules that needed to be followed. Can't have the neighborhood looking like it's going downhill, can we? She knocked again. Nothing. She peered in the window as best she could but heavy drapes blocked the view. *In my book, they've got to have sheer curtains so I can see something. Paper and pen, paper and pen, why didn't I bring any?*

She walked over to lawnmower man and flagged him down. He stopped beside her and shut off the motor.

"Hi, I wonder if you've seen a man and woman here?"

"No. Why?"

"I, um, sent them over here to look at the house. Never got any feedback."

"Oh, I just assumed it sold when I noticed the real estate sign was gone. So, it hasn't sold?" he asked.

"No, not yet."

"And you know this because?"

"I'm the real estate agent."

"And I thought the housing market was in a slump." She gave him a puzzled look. "I saw the Hummer you drove up in."

Well, so much for moving it so nobody would notice me. "Yes, well, they were supposed to call me and give me the extra set of keys back that I loaned them last week; they never did." She pulled Viva's ring of keys out. Hopefully one of these opened the door. "I think I'll go check on the house and and see if they left the keys inside. Thanks." *And if none of these keys work, I'll just break in.* She strolled back to 1515. Now her going inside the house wouldn't seem strange.

She held her breath as she tried several keys in the front lock; eventually she heard the sound that made her smile: click.

DeMaris walked in and shut the door behind her. For some reason she had expected the same awful odor to hit her here as when she had entered the apartment. She was relieved to find it not so and . . . the rooms empty.

Well, empty until she reached the last room down the long hallway. DeMaris was startled and gave a slight scream when she saw a blow-up mattress complete with sheets on the floor. "Hello?" she asked tentatively. Silence. Slowly she walked in the room and quickly looked behind the door. She could see into the bathroom and saw toilet paper and a washcloth.

She hurried back into the kitchen. Although it appeared unused when she had first looked in here this time she opened the refrigerator door. Food. She opened the cabinet doors. Snacks.

Okay, is someone hiding from me or is no one here? Lawnmower man said he hadn't seen anybody; yet someone's been living here. Okay, time to get down and dirty. Wish Kirk were with me. He was always good protection at this kind of thing. Greg has yet to be tested. Yeah, I really wish Kirk were with me.

DeMaris grabbed the ring of keys. Taking two at a time, she placed the keys so they poked out between her fingers. She balled up her fist and walked as quietly as she could to the two doors opposite each other in the tiny entryway that she hadn't yet opened. Taking several deep breaths, and telling her imagination to shut up and go take a hike, she flung the first door wide open screaming, "Yeah ha!" as loud as she could. Fortunately she didn't spring forward as she had planned. She would have tumbled into the basement.

Yeah, I really need Kirk to go down to the basement.

She shut the basement door, turned, and looked at the second door. *This has to be a closet—and now I've lost the element of surprise.* But she could still do some damage with the keys, she reasoned, and eventually somebody would find the Hummer if she didn't turn up. Besides, Viva knew exactly where she had gone. DeMaris swung open the door and stopped. There was only one item in the closet: a 'For Sale' real estate sign.

Viva's real estate agency to be exact.

Chapter Sixteen

DeMaris's head was spinning as she locked up the house and sprinted to the Hummer. Experience had taught her that when she was like this she should try something entirely different. *Maybe I should see if my cell phone works and call Greg.* She was happy to hear it ring.

"Love to hear your voice," he answered.

"Hey, love to hear yours too. And, I do miss you but . . . what did I tell you before I left? That all of us had new identities and that I was going to tell the girls I was dating a TV star. You couldn't back me up, huh?"

"Sorry," said Greg.

"I ask you to do me one favor."

"I'm sorry—but, did they believe you?"

"It's not about believing me. This is my character for a week! God, you suck at this as much as they do," she cried.

"Really sorry."

There was silence for several seconds before DeMaris said, "God, I really miss you."

"Come on home. I'm here."

The man rummaged through the grocery cart until the woman came out of the restaurant. "Hey!" she yelled.

"Where's your purse?" he demanded.

She didn't like the looks of him. "Don't got no purse for you, sissy." She pulled her food up tight against her. He continued rummaging through her cart. "No! Get out! Get away! Not for you!"

He was as tall as she was and he didn't hesitate. He grabbed her by the collar and shook her. "Where is it?" he growled. "Where's the Coach purse?"

She stared blankly at him.

"What did you do with the purse that had a stain on it?"

"Pretty purse."

"Yeah. What did you do with the pretty purse?"

"Got hundred dollars for it."

"What? You sold it?" he screamed. He shook her again and she screamed. "Shut up! Who did you sell it to?"

"Lady who bought food."

"Lady who bought food? Somebody from the restaurant?"

She shook her head. "Stranger. Likes to row."

"Row? You saw her on the lake?"

She nodded.

"Does she have a name?"

"Don't know."

"Well, you'd better." His hands squeezed her arms like a vice.

"Don't know! Don't know! No!"

⚊ ⚊ ⚊

What am I missing? After talking with Greg for a half hour, DeMaris drove into town. She looked up at the restaurant sign, looked around again, and went inside.

"Hi!" She flagged down the waitress in the nearly deserted place. "Where's the bag lady?"

"I don't know. She left with some guy."

"Some guy? Who?"

"How do I know? I just looked out and the two of them were disappearing down the street."

"When was this?" DeMaris demanded.

"What, are you a friend of hers? Relative?"

"No."

The waitress looked at her. "So, what's your interest?"

"Good Samaritan? I paid one hundred dollars to have you feed her and— *What?*" DeMaris saw a look come over the gal's face.

"Nothing. Nothing. Can I get you something to eat?"

"No." DeMaris almost got to the door when she realized she was hungry. *Maybe I should get something to eat while I'm here.* She started back to the waitress when she noticed her on the phone, back toward her. The girl turned around, they made eye contact, and then she quickly turned back around.

I'm hungry but not that hungry. DeMaris almost ran out the door.

She went into the next restaurant she found that had several people in it. She sat down far away from any doors or windows and placed herself where she could keep an eye on the entrance. She wondered about the bag lady.

Who was the guy that suddenly showed up? Does she have a place to stay now, so I can quit worrying about her? I should have asked that waitress how much of the gift certificate had been spent. Some guy wouldn't have rolled her for that, would he? Of course, in my book, she's dead by now. Okay, this is reality. She must have found somebody to stay with. And yet, I don't feel right about that guy. Why?

I find it strange the waitress didn't know anything. Correction: she does know something, she's just not telling me. Why? Who would she have called?

And then it struck DeMaris: the woman's cart was still there. If she had left voluntarily with some man, why wouldn't she have taken her belongings with her?

"Excuse me, it's DeMaris Azaygo, right?"

DeMaris was on her way back to the Hummer when she turned to see Brian. With a smoothie in hand she wondered if she needed to douse him and run. She tucked her chocolate in her fanny pack for safe measure. "Just for the time I'm here. In real life I'm DeMaris Pala."

"Huh? Never mind. I'm Brian Fox. I met you before." DeMaris said nothing. "You were on the rowing team with Gloria."

"Yes, I remember you." *The bank manager who tried chasing me down.*

"I was wondering if you ran into that woman again, you know, the one you described as possibly taking Viva's hat." He looked her up and down and DeMaris struggled to keep a straight face.

"No, I'm sorry. I haven't."

"Um, do you know a woman by the name of Blanche Fox?"

"No, I'm sorry. I don't."

125

He stood there for a moment. "Can I ask why you paid a hundred dollars for a gift certificate to give to a street person? Do you know her?"

How does he know that? "I can explain . . ." *No, why should I explain anything to him? Who knows what he had planned for me if he had caught me that day.* "No, I don't know her—is that a crime in this city?" she countered. *Think! Think! How does he know that and why does he care? What would a bag lady have to do with him—the waitress and her phone call!* DeMaris gave him a puzzled look. "The woman I described to you wasn't the same woman I gave the gift certificate to."

"No, no. I realize that. I was just wondering why you would do that."

Don't embarrass Viva. Stay calm. "I don't mean to be nasty, but what business is it of yours what I do with my money? What, as a banker you're trying to keep track of *everybody's* busi— money?"

Brian smiled. "No. I was only trying to find out your relationship to her."

"I don't have a relationship with her. What is your concern?"

"Well, I myself have been paying for meals for her—"

"You?" DeMaris's face showed disbelief.

"Yes, believe it or not, I am a decent guy."

Yeah, that's why I was chased down the street and had to hide to avoid you. DeMaris chuckled. "I'm sorry. I didn't mean to insinuate . . . are you related to her?"

"No," he said quickly. "I just can't stand around though and watch someone starve. When I found out that you had paid for her meals, I thought perhaps you knew her. Nobody here seems to know her and there are those of us who would like to let her family know her whereabouts."

"Well, I'm sorry I can't help you." DeMaris turned to go. "I was just being a Good Samaritan myself."

Brian studied her for a moment. "Nice haircut and dye job. My sister does excellent work, doesn't she? Where did you get the clothes you were carrying under your arm that day?" DeMaris had already turned her back on Brian, so fortunately he couldn't see her face.

Holy shit! I can't believe he put two and two together. What am I going to say now? Sorry Viva. DeMaris turned and gave him a haughty stare. "Are you insinuating I stole clothes from a bag lady?"

"No!"

"How dare you!"

"I was only curious—"

"You think I helped out a street person and then took her clothes? I don't think I have ever been this insulted!"

"Please! I didn't mean—"

DeMaris turned and stomped off. She let out a deep breath. Hopefully he would never ask her that question again. *But how was he able to figure out I was the fake Blanche? And yet, he was careful not to outright accuse me. Why would he even care? What is he up to?*

——— —— ———

"I did not steal your precious Hummer!" DeMaris had been unceremoniously shoved into a chair upon returning. Arms crossed, she glared at the two people screaming at her.

"Oh! You couldn't take the Porsche or the—"

DeMaris looked at Viva. "You have a Porsche? Can I test drive it?"

"No!"

"You don't even drive!" Harlan was still yelling.

"I do too drive. I just hate doing it, that's all."

"No more taking our cars!"

"Cripe, I feel like a teenager who's just been caught coming home after curfew. Yes Mom, yes Dad," she glared at each one in turn.

There was finally silence. "We need to get going. We're late," Viva said.

"Which one of you wants to tell me the story of Blanche and Owen?" The silence was longer this time. "How did you acquire Sophocles? I mean, I like the Walmart story. I'll probably use it in my book, but for the record, what's the real story?"

Viva sighed. "Those birds can live for fifty years or more. He actually belonged to Blanche's grandmother. Owen hates the bird. He is always threatening to kill it. God, he is a big, awful, mean man. I told Blanche I'd be happy to take the bird anytime. She called me one day, asked me to come and get it. They have an apartment in Spokane. The minute I opened the door from the street, well, we nearly collided. She yelled, 'leaving' as she ran by me. I could hear two men screaming at each other so . . . I took off after her and I put her up temporarily in one of the houses I'm trying to sell."

"Why didn't you go to the police?"

"To say what? Owen threatened *again* to kill her bird?"

DeMaris sat there for a moment. "Do you know who was upstairs?"

"Why?"

"Just something I was thinking about." DeMaris thought for a moment and then asked, "Why don't they just get a divorce if they're so unhappy with each other?"

Viva shook her head. "They're brother and sister. They live together because of finances."

DeMaris continued to stare to her.

Viva sighed and continued, "They lived with their mother, before she died. She was fine but . . . Blanche and Owen are just strange. Even the husband, Blanche and Owen's father . . . I never met him. He always disappeared and was never around whenever I showed up. But their mother talked about him all the time and I attended his funeral. The woman worked for me for over twenty years and seemed normal. I can't say that about her family."

Hmm, I've got to look through the papers—or call Chuck—and find out what/who was in that closet. If he's as big and mean as she says, then it wouldn't be Owen and I met their neighbor. So who?

"I had an interesting talk with Brian, the bank manager," DeMaris said.

"Really?" asked Viva. "I've never found him particularly interesting."

"Is he the Good Samaritan type?"

Viva laughed. "Brian?"

"Yeah, that's what I thought. First, he wants to know if I know someone named Blanche Foxx."

"Why would he think you knew anybody by that name?"

"I don't know," she said slowly. "Then, he wanted to know why I was buying lunch for the bag lady."

"What bag lady?"

"The one in front of Wiley's Restaurant. The one who sold me the Coach purse."

"I thought you bought that at the Salvation Army in Michigan."

"That was the first story. This is the second story. Keep up with me." Viva glared at her. "Where are Blanche and Owen now?"

"I don't know." Viva shrugged her shoulders.

"Oh, my God!" DeMaris's mouth dropped, her eyes bugged out, and she clasped her hands to the top of her head. "Why didn't I see this before? Well, I'm some freelance writer. Blanche and the bag lady are the same person!"

Viva clamped a hand over DeMaris's mouth. "Shut up!" she hissed. "What did this bag lady look like?"

"Old. Fat. I mean, huge woman. Really tall, at least six foot if not taller and carrying a lot of weight. Gray hair that hasn't seen a brush in years . . . poorly dressed."

"My God! What is she doing out and about? She's supposed to stay in the house!"

"The house at 1515 Deacon? She wasn't inside earlier in the day."

"Inside? Earlier in the day? Like today?" Viva shrieked. "How could you get in— When did you— I don't see how . . . you don't know your way around . . ." Viva stared.

"On the other hand I didn't go in the basement," mused DeMaris.

"Wow," said Harlan. "So this is how it all begins with you girls, huh? And all of us guys thought you sat around on your last night together and concocted a story for our benefit."

Viva glared at him, pressed a hand to her head, and then looked at DeMaris. "I still haven't gotten an explanation as to how you know that address and put two and two together."

"Well, actually I meant Blanche and the bag lady were one and the same in my book—*not* real life. And the house part I just guessed at."

"At what point did you decide I was stupid?" asked Viva.

"I don't think you're stupid. I just think you are better off not knowing what I know."

The two of them sized each other up. "What did you do inside all those banks we took you to?" asked Viva.

"Ninety-nine percent of it was legitimate stuff. I could maybe tell you about that."

"Ninety-nine percent and *maybe*?" screeched Viva.

"Maybe not."

Viva started to walk away and then stopped. "Don't get— Are you involved with Brian?"

"I think he's a little too young for me."

"Oh, but you don't see the correlation between you and Greg?"

"Let's keep Greg out of this and continue with our discussion."

"Fine. Stay away from Brian. The guy is scum and I have no idea why Gloria thinks he's so great."

"Why can't Blanche come out of the house?"

Viva walked up to DeMaris and said quietly, "Because it could get her killed."

"By Owen or Denny Caldwell?"

"My God. How do you . . . Who told you? How could you possibly— You're good."

"Thank you."

They were both silent for a moment then Viva shook her head and said, "No, I don't want to know."

"Yeah, it's probably best you don't." Then DeMaris brightened, "Should we go find her?"

Viva nodded. "I need to get her off the street. After our appointment, I'm dropping Harlan off at the airport. You be ready to leave and make some excuse so the girls don't want to come."

DeMaris nodded.

"Viva," Harlan checked his watch, "we really need to go."

"I'll take care of everything at this end," offered DeMaris.

"Gee, I feel so relieved," said Viva as she walked out the door.

DeMaris chuckled and took off to find the girls.

They were getting ready to head into town, did she want to come?

DeMaris took one look at Jacyne and said, "Take that off."

Jacyne stared down at her outfit and then at her. "I beg your pardon?"

"In fact, it just dawned on me. Attention everyone—all those clothes that I borrowed from you and wore into town the other day can never be seen around here again."

Jacyne ripped her sweater off. "Great." Melissa headed back to her room to change her skirt. No one bothered to ask why.

———

Viva drove up and DeMaris hopped in. "What did you tell the girls?"

"Well, if you'd arrived fifteen minutes earlier, we could have just left. They weren't here. However, I guess it's better they are back from town so now we won't run into them. I told them you weren't going to be home until late as you were going to spend some time with Harlan before he headed back; and that I was going for a walk."

———

They stood in front of Wiley's Restaurant and looked around. "Are you sure you saw her here?" said Viva.

"Of course, I'm sure," yelled DeMaris. "However, she wasn't here earlier in the day. I was hoping she'd be back by now."

"Well, I'm just remembering the time . . . okay, where would she go from here?"

"Her cart is still here so I'm thinking she hasn't gone far." *Better not tell her about the bag lady leaving with a man, Viva'll really freak.* DeMaris ducked inside the restaurant and came out five minutes later. "They have no clue about anything she does. They don't even know her name."

"Thank God."

"Let's go to the house you have her in then. Maybe she went back there."

Viva deliberated with herself for a minute and then they returned to the car. "Just for the record, did you really go to 1515 Deacon?"

"Yes, why do you think I took the Hummer?"

Viva shook her head. "It is beyond my comprehension—everybody's comprehension—that you always fall into these things. You're a magnet."

"Exactly. I ask the universe to send me a book idea and I get one. I've just been a little more involved in this one than usual. Isn't it exciting?"

"No! It's dangerous. You don't know—" Viva stopped.

"Yes?"

"You don't know and we're gonna leave it that way."

"Fine. But you might find down the road that you want to trade a secret for a secret."

They rode in silence until they pulled up in front of a small house on the far side of town. "Okay, I thought you had her staying at 1515 Deacon. Who's over there if Blanche is here? Oh! Owen! Of course. Thank God I didn't run into him while I was there."

Viva stared at her for some time and DeMaris braced herself for a verbal assault. Instead Viva asked calmly, "What did you find there?"

"Nothing much. Food, toiletries, mattress, sheets, stuff like that."

"But no person?"

"No."

Viva stared out the side window. "I had Blanche at the Deacon address. I snuck her in there and told her nobody could know she was there. No lights on, keep the curtains drawn, and that I would bring her food and check in on her. But somehow Denny Caldwell found her there and she doesn't want anything to do with him. I don't blame her—I was always telling their mother she shouldn't trust Denny but she thought he was all right. I don't know how he found Blanche."

Probably the same way I did. Let myself into her apartment and found your business card with that address on it.

"Blanche saw him coming and went out the back door. She found me and so I put her up here. But I can't keep moving her from house to house. Why did she leave this house? Did Denny find her again? How could he? And if somehow he did find her, why didn't she tell me? Does she think I'm the one giving him information? Oh, God," she sighed. "I've got to find a permanent remedy for her . . . and Owen . . . and do something about that scum that keeps following her."

"What does he want with Blanche?"

"I don't know. Blanche won't talk and I am not about to confront him."

Standing on the little porch Viva pounded on the door. "Blanche!" she yelled. "It's me, Viva!" She repeated this several times. Nothing. She tried the door; it was locked. Viva got out her set of keys, inserted one, and then stopped. "What if she's dead?" she whispered.

"Then we'll call the cops."

"I don't want them to know that either one of us knows her. What story could we possibly give as to why we're here? Or her? I mean, she's not supposed to be living in the house, I'm supposed to be selling it!"

"I'll think of something," DeMaris snapped her fingers. "I'm thinking of buying around here and you decided to show me this. Look what we found."

Viva nodded. "Yes, that active imagination of yours does come in handy. You do it."

"Fine." DeMaris unlocked the door and linking arms they slowly made their way through the house room by room.

"This is not good," Viva kept whispering.

"I think it's good we haven't found a dead body."

"But where is she?"

"Why don't you tell me—"

"No."

After canvassing the first floor DeMaris said, "We have to look in the basement."

"Do we have to?"

"Yes."

Hesitantly they made their way down the stairs. The basement was one large finished room. Nothing.

"What do we do now?" asked Viva.

"I say we check out their two addresses."

"Their two— How could you— God, why me? I don't see how she could have gotten back to either place. She has no car or friends."

"Well, we could check around downtown, ask all the merchants—"

"I can't let people know I'm looking for a street person!"

"Fine. I'll do it."

"Everybody knows you're with me."

"But I'm the crazy one, remember? I'm doing research on a book. Besides, Denny may have already found her."

"What?" DeMaris told her the conversation with the waitress.

"Oh, God," Viva nodded. "Okay, I'll drop you off in town and go back to the house."

As Viva pulled into a parking spot in town DeMaris said, "We may need to check the morgue. Here and in Spokane."

Viva visibly shivered. "Why Spokane?"

"Because," said DeMaris getting out, "we both know that's where their apartment is." They stared at each other for a moment and then Viva reached into her purse.

DeMaris waited to see what Viva was going to pull out. "No!"

"Take it," Viva waved the money at her. "You might need to take a taxi home."

"Give me an hour and come back and get me or I'll borrow a boat."

"Take it."

"I have money," DeMaris gritted her teeth.

"This isn't a time to be proud."

"I have money. I can take care of myself." DeMaris stormed off down the street.

Just what I need, thought Viva as she drove away, *DeMaris inquiring about a street person and bouncing checks all over town.*

Chapter Seventeen

DeMaris visited most of the shops and restaurants on Main Street without luck. No one had information about the bag lady. As she was walking and pondering the situation, she suddenly remembered what Viva had said: "What is she doing out and about?" *Why can't Blanche be out? Why can't she be seen? If Blanche isn't supposed to be seen why is she hanging around Main Street? But she has been on Main Street. She's been in front of the restaurant. And, somebody found her. Where did they go?* DeMaris turned in both directions not sure what she was looking for. *What would a man want with Blanche? Did she go willingly? Was she murdered? That's what will happen in my book but here . . . I guess I'll check out behind the stores. There's no place else left for me to look.*

For three blocks DeMaris wandered around the back of shops. She debated looking through the commercial trash compactors but couldn't bring herself to do it. As she considered her next move, she watched a Mexican woman carrying out the garbage from one of the restaurants. *This is useless. I'll call the girls and—where's my phone? No! No! I could not have lost my phone! My brand-new phone!* The trash was compacting when she heard one shrill scream followed by another.

The first scream came from inside the compactor. The second was the Mexican woman.

"Turn it off!" hollered DeMaris as she ran toward her. "Turn it off!"

DeMaris's college Spanish was rusty, but she understood several Bible references while the woman crossed herself. DeMaris hit the red button with the palm of her hand. Slowly the compactor came to a halt.

"Shut up!" yelled DeMaris. *"Alto! Alto!"* The woman was flinging her hands and screaming Spanish in DeMaris's face. "Would you just shut up? We need to get the police! *Policia! Policia!*"

The woman stopped in midsentence, her mouth hung open as if DeMaris had slapped her. *Good, finally got her attention.* Someone inside the trash compactor was sobbing.

"You," DeMaris pointed at the woman, "need to get police. You. *Policia.* Get, get!" She waved her hand.

For several seconds the woman stood still, then turned and bolted across the parking lot. *I thought the police station was to the right.* The woman yelled something over her shoulder and suddenly DeMaris saw two Mexican men running with her. "Wait! *Alto!* I'm not calling the police *on you*! Wait! *Misunderstanday!* Hey! Crap, now I'm going to be blamed for that too."

The sobbing continued inside the trash compactor. DeMaris opened the door and hollered, "You can come out, it's safe."

"Bad man! Bad man put me here!"

"Oh! Bag lady, is that you?" DeMaris said excitedly; then grimaced when she realized what she had just called the woman. "I mean, are you the Coach purse lady? Ah, Blanche?"

The crying ceased. *Well, I'm two for two getting people to shut up.* DeMaris leaned into the compactor. "I'm looking for the Coach purse lady. I think that's you. At any rate, whoever you are, I'd think you'd want to come out . . . Hello?" She was suddenly showered with garbage.

"Get out! Bad man! Get out!"

DeMaris didn't even want to look to see what had hit her. It smelled, that's all that mattered. It was in her hair, on her face, and covered her from the waist up.

"Go away! Go away!" came from inside.

DeMaris grabbed the door, slammed it shut, and secured the latch. She didn't want the woman to get out and disappear on her again. She looked around. Hopefully while she was gone no one would try to compact any garbage. She walked into the closest business, a restaurant.

"Stop right there!" someone yelled. A waitress was pointing a finger at her. "Not in my establishment!"

"If you promise to call the police right now and ask them to meet me out back by the trash receptacle, I'll leave. If I don't hear sirens in one minute, I'm coming back inside and sitting down."

The woman ran over and grabbed the phone.

Ten seconds, not bad, thought DeMaris as she heard sirens. She watched two more Mexicans running across the parking lot. "Wait! I can explain! Oh, what's the use?" She picked some of the garbage off and waited.

The two police officers hesitated as they drew closer to DeMaris. "There's a woman in the compactor. You need to get her out."

Tentatively one knocked on the compactor. "I don't hear anything," he said.

"Maybe's she unconscious," offered DeMaris. "I assure you, someone is in there."

They opened the door and were showered with food. "Bad man! Bad man!"

"We're the police! We're the good guys!" yelled both officers.

"Go away! Leave me alone."

"You can't stay in there, it's dangerous."

"Real cops?"

"Yes, we're real cops. See our uniforms?"

Carefully the woman peeked her head out. "I've been looking for you," said DeMaris.

The woman looked at DeMaris and then broke into a smile. "Nice lady. Buy food."

"Yes. Not nice to throw food at nice lady."

The woman refused to give her name and only said 'bad man' when asked why she was inside the compactor.

"Is this a friend of yours?" Officer Mahoney asked DeMaris.

She had just started to answer him when the woman threw her arms around DeMaris and said, "Friend." She looked adoringly at DeMaris.

"Oh, God." DeMaris stood still as the woman continued to hug her. At least they both smelled the same; so they cancelled each other out. "Listen, bag la— Can you tell us anything about the bad man?"

"Bad man!"

"Yes, was he tall? Bald? Lots of hair? What?"

"Don't like him."

"I don't like him either. That's why I want the cops here to find him and arrest him. But you need to tell us who it is."

"Wanna go home."

DeMaris looked at the two officers. "I'm staying with a friend here, in town. Perhaps you could drive us both to Viva Zimmer's house?"

They both laughed. "You must be DeMaris. Sorry lady, but there's no way in hell the two of you are getting in our car."

She gave them a disgusted look. "How about going into the restaurant and asking for a couple garbage bags for us to sit on?"

"Oh. That's an idea."

DeMaris and the bag lady had just entered the house by way of the kitchen when she heard, "For God's sake, De! Take a shower."

Liset was at the stove preparing dinner. She had not turned around. *We must really reek if she can smell us over that spicy dish she's working on.*

"Oh, my God!" Melissa.

"What did you do this time?" Sara.

"Why were you with the cops?" Jacyne.

"Blanche!"

"Viva!"

DeMaris looked from one to the other.

"No! No!" said Viva as Blanche ran toward her and flung her arms around her.

"Blanche! Feed that damn bird!"

Blanche's eyes widened. "Owen!" She ran in the direction of the voice. "Sophocles!"

"So, that's Blanche, huh?" asked DeMaris as Viva came to stand next to her. "I'd ask for an explanation except I'm afraid it'll clash with the story I have in my head and I don't want to confuse the two. Why don't you get Blanche to take a shower while I sit on the porch and write?"

Getting Blanche to take a shower was a major production. Whereas DeMaris hated taking them but knew she had to Blanche hated taking them and truly saw no reason to. Liset finally won her over with the promise of chocolate cake.

DeMaris could hear Viva through the bathroom window. "You *have* to use the shampoo and you *have* to use the soap."

"No shampoo."

"No chocolate cake."

"Meany!"

"Yes, I am."

"Want my clothes back."

"After they've been washed."

"Washed? Don't want 'em clean!"

"And you all thought I was bad," said DeMaris to Jacyne as she walked up.

"That'll be you in ten years. We can't wait. Here," she held out DeMaris's bathrobe. "Take your clothes off in the garage. Might as well wash your stuff along with Blanche's. Oh, Viva found your phone in her car."

"Thank God. Thank you," DeMaris said as she took the phone and bathrobe. After removing her clothes in the garage, she returned to the porch, where Liset brought her dinner.

"The soap goes under the arm," they could all hear Viva.

"No!"

"Yes!"

Over an hour later, two disgruntled women came out of the bathroom. Viva, for the most part, had sat on the toilet with the lid down dispensing instructions; while Blanche shouted, "no" at everything. The only thing that got Blanche moving was when Viva told her the cake was out of the oven and the other girls were going to eat it. Although making her take a shower had been a chore, getting a brush through her hair was impossible. Blanche's hair was so long and wild that Viva actually cut out chunks of it that were severely matted while Blanche was occupied with Sophocles and chocolate cake.

DeMaris, an avid recycler, conservationist, and environmentalist took a long, fifteen-minute shower instead of her usual five. And she enjoyed it.

Blanche was happy to be reunited with Sophocles. She curled up underneath his hanging cage on the floor and talked to him until she fell asleep. Viva threw a blanket over Blanche but nearly burst into tears when she discovered Blanche was drooling on a designer pillow she had taken off the living room couch.

"She's finally quiet," whispered DeMaris. "And you finally have her off the streets. Be happy."

"Key!" The girls had taken a snack and their drinks out to the pool so they could talk while Blanche slept. Now they turned in her direction.

"Key! Where's key?" Blanche's shrill voice came from the living room.

Everyone out by the pool stopped talking. "Hang on, Blanche," yelled DeMaris. "I'll get it for you." DeMaris went into her bedroom and pulled out a handful of keys on a ring. *Ah, this one will do nicely.*

Everyone was consoling Blanche, who could only blubber, "Key. Lost key. Owen mad." She stopped as soon as DeMaris held out Kirk's house key to her.

DeMaris held her breath as Blanche's face changed to puzzlement. *Shit, does she recognize that it's not the right key?* "I found it in the birdseed. Is this Blanche's key?"

A smile spread across Blanche's face and she wrapped a hand around it. "Blanche's key."

"All right, where's the real key?" hissed Viva in DeMaris's ear.

"In a safe place," DeMaris whispered. "We're all happy, okay?"

"None of us are happy until you dump geriatric Greg."

Chapter Eighteen

The next morning the women were having breakfast while they waited for DeMaris to return from rowing practice. Although after watching Blanche grab food with her bare hands and stuff it in her mouth, several opted for just coffee.

"Okay," said DeMaris cheerfully after she had showered. "I thought we'd have fun by going on a treasure hunt today."

They eyed the torn yellowed sheet of paper she had gotten from the safe deposit box. "Where'd you get this?" Liset asked.

"Let's not take the fun out of it, okay?"

Shay looked at it. "Who wrote this? It looks like a child's handwriting."

"I didn't ask you to analyze it."

Viva grabbed it. "You're not familiar with this area. How did you come up with these road names?"

DeMaris stared at her for a moment. "Chuck helped me. And I wrote with my left hand. Satisfied? God, you people take the fun out of everything."

"But this is old paper," pointed out Caroline.

"Chuck works with paper. It comes in all shapes and sizes . . . and looks."

The girls looked at one another.

DeMaris held her breath as Blanche examined it and then reached for another muffin.

Viva studied it. "Okay, I know where this is . . . sort of."

"Let's drive and see where it leads." DeMaris looked around at the doubtful faces. "Come on! Live a little. Let's have some adventure."

"Didn't I tell you, nice and quiet couldn't last?" sighed Jacyne.

"Let's go."

They would take the van. With nine people, Liset and Melissa volunteered to stay home. "We'll be here when you need help. We'll come to your rescue."

When DeMaris came out of the garage with two shovels, Caroline and Sara tried to bow out also.

"Fine," said DeMaris, "but when we find buried treasure, I'm only splitting it with those who came with me."

"Where did you get the map? We don't buy your explanation."

"I think Chuck and she buried something," said Jacyne.

"Do we really want to know what it is?"

"They talked about D. B. Cooper's money. Do you think the two of them found it and buried it again?" This got laughs.

"Sneeze or snooze," said DeMaris as she got in the van.

"Sneeze or snooze?" They all looked at each other.

"Snooze or lose?" offered Jacyne.

"Whatever!"

Slowly they got into the van. With one extra person, they thought it'd be crowded but they were wrong. Blanche threw herself on the floor and laid down. *Okay.*

"Wait a minute," said Shay as they drove out of the driveway. "If you snooze you do lose."

"It's 'use it or lose it,'" said Liset.

"Ya snooze, ya lose," said Sara.

"Well, I'm glad we got through that mystery," said DeMaris. "Now, let's try to enjoy this one."

"I'd enjoy it more if I believed your story about where you got the map," demanded Caroline.

"What difference does it make?"

Jacyne leaned forward in her seat. "Did you come by it through legal means? I mean, we no longer have Kirk to come and get us out of a jam."

DeMaris turned around and glared but said nothing. There was a collective groan through the van.

"I can explain, but for the moment, trust me."

They drove north of town. At least the scenery was gorgeous.

"Okay," said Viva. "The map is not to scale. We're on the right road but how do you know where to stop?"

"There's a square marked on the map. I thought there would be a building or something."

Blanche was kneeling and looking out the window. "Home."

DeMaris looked at Viva. She couldn't read her face.

"Stop! Stop here!" Blanche pounded her fist on the front seat.

"Okay! Okay!" Viva pulled over to the side of the road. The girls had to physically stop Blanche from opening the door before they'd come to a full stop. She started screaming and hitting.

"Okay, now you can get out!"

Blanche flung the side door hard, nearly knocking it off its track. She ran down the tree-packed hill while the girls followed slowly. DeMaris grabbed a shovel. Sara grabbed the other.

Viva walked up to DeMaris and said quietly, "I know why Blanche wants to stop here—but what makes you think the map meant here?"

"I just have a good feeling," DeMaris smiled.

"Hey, look! There's a building," Sara pointed out as she and DeMaris walked together.

It was not a building they would ever have seen from the road. It was a dilapidated two-story house with its roof caved in on one side and the porch looked unsafe. Blanche stood in front of it. From her face they could see she was near tears. "No home."

"You and Owen have an apartment in the city," Viva said gently.

Blanche sniffed. "No home. Can't go home." They were not sure if she meant this one or the one Viva mentioned.

"Okay, everybody start looking for a big oak tree somewhere in that direction." DeMaris pointed south. But the girls mainly wandered around checking out the flowers, squirrels and poison ivy. While nobody paid any attention to her, DeMaris quietly walked onto the porch. Ever fearful that she might fall through, she nonetheless pulled out the other key that she had discovered in the safe deposit box and inserted it. Voilà. It worked. *Okay, figured out both of those clues. Extra house keys.* DeMaris hurried to join the others.

"Here." They turned to see Blanche pointing at a huge oak tree. *Hmm, maybe Blanche was the one who drew the map. No, she would have said something. Must be Owen then.*

Jacyne looked over DeMaris's shoulder at the map and pointed. "What do these three circles represent—and why are they X'ed out?"

DeMaris smiled. "Don't you read? X marks the spot. Look for three things—that way." She pointed.

"When did DeMaris come out here to set this up?" whispered Sara.

"I'd say she didn't," replied Shay. "She's just playing us like she usually does."

"Here." Melissa pointed to the ground. Sure enough, although it was very overgrown, there were three large rocks laid in a line next to each other. "Let's start digging," said DeMaris happily as she stuck the blade of her shovel in behind a rock and pried it up.

Sara groaned but jammed the other shovel in none the less.

They took turns digging.

"I wouldn't do that," Blanche warned without much conviction.

"How deep are we going?" asked Sara.

"I don't know." DeMaris looked at Blanche. She was perched on a huge rock watching them with a look that clearly indicated she was miserable. DeMaris walked over to Viva and said quietly, "Is Owen as . . . handicapped as she is?"

"No, but he's not the brightest bulb."

DeMaris held out the map. "If Blanche or Owen made this map, they couldn't have dug very deep."

"Probably not. Owen's not in very good physical shape. But Blanche didn't seem to recognize it; so I doubt she drew it."

"I don't think her memory's all that great."

DeMaris walked over to Melissa and Jacyne who were digging. "I think that instead of going down any deeper we should dig toward each other."

"Your turn." Melissa handed the shovel to DeMaris. By now they had dug two good size holes, one at each end of the three rocks. Jacyne had started to carve her way to DeMaris when there was a definite whump. All chattering stopped. DeMaris jumped out of her hole and began to dig near Jacyne.

"I can see a plank!" said Jacyne.

"I see a top!" said DeMaris.

The girls crowded around excitedly. Even Blanche got off the rock and came over to look.

DeMaris ran her shovel across the top. A few minutes later Jacyne declared from her vantage point in the hole, "I think you can pull the top off. There's nothing holding it."

Four pairs of hands, one on each of the sides, two on the back of the approximately three foot long top and Jacyne with her shovel in the front ready to pry, carefully pulled. Slowly the top rose. Blanche was on all fours and saw what was inside before the rest of them. "Emily!" she screamed.

They dropped the lid, each one looking at the other.

"Her dead cat?" Sara asked hopefully to Shay.

"Her dead dog?" Caroline asked Liset.

"Her mother?" asked DeMaris to the group.

"Too small a box," said Melissa. "Baby sister?"

"It's a doll," said Jacyne.

Blanche had pushed the fallen lid away and had grabbed up Emily, hugging her fiercely to her chest.

"Well, shit," said DeMaris. "It's a damn toy chest. I can't write that in my book."

There was silence—and then a burst of laughter. "Nancy Drew strikes again."

"Or stinks again."

"Sinks again!"

"Oh, no. Remember," said Shay striking a pose, "Trixie Belden is so much *more*." All of them had read Nancy Drew mysteries as young girls, only two had even heard of Trixie Belden—DeMaris's favorite young detective when she was growing up.

"*Trixie Belden and the Mysteriously Dirty Toy Chest.*"

"*Trixie Belden and the Three Rocks.*"

"In her head."

"Yeah, laugh it up," said DeMaris disgustedly. "Just for that, I'm not sharing any dirt-encrusted toys."

"They're not yours, anyway," Viva pointed to Blanche who still hugged Emily tightly.

"Ya know," said Melissa, who was now on her hands and knees, "these could have been worth something if we'd found them in decent shape." Melissa frequented antique shops and was knowledgeable about this. "Gosh, look at the Tonka trucks, all rusted and broken. That's a shame." She picked through the toys, absolutely nothing of value.

They put the top on the box and threw dirt back over it.

"Owen wants trucks," Blanche reached a hand out still with her death grip on Emily.

"Then Owen can dig them back up," DeMaris said uncharitably.

Blanche stuck her tongue out at her.

DeMaris suddenly asked, "Where is Owen?"

"Don't know," said Blanche.

DeMaris looked over at Viva who shrugged her shoulders.

"Are we filling the holes back in?"

"I'm not."

"I'm not."

They walked back to the van only to discover a flat back tire. "Well, that's just what we need," said Viva disgustedly as she opened her cell phone. "Nope, no cell coverage. Great."

"No fear," said Shay. "This is what I do for a living this week." The girls watched while Shay pulled out the jack and spare tire and went to work. They were on their way in no time.

They decided on take-out food for lunch as they didn't want Blanche's unruly manners to gross out patrons.

They ate on Viva's deck overlooking the peaceful lake.

"I really can't be seen in public with her," whispered Viva.

"For all the charitable work you do, you act like this?" asked Jacyne.

"No, that's not what I meant. *Blanche* shouldn't be out in public."

"Care to elaborate?"

"No."

"What are we going to do with her?" asked Melissa.

"Take her back to her apartment and make her stay there."

"I'm thinking that's not a real good idea." However, the only person who listened to DeMaris was Viva who nodded her agreement.

"No!" Blanche stomped her foot when told this.

"We'll stop and buy groceries," offered Jacyne. "Why were you in front of the restaurant if you have a place to stay?"

"No home."

"Yes, you do have a home—an apartment. And that's where you are going."

"No!"

DeMaris looked at Viva who said nothing and stared at the ground. "Blanche," DeMaris turned to her. "What happened—did something happen to you in the apartment?"

Blanche stared at her. At least she had stopped the weaving of standing on one foot and then the other. "We're your friends. You can tell us. Can you tell us what happened there?"

Blanche finally said, "Owen mad."

"Mad at you?"

Blanche shook her head.

"Mad at who then?"

Blanche started to hum and look around. "Emily? EMILY!? *Where's Emily?*" she screamed.

"I'll get her, I'll get her." Liset raced through the house and brought the doll back wrapped in a towel. "I was just letting her soak before giving her a bath."

Blanche ripped the doll out of Liset's hand and hugged her letting the water drip down the front of her. "Smells funny." Blanche made a face.

"That would be detergent."

"Blanche," DeMaris tried again. "Who was Owen mad at?"

Blanche played with Emily's hair. "Denny."

"Who's Denny?" asked Liset.

Silence.

"Um," DeMaris looked around. "Is he a neighbor, perhaps?"

Blanche nodded.

"Denny Caldwell," stated Viva.

Again she nodded.

"Who's Denny?" asked Caroline.

"Oh," Viva stood there and shook her head. "He's a real work of art."

"Denny's no artist," Blanche looked up at this and then leaned into DeMaris. "Viva thinks she's smart, but she's not."

"What did they quarrel about?"

Blanche said nothing for a long time, then she smiled, straightened up, looked at DeMaris and announced, "Emily."

"No," DeMaris said firmly. "They did not quarrel about your doll. Is there another Emily?"

Blanche's face drooped and she shook her head.

"What did they argue about?"

Blanche once again felt cornered and became highly agitated. "No. No. Can't tell. Secret. Owen mad. A secret. A secret!" She began to stomp her feet.

"Okay, okay," DeMaris said. "If it's a secret, then you're right not to tell."

She stopped her tantrum. "Really?"

"Yes, really. We all have secrets. We don't tell."

As Blanche looked around the room at the girls they each smiled back reassuringly. "Tell me a secret," she said eagerly.

"No, we can't tell; you can't tell. That's how secrets work." DeMaris tried a different tactic. "Can you tell us where Owen is?"

Her face crumpled. "Don't know."

"When was the last time you saw him?"

"He and Denny fight."

"Okay, when was that?"

Blanche shrugged.

Out of the corner of her eye, DeMaris caught sight of Viva. She was getting nearly as distressed as Blanche. *What's her problem?*

"They fought in the apartment?"

Blanche nodded.

"And you never saw Owen again?"

Blanche's eyes welled up as she shook her head no.

It was silent for a long time while Blanche sniffled. Viva mumbled something and left the room. DeMaris suddenly had an idea. "Your last name is Fox, isn't it?"

Blanche nodded.

"I know another Fox. Brian Fox."

Blanche made a distasteful face.

"Do you know Brian?"

Blanche nodded.

"Is he— your son?" *God forbid.*

"No. Weasel."

"Where have I heard that name?" asked Sara.

"He's the bank manager in town," said Viva standing in the doorway. "You met him at the festival."

"Oh, the young guy who couldn't take his eyes off De," offered Caroline.

"Hey, I've still got it."

"I've still got it," Blanche smiled.

"What have you got, Blanche?"

"Key." She fished it out of her pocket and held it up.

"Do you know what that belongs to?"

She quickly shoved it back in her pocket. "Secret."

"Okay. Do you need us to take you some place so that you can use it?"

"No. I keep it and keep quiet." She whispered the last word.

"Let's get back to Brian. Is he a relative?"

Blanche looked at the floor. "Maybe."

"Is he a . . ." DeMaris was stuck.

"Brother?" asked Caroline.

Blanche snorted at this.

"Nephew?" asked Shay.

Blanche shook her head no.

"Cousin?" said DeMaris.

"Don't know. Don't know. Don't KNOW. DON'T KNOW. DON'T—"

"Okay, okay! Calm down. It's okay not to know. We got it."

Blanche giggled. "Owen had him spell his name. He's smart that way." She saw the confusion on their faces. "Brian has one X. We gots two. But *he* was always after—" She stood with her mouth hung open.

Say it, DeMaris wanted to scream. *The safe deposit box? The money? Something I don't know about? Just tell us!*

"The secret."

DeMaris digested this. "Did Brian know what the secret was?"

"Weasel. He and Denny— Owen's friend. Not a friend anymore."

"So, Denny knew about the secret?"

Blanche nodded.

"And he told Brian?"

Again she nodded.

"But . . . he doesn't know where?"

"Denny *says* he knows where, but Denny can't get to it. Owen told him no."

If we're talking about the bank; then no, Denny couldn't get into the safe deposit box but Brian possibly could—if he had the key.

Which is why he ran after me.

Chapter Nineteen

"While I was in town this morning for rowing," DeMaris announced, "I saw a nice restaurant. Why don't we eat at Bugzys tonight?"

"That's expensive," hollered Viva over everyone else agreeing.

"I checked it out while I was there. It's really neat. The menu looked great and we all deserve a treat. I've got money from Liset for the purse so I'll be paying with cash."

"Okay."

When it was time to leave, they all went in the van—everyone except Blanche, who they left at home happily talking to Sophocles.

"This place is packed," said Jacyne upon arrival. "Let's go somewhere else."

They were all headed out the door when DeMaris stopped them. "Just wait."

She made her way forward when they suddenly heard, "Welcome Ms. Azaygo! I have your table ready. I hope it's to your liking."

"I'm sure it will be," said DeMaris graciously. They were to be seated in an alcove. She turned and saw the horrified looks. She gritted her teeth. "Roll with it," she hissed and then smiled. "I told you I was in town and scouted this place out. I made us a reservation."

"Great."

"Wonderful."

"How thoughtful, Ms. Azaygo."

"I thought so too."

They enjoyed a wonderful meal and were commenting on how they couldn't have dessert as they were too full when two servers arrived with tiny cakes. "Let me see," said DeMaris, "Lemon is Caroline's, chocolate with butter cream is Sara's right there . . . this one is mine . . ." The women stared at her as each received an individual cake. "I went to the bakery two doors down and ordered one for each of us. We haven't celebrated birthdays in a couple of years. Just eat what you want; there are boxes for the leftovers. Isn't this fun?"

They ate in shocked and satiated silence.

"What's De doing?" there was an edge to Viva's voice; they all turned to look. Viva was out of her seat with Shay right behind her. They both arrived at the doorway to see DeMaris handing money to the two servers.

"You two did a great job. Thank you."

"Oh, thank you, ma'am," they both said and walked away.

"What did you just do?" asked Shay.

DeMaris brushed past them and returned to their table. "Okay, we're all set."

"You didn't just—"

"—pay for everybody—"

"—did you?"

"Don't get your panties bunched. I paid in cash. Don't forget your cakes."

"Oh, Ms. Azaygo, you won't forget?" The owner of the establishment stopped her on the way out.

"I have it all right here." DeMaris held up her phone. "I promise you, Greg will call on Wednesday."

"My daughter will be so thrilled. She has his pictures all over her room. You're sure he won't mind?"

"I'm sure. He'll be happy to do it."

"This will be the best birthday present ever. I can't thank you enough."

"No problem. I am happy to do this. Dinner was wonderful, the staff, everything. Thank you."

Once they were settled in the van, they all began rummaging around in their purses. "My dinner was around thirty dollars. Did anybody pay attention to how much the wine was?"

"I told her to put the appetizer on my bill. Mine's got to be close to fifty dollars."

"No!" Those in the back looked up. Viva was trying to hand money to DeMaris. "I did this as a thank-you to my friends," said DeMaris. "You've always been there for me and I wanted you to know how much I appreciate it."

"That's kind of you," said Sara.

"But you need to hang on to your money," added Shay.

"How often do we have to keep telling you that?" yelled Jacyne.

"It's my money to do with as I want."

"That's all well and good, but you should have something in your savings account—"

"I have enough in my savings and my checking. Greg also owns his own house and has a nice pension. I'll be all right whichever way I choose. I know you mean well but I need to make my own decisions and you all need to let me."

"You need—"

"Thank you for dinner," cut in Liset.

There was silence for a moment and then the rest thanked DeMaris.

"However," added Viva, "I wish you'd stop telling people you're DeMaris Azaygo!"

"It's fun! We got the royal treatment, didn't we?"

"And what happens if the *real* DeMaris Azaygo finds out?"

"How is she going to find out? She's a recluse! Nobody knows what she looks like. She's never going to come here. And, it's not like I gave her a bad name. I was very pleasant and I tipped well. She should thank me. Hey, how about this scenario? She shows up to complain and everybody says, 'Sorry lady, the real DeMaris Azaygo was here and you're not her.' Huh? Wouldn't that be funny?"

Caroline groaned and rolled her eyes.

"We're all leaving in a few days," continued DeMaris. "Viva is selling her house. Nobody will ever know we were here."

"Yeah, after ten years, *nobody* here knows Harlan and me," Viva said sarcastically. "We are selling the house because it's too big; Harlan and I love it here. We had planned on buying a smaller house and staying!"

"Oh . . . I didn't know that. Sorry."

"And, what was that about Greg calling the owner's daughter?" asked Melissa.

"Oh," DeMaris laughed. "His daughter is a big fan of the TV actor and as DeMaris Azaygo I am dating him, remember? So I said he would call her on her birthday next week."

"DeMaris!"

"And *Greg* will be calling. I didn't *exactly* lie."

"And as a fan," said Jacyne, "you don't think she'll notice that he doesn't sound like the TV guy?"

"People sound different in real life, over the phone, and on TV. Maybe he'll have a cold. I'll come up with something. I mean, she's not meeting him. That would take a little more imagination. All these years and you girls still haven't learned to relax. I always come up with *something*."

When they returned to Viva's, Blanche was sitting at the kitchen table. "Hungry," she announced.

Everyone unconsciously pulled their leftover dinner and cake closer to them.

"We have some leftover lobster," Liset volunteered.

"Yuck!"

"I think I saw a can of soup in the cupboard," offered DeMaris.

"Tooth hurts. Want soup."

Chapter Twenty

DeMaris hauled—and hauled was the word—Viva out to the porch. "I really don't want to talk about this now," Viva said before DeMaris had her mouth open.

"Well, I'm sorry, but we have to. Where's Owen?"

Viva looked nervous. "I don't know."

"How 'bout looking at me and saying that?"

Viva gave out a huge sigh, ran a hand through her hair, and looked at DeMaris. "I don't know. Believe me. I wish I did."

"How do you know these people?"

Viva wrestled with herself. "Their mother, Maureen, worked for me and when she keeled over in my office quite unexpectedly from a brain aneurism I felt obligated to look after Owen and Blanche. Maureen had bought them an apartment that they were living in in Spokane. It's downtown and they can walk to whatever they need—obviously neither one drives. A few weeks ago, I went to check on them and Blanche comes flying down the stairs with Sophocles, screaming at the top of her lungs that Denny and Owen were having a big fight. I got Blanche and the bird in the Hummer and we drove around while I tried to decide what to do. Denny had always seemed rather squirrely to me but Maureen and the twins thought he was a good guy. Who was I to say otherwise?"

"The twins?"

"Yeah, I told you, Blanche and Owen are brother and sister."

"We sat in a parking lot down the street for a good hour while Blanche calmed down. This wasn't the first time that Denny had been a problem. Maureen had told me some things that I thought were kind of odd—but she brushed them off.

"After she died, Denny started getting physically abusive. I'd been urging the twins to move and now Blanche finally agreed with me. I drove back to the apartment to get Owen and . . ." Viva stopped. "Denny met me at the door. Told me Owen had gone berserk on him for no reason and had left. Said he was in the apartment cleaning it up because he knew how particular Blanche is. Didn't want her coming back to find a mess. I wasn't about to question him. He is one sick person. I just left."

"Please tell me you've seen Owen since then."

"I have not seen Owen again," Viva whispered.

"And the police haven't found him?"

Viva rubbed her fingers across her forehead. "I didn't call them."

"What?" DeMaris couldn't believe her.

"Blanche was hysterical when I ran into her. It had taken me an hour to calm her down and that wasn't exactly calm. To call the police and have them come and interrogate her—I thought I'd call them after I got her away from the apartment. I drove us back here and when I was finally alone and able to think I thought, how am I supposed to tell the police that I waited a couple of hours before calling them? I didn't see anything, so what could I tell them? And, I didn't want them questioning Blanche. All she has is Owen and that bird."

"Which you took."

"I am taking care of Sophocles. That bird is old. How long do you think he'll live under Blanche's care?"

"You could have at least told the police to look for Owen—even anonymously."

"Look, I panicked. Plus, if I told the police, they'd question Denny and he'd know who had told them. He'd come looking for me and . . . the guy scares me, all right? Trust me. I want to find Owen. I do not want Blanche around and underfoot."

"Well, do you think Brian is a nephew? A cousin? Can we dump her on him? He was looking for her."

"I doubt it. As far as I know, Maureen didn't have any other children and she never spoke of any other family. Not her parents, in-laws, siblings, no one. I never saw her husband, although she talked about him. He kept to himself and played the stock market. Or so she said. Supposedly he was pretty good at it. But he didn't trust banks so he'd never let her have a bank account. I talked her into that after they had a funeral for him. And that was closed casket so, to the end, I never saw him. Maureen seemed normal but her family . . ."

"Blanche is an embarrassment to you, isn't she?"

"DeMar—"

"Don't you and your high society friends ever help those less fortunate? Or is your nose too high in the air to notice people in need?"

"Oh, come on. Is this how you want to finish out your vacation? Baby-sitting Blanche? And I donate plenty in this community, and in Nevada."

"You throw money at the problem, huh? Have you ever taken food to a neighbor in need? I'm not talking caviar when your friends phone crying. Ever driven a neighbor to work every morning at the crack of dawn because that's the only way he can get to work? Ever gone out of your way for anybody?"

"Yes, I have," Viva said evenly.

"Just throwing your money around is not the only answer—" DeMaris suddenly stopped. She looked toward the house and then slowly turned to Viva. "You," she said softly, "all of you think I'm a charity case. I don't believe it. My God," she raised her voice. "How do you all put up with me? The embarrassment of the group. I'm the Blanche in this group, aren't I?"

"Let me remind you," said Viva hotly, "you were born into the high society crap you supposedly loathe. You were the one who stuck her nose up to live the Bohemian lifestyle. You have an education, intelligence, and there is not one of us who doesn't believe you could have made something of yourself with your writing. You're talented but you've thrown it all away—and for what?"

"Thrown it away? I'm not unhappy with my life nor with the way things have turned out. I've done exactly what I please . . . and always have."

"Yeah, you have—and at who's expense?"

"Expense? I've always paid my own way!"

"Yeah, at a discount," yelled Viva.

"A discount? What are you talking about?"

"Whenever we've planned anything, we've always had to go second-rate so that you could afford to go with us."

DeMaris was in shock and dismayed. "Why would you girls do that?"

"Because we enjoy your company. We want you to come with us but . . . we've all worked hard while you and Kirk have lived on part-time jobs and government handouts and—"

"I have *never* asked for a government handout," yelled DeMaris. "I don't know where in the hell you got that idea! Or any of your ideas. If you wanted to live high on the hog on vacation why not say so? I have *never* told you I couldn't do something because of money. Never."

"You don't have to. We've all seen how you live. You stayed home to raise the kids and have never worked a day in your life except here and there. Have you lasted a year any place? Oh, and your freelance writing. Kirk had that college professorship that lasted what, five years? And then he up and quit. He's worked odd jobs ever since. You've got a garage full of old cars, none of them work—"

"A few of them do. Kirk's working on them."

"Kirk's always working on them—"

"It's his hobby!"

"—or the house. I'm sorry that you can't afford a builder to come in and remodel but maybe you should get a real job instead of writing little articles for small-town magazines."

There was a long silence.

"Well," DeMaris recovered, "I had no idea that any of you thought . . . I've never complained about not having money. I've done all the stuff I wanted to."

"You don't fly. You used to love it."

"Yeah. I don't know where the fear came in. I'm getting better about it though."

"It seems to us you quit flying right after Kirk quit being a professor."

"Ah. I see. I couldn't afford a plane ticket. Fear was just an excuse, huh?"

"Well, if the shoe fits . . ."

DeMaris stood thoughtfully and then said, "I'm sorry I'm not as materialistic as the rest of you. Yes, I lived in an old farmhouse, but Kirk and I enjoyed fixing it up. Do all the girls feel the way you do?"

"No," Viva answered honestly. "Shay says you live exactly the way you want. Liset doesn't say a word, and Sara is starting to believe your story about *really* being DeMaris Azaygo."

DeMaris chuckled. "Sara's always been the gullible one."

"Uh-huh."

DeMaris pondered the lake and ran her tongue over the back of her teeth. "I think it was Socrates, or Plato, who said something like, 'I'm amazed by the number of things in this world that I don't need.' I have what I want. It's not a big fine house, a new car, or fancy clothes—although I did splurge for this trip. Greg has a thing for expensive clothes—one of his rare flaws. Well," DeMaris took a deep breath and slowly let it out, "I need to make a phone call."

DeMaris found Viva a few minutes later. "We need to go to Spokane."

"Why?"

"On a hunch I called the morgue. They have one John Doe. Large. Somewhere in his forties, starting to bald. Five feet, ten inches. What does Owen look like?"

"You're not serious. What would make you think to call the morgue?"

"I'm just being the mystery writer here. A fight, the person vanishes and doesn't return to take care of his mentally disabled sister—"

"A reason to skip town, don't ya think? Let somebody else take care of her for a change."

"Maybe so. But if somebody disposed of his body and it was found, who would claim it? What other family does he have? Plus, I want to see inside the morgue so I can write about it."

"I'm sure it's not him."

"So . . . you do know where he's at?"

"No, I just— I just can't look at a dead body!"

"Look," DeMaris moved in closer. "You should have called the police. You didn't, so now you get to do this. Or have Blanche do it."

"Oh, yeah, right. I'm gonna have her do it."

"You have to go see if it's Owen. Does the description match?"

Viva wavered. "Maybe."

"I'll go in with you. This is the least you can do for Blanche. If it is him, then you need to proceed to the next step and if it's not him, you need to file a missing person's report."

"Understand me, I will not tell the police I knew there was a struggle and I did nothing."

DeMaris shook her head. "No, you recently ran into Blanche who was distraught because her brother was in a fight with a neighbor and she hasn't seen him since. Since she's not all there, you took it upon yourself to alert the police."

Viva shook her head. "I know I should have called the police . . . I don't want to get mixed up with Dennis Caldwell. He is one mean son of a bitch."

"I know. I've met him."

"When?"

"At their apartment."

"Their apartment? How? When? How could you possibly know where they lived?"

"If I ever get this book published, you can read all about it."

"Very funny."

"Come on, we need to go to Spokane."

"You can't tell the girls."

She linked her arm through Viva's and propelled them both through the house. "You're taking me to meet up with Chuck. The girls just want to lounge around on the lake."

"Yeah. I'd prefer to do that instead of look at a dead body."

"Well, here's an idea. We'll call Dennis Caldwell and ask him to go down to the morgue and check it out."

"You can be such a bitch at times."

"Yeah, but you enjoy my company."

Chapter Twenty-One

"Whenever you're ready, I'll slowly pull the body out."

DeMaris looked at the coroner across from her. Viva was standing in the distance. "Thank you, but this isn't the first dead body I've seen. Pull away."

"Oh, you're in law enforcement?" he asked.

"No, writer."

He stared at her for a moment and then pulled the drawer out.

"Oh shit, oh shit, oh shit."

"Okay," DeMaris broke into Viva's repetition. "Are you upset about looking at a dead body or because it's Owen?"

"I'm thinking it's a positive ID. Most people look relieved when they discover it's not a loved one. She doesn't look relieved," said the coroner.

Yeah, well, Owen's not a loved one either. DeMaris stepped between Viva and the corpse. "Is it Owen?" she said slowly and loudly.

Viva just shook her head. *My God, she's gonna burst into tears.* DeMaris turned back to the coroner. "Should I slap her?"

"Don't even think it," said Viva. DeMaris turned back around to face her. "Yes, that's Owen."

The coroner picked up his clipboard. "Last name, please?"

"Foxx. That's with two X's."

"Thank you."

"What can you tell us about how he died?" asked DeMaris.

"I'll direct you to the police station," he answered.

The police officer escorted them to a room and then left to get the detective. DeMaris sat relaxed while Viva sat with her elbows on the table and

159

her head in her hands. DeMaris tried to think of some comforting words but soon realized she'd used them all before so she, for once, sat quietly.

Viva heaved a sigh. "Just once. *Just once* I'd like to have a vacation that did not involve the police. I thought . . . my house, being on the lake, nice town . . . what can DeMaris possibly do here?"

"This isn't my fault—" she stopped talking when Viva glared over at her. The two sat quietly after that.

Detective Morgan went through his questions which Viva answered. She then asked, "What happened to Owen?"

Detective Morgan looked at her. "Don't you get the paper?"

"Yes, but I have company and no chance to read at the moment."

He nodded. "He was found in his own apartment but we never found anybody to contact for a positive ID. I mean, that side of town, it could have been anyone. He was beaten. Any idea who might have done this?"

The two women exchanged glances. Viva was shaking her head no; so it was DeMaris who announced, "His neighbor Dennis Caldwell. Owen's sister positively identified him as the person who was arguing with her brother the last time she saw him."

The detective nodded and wrote it down.

"How did you find him?" ventured Viva.

"Anonymous tip called in."

"Oh. When?"

"A few days ago."

"Where did they find him in the apartment?"

"Stuffed inside a closet."

Viva made a face. "I can't tell you how many times I've called his apartment. I've gone over there and knocked on the door. He never answered. I just never thought . . ."

"He's been dead about two weeks."

DeMaris could see the wheels turning, Viva calculating how long ago it was that she picked up Blanche and Sophocles. "But, if he's been dead all this time . . . who would suddenly call it in? Why not call as soon as it happened?"

"That's another mystery," said the detective looking over his notes.

Viva suddenly caught sight of DeMaris giving her a wide smile and batting her eyelashes. "Oh. My. God."

"What?" asked Detective Morgan.

"I just realized . . . his sister is all alone now."

The two women walked out of the station. "How— When— I don't see how— How did you know to call?"

"Because of the smell."

"How did you even know Owen?"

"I didn't. I just happened to be in his apartment."

"You were in Owen's apartment? How? How could you possibly . . .? For what reason would you be . . . Oh God. Do I even want to know?"

"No, not really. I needed to use the bathroom. How fortuitous it was that I picked that apartment, don't ya think?" DeMaris looked at Viva's dumbstruck face. "Let's forget that part of the conversation. I was smiling at you, trying to cheer you up, you jumped to a faulty conclusion. I have never met Owen . . . at least, not alive."

"Oh, God." They walked silently toward the van. "I worry that Dennis will come after me," bemoaned Viva.

"Why would he come after you? We pretty much laid it all on Blanche, and if he goes after her then she'll be out of your hair as well." They both slammed their doors shut.

Viva stuck the key in the ignition but didn't turn the MINI Cooper on. "You think I'm just slime, don't you?"

"Viva," DeMaris looked at her, "we've been through a lot together—all of us. We all have our faults. I've done stuff I'm not proud of. Stupid stuff you guys don't even know about—you should really read up on Velcro woman. I think you panicked and Owen was probably dead when you ran into Blanche or he was shortly thereafter. I don't think you could have prevented it. But, your silence is preventing his killer from getting caught. You don't want that, do you?"

"No, of course not. But . . . Blanche? How do I tell her? Owen was all she had."

"I don't have an answer for that."

"I feel responsible for her. I mean, there's nobody left to take care of her. I can't have her living on the streets, and she certainly can't live alone—but I hate to commit her to a home."

"For a price, some of those homes are decent."

"And you think I should foot the bill for that?"

"No. Sell her apartment, the wooded property. Besides, maybe Blanche has some money stashed away."

"Yeah. In your book, I'm sure she does."

"You never know how life is going to turn out. Humph." DeMaris sat, thinking. "Is there a statute of limitations for bank robbery? If you keep it long enough, do you ever get to keep the money you stole?"

Viva stared at her. "What does your sense of morals tell you?"

"Well, that stealing is wrong. Stealing is always wrong. I mean, I do *know* that. But shouldn't banks have the same moral code? They've been stealing from the public for years. Probably since they first opened their doors. And if somebody really needed it, say, a handicapped person, then . . . maybe they're just getting their money back . . . don't you think?"

Viva shook her head in disgust and then suddenly said, "You're not thinking of robbing a bank, are you? For God's sake, De, we are here to help you—"

"So, you think I'm handicapped? Since everything works on me, I'm going with mentally handicapped. Thank you. The compliments just keep coming on this trip."

"Well, I think about the time you tried to commit suicide and nearly succeeded—"

"I'm sorry I tried doing that! I wish you people could let that go! One time. I did it one time. I am very grateful to be here. I'm very glad I botched that up. I *do* have a wonderful life and I'm glad I am living it." DeMaris motioned with her hand to go down the street. Viva started the car up and moved into traffic.

"Going inside a tiger cage wasn't suicidal?"

"I was doing research. I've told you guys that a million times."

"How about the body cast you were in for months?"

"Research! I botched that up too . . . obviously. But the point is, I was *not* trying to kill myself!"

They were both silent for a moment. "You do a lot of research for someone who doesn't want to be published," Viva looked at DeMaris.

"I'm published. I sold that tiger story to an animal publication and the body cast actually netted me around a thousand dollars. It went to a stunt magazine. Ya know, what *not* to do. Hopefully I saved some people's lives."

"Oh, I didn't realize. You never told us that."

"Do you call us every time you sell a house?"

"Okay, good point. So, you do make . . . some kind of living . . . writing."

"Yeah. Somewhat. Turn here."

Viva turned down the street. "What's here?"

"The newspaper office. I thought as long as we're in Spokane we'd go see Chuck so we wouldn't be lying."

Viva smiled. "Okay, when are you going out with him again?"

"Not sure."

They were ushered into Chuck's office. "What a surprise!" He was all smiles for DeMaris.

"We happened to be in town and I thought we'd swing by to see if you had those newspaper clippings for me? Save ya the trip." Having found out that Viva spoke the truth—there was no internet connection at the house—DeMaris had called Chuck and asked him for the D.B. Cooper story.

He picked up a manila envelope. "I would be happy to drive over and hand-deliver this; however, since you're here . . ."

"Thank you. I really appreciate it." She held out her hand.

"Dinner tonight?" He held onto the envelope.

"I'm sorry. I'm going out with my sisters."

"Oh," interrupted Viva, "I forgot to tell you. While you were in the bathroom, Jacyne called and Liset finally got talked into making her famous prime rib." DeMaris glared at her. Viva turned and smiled at Chuck. "Perhaps you'd like to join us?"

"I could do that—if it's not an imposition." He handed the envelope to DeMaris.

"Not at all. We look forward to seeing you."

Out in the parking lot DeMaris said, "The last time I was in the bathroom was seven-thirty this morning at your house. Jacyne *called* you then? From where? The bedroom?"

"Hang on." Viva put out a hand while the other flipped open her phone to call her land line. "Jacyne, go into town and buy prime rib and have Caroline start in on Liset about having it tonight. We've got company coming. I'll pick up dessert and Liset's favorite bottle of wine."

DeMaris sat with her arms folded across her chest. "You shouldn't be leading Chuck on. I am very happy with Greg."

"Greg may be a nice man but he's too old."

"Not your decision. Besides, old is a state of mind. Greg is very young thinking."

"Well, you should at least consider Chuck."

In the winery Viva found the bottle she was looking for, paid for it, and looked around for DeMaris. She was sitting at the tasting area talking to the man behind the counter.

"I'm ready," announced Viva.

"Hang on. I get to try six for free."

"I bought Liset's favorite and I have some at home."

"Yeah, I know, but I like mine a little sweeter than the rest of you. Thought I'd get my own bottle."

"Your own? Do you know how expensive it is here?" Viva lowered her voice.

"I think it tells me that on this sheet." DeMaris held up a price sheet as she finished sampling #5.

"We need to go."

"Last one," DeMaris said as the man set the glass down in front of her. She slowly swished it around in her mouth and swallowed. "Yeah, I still like #3 best."

"You are not buying that."

"I'd like one of these—"

"Excuse us," interrupted Viva. She then whispered, "That is a $100 bottle."

"Yes, I saw that."

They eyed each other. "How do you intend to pay for it?"

"I'll write a check."

"No!" Viva had finally had enough. "You don't have any money. We're leaving."

Embarrassed to have the man behind the counter hear this, DeMaris bristled. "I most certainly do have money. I don't know when you all became so fixated about my spending. Stop it! It is *really* annoying."

"Oh, come on! This isn't rocket science. You and Kirk never had anything and half of that is nothing. You're living on the streets and you don't have a job."

DeMaris sat stonefaced for several seconds. Slowly she turned to the man behind the counter and said, "I'd like a bottle to go and a case shipped to a friend."

"A case?" screeched Viva.

"I get a discount that way," DeMaris answered dryly. "Don't worry, I'll charge it."

"Fine." Viva left. She didn't want to be around when they declined DeMaris's card.

———

Neither spoke on the way home but they all heard DeMaris talking to Shay when she cornered her. "I want all of you to stop telling me what to do with my money! You've all been treating me like I'm some kind of idiot—thank you ALL very much."

"We are only trying to help," said Shay as DeMaris stomped out of the room.

The rest of the girls had scattered themselves through the house so

DeMaris shouted, for all to hear. "What if I *was* DeMaris Azaygo? Is this how you would treat me?"

"But you're not," Caroline happened to be in the room where DeMaris was doing all her shouting. She uncoiled herself from the chair she was sitting in, threw her book down on the table, and stood up. "You've always lived in a fantasy world and you've got to come out and join *this* world now. You've got to get a job."

"What makes you all think I got nothing from my divorce settlement?"

"Because you had nothing to begin with."

"I've got a house! Land! And Kirk's got lots of cars!"

"You and Kirk did a lot of work on your house and you've got a few acres," said Viva. "Let's say, for the sake of argument, that you paid off your mortgage. It still won't fetch much in today's market. And half of that, particularly with the way you're spending money, is not going to last long. And your cars are old."

There was silence until DeMaris finally spoke. "If you are all so worried about me, let me assure you. I will live on the street before I come and live with any of you!"

"DeMaris!" several shouted.

"And," she brought her finger up to make her point, "to teach you all a lesson—I AM NOT TAKING A SHOWER FOR MY DATE TONIGHT!"

DeMaris sat and fumed and at the same time was grateful that she had friends who were concerned about her and who had stuck with her through thick and thin. Still, she needed to spout off. She grabbed Viva's home phone and punched in a number.

"Hi," her voice cracked when he picked up.

"What's the matter?" asked Greg.

"Viva embarrassed me today when I was writing a check." She told Greg her story of woe. "Now I'm going to have to charge everything. God, I hate that."

"I'm telling you, you've got to get a debit card."

She sighed. "Maybe you're right. I just hate change."

"I'm beginning to realize that."

"Well, I can tell you one thing I charged: wine." She smiled and then plunged on, "Don't be mad. I mean, I was really mad; that's why I did it."

"I don't care if you charged wine," he said.

"No, not that . . . I can explain."

"DeMaris," he said after the long silence.

"Well, I was really mad at Viva—and all my sisters. They're treating me like crap! Okay, maybe not crap, but treating me poorly, like they think I'm poor! So . . . I name dropped."

"Who did you tell you were DeMaris Azaygo?"

"No, I didn't . . . do that . . . The guy I bought the wine from . . . well, I bought a case . . . and had it sent to your address. But instead of putting my name on it I said . . . Greg Delray."

"Still playing that card, huh?"

"Hey! I am DeMaris Azaygo on this trip and my time here is not over with yet! The guy that took the information is apparently a big fan. Viva wasn't around, fortunately. So, he's hoping to drum up some business with someone famous. He asked me what your favorite wine was. I'm interested to see if you get a complimentary bottle or something."

"Well, I hope it's good."

"Um, the girls are really on me about my spending. And, Shay told me a few days ago that I could stay with one of them while I get back on my feet."

"What about my place?" he said indignantly.

"Honey, they think you're too old. I'm sorry!"

"You've got to be kidding me."

"I told you before I left that I was going to tell the girls I was dating a TV star. You should have stuck with the story."

"I thought we agreed, your sisters wouldn't buy that."

"That's not the point. But still . . . I think I'll tell them I'm staying with Melissa. She's the one who lives just a couple of hours from you."

"I believe we figured out she was six hours away."

"Well, I'll either take the train to you or you can drive up and get me and meet one of my sisters."

"I'll come get you."

"I thought you would." Greg had been pressing her to meet the group. "Maybe that's a good thing. Melissa can report back to the girls that you're in good physical shape and they don't need to worry about me. Hey! I've gotta go. Viva's in my stuff!"

"I love . . . you." Greg was already listening to the dial tone. He shook his head. *That woman is going to make me old before my time.*

He realized what he'd said and burst out laughing.

Chapter Twenty-Two

DeMaris wasn't upset that Viva was looking through the newspaper clippings she had spread out on the table. After all, thousands of people had already read them. What she was worried about was Viva reading her notes.

Viva sighed deeply. "I told Blanche about Owen. I'm not sure it sunk in. She just stared at me blankly and then went into the garage to tell Sophocles." Viva had a drink in one hand and newspaper clippings in the other. "Boy, this story's old," she mumbled. "Why are you reading about D. B. Cooper?"

"It's an idea I have for a book. I watched *Catch Me If You Can*, the movie where Leonardo DiCaprio's character escapes out the plane by way of the bathroom. My character is going to do the same thing. Ya know, fly around like D. B. Cooper but in reality he's still on the plane."

"Some of that money was found, you know."

"Yes, I read that. But if I wanted people to think I'd jumped, I'd throw some money out the door too."

"You're trying to solve this?"

"No, I'm just writing a mystery. I got the idea from D. B. Cooper and *Catch Me—*"

Viva slammed her drink on the glass table and sat upright.

"What?"

Viva threw down the newspaper article she was holding and stared into space. "Oh, my God. Oh, my God. That's why I never met her husband. All the times she told me I had to call first if I was ever coming over. The times she'd meet me out by the road . . ."

"Who?"

"Maureen Bloomgarde."

"She was one of the stewardesses on the plane with him," said DeMaris.

"Yeah. And she was my secretary and Blanche and Owen's mother . . . and, apparently, D. B. Cooper's wife."

The two stared at each other. Slowly DeMaris turned and looked out at the lake. "Oh, my God," she said softly as she thought of the money in the safe deposit box and the signature on the card. "That's where it came from."

"That's where what came from?"

"My God, don't you see? Life is imitating art," she banged her hand on the notepad she'd been writing on. "Or is art imitating life? Anyway," DeMaris said excitedly, "my story is that the bank robber had an accomplice—a stewardess—and I think that's what really happened!"

"You're saying that Maureen stole the money?"

"Come on, you just read the articles and said she was married to D. B. Cooper."

"Okay, I always found it strange that I *never* met her husband. And, now that I think of it, she never said she was a former stewardess or that she knew the man. I mean, on occasion, a group of us would be sitting around talking about it. Nothing from Maureen. Ever. Why wouldn't she have said, 'Yeah, I was on that flight. I was the go-between for Cooper and the FBI.' But she never said anything about it. So, what do you mean 'that's where it came from'?"

"Oh . . . right. I was talking about my book. That's how it happens. My character has an accomplice. The stewardess takes the money off the plane while he, I don't know, escapes out the bathroom. One of them buries it, realizes it's starting to mildew or animals are chewing on it or something; and so, he/she/they decide to put it in a safe deposit box. Actually, several safe deposit boxes."

"If you saw where Blanche and Owen lived—you saw where they lived. They don't have any money. They were living off the government after Maureen died. She left them a little something, but I'm sure they went through it in short order. Besides, I have to think that at least some of that money, if not all of it, was marked. They couldn't spend it."

"You don't know that. There is nothing that I've read that says it was marked. Somebody could have been spending it all along. If it wasn't marked, no one would ever know. And even if it was marked, people can't be expected to check every twenty dollar bill—that's what D.B. Cooper asked for—that comes to them. As the years passed, it would be easier and easier to spend."

"What is it you're not telling me?"

"Nothing. I'm just playing with storylines."

"De, we are too old to be playing games."

"Okay, you're right. I'm simply not going to tell you." DeMaris returned to writing and then suddenly looked up. "What size was Maureen?"

"Size? You mean, dress size? She was average, probably wore a medium."

"She wasn't as big as Blanche?" asked DeMaris.

"No. Why?"

DeMaris shook her head and went back to making notes. "Just wondering." *The clothes in the boxes had to be Maureen's. That would make sense: packing up a dead person's clothes to give away or store.*

Viva sat for a moment, her mind whirling. "You've been very interested in banks . . . you've been here by yourself . . . alone with Blanche . . . safe deposit boxes . . . I let you keep that key . . . big mistake.

"DeMaris, you would have to prove you had a legitimate claim to get into someone's safe deposit box and your name would not have been on any signature card on file. You couldn't have gotten in to see— How did you get in?"

DeMaris smiled at Viva. "I don't know what you're talking about."

"Oh, God. I know that look." Viva leaned back in her chair. "How could you? What's in the box? Money?" DeMaris just smiled. "Don't forget it could be stolen money. If there is anything in there that could help Blanche—there has to be a reward out for that—that poor woman needs help a hell of a lot more than you do. She *is* living on the streets."

"She doesn't have to. She's got an apartment and a beautiful piece of property."

"You have friends who are willing to take you in, you have a college degree, and you're not handicapped."

"Whoa! You are *not* accusing me of stealing from her! First, all of you telling me how *not* to spend my money—and now this! I don't believe you!"

"You've been throwing money all over town. That expensive meal— paid with cash! She could have bought a couple of month's worth of food. Besides, if it's what we're both thinking, it's stolen money!"

"Since when have I become a thief?" yelled DeMaris hotly.

"Look, divorce, losing the home you loved, being uprooted and being involved in a train accident—well, that affects people and can make them do things they wouldn't ordinarily do. I've seen it happen; I understand. I'm not judging you. You know the stupid stuff I've done. But De, Blanche is handicapped. You need to pay the money back and if you can't do that, at least stop spending it! It's not yours. It's not even hers, realistically, if it's what we think it is. I wonder if she could get some reward money though. I mean, it's not like *she* stole it. Wait a minute. Is this why you were asking me if the statute of limitations was ever up on a bank robbery? *You knew?*"

DeMaris stood up. "You have gone too far! I *borrowed* twenty dollars; that's it! I still have it and I will give it to Blanche, although I doubt she'll get far on it."

"How did you borrow money that belongs to Blanche? Wait, you were in her apartment . . . you couldn't possibly have gotten into their safe deposit box . . . Yes, *you* could have . . . but . . ."

The other sisters were gathering to listen to the heated dialogue. DeMaris waved at them. "Bring me a glass of my wine. Forget it, just bring the whole bottle, and all of you come out here." Silently and quickly they all obliged.

Shay was getting ready to pour some wine into a glass when DeMaris ripped the bottle out of her hand and guzzled. "All right, girls, sit down and listen to me! I am not a thief!" she yelled.

"What did you say to her?" whispered Jacyne. Viva waved a hand at her.

"You people have treated me like dirt since I arrived!" DeMaris saw the shocked looks on their faces. "I'm the poor relation in the group and you want to keep me that way! It took a lot longer for Kirk and me to get out of the hippie movement than the rest of you, but you know what? For a long time, we were happy. We were environmentalists. We grew a lot of our own food, did our own house repairs—which a couple of times has helped some of you out." She pointed at Sara. "The time the furnace went out and we were caught in that blizzard. We didn't have to stay in your house and freeze. Kirk went into the basement and fixed it." Sara nodded.

"You've all enjoyed our free-roaming beef and chicken—and now you think I've hit rock bottom and my years of doing my own thing were a waste. Well, let me tell you something: they weren't! Kirk and I did precisely as we pleased and raised our kids to take care of themselves." She whirled on Caroline. "When our boys went on their cross-country trip and your fancy Jeep broke down in the middle of nowhere, who knew how to fix it? Your sons don't know how to fix a flat tire let alone work on the engine. My son fixed the Jeep and got them on the road again, didn't he?"

Caroline nodded.

"You live in your fancy houses that you don't know how to keep up, you drive fancy cars that you don't know how to fix—"

"What can of worms did you open?" hissed Liset at Viva.

"You eat food that you don't know where it comes from or what's in it—and I'm the dummy here?"

"Nobody here thinks you are dumb," hollered Shay standing up. "But you *have* lived a different lifestyle than the rest of us. We never understood it; although you've made a few good points here. But, your free spirit has gone a little too far. You're spending money right and left, money that you don't have, you've lived out on the streets, and you're dating a seventy-three-year-old man. You have no income, and you're traveling the country by yourself. You are not close to Social Security benefits, and even if you were, how much would you get? You haven't put anything into it. Your free-wheeling lifestyle is affecting all of us. Kirk is no longer taking care of you. Your daughter's in college and your son is working in Europe. Who is going to take care of you? Us."

There was silence while everyone held their breath and their wine glasses near.

"I see," said DeMaris softly. "Well, let me relieve your minds. If it's any of your business, my parents left me a sizable estate."

"I told you," whispered Jacyne.

"I don't recall telling any of you what the terms of my divorce agreement are but I do have money, a new lease on life, and a new *boyfriend* who is collecting Social Security and yes, he did put in! And gosh, think of this—he has a savings account too!"

"But you are running through your money—or his—at quite a pace."

"No, not *his*. Key word here—*your*—meaning *my* money. I promise you, I'm not going to be a burden to any of you. That is certainly not my wish."

"Why did you get divorced?" asked Shay.

"Okay," DeMaris nodded. "If it was one of you, I'd be asking the same thing. We had a lot of good years and I wouldn't change them for anything, but I grew tired of that life and wanted something different. I decided I didn't want all my clothes from the Salvation Army and resale shops. I liked buying new stuff. I'd like to have a new car instead of one of Kirk's cheap fixer-uppers. Traveling is fun. I wanted to do more things and Kirk just wanted to stay put. He doesn't want to change in the least; and so we agreed to go our separate ways. It was quite amiable and we're still friends. He and Greg have even met."

"You're kidding."

"No. If anything, Greg was the nervous one. He was weirded out by it, but he got over it."

"No, I mean, you don't want to be a recluse anymore?"

But Sara was drowned out by DeMaris still yelling. "The three of us are fine. Why can't you all be?"

"You're right, it's your life," said Melissa.

"Let me just say that a twenty-three-year gap is not good," said Caroline. "He could have a heart attack, a stroke—"

"So could I! We're not repeating this conversation."

"Listen!" Caroline, was on her feet now. "You marry Greg and something happens, what memories do you have to sustain you? Trust me, I'm struggling as it is! I have no life. It was all I could do to find three people to take care of Bob for this vacation—which I desperately needed."

"It takes three people?"

"Yes, because nobody was willing to stay the entire time I was gone."

"Well, I admit it's something to think about," said DeMaris. "But in the meantime, it's my life and I intend to live it my way. You can either join me . . . or not."

They all nodded and raised their glasses. "We're with you."

"Except Blanche," Jacyne pointed. "She just left."

Chapter Twenty-Three

"So, do I get to find out why you needed the information on D. B. Cooper?" asked Chuck at dinnertime. They had all made quite a fuss over him when he had knocked on the door and entered with a bottle of wine. All except for DeMaris.

"I'm using it for my next story."

"The next story you're not going to publish?" asked Caroline.

"Chuck, do you know any agents or publishers?" asked Shay.

"Yes, actually—"

"No!" both DeMaris and Liset yelled.

They all looked at Liset.

"I have sent not one, not two, but *three* agents DeMaris's way and they reported back that she was . . . difficult. Don't embarrass yourself," Liset said looking at Chuck.

"Liset, I'm sorry," said DeMaris, "but I've told you all a number of times that I don't want to be published, at least not in a big way."

"Why?" asked Chuck.

She sighed. "Because I don't want people to know how I think; especially my kids. I don't want people to know who I am. I'm too private a person. My friends here can tell you that I dream of being a recluse." They all nodded. "I just want to be left alone. My kids can sell my stories when I'm gone and live off the profits if anybody thinks what I write is any good."

"Ya know," said Sara, "maybe you could use a pen name."

"Thank you for the suggestion," said DeMaris, "but no." She had had this conversation with each of them. Now that they were afraid they'd have to support her, she was being hit again from all sides. "Please, please, don't worry about me. I promise you, I have a plan and it's not living on the streets—or with any of you."

Several of them opened their mouths to say something; and then thought better of it.

The superb prime rib Liset cooked was enjoyed in relative quiet.

—　—　—

After dinner, they sat around the table and talked until Melissa noticed the moonlight out the window. "Why don't the two of you go out on the lake? It's a beautiful evening."

Chuck was agreeable; what could DeMaris say? "I get to row."

The girls brought their drinks out on the deck and watched.

"Do you feel like you're living in another century and all my sisters are chaperoning us?" asked DeMaris.

Chuck chuckled. "They mean well, but if I wasn't so smitten, I'd tuck tail and run."

"I'm flattered. But trust me, I'm not worth it."

"I'm forty-five years old. Surely I can beat out someone who's nearly thirty years my senior."

She smiled. "So, the girls told you about Greg."

"Yes, and they're rooting for me."

—　—　—

"He's kissing her," Sara hissed.

All heads turned toward the lake.

"She's not pulling away," said Jacyne.

"I've got an extra blow-up bed," said Viva.

"No," Shay shook her head. "I don't want him in our room."

"No, the blow-up bed is for you, in my room."

"What? Oh . . . no. De will not sleep with him tonight." She looked at their faces. "Okay, she's not sleeping with him *here*. She may go back to his house but she's not doing anything with him here. Not with us around."

An hour later they heard DeMaris say good night to Chuck. The car door shut and they heard him drive away. She came out on the deck all smiles.

"So, it went well," said Melissa.

"Yes, very well. I'm getting married."

"What? All ready?" said Shay. "I mean, we like him—but you don't really know him. Get to know him a little better." *My God, she's just getting more and more irresponsible. I don't even know if her divorce is finalized!*

"You're not marrying him so that you don't have to work, are you?" asked Jacyne.

"Or worse, so you don't have to live with one of us?" asked Caroline.

"No, no, no," DeMaris laughed. "I'm not marrying him for either of those reasons. In fact, I'm not marrying Chuck." She turned on her heel and walked toward the house. "I'm marrying Greg."

Jacyne had volunteered to make breakfast so the rest of the girls were having their coffee out on the deck waiting. DeMaris was just back from rowing practice.

"We shouldn't have pushed." Viva.

"Maybe we should have listened." Shay.

"Maybe we need to support her decision." Sara.

"No, we need to talk her out of this," Caroline said decisively.

"Oh, I don't—"

"Look, I've got a husband my age, he's had a stroke and it's well, you just can't imagine the challenges we're going through. De doesn't need that on top of everything else she's going through."

"Maybe we could talk her into just living with Greg. She doesn't have to marry him. She just wants companionship."

"And a place to stay," added Liset.

"Ta-da!" DeMaris walked onto the deck flinging her arms out. "You can all rejoice and breathe easy: I took a shower."

Jacyne came out carrying a casserole dish. "I seem to have forgotten an ingredient. It's missing something." Tentatively they all took portions of bread soaked in eggs with granola on top.

"What are we doing today?" asked Melissa.

"I say we go for a drive and see what we can find," said Viva. This, they knew, would be an all-day excursion. They would get a brochure and read up on what was happening in the neighboring towns. Basically going wherever the road took them.

"Sounds great," said DeMaris cheerfully, "you guys do that and drop me off in Spokane."

"Why?"

"I need to do more research for this newest book. Chuck will bring me home."

"What makes you so sure he'll be willing to bring you home, since you're marrying Greg."

"Well, I'm not telling Chuck that. Besides, we have a dinner date. I mean, I have to eat and Greg's not here."

"Okay, so she's not entirely committed to Greg if she's still thinking about Chuck," whispered Jacyne. Caroline and Liset nodded.

"Sounds like a plan."

They dropped DeMaris off where she directed, making sure she had her cell phone and that it was turned on.

Okay, what to do first? Should I risk going to the bank again? For what? There's nothing I need. The Foxx's apartment? Might be an idea.

She wandered around Spokane to get a feel for the setting of her story and fingered the key to the Foxx's apartment in her pocket.

It couldn't hurt to just walk by. She got to the street door and looked up. *Well, looky there, windows are open. They weren't before. Is Blanche up there?*

I really need to investigate that. I'm checking on Blanche. Making sure she's all right. And if she's not there . . . then I need to look around. I mean, look what happened last time. Owen would still be in the closet if it weren't for me.

DeMaris made her way up the stairs, stood in the hallway, and looked around. It all looked like she remembered it.

She leaned over and put her ear to the door of apartment #2. She tapped on it loud enough for someone inside to hear, but hopefully not loud enough for the neighbors to hear. Nothing. For good measure she tip-toed over to Denny Caldwell's apartment and pressed her ear to his door. She smiled, still nothing.

She tip-toed back to the Foxx's and knocked once more. Silence. *Okay, I really need to check and see if Blanche is here. We haven't seen her since she walked out after being told about Owen. Who knows what she'll do in her mental state? And, where else does she have to go?* As quietly as she could, DeMaris slipped the key in the lock, turned it, and let herself in.

It did not have the horrible stench this time. "Blanche?" DeMaris called out softly. Nothing looked out of place. She did a quick walk through to discover nothing had changed, not even in Owen's room. *Okay, nothing more in here.*

She looked through the peephole. Nobody was in the hallway. She opened the door, stepped out, locked the door behind her, and was just on the first step, when the door below opened. *Oh, no!*

"Well, hey, look who's here!" Denny shouted when he saw her. "You gonna take the apartment?"

"Ah . . . ya know, I still can't make a decision. Street noise bothers me."

"You'll get used to it. I think you should take it." He was level with her now. "Why not come in my place? I'll fix us some coffee. Or something stronger, if you like."

"I really don't think . . ."

"Come on, come on." He grabbed an elbow and propelled her around. "Give me a chance to talk you into being my neighbor."

Knowing this wasn't the smartest move she'd ever made—no one knew where she was—she slowly made her way into Denny's apartment.

⌐ ——— ⌐

Not only did she not want to drink anything, she didn't want to touch anything either, including sitting in a chair. "You know, I've been sitting all day, think I'll stand. Thank you, anyway."

She looked away from the needles on the table. He quickly picked them up and threw them in a drawer. "That's for my, ah, what do you call it? That disease . . ."

"Diabetes?"

"Yeah, that's what I got."

She did not care for the way his eyes roved over her and she mentally counted the steps to the door.

"Unless, of course, you're interested." Denny arched an eyebrow at her.

She decided to play dumb— as her friends said she always carried this act off well. "And take insulin? No thanks. I don't think that'd be a wise idea."

He shrugged. "Oh, right."

"I really need to get going," DeMaris said as she watched him dump out two mugs into the sink, rinse them with rusty water, and then turned them upside down to drain while he filled the coffeepot. *I'll pour that hot liquid all over me before I drink from that cup,* thought DeMaris. She looked around the room. The layout was nothing like the Foxx's. *Yes, Owen and Blanche have the nicer of the two apart—* She froze and then glanced at Denny. Still with his back to her, DeMaris took the opportunity to look again at what had caught her eye. A piece of yellow tape with black lettering hung over the rim of the wastebasket. She leaned so that she could look directly into the basket. POL . . . DO. DeMaris didn't need to see the entire tape to know it said: POLICE LINE DO NOT CROSS. *Why would Denny have it? It has to be from the Foxx's apartment. Was he thinking that I might come back and that the tape would scare me off so he took it down? No, not me—Blanche. Viva said Blanche was hysterical when she ran into her. If Denny killed Owen, Blanche would be the one person who could identify him. But Owen was a big guy, from what I saw of him. Would Denny be able to move him to the closet? Maybe. Blanche definitely could. Was she hysterical because she'd just hit her brother with a baseball bat and she realized she'd killed him? Denny and Blanche as lovers? I don't even want to put that in a book! I've gotta get out of here.* DeMaris started for the door.

"Hey! Where ya goin'?"

"I—I have other apartments to look at. Thank you but—"

"You don't want one of those."

"I really need to look at all my options before I make a decision. I'm still not sure that I want the apartment."

"Oh, honey, of course you do," he smiled. "You and I could have a lot of fun."

DeMaris had to bite back telling him to brush his teeth. "Well, I don't have to be right next door," she pointed out. "I know where you live. Wherever I decide to move, I'll come by and let you know."

She had managed to reach the door and turn the knob when he brought his hand up and laid it on the door. "What's wrong with the place? I want you here."

"I'm flattered but the street noise—"

"Close the windows."

"The smell—"

"That's why the windows are propped open."

Mom, Dad, I need something! "Well, I just think— I just think— It's haunted."

He glared at her and stepped away. "You been readin' the paper? It wasn't that apartment. It was the one across the way. I don't believe in no ghosts anyhow. You shouldn't either."

"You're probably right." They could both hear the water boiling.

"You stay put," he growled and went into the kitchen.

DeMaris had had enough. "You don't ever tell me what to do." She jerked open the door and ran down the stairs. She heard him yell but he didn't chase after her.

She made her way safely and quickly to the newspaper office. "Is Chuck here?" she asked Doris at the front counter.

DeMaris didn't have to wait long, but in the space of a few seconds she suddenly asked herself what she was doing here. She'd gotten scared and run to safety. How was she going to explain this to—

"DeMaris!"

"Hi Chuck." She supposed she shouldn't have been surprised when he gave her a big hug and kiss.

"Gosh, I thought we were having dinner together, not lunch. Did I mess up?" he asked.

"No. I got a ride into town and have been doing some research. I'm done so . . . I came here. Ahh, ya know what? I'll just go grab something quick now and I'll come back at what? Five o'clock?"

"I was just wishing I had someone to eat lunch with and in you walk. What does that tell ya, huh? Lunch *and* dinner. I'm the lucky one. How hungry are you right now?"

"Ah . . . well . . . I'm up for Italian, hint, hint."

He smiled. "I know just the place." They walked out to his car and he held the door for her. It was a ten-minute drive to the restaurant.

"I'd like a bottle of wine," DeMaris said to the hostess who seated them.

The woman glanced at Chuck who, although taken aback, nodded. "I'll tell your waitress."

"What's the matter?" he asked.

She folded her hands and twisted them several times. "I'm just nervous."

"Darling, you don't need to be." He placed his hand over hers.

"Do you know anything about a Dennis Caldwell?" she suddenly asked.

He nodded. "He's had several brushes with the law. How do you know him?"

She shook her head and then said, "The research I'm doing for my . . . I ran into him. He gives me the creeps."

"He should. My advice is to stay away from him." Chuck studied her. "When did you see him?"

"Today, just a little bit ago."

"I happen to know the police are looking for him to question. They can't find him. Where was he?"

"In his apartment on Jones Street."

Chuck pulled out his phone and made a quick call.

"Yes," she smiled as the server set down two glasses and the bottle of wine. "I plan to stay far, far away—but here's my thing: I still want to know about the dirty money in the safe deposit box and what was up with the treasure map?"

"What are you talking about?"

Crap. I told Greg what I did, not Chuck. I need to learn to keep my men straight. She remembered when she had started to tell Kirk. He'd yelled into the phone: "Stop! That was part of our divorce agreement. That you wouldn't tell me anymore of the stupid stuff ya did. You're not making me an accessory ever again. My life is finally quiet! I'm happy."

"I'm sorry. My book . . . I have my characters stuffing a safe deposit box full of money but I haven't figured out a reason why they would do that and I'd like to use a treasure map but I haven't found a reason for that either. I'm really frustrated."

"You told me you had a mystery to solve here—"

"Spokane is where the story takes place." She gave Chuck the you-obviously-haven't-been-listening-to-me look.

"Okay."

Lunch was quiet. DeMaris had no problem polishing off the bottle of wine and Chuck wondered if he'd have to carry her out to his car. But no, she was fine. In fact, she was remarkably unaffected.

As they drove through the countryside, Chuck interrupted her pointing out the beautiful scenery. "How serious are you with that old man?"

She was surprised and hesitated a second before she said, "He's asked me to marry him. I have this vacation to figure out an answer."

"You don't belong with him. You belong with me."

"We've seen each other, what? A couple of times?"

"You are going to sit there and tell me you don't feel a spark? Well, answer me," he said as the silence grew. "I can say the same thing to you that you said to me: if you want your marriage to last, don't marry someone who's old enough to be your father."

"He is not old enough to be . . ." she sighed. "You're right. I am crazy about Greg but I do have my doubts."

"What do you think of when you think of me?"

She sighed. "That you are moving on me much too fast."

"I have to! If I take my time, you'll be married. I suppose I should ask this: do you think about me?"

She mumbled something into her window.

"What?"

"Yes. You've crossed my mind a time or two. I worry about the age difference between Greg and myself—but I really do love him."

"So, why think about me?"

"I don't know," she answered honestly.

"Maybe you should not get married until you've resolved that question."

"I'm sure you're right."

"But you're going to do it anyway."

DeMaris looked at Chuck. "I really don't care to be divorced a second time. I really don't care to have my friends, including you, say, 'I told you so.' My other thing is: I want to be a hermit. That has always been my dream. I certainly have not had a bad life living with my husband and raising two kids. I'm very glad I did but . . . this is *my* time. I've earned it . . . Oh God, that's what's bothering me. Kirk, my ex-husband, understood when I wanted to be alone. He didn't take it personally. Greg does. He gets upset when I want to be by myself. Oh, my God." Chuck looked at her. "*That's* what's really bothering me, not our age difference."

"So what does that tell you? Greg is the insecure type," he pointed out. "I would be understanding."

"Yeah, so you say," she said absently as she realized what was really bothering her. If she married Greg she would have to be constantly feeding his ego, constantly doing stuff with him, constantly on the go . . . and so far, she'd really enjoyed it. Hadn't she already pretty much led the hermit life with Kirk and the kids? Of course, she'd been around and had been willing to go places and do things, *but admit it,* she admonished herself, *there were a lot of days when you stayed in your studio writing away, letting your family fend for itself.*

And now? Now she wanted to travel, get new ideas, meet new people, do crazy things . . . which Greg was more than willing to do. Kirk had actually become the hermit, not wanting to leave the house much, staying in his own world, and pretty much holding down the fort while his ex-wife and kids took off for the world. *Wait a minute, didn't Sara say something last night? 'You don't want to be a recluse anymore?' So . . . my midlife crisis is that I've given up one dream and started another? No, I've achieved one dream; now I'm starting another. But do I want that dream to include Greg or do I want to wander off by myself? THAT'S the question.*

As they turned into a long driveway, DeMaris looked around. "Where are we?"

Chuck smiled. "I want to show you something." *Great,* thought DeMaris. *I have no clue where I am, even if I did call the girls to come rescue me.* They pulled in front of an elegant, stately home in the country. Three stories showed off white pillars. The door sported an elaborate knocker and there was a wide wraparound porch. "What do you think?"

"It's gorgeous."

"My grandfather built this house at the turn of the century. This is where I live." He opened his car door and DeMaris did the same. They walked around the property, complete with a golden retriever that ran up to greet them.

DeMaris smiled. "I see your grandfather was a visionary—a pool in the backyard."

Chuck nodded. "Second wife thought she'd like one. Seems she just wanted an excuse for the pool man to come over."

"I see . . . How many times have you been married?"

"Just the two. You?"

"Just the one. Kids?"

"Two. You?"

"Two also."

"Have your kids met the old man yet?"

"I really wish you'd stop calling him that. His name is Greg. And one has; one refuses to."

"Doesn't that tell you something?" he said.

"I'm not going to live my life by what my children think. I realize my daughter is not happy with me—my son isn't either for that matter, but he acknowledges that I need to live my own life just as he would like to live his own life without my constant interference; so, we have come to an agreement." DeMaris's cell phone suddenly rang. "Hello . . . Yeah, okay . . . No, go on without me . . . Hang on." She cupped the phone against her shoulder. "Can you take me back to Viva's or should they come get me after the show?"

"To have you all to myself for the day?" He smiled. "I'll take you home . . . late tonight . . . if you decide you want to go."

She shook her head at him but said into the phone, "Chuck will bring me home."

He found a bathing suit left behind by his ex-wife and he and DeMaris sat out by the pool. They talked and discovered they had several interests in common. *Dang,* thought DeMaris, *if I hadn't met Greg I could definitely go for this guy. There's no real age difference here. What am I thinking about? Chuck is a great guy and so is Greg. And I am definitely in love with Greg. Another time, another place it could have been Chuck—but it's not for today. Hmm, a backup man if things don't work out with Greg. What a lovely thought.*

Chuck cooked them steaks out on the grill and they watched a gorgeous sunset. "I need to get back," DeMaris sighed.

He reached over and took her hand. "Stay the night."

"No way."

"At least let me see you again while you're here."

"I feel bad. I really haven't done that much with my sisters. I've been out on the lake with the rowing team, I've been off investigating a story, and spending time with you. I really need to do something with my friends."

"Fine, but please don't cut me out altogether."

"Chuck . . . I am . . . I think I am going to . . . marry Greg."

He shook his head. "You're having doubts. I can see it in your eyes, hear it in your voice. I'm hangin' around."

He drove her home and gave her a long kiss before she finally wrestled herself away from him. "Don't do this to me," she said.

"Until you're married, I'm not quitting. I might not quit then either."

"Look," she said. "You may be in love with DeMaris Azaygo but you're not in love with me."

"Oh, I thought you said you weren't her." He smiled at her.

She chuckled. "I'm not, but you seem to think I am. Some of the things you said today out by the pool. I think you like the idea of *imagining* that you are dating DeMaris Azaygo. And for this week, you can tell people that—as long as you don't mind telling everyone later it was a lie.

"And DeMaris Azaygo has a lot of money, I would have to think. I know that newspapers are dying off and . . ."

"Ah, I'm after you for your money—if you were her."

"Trust me. I don't have any extra to give. In fact, my sisters can vouch for that."

"Well, I'm not exactly a pauper. I own my house outright and I have some other investments."

DeMaris held up her hands. "None of my business."

"If these are the concerns you have about me, I need to tell you." He looked at her for several seconds. "You know what? You may be right about the DeMaris Azaygo thing. I am a huge fan and I do . . . okay, fantasize. But deep down, I know you're not her and I have not been this interested in a woman in a very long time. I think you need to give us a chance. Think about us, please."

"No," she put her finger up, "don't kiss me again." She got out of his car, grabbed her fanny pack, and looked at him. "I will think about what you said though."

She stood up and stopped.

"What?" he asked.

DeMaris looked toward the house and then the garage, which was closed. "Odd. We didn't leave any lights on when we left but there's a couple on now. The girls shouldn't be home yet. They were going out to eat after the movie; unless something happened. But if they are here why is it so quiet? Usually we sit out back with drinks and music blaring. We're loud and obnoxious." She shook her head. "I hope nobody's received bad news from home. I've gotta go."

She took off at a quick walk and ran smack into the front door when it didn't give as she turned the handle and shoved. Locked. She pounded on the door, "Girls! It's me!"

"DeMaris! Get in the car!" She heard the urging in Chuck's voice but couldn't imagine what the problem could be. "DeMaris! Now!"

She turned to holler back at him when the front door opened. She whipped back around. "Hey, is everything all—"

Two people wearing dark ski masks over their faces stood before her. One cleared his throat and spoke quietly, "That's her."

"*That's* her?" said the other. "Oh, great."

"DeMaris!" this from Chuck.

As the men reached out for her, she turned and bolted.

Chuck had the car door open. She flung her fanny pack inside and just managed to get in when he drove away with the passenger door still open.

"Hey!" There was a thump, and a scream. Chuck grabbed DeMaris by the jacket to keep her in the car and raced down the street. He watched in the rearview mirror and stopped after two blocks. "Hurry up!"

She hauled herself in and slammed the door. "What the hell just happened?" She fumbled with and then heard the snap of her seat belt and let out a big sigh of relief as Chuck floored it.

"I turned around in the driveway. The second you knocked on the door, all the lights went out. Who were they?"

"I don't know. It was dark inside and they were dressed in black. Two men by the sound of their voices. Did you hit one of them?"

"Ran over his foot, I think. I had to leave—he was just reaching out to grab you."

"Yeah, I know," she said quietly.

"We need to report this to the police."

"I know." *But I don't think I'm going to tell the police or you that I think both of those men knew who I was.*

Chapter Twenty-Four

Viva had gone through the house and the girls their suitcases and closets. It appeared nothing was missing. Viva knew both police officers who came out and they offered to patrol the area during the night. The girls all nodded their relief at this suggestion.

Today the girls were taking the speed boat to an island that had some cute shops. Although Paula was back from her daughter's and DeMaris was no longer needed on the rowing team, she wasn't interested in shopping.

"Why don't you guys go and then come and get me for dinner?" said DeMaris guiltily as she remembered telling Chuck she should spend more time with her sisters.

"What do you have planned?"

"Um, a shower for one," she said hoping to appease them, "but I have all these ideas running around in my head. I've got to get them down on paper; and hopefully I'll find the time to stencil my bedroom."

"Oh, you don't have to do that."

"I told you I would. You girls go and enjoy the day."

The girls left. DeMaris went back in her bathroom, studied the shower stall, tried to remember when last she'd showered, decided it was fairly recent and dosed herself with perfume. Now she was ready to write.

She wrote a few pages, scratched it out, wrote some more, stared off into space, then scratched the last idea out. As she was concentrating on her character's next step, the whole house shook with the slamming of the front door. *Crap! Who is that? The girls didn't bother to lock up when they left? Oh God, those guys probably had their eyes on the house and they think it's vacant!* DeMaris frantically looked around for something to protect herself with when she heard behind her, "Want stuff."

"You can have anything—Blanche. You scared the devil out of me!"

"Want stuff."

DeMaris followed Blanche's finger out across the lake.

"In town?"

"Want stuff. Clothes, purses."

DeMaris let out an exasperated sigh. *Oh, what the hell? My story isn't coming to me anyway. Might as well take a break.*

"Fine, let's go get the oars."

— — —

DeMaris was reflecting on the fact that Viva would probably not be happy to know that Blanche and she were strolling down Main Street. As far as Viva was concerned, Blanche should be shut away so that nobody saw her. *Hmm, she probably feels the same way about me.*

Suddenly Blanche came to a grinding halt. DeMaris saw the frozen look on the woman's face. DeMaris looked around. They were near the restaurant and the grocery cart was nowhere to be seen.

"Bad man!" blurted Blanche.

"What?" asked DeMaris.

"Bad man! Bad man!" Blanche's voice began to rise, her fists pumped the air, and she began to stomp her feet. "Bad man!"

"You mean the guy who threw you in the dumpster?"

"Bad man!" DeMaris followed Blanche's gaze to a blonde-haired man who had picked up his pace. He turned slightly to look at them and then whipped back around.

"Oh, no, no," said DeMaris trying to calm Blanche. "That's Tim. He bought me a box of chocolates."

"Bad man!" she screamed.

"Oh, God, Blanche. Please," hissed DeMaris. *Great, I'm getting a taste of how the girls feel when they say I'm acting up.* She glanced at Tim and then looked again.

Crutches. The man had one foot bandaged—no cast—and he was using crutches. *For a plaster cast, one would have to go to the hospital and if your foot was run over when you had broken into a house . . .*

Tim was getting away. Blanche was riled up and screaming for all she was worth, while DeMaris just stood there watching the scene unfold.

What to do? Well, my character would tackle him. And in keeping with living her own mystery, whether her assumption was right or wrong, that's what DeMaris did.

She ran down the sidewalk and made a flying leap onto Tim's back. Unfortunately Tim had just stuck his crutches forward which held him upright. DeMaris basically looked like she was asking for a piggy-back ride.

"What the hell are you doing?" he growled turning to look at her.

"Ah . . . well . . ." *Mom! Dad! Say something!* DeMaris frantically tried to think of a story when suddenly she was slammed from behind.

Blanche had decided to follow DeMaris's example. Between Tim turning with one foot up, making him off balance, and Blanche's considerable weight, the three of them fell to the pavement. The wind was knocked out of DeMaris and she suspected Tim was in the same boat as she saw his one hand going up and down as if to say uncle, uncle.

Get her off! Get her off! De did her best to yell—but no sound came out. She was squashed between the two with Blanche screaming, "Bad man!" in her ear.

I thought she was around three hundred pounds. I was wrong! So wrong! Its gotta be closer to four—five hundred pounds! Somebody get her off me! I'm dying here! I can't breathe. God, Mom, Dad, don't let me die like this!

She had a sudden vision of Kirk talking with her friends at her funeral: "DeMaris was found dead lying between a man and a woman. First the divorce, and now this. I just can't talk about it." No! No! She squirmed and wriggled but to no avail. *What will the girls tell Greg, the man they don't like? Oh, probably the same thing that Kirk tells all our friends!*

She was stuck. Tim's hand was no longer moving and she wondered if she was going to die first or go deaf. *Doesn't anybody hear her screaming!?*

DeMaris saw spots before her eyes, then finally, strange feet and hands. Blanche was unceremoniously rolled off her one way while someone rolled DeMaris the other way. She landed on her back on the sidewalk next to Tim.

DeMaris gulped air. She saw people standing near her with their mouths moving. "I can't hear anything with this ringing in my ears," she said.

She turned to look at Tim. He was not moving. "Hey," DeMaris tried to smack his arm but found she was too weak. *My God, I wasn't this bad after the train accident.* She ended up giving him a feeble pat on the back. "Tim?" He blinked. "Breathe." She watched him slowly gain awareness while her hearing improved.

". . . in the dumpster?"

187

DeMaris rolled to her side to see Blanche talking with the police officer who had pulled her from the trash compactor. Blanche was pointing at Tim.

The two of them were helped to their feet. There were several people standing around. "This woman says you stuffed her in a dumpster," said the police officer.

"She's crazy," Tim sneered.

Immediately Blanche's fists started to hammer the air as she stomped her feet.

"You're gonna get tackled again," warned De.

"You keep her away from me!" he yelled. "Anybody can see she's crazy. You can't trust anything she says."

"You did, you did, you did," Blanche continued to chant while others tried to calm her.

DeMaris looked down at his foot. It was crudely wrapped in ace bandages. No doctor did that.

"This is the man who broke into Zimmer's house."

For a second all Tim could do was stare at her. "You're crazy, too!"

"I can positively identify him."

"No way!" he yelled. "There is no way in hell you can identify me! I had a ski mask on the entire time I was there!"

"Inside Zimmer's house?"

"Yeah!"

"Last night?"

"Yeah!"

"Can anybody vouch for your whereabouts?"

"Yeah! My friend—" Tim suddenly stopped and stared at her. "You bitch."

"Lack of oxygen will do that to ya. I know. I suffered from it too. Saw my own funeral. It wasn't pleasant. Rachel will be very disappointed, as am I."

"Oh, shut up!"

"Let's go," said the cop.

As Tim hobbled to the police cruiser, DeMaris heard him ask, "Can we go to the hospital first? My foot's killin' me."

When the girls arrived home several hours later to pick up DeMaris for dinner they found her at the kitchen table writing furiously. They changed their clothes and then stood around her. Finally she put down her pen and looked up. "Have fun?"

Yes. They had gone walking in a nearby park, found an antique shop, some cute clothing boutiques she would have enjoyed. They'd go back if she wanted—

"I don't have any money, remember?"

That stopped them for a second, but then they plowed on.

"But this weekend—"

"Money or no money—"

"We are taking you to—"

"The big art fair!"

"You guys found an art fair?"

"Here's the brochure."

Viva walked into the room. "Thank you. The stenciling looks great," she said stiffly.

"You don't like it?" asked DeMaris with dismay. "Caroline can always paint over it."

"No, no. I really do like it. You did a great job as always. What I didn't like, is what I found in my bed." She glared.

"Oh," DeMaris chuckled. "That. She and I had a full day in town—and just so you know, we kept as low a profile as the two of us possibly could."

"Great. Thank you. But you didn't suggest a shower or a bath to her?"

"I did suggest it. She didn't want to; I understood."

"I take it Blanche came back," stated Shay.

"Yes, and she crawled into my bed," growled Viva.

"Well, at least we know she's safe," offered Melissa.

"Yes, and stinking up my entire room!"

DeMaris grabbed her fanny pack. "Are we taking Blanche with us? If not, I suggest we leave before she wakes up. Oh, and just in case the police show up," all of them turned and stared at her. She put a hand up, "Blanche and I caught one of the guys who was in the house last night."

"How did you do that? Who was it?"

"Tell ya in the car." DeMaris headed out.

"Is it safe to leave Blanche here?" asked Sara as a few of them followed DeMaris's lead.

"I don't think she'll steal anything," said Viva. "Plus, I'd say she's out for the night."

"Yeah, she seemed pretty exhausted," said DeMaris, "and she only laid down about an hour ago. Good thing you've got that extra blow-up bed Shay told me about."

Viva didn't find this funny.

—— —— ——

In the evening DeMaris was out on the porch trying to write when the next crisis arose.

"No! No! No!"

"Blanche, honey, a shower will get you all clean—"

"No!"

"What's your favorite dessert? Would you like a cookie? Look here—"

"No! No shower! Hate shower!"

"Well, if you got cleaned up—"

"No! No!"

"I can't get anything done out here," DeMaris slammed through the house. "Blanche!" she roared.

Blanche had been stomping her foot with each "no." Her head shot up and she looked at DeMaris bug-eyed. "Does your tooth still hurt?"

"Yeah."

"Do you want it to stop hurting?"

"Yeah."

"Then go take a shower!" yelled DeMaris pointing down the hall.

"Meany!" Blanche stuck out her tongue but slowly proceeded down the hall.

"She's a child," hissed DeMaris. "Treat her like one."

"Wow, you're a mean mom."

"Damn straight I am. I'm in the middle— I can't lose this." She ran back outside to write.

—— —— ——

The girls roamed the makeshift aisles of the art fair that was being held in a large park. They were surprised when DeMaris eyed some rings and bracelets.

"When have you ever been interested in jewelry?' asked Shay.

"All I have is costume jewelry. I need some decent pieces."

"Not all costume jewelry is cheap."

"I know. I have a friend who's really into jewelry and she's been educating me. I'll take this one."

"Stop," hollered Caroline. DeMaris could feel herself doing a slow burn—but Caroline was only interested in getting a deal since four of them saw pieces they wanted from this vendor. After some negotiating they all left with less money but happy with their deal.

They were near the end of the third aisle when DeMaris stuck her nose up. "Ah, French fries . . . corn on the cob. I'm gone. Anybody?" They shook their heads. Liset and Melissa had wandered off an aisle back. DeMaris took off for the food. She stood behind several men who clearly hadn't showered in days. *A date for Blanche.*

She glanced over and noticed the rides for children. *Carnival workers. Oh. Oh!*

She smacked her hand against the man's back in front of her wondering at the same time if she had her anti-bacterial hand gel on her.

He had to be seven feet tall. Slowly he looked down on her and leaned forward. "You're from the carnival, right?" she pointed.

"What's it to you, bitch?"

DeMaris had been called many things; so she continued undaunted. "Are you hiring?" *This would be perfect for Blanche. No showers, travel the country—maybe even Canada. A foreign country. Make some money —if she's capable of doing anything.*

He smiled showing his two teeth. *Okay, no dental plan comes with the job.* "Sure."

"Out of my way. Out of my way!" said the man in front of 'leaning tower' quickly switching places with him. He stood about five feet but had most of his teeth and possibly cologne on.

"I'm Hewitt." Fortunately he did not extend his hand. "Owner over there. Did I hear you were looking for work?"

"No, not me." Hewitt's face fell. "I have a friend who really needs to get out of town."

"Don't they all," he muttered. "Is this person intelligent?"

"Um . . . is that really a requirement?"

He stared at her.

"Yeah, okay, um, halfway. What if I paid you to feed her and . . . keep an eye on her? Not you personally, of course—someone you know who needs a little extra cash? For say a year?"

They looked at each other for a moment. "How badly are the police looking for said person? I don't take on murderers or rapists. I draw the line there."

"Oh, heavens no! Not even the police. Relatives. They want to commit her for all her money and try to take over her estate. I admit she's a little eccentric but she certainly knows what's going on. People are so greedy nowadays." She had expected him to jump on the money part but he stood there in thought.

He had a faraway look in his eyes when he said, "Yes, family members do love to mettle, don't they?" He reached into his wallet and pulled out a business card. "I'll want to meet her before taking her on."

"Of course. How much longer will you be here?"

"Through the weekend. Next county over all of next week. My cell number's on here."

"Thank you, Hewitt."

"Your name?"

"DeMaris."

He looked up at her. "DeMaris Azaygo?"

She laughed. "No, afraid not. Pala." *Well, I'm glad the girls aren't here to hear me goof up after all the yelling I did at them to be somebody different while we're together.* "You're a reader?" she looked unconvinced.

"No," he shook his head. "Love the movies though. I'm a real movie buff. Not just the actors. Name a movie and I can tell you who directed, produced, and wrote it. I haven't missed one of Azaygo's."

"I think there's only been a handful."

"Yeah, but they were great. She has some classic mysteries. And then in others some of her characters do the stupidest stuff, the trouble they get into and yet it all makes perfect sense. Those three movies with the sorority sisters . . . ya know, ya wanna like the main character . . . even while you're strangling her."

DeMaris nodded. "I bet her friends feel the same way."

By now they had worked their way up to the counter. "Two of the works," Hewitt hollered.

DeMaris was waiting her turn when he turned around and handed her a loaded tray.

"What? Oh, no. Thank you. I couldn't."

"Sure, ya can. I own food concessions here too. Take it."

"Oh, well . . . thank you."

"I can expect to hear from you?"

"Sure." She grabbed a handful of straws and napkins and took off.

Shay saw her coming. "You're that hungry?" The tray was loaded with a large soda, two hamburgers, two fries, two ears of corn, and a bag of chips.

"No. I ran into the owner of the carnival slash concession stand and he gave me all this."

"You don't need to be sarcastic, I asked a simple question."

DeMaris handed out straws. "You're gonna have to help me eat this."

"I gave up asking those kinds of questions long ago," whispered Caroline.

"Oh, I just ask to see what she's gonna say," said Sara. Liset nodded. They all munched on the food and took off down the next aisle.

DeMaris was throwing away the trash from the food when she looked up to see hot air balloons in a nearby field. *Why didn't Viva mention this? She could have taken some of us up. Maybe she knows somebody here and I could try it out—my character could try it out.* DeMaris started slowly walking toward the field. *I could at least ask questions about ballooning while I'm here—I mean, think about it, what does Viva know?* She was rummaging around in her fanny pack to make sure her trusty notepad and pen were handy when she heard a commotion from behind. She glanced over her shoulder and did a double-take when she saw Brian. He was running straight at her. There was no question he was focused on her while DeMaris stood there with a deer-in-the-headlights gaze. *Think! What would my character do? Well, she wouldn't stand here waiting to get caught, tackled, or whatever it is he has in mind! Run!*

She took off, dodging around people. Being short and as fleet of foot as she was—thanks to Greg making her jog—Brian soon lost sight of her. DeMaris stopped to catch her breath but kept her eye on Brian while he looked around for her. As she watched him her ears picked up on a conversation behind her. ""I'm sorry, Mrs. Smith, we have to launch."

"But my friend's not here yet!"

"I told you what time you had to be here. I've waited fifteen minutes. We need to go."

"Just wait. I'll go look for her."

"No!"

DeMaris turned slightly to see two men and a woman standing near one of the balloon baskets. The woman took off running toward the parking lot. The one man stood there for a moment; then turned to the young man helping him and said, "I'm not waiting any longer. Let's go."

DeMaris looked to see that Brian had his back to her and the woman had disappeared in the crowd. "Excuse me," said DeMaris walking up to the balloonist. "Am I at the right balloon? I'm here with," not knowing the woman's first name, she coughed and mumbled, "Smith. I've been looking all over—"

"You've got the right balloon, lady, but your friend left to go find you. I'm leaving now. You can either come with us or go find your friend. Either way, I'm gone and there are no refunds."

"I'm in," said DeMaris.

As they left the ground DeMaris peered over the basket. The thought dawned on her that maybe she should let her friends know where she was. She searched the crowd. "Viva!" she yelled. "Viva!" She saw the girls looking around and then Sara pointed up.

"Nnnnoooooo!" she couldn't hear it but that was definitely what Viva was yelling. The girls started to run and then realized how fruitless it was and stopped.

DeMaris waved and smiled happily until she saw Brian looking at her. Clearly he was not happy. DeMaris smiled and waved at him too. As the people on the ground started to get smaller and smaller it dawned on DeMaris to finally question herself. Why had she run? Brian didn't pose any threat. There were hundreds of people around. What did she think he intended to do? Yes, he wanted the key but it wasn't likely he was going to kill her for it . . . at least, not in public. Once again, her character's personality had taken over and DeMaris had acted accordingly. She sighed. *I always seem to be doing stupid stuff. Why don't I ever learn?* She smiled. *This is fun though!*

Near the end of the balloon ride the pilot said to her, "I see you're a friend of Viva's."

"Yeah."

"I'm going to take a wild guess and say you're not Mrs. Smith's friend."

"No. But hey, you were leaving with or without them so . . ."

"You wouldn't be DeMaris, would you?"

"Yeah."

The man chuckled softly, "My wife, Ann, rowed with you."

"Oh, yes. I had a lot of fun rowing with the girls."

DeMaris turned to look out over the countryside. *The girls are really missing out. This is so much fun! Not scary like flying in an airplane.*

"You do realize," he said, "you owe me for this ride."

DeMaris looked up. "You had two people who didn't show. I'm thinking if I owe anybody money it's Mrs. Smith or her friend."

"I was leaving without them. There are no refunds. I thought you were a paid customer."

They stared at each other. DeMaris looked at the two other people in the basket. They stared back at her. "Fine. I'll write you a check. How much?"

He gave a slight groan.

"What's wrong? My check's good!"

He thought for a moment and then nodded. "Yeah, okay, I guess it is."

Chapter Twenty-Five

"No lawyer!" Blanche pouted and pounded her fist on the kitchen counter.

"Blanche, this is for your own good. I'm helping you," explained Viva. They had just finished breakfast. "Your mother often said to me that she worried about what would happen to you if she and Owen were both gone. And honey, they are. Let me take care of your finances for you. Your mom bought that apartment that you and Owen lived in—"

"Won't go back."

"Okay. Let's sell it." Viva spoke slowly and softly. "And we'll find you a nice, clean place to live."

Blanche folded her arms across her chest. "No hospital, no mental ward."

DeMaris laughed. "See, Viva. She's not as dumb as you thought."

Viva glared but got the last laugh when Blanche turned to DeMaris and said, "Go home with you."

"Ah . . . I'm homeless."

Blanche smiled. "Go with you."

"No," Jacyne said firmly. "Neither one of you is leaving here homeless. Now, Blanche, there are some assisted living places—"

"No!"

"She can't stay there," said Liset. "She'll just run away. Blanche, where would you like to stay?"

Blanche looked at each of the girls. "Here."

"No," said Viva. "I'm selling this place."

"Basement."

"No." Viva put her head down. "You're not coming with the house."

196

"Like street," she smiled at DeMaris. "We have fun."

DeMaris downed her glass of milk. "Yes, won't we?"

"All right, look," Viva decided to try a new tact, "let's think about where you're going to live later. You can stay here for now. I know your mom left you and Owen some money. Hopefully the two of you did not spend all of it."

"Owen cheap."

"Good. I can invest that, help it to grow. Maybe I could find you a little job. But we need to sign some papers so that it's legal for me to help you. So, we need to talk with a lawyer. I have the appointment—"

"No."

Viva picked up her purse. "This man is doing me a personal favor. We're going now." She got behind Blanche and began pushing her toward the door.

"No! De! De!" Blanche reached out for DeMaris. "Help! De!"

Viva slammed the door behind the two of them.

DeMaris groaned. *Why me? Hmm, maybe while we're in town I can call Greg.* DeMaris grabbed her fanny pack and looked at the group. "Nice choice I've got, huh? Live with an old man on Social Security or live out on the street with Blanche." She hurried to catch up.

"Don't forget Chuck!"

"Maybe you should go back to Kirk!"

"Maybe you shouldn't have gotten a divorce!"

DeMaris whirled around. "Thanks for the support."

At least a couple of them had the decency to cringe.

"I'm here, I'm here," said DeMaris buckling herself in the backseat while Blanche boo-hooed up front.

"Okay, you two," Viva pointed a finger in the vacant attorney's office for the two of them to sit. "I need you both quiet. Just stay here and be quiet. I don't know how long I'll be. Just . . . be quiet."

DeMaris stuck out her tongue. After all, if she was going to be treated as a child . . . Blanche laughed, stuck out her tongue, put her thumbs in both ears, and wagged her fingers at Viva.

"Don't encourage her."

DeMaris made an exaggerated frown and Viva rolled her eyes. The attorney was standing in the doorway watching.

DeMaris could see Viva was getting ready to lambast her when they both noticed Blanche. On the end of Viva's string of keys was a small ball-shaped compass. Blanche was fixated on it. Viva shook the keys in her hand. "Blanche, honey, would you like these?"

Blanche gave her a vacant stare and nodded. At least she was quiet. Viva handed her the keys.

Just before the office door closed they heard, "Which one is it that's handicapped?"

— — —·— —

Blanche sat and slowly turned the compass this way and that while DeMaris slumped on the bench, feet crossed at the ankles, arms crossed over her chest, staring at the ceiling. She had found a glitch in her book and was deciding how to fix it when Blanche spoke.

"I know my mom trusted Viva and I don't mind her taking over the finances. Owen did all that. I wouldn't know where to begin, plus she can invest it whereas I can't—but if I sign those papers, she'll put me in a home. I'll be locked away forever. We both know that."

Slowly DeMaris turned and looked at Blanche. Even with the yellow teeth and hair sticking up on end, she looked, well, no, still insane. *Maybe I'm the one who's finally lost it.* "Huh?" was all DeMaris could manage.

Blanche leaned back against the wall. "People leave you alone when you act weird and don't talk in complete sentences."

"I'll have to remember that. On the other hand, it doesn't seem to have worked with my friends."

"No, you have friends who care. Other than my mom, I never had that."

"You had Owen who looked after you," DeMaris reminded.

Blanche blew air out between her lips. "That son of a bitch ruined my life. I guess I did go crazy for a while. I never forgave him for what he did to me. Then Mom died and . . . that was the last friend I had. Owen was always the bully, but Mom could usually hold him in check. Once she was gone, I barely spoke to him. But where was I going to go? We had that one little apartment and all that land on the outskirts of town. I could stay there while the weather was good but I was stuck in Spokane in the winter.

"By then, he was chummy with Caldwell. I'm sure they were plotting to do something to me—not sure what—but they got to arguing. I truly feared for my life. One day I heard them yelling and screaming at each other and when I confronted them Caldwell got really nasty with me. We had a baseball bat—not the best neighborhood. I caught Caldwell a good one. Owen yelled at me to get out. I grabbed Sophocles and left. For a long time I thought Owen had thrown me out, taking up with Caldwell instead of watching out for me—his twin sister. But now . . . I think he told me to leave to protect me. Anyway, I never saw Owen again."

"Well, what about Brian Fox? Is he a relative?"

Blanche snorted. "He apparently believes we were stupid enough to think that, but no. We have no relations. He said he was a long-lost cousin on our dad's side. Daddy always talked about how sad he was that he never had family. He was sent from one foster care home to another. Personally, I think Foxx is a name Daddy made up. We asked Brian for proof and that was the last we saw of him.

"Thank you for finding that key by the way. The last thing Owen did was to tell me to take it and go. I thought I'd lost it. I knew Mom kept a key in the birdseed so I dropped the one Owen gave me in the bag. Mom always said if we ever got robbed nobody would think to look there." Blanche shook her head. "Who was gonna rob us? We had nothing. I knew Viva would take good care of Sophocles so I didn't think anything about giving him to her and the birdseed. It hit me days later . . . When I finally got to Viva's house and couldn't find it I thought Viva had gone through the original birdseed and that that was a new bag. I just panicked searching through that bag and not finding it. Still don't know what it goes to but Owen thought it was important and Mom always told me that Owen would take care of me after she was gone. He would be the man of the house. She just refused to believe that we didn't get along. He was never gonna take care of me," she said bitterly but then reflected. "I wonder what the key goes to. Why he thought it was so important for me to take it and leave."

DeMaris sat there looking around the room. The money obviously belonged to Blanche but how sensible would she be with it? Viva would know how to take care of it. Better to wait until the papers were signed.

"So . . . does Viva know," DeMaris paused to find the right word, "that you're normal?"

"No," Blanche chuckled. "Why do you think she's drawing up papers? Probably expects me to sign with an X."

"You—you know how to write?"

"I love to read. Mom and I particularly loved DeMaris Azaygo. We would read to each other every night. We read her books through twice. That's why I latched onto you, you know." She looked at DeMaris who raised an eyebrow at her. "I know you're not her but you have the same first name. I feel connected to you."

DeMaris smiled. *Well, my friends have often thought I was insane.*

"I even have," Blanche leaned over and whispered, "an education."

"You're kidding."

"No! Owen and I both have high school diplomas. Those were awful years. Not only did the kids tease us but Owen was always so hateful toward me."

"Why?"

"I had something he didn't." She stared off into space and sighed deeply. "I had someone who loved me."

"Your mom didn't love Owen?"

"Oh, yeah. I meant, I was in love and he loved me."

DeMaris was glad Blanche wasn't looking her way as she had to bite her lip to not burst out laughing as she imagined Blanche with a boyfriend. *Good grief, what would he have looked like?*

They sat silently for several minutes. Finally Blanche spoke. "I can't. I won't let Viva commit me."

"Well, I had the grand idea of you running away with the carnival when it was in Coeur d'Alene."

Blanche chuckled. "Not a bad idea."

DeMaris reached into her fanny pack and pulled out the business card. "Yeah, I talked to a—" She held it out at arm's length. "Hewitt . . . LaChance. Seemed like a decent guy."

She knew immediately that something in the air had changed. Was it the sudden noise that escaped Blanche's lips or the sound of her sitting upright? Slowly DeMaris turned and looked at her.

Blanche's eyes were bugged out, her mouth moved, but no words escaped, until she finally whispered, "Hewitt? You said Hewitt *LaChance*?"

DeMaris nodded. Cautiously, as if it might bite, Blanche pulled the card out of DeMaris's hand. She stared at it and then, closing her eyes, pressed it to her chest. She leaned against the wall and tilted her head back. DeMaris could see tears slowly running down her face. "Hewitt," she whispered again. "What did he look like?"

"Well, not a bad-looking man. His hairline is starting to recede, but it's brown. He had all of his—well, most of his teeth. Brown eyes, straight nose. In his forties I'd guess, maybe early fifties."

"How tall?"

"Short, for a man. He was about my height. He was solid though. Must work out."

"It's him," Blanche cried.

"Who?"

She shook her head. With her eyes still closed Blanche said, "All these years . . . I thought he was dead. You have no idea what it was like for me to watch while you girls dug up that toy chest. I thought . . . that Owen had killed him. He'd threatened to.

"I still remember that night like it was yesterday. Owen coming to me and saying he'd fixed my boyfriend but good. That I was never going to see him again. I didn't believe Owen. Sure, Hewitt was a small guy, but he was no coward. And then, days went by . . . and I heard nothing. I walked to our favorite spot, which Owen had found out about and. . . the ground was all dug up. You know, like something had been buried there. I realized that Owen had killed him. That's the only thing that would have kept Hewitt from me. I couldn't go to the police. Daddy was always insistent that the police never come around us. He was really pretty paranoid. And it would have destroyed my Mom too knowing that Owen was capable of murder. Plus I had no proof. There was no way I was digging him up." Blanche stared off into space going through her memories. "Oh, we had a real love. Not that trashy-romance, cheap-novel crap. This was the real thing. And all this time . . . Wait a minute." She sat up and read the card again. "He's the *owner* of the *carnival*?"

"That's what he said—and the food concessions."

Suddenly Blanche started stomping her feet and hitting herself in the head with her fist. "I am stupid, stupid, stupid!"

"What? What?"

"The carnival! The last week we were together, Hewitt and I went to the carnival. Owen followed us, like he did most of the time. Hewitt and I joked about leaving town with the carnival, traveling the countryside. That last night . . . Hewitt said he thought we should run away. It was the only way to be free of Owen. But I couldn't do that to my parents. Plus, I would miss them. I asked Hewitt to wait but . . . Owen must have done something. Hewitt would not just leave me." They sat silently for several minutes. "Is he married?" Blanche suddenly asked.

"My conversation with him wasn't that personal. I have no idea. However, he did say something about families meddling. I bet he was thinking of you." DeMaris smiled thinking this would console her.

"Call him."

"What?"

"You've got a cell phone." Blanche thrust the card at her. "Call him and find out if he's married."

"Wha . . . who . . . how . . . you don't . . . huh? How many years has it been?"

"I haven't seen my beloved for more than twenty-five years. I don't want to waste another minute."

"But if he is . . ."

"At least I know he's alive. But—if he's *not* married," she shook the keys in her hand, "you're driving me to wherever he is."

"Aaahhhh, I don't like to drive; I don't enjoy driving . . . I don't drive."

"No, *I* don't drive," said Blanche. "You do."

"What I do isn't technically called driving."

Blanche stood up her six feet three, large boned frame towering over DeMaris. "I didn't get these keys away from Viva for nothing. *You* are driving me somewhere."

"Okay, okay," DeMaris scooted down the bench. Blanche followed. "Just hear me out. I've seen Hewitt. He's not bad-looking. If— if you were going . . . to see him . . . after twenty-five years . . ."

"Spit it out. You're wasting time, my time. Viva's gonna come out any minute."

Yes, Viva. That would be good. "Well, you would want to— to look your best, wouldn't you?" DeMaris moved to the end of the bench and realized she'd have a better chance of escape if she was moving instead of sitting. She stood up. "You would have to . . . take a shower . . . and do something with *that* ha— your hair. Dress a little nicer and . . ." She looked at the nearest door, "Get your teeth cleaned."

"I'll do all that for Hewitt. After all, there are a lot of pretty girls who go to the carnival."

"Uh-huh. And if he's married?"

"Then you'd better start running cuz I don't have Owen to kill."

"That's what I was afraid of," said DeMaris as she flipped open her cell phone.

⸺ ⸺ ⸺

"Okay, Blanche," Viva said as she walked out of the attorney's office and into the waiting room. She stopped when she realized it was empty. "Blanche? Blanche, honey?"

Viva stomped across the room and flung open the door that led to the elevators. The eerily silence was shattered when she screamed, "DeMarrrrisssss!"

Chapter Twenty-Six

"Oh, DeMaris. I want to thank you for saving my dad's life," Gloria hugged her as DeMaris walked into the shop.

DeMaris looked beat but she smiled. "I understand he's going to be all right. I'm glad. Um, I've had a long day but as I was just coming through town I remembered that when I was in here the other day a picture caught my eye. Here, this one. Can you wrap this and send it to my daughter? Her birthday is next month and she would love it."

Gloria stood there for a moment and then brightened. "Sure, I can do that. In fact, it's on the house. A thank-you for what you did for my dad."

"Oh, no, no. That's not necessary."

"DeMaris, please. It's the least I can do. Think about it. You were the only one who knew how to land that plane."

"I don't know about that. Melissa's never flown a plane but she's certainly picked up a lot from her boyfriend."

"But she wasn't in the front seat and as you just said, she doesn't have the experience. Dad would be dead; you girls too. Who knows where the plane would have crashed? It could have hit a house, an apartment building. A lot of people could have been hurt or killed. I am so very grateful that none of that happened. Thank you. Please, let me have your daughter's address. I'll be happy to ship it."

"Well . . . okay, thank you." DeMaris wrote out the address while Gloria fished around in her cash drawer.

"Here, you might as well take these too." Gloria thrust a handful of checks at her.

DeMaris took them and thumbed through them, perplexed. "I don't understand. These are checks that I've written. That I've written all over town. How is it you have them?"

"I was trying to find a way to thank you," Gloria unhooked the picture from the wall and set it on the counter, "and then I remembered the shop owners were holding onto your checks so I thought, why not pay a few—all—as a thank-you? So, thank you. *I* paid *all* of them; so there's your checks back."

"Why?"

"For saving my dad!"

"No. Why were the shop owners holding onto my checks? From before the plane incident?" DeMaris pointed out the date on one of the checks.

Gloria's mouth dropped and her eyes widened. "I— we— because you— it's because they're from out of town, out of state, *way* out of state. That's— that's how things are done here."

"No," said DeMaris loudly, "that's *not* how things are done. Why are people holding onto my checks in this town?"

❦

"Here she is! Here she is!" yelled Sara as DeMaris walked in the house. "We've been worried sick," Sara said as she hugged her.

"I told Viva I was fine."

"No," said Viva, who was surrounded by the rest of the sisters. "Saying 'I'll be home late seeing as how I'm lost' and hanging up the phone, and then not answering it again, is not the same thing as saying you're fine. Where's Blanche?"

"You're not going to believe this," DeMaris held up both hands excitedly, "she fell in love and ran away with the circus."

"Oh, honestly!"

"Come on!"

"DeMaris!"

"Where is she?"

"Okay, fine. In actuality, it was a carnival, but I don't think it has the same ring as 'ran away with the circus.' Think about it 'ran away with the carnival'—"

"DeMaris!"

"Remember at the art fair, all that food I brought back? It was Blanche's long-lost love who bought me the food. She thought Owen had killed him twenty-five years ago."

"Earth to DeMaris! We know *you* bought that food," said Melissa. "I mean, why would anyone give you a tray full of food when he just met you?"

"This is part of your book, isn't it?" asked Caroline.

"You didn't say you were DeMaris Azaygo, did you?" asked Shay.

"We've been reading your notes," said Sara.

"You've been reading my notes?" yelled DeMaris.

"We're worried about you," said Jacyne. "You've been strange since—well—always but we've noticed something is different. Ever since you burst in here with 'I'm living my own mystery' you've been . . . preoccupied."

"How dare you!" said DeMaris. "I've always told you you're not allowed to read my notes. They're private."

"And we've always respected that," Shay stepped in, "but you have been a little off the wall, even for you. We were getting ready to call the police. Then we thought maybe we'd find something in your notes. It will certainly make an interesting story. We found it quite entertaining."

"Where is Blanche?" Viva enunciated each word.

"She learned the love of her life was waiting for her; so I took her to him," smiled DeMaris.

"Get out of book mode!" snapped Viva. "What really happened?"

"Don't yell at me," DeMaris yelled back. "It was your smart idea to give her your car keys."

"No! Don't tell me! It was bad enough thinking you were driving my car! Blanche? Oh no, no, NO!" Viva wailed.

"It's fine. At least, I think so. I went to the grocery store and looked under the lights. It appears to be fine."

"What happened?" asked Jacyne.

"Well," DeMaris hesitated. *Where to begin?* "While we were waiting for Viva and the attorney, Blanche started waxing nostalgia—"

"Stop!" Viva put up a hand. "Just get to the point. What *happened to Blanche*?"

"She understands things better than you think. She was afraid you were going to put her away forever and then she thought of a friend for me to call. She didn't like the answer and decided to take it out on me. I had to run for my life!"

"Oh, come on, DeMaris."

"What friend does she have living on the streets?"

"You've seen how she gets. Blanche is a large woman. A large, scary woman! I did yell for you—"

"Never heard ya."

"How convenient. I took off running with her right behind me. But thanks to *Greg*," DeMaris emphasized his name, "I was able to outrun her."

"Yeah, that took effort," mumbled Liset.

"Once she realized she couldn't catch me on foot, she got in the car and just took off. I chased her for a while but I lost her."

"She doesn't know how to drive!" wailed Viva.

"Tell me about it. You guys thought I was bad."

Viva ran outside to check the car.

The girls stood in a half circle. Finally Sara said, "You've got the makings of a good story."

"Thank you," said DeMaris dryly.

"We've never read your notes before," Shay said.

"We think you have a good chance of publishing this one," this from Melissa. "We like it."

"Have you got an ending for it yet?" asked Liset.

"Maybe. It's just a rough outline."

"We're kind of curious to know how it ends," said Jacyne.

"Well," clearly DeMaris was pissed. She folded her arms across her chest and said, "I am going to write that my character took a shower at her own apartment, had her hair colored and styled, her nails done, and even used makeup. They found a dentist whose hygienist was willing to clean her teeth. She will still need some dental work but her teeth look pretty good. Then, some new clothes were bought for her WITH A CHECK. They make it to the bank in Spokane before they close," DeMaris looked toward Viva who had just walked back in from the garage, "She was quite happy with the contents of her safe deposit box, although I— I mean my character is still wrestling with some of the moral issues of that." DeMaris noticed their puzzled faces—except Viva who gritted her teeth and shook her head. "They went to the carnival—nope, I'm still liking circus—to unwind and there, lo and behold, was her long-lost love.

"I hope I can do the looks on their faces justice when I write about the moment they saw each other for the first time in twenty-five years —across the crowded fairway. Blanche was a transformed woman; she didn't look half bad. I doubt you girls would recognize her. I mean, in the book my character looks so changed.

"Her long-lost love had never married. He left notes for her in their secret spot whenever he came to town, making sure he didn't run into the evil twin brother. But she— my character had thought her brother had killed him and buried him by the old oak tree; so she could never bring herself to visit their secret spot. What was actually buried there was a . . . hmm, a toy chest. No, I'll have to think of something else. It also explained why his parents never filed a missing person's report."

"Gosh, you think of everything."

"Now, in my story, I think I'm going to have him walking through the woods, getting bashed on the head from behind, and waking up some time later to discover he is with the carnival, er, circus. Should I give him amnesia or just write he thought it'd be best to lie low for a while? He would come back when his love told her she was ready to leave with him. But remember he continued to leave notes as to where she could reach him, and she never responded. So, what was he to think?"

"I think it sounds great."

"Yeah. You really need to try to publish it."

"Yes!"

"Uh-huh. Well, with that nine-to-five job you all keep saying I need to get, I doubt I'll finish it let alone see it published."

"My car looks okay," volunteered Viva, unimpressed with the story. "Did you ever find Blanche?"

"No, I've been all over town, asking everybody, even the cops. Nobody has seen her and I figured I couldn't come home empty-handed so I've wandered every street there is. That's how I found the car. She left the keys in it. I drove around looking for her some more, nothing. Finally came home to face the music."

"We'll look for her tomorrow," said Viva. "You do know where you found the car, right?"

DeMaris just glared at her.

"Yes, of course you do."

⁓   —⋅—   ⁓

The girls could hear Viva on the phone but only DeMaris perked up when she heard, "Fine, but I assure you there is no Lisa Caldwell staying here." Viva hung up the phone and immediately turned to DeMaris.

"I can explain," said DeMaris, even though she had no idea with whom Viva had been talking.

"Yes, you always can, can't you?" Viva said.

"I try," DeMaris smiled. "What's up?"

Viva folded her arms across her chest. "That was the police. They found the other guy who broke into the house. In fact, they had recently picked him up for something else."

"Well, that's good, isn't it?" asked DeMaris.

A few of the girls came into the room. "Who's the other guy?" asked Shay.

"Well, it turns out it's somebody DeMaris knows," said Viva.

All eyes turned to DeMaris who screwed up her face. *Who do I know? Oh!* "Brian! I knew he was no good!" DeMaris said triumphantly.

"No."

"Good gravy! Chuck? But he was with me— "

"No," said Viva quickly. "Denny Caldwell."

"Oh, that's right; you did mention Lisa Caldwell, didn't you."

"Yeah, and exactly who is that?"

"Nobody. Just somebody I made up."

Viva put a hand to her head.

"How does De know him?" asked Sara.

"Yes," said Viva. "Maybe now is the right time to tell us."

"Yeah— I— Well, this is where I can explain," said DeMaris. "I met him—" *At Blanche's apartment? At his apartment? Then I'd have to explain how I got their address. They'll never let me keep the key after this if they think I'm actually using it . . .Well, Viva knows I did . . .but she didn't really pursue that, did she? Boy, they are getting just like Kirk. They no longer want to be accomplices.* "—at Gloria's shop. Yeah, I needed to use the bathroom one morning during rowing practice and her assistant was talking to some guy and we got to talking and he said his name was Denny Caldwell."

"Oh, really? Because Denny tells a different story. I'm sure the police will be interested in yours though. They're on their way over." Viva smiled.

"Oh. Thank you for the heads up. Guess I'll have to . . . stick with . . . the truth."

"Yeah, guess so."

"So, why not try it out on us?" offered Shay.

"Fine. When we were shopping at Walmart, I looked up Foxx's in the phone book. Got an address and I went there. Denny lives next door. I bumped into him."

"And you had to mention *me* to him." This was clearly why Viva was upset.

DeMaris thought for a moment. "No, I never mentioned your name. I never mentioned anybody's name."

"Denny told the police he met a woman coming *out* of the Foxx's apartment. She mentioned that she was thinking of renting the place and that she was working through a *real estate agent!*"

"Oh. Yeah. I did say that. But I didn't mention your name."

"No. He already knows me through Maureen. He put two and two together. He refuses to say what they were looking for here. Any ideas?"

"What else do we have here that would interest him?" asked Liset.

"Blanche?" offered Jacyne. "The bird?"

They all thought about this for a moment.

"No," Viva shook her head, "some of my drawers were rifled through. They were looking for some *thing*."

"And, Blanche is safe now," said DeMaris.

"What? With the carnival?" snarled Melissa.

"Hey, if we can't find her, nobody can." Everybody looked at DeMaris. "Maybe the key?" she offered.

"No, Maureen gave him one," said Viva.

"Maureen was stupid enough to give him a safe deposit key?" asked DeMaris.

"No. I meant the apartment key. You're right though . . ." said Viva.

"Why are the police coming over here?" asked Liset.

Viva smiled. "Well, as I said, Denny described the woman he met coming out of Blanche and Owen's apartment. And, gosh darn, if one of the police officers didn't think the description fit the same woman who has been seen around town with Blanche, at the dumpster and when they arrested Tim Farley. Although, I did tell the police that there was no Lisa Caldwell staying here."

All eyes turned to DeMaris.

"So?" asked DeMaris, "What do they want to talk to me about?"

"Well, it seems that Owen Foxx was murdered in his apartment. Denny said you did it."

Chapter Twenty-Seven

It was their last night together for another year; they sat around the pool, drinks in hand, enjoying appetizers prepared by Liset and Viva. Viva looked around. "Where's De?"

"I'm coming," DeMaris strolled out of the garage carrying Sophocles in his cage. She smiled at Viva as she hooked him to his stand.

"Oh, God," groaned Viva. "You've been teaching him swear words, haven't you?"

DeMaris laughed. "You're always so suspicious. I promise you I have not taught him any swear words. I just thought he'd like some company."

In between taking the boat out, shopping, eating and lounging, the girls had split up and scoured the city and countryside looking for Blanche. Well, seven of them had—DeMaris had not. "She's been taking care of herself for years. When Blanche wants to come back she'll find us—well, Viva anyway," said DeMaris.

"I am selling this house," said Viva.

"So? Tell the buyers to be on the lookout for an extremely large woman with ratty hair. And to send her your way when she shows up."

"Oh, yeah, there's a selling point."

"Viva, she's fine. Trust me on this."

"What? That she's found her true love and is living with him?"

"Something like that, yes."

"So, DeMaris," said Liset as she sat down next to her, "what was it like telling the police the truth? You did tell them the truth, didn't you?"

"Yes! It actually worked to my advantage!" DeMaris looked surprised. "I mean, Owen had been dead for a while, even before I was in town. I had no reason to kill him—obviously, as I'd never met him. Denny, on the other hand, has a rap sheet which includes assault and battery. Plus, the police had an eye witness who put Denny in the apartment at the approximate time of Owen's demise. Also, as I was talking to the police it suddenly hit me: When I first met Denny he asked me if Blanche was renting out the apartment. Not Blanche and Owen. Because he already knew Owen was dead. *And*, I was able to prove that I was the one who made the anonymous tip to go look for Owen. He'd still be rotting in that closet if it wasn't for me." She raised her glass slightly.

"How did you prove that?"

"I told them where I made the call, what day, approximately the time, and the fact that I used a very robotic voice. Only the person calling it in would have known all that."

"So, Denny killed Owen?"

"Yeah, he slipped up about a couple of things and then finally admitted to it."

"Why did he do it?"

DeMaris squirmed in her seat. "Well, for some reason Denny got it in his head that the Foxxes had a lot of money. Thought they had it squirreled away someplace and patience wasn't his thing. He wanted the money and decided he was going to get the answer out of Owen and Blanche one way or another. Blanche left and . . . that just left Owen."

"So," Shay smiled, "you did actually solve a mystery—at least helped solve a mystery."

"Yes! Gosh, it was fun! I'll have to do this more often—"

"No!" four yelled.

"You have the makings of a good—a great story," offered Liset. "Please, let me send you the name of my friend who is an agent."

DeMaris put a hand up to stop her. Liset sighed and leaned back in her chair.

"Guys," said Jacyne after it had been silent for a moment, "I have some news to share with you." She smiled and they waited expectantly. "You know how we all changed our identities this week? Well . . . I really am a general, for real."

There was silence for a second and then squeals of joy and congratulations. After they calmed down, they listened as Jacyne told them about her promotion. "I know I should have told you, but I was afraid if I did, it would never happen. It's been sitting in Congress for months."

The conversation took an hour-long detour down memory lane and then they were all lost in thought.

"Ya know," said DeMaris, who had been quiet through most of the discussion, "I don't remember you treating me like I'm an idiot before this. Or have I just not noticed?"

The girls exchanged glances and then looked at Shay to answer. "De, you've always done crazy stuff, but this time you do have us concerned about your sanity. Out of the blue you and Kirk get divorced after how many years? Twenty-five? We hear you were living on the streets . . .you have us change our identities and you really go far with yours . . . pretending to be a famous writer and then telling us you're living with a thirty-seven-year-old actor when in actuality you're considering marrying a seventy-three-year-old retiree. Clearly, you didn't want us to know about him. You've always been prudent with money and this year, when you have no means of support, you're just throwing it around. You've been 'living your own mystery' which has taken you literally to the dumpster. You got us mixed up with a mentally handicapped woman that you've lost—"

"She's not really handicapped."

"The fact that you think Blanche is *not* handicapped . . . and not looking twice at Chuck, who we all think is a really decent catch."

"You don't even know him!"

"He's good-looking, owns his own business, and seems very interested in you."

"He does have a good reputation in the community," Viva added.

"Well, lah-de-dah. Do you realize newspapers are on the downslide? He truly believes I'm DeMaris Azaygo. Maybe he's after my money." She had meant it as a joke; however no one cracked a smile let alone a laugh.

"You seem to be making . . . a lot of bad choices," said Melissa.

DeMaris stared. They couldn't tell if she was mad or thinking. She swirled her wine around. "But, it's my life. I've always been cautious. For the first time I'm *living* and loving it."

"I'm sorry," said Jacyne, "*cautious* is not a word we have ever used to describe you."

"Well, I feel I've always been a cautious person. I stayed home and raised my kids. I've kept to myself. I've lead a sedate life. I'm not complaining—it's what I chose. It's just now I'm choosing something else."

"It's called a midlife crisis," said Caroline.

"So? I'm enjoying my midlife crisis. Apparently it's not a crisis to me, just to you guys. Look, I did all the things I was supposed to, it's finally my turn. I'm having fun—be happy for me."

"We are happy for you," said Liset.

"We just want you in the real world," this from Sara.

"You mean your world. Your world is no fun. I like the world I'm living in. Your world stinks."

"Yeah, talk like that doesn't scare us," mumbled Shay.

DeMaris sighed and sat up. "It's our last night together. I've been wrestling with something and . . . you're my best friends, you're my sisters. You need to know something."

"Oh God, she *is* dying!" cried Sara.

"Is it cancer?"

"You can beat this."

"We're here for you."

"What the hell?" DeMaris stared at them.

"We figured out that you were dying—it's the only explanation."

"Or that you were just seriously ill with something that is treatable. Just tell us what it is."

DeMaris burst out laughing. "I guess I have to tell you now. I don't want you all leaving here thinking you've seen the last of me. But, you all have to *swear* you won't tell a soul, especially the news media."

"Sure, De."

"No, I'm serious. My attorney wants you all to sign a letter to that fact— but I'm not going to make you do that. If I can't trust you after all these years to keep your mouths shut, a piece of paper's not going to do it. You truly cannot tell anyone what I'm about to tell you until . . . well, until I tell you you can. This is really big, people."

They all leaned forward.

"I haven't heard anybody swear an oath yet."

"I swear!" they yelled in unison.

"I am *dead serious* about this. Not a soul. Not your husbands, significant others, parents, *nobody*."

"Between us, we've kept a lot of secrets," pointed out Jacyne.

DeMaris nodded and took a deep breath. "I am— No, let me back up. Viva, you don't need to worry about DeMaris Azaygo ever coming here or finding out anything and slapping me with a lawsuit for defamation of character or whatever you think because . . . I am DeMaris Azaygo." She smiled and waited expectantly.

Silence.

And then, "Have you completely lost it?"

"*Why* would we believe that?"

"How stupid do you think we are?"

"You need to snap out of this delusion!"

213

"Have you immersed yourself so completely that— that— that you actually think you are her?"

"Can any one of us have her committed—I mean, just for a little while."

"I don't think so. We don't have—"

"Enough!" DeMaris yelled, raising her hands. "And no." She looked at Caroline who had asked the commit question. Taking a deep breath, she said, "Let me rephrase. I am going to be the *next* DeMaris Azaygo."

"The next?" queried Liset.

"Yes. I have a friend—some of you have met her—Sabrina D'azayga. She is wheelchair bound and dying of cancer. DeMaris Azaygo is our collaboration. Sabrina can't get out and do things and I'm always having something happen—how I fall into these things, I have no idea. Anyhow, she has always enjoyed me coming over and telling her about what happens when we get together each year. She knows all of you through my stories. Well, sitting in her house all day long, she started writing down our adventures and, of course, embellishing.

"Liset sent Liz Brown my way. I showed her my stuff and on a lark I showed her my neighbor's writing. My story was nice, but Sabrina had a special way of telling it which is why—sorry Liset, but I had to be kind of unpleasant to the other two agents you sent my way because I/we already had Liz. But I couldn't tell them that because we never wanted anyone to know who DeMaris Azaygo was."

"Yes, I was surprised when they said you refused to send them anything."

"So, Sabrina and I have collaborated on the books and I do get a percentage, and I will continue. She doesn't want the books to stop just because she won't be around. I've gotten to where my writing style is a lot like hers."

"Yes, I've noticed that," Liset stared at her.

"Noticed what?"

"Your writing style. Come on, you've sent us plenty of letters over the years. The little stories you put in. I've read all the Azaygo books and I don't see any difference. But when you tell people she's passed on—"

"Who said I was going to do that?"

They sat there for a minute. Liset leaned forward. "That's what you meant by being the next DeMaris Azaygo?"

DeMaris nodded. "I'm the one having the adventures. And I have helped write the manuscripts; so I'm not really being deceitful."

"What does Sabrina think of this?" asked Melissa.

"Oh, it was her idea. Now, DeMaris Azaygo can come out. Go to book signings, meet her fans, talk to reporters, have interviews, et cetera."

"Why didn't Sabrina do it?"

"She refused. Trust me, I tried to talk her into it. She's not someone who wants to go anywhere. She won't even go to the grocery store or the mall with me. She has a nice little home; she is comfortable and wants to be left alone for the most part. If she wasn't going to go out to do the everyday things she certainly wasn't going to do well meeting the public."

"Why didn't you do the publicity for her then?"

"I couldn't. You know I've always been a private person. I don't want—didn't want to do those things. I mean, yeah, I was living it and giving her all the ideas but she pretty much wrote them. I proofed and made corrections but . . . Now Sabrina would really like to hear about book signings and her fans. She wants to experience some of that before she passes on; so, although I was against it for a long time, now that I'm divorced, why not? The kids are grown. Kirk doesn't need me. I've found someone new. Why not give this pleasure to Sabrina? I finally realized I was being selfish in not granting her last wish. So, when I return home, I am going to announce—actually Liz is going to announce—my coming out."

"I hope she's going to clarify that," said Caroline.

There was silence while they absorbed the news.

"So," Shay cleared her throat, "what exactly are we swearing to?"

DeMaris held up her hands and with her right index finger tapped her left index finger. "You can't breathe a word of this until it's on the news." She hit the middle finger, "You are *never* going to be able to speak about Sabrina. The secret dies with her." She landed on the ring finger, "I see no reason why you would need to say anything to anybody about me being delusional about the actor Greg Delray." They laughed. "I think it would only make my Greg feel bad."

DeMaris held her left hand out palm down. Immediately seven hands were on top of it.

"We swear."

Chapter Twenty-Eight

As DeMaris hauled herself out of the cab, Greg stood on the porch and smiled at her.

"They insulted me!" she screamed at him.

He raised an eyebrow. This was not the welcoming response he was expecting.

"My sisters, my friends for thirty years, didn't believe a word I said!" She stomped up the porch lugging her two suitcases. "They treated me like some poor relative they had to rescue. I'll have you know," she was still worked up as she came face to face with him, "Kirk and I own several thousand acres of *prime real estate* that we've been offered millions of dollars for! And they think I'm a farmer! A nonworking farmer! Yeah, well, try eating without one!"

"Honey, if you're a nonworking—" Greg started to comment but then stopped when he saw the look on her face. "I like your hair."

My—" she touched a hand to her head. "Oh, yeah, my hair. I had to change it because . . . I can explain . . . well, I needed a change."

"It looks nice."

"Thank you."

"I appreciate you letting me know you were coming here, instead of having me meet you at Melissa's. Odd the phone cut out at that point. I would have picked you up at the airport if I had known what flight you were on."

"I wasn't in the best of moods. You wouldn't have been happy to see me. All I thought about was *them* and various ways to do them in. I may kill them all off—in my next book. Serve them right. And besides, I took the train," she mumbled this last bit.

He smiled. "I'm glad you're back. I really missed you."

She smiled back. "God, I missed you too." Her face softened as she gave him a loving look and then suddenly, "Out of my way; I have to use the bathroom."

He leaned against the door frame and crossed his arms, blocking her path. "What's your answer?"

"Greg, I really have to go!"

"Yes or no. You're not getting in without an answer. And the wrong answer won't get you in at all."

"You know the age differ—"

"No. We've hashed that around enough. I gave you this time away to think about us."

"Did you think about us?" she countered.

"Yes, and my feelings haven't changed any, except that I missed you terribly." He leaned over and gave her a long kiss.

"Oh," she moaned; then opened her eyes. "Don't do that. I'll wet my pants!"

"I've never had a girl say that to me. What a turn-on."

She slapped the back of her hand against his arm. "Please! I really have to go to the bathroom." He didn't budge. Finally she smiled. "I wish the girls could see you. I wish they could see what great shape you're in. They're worried I'll end up taking care of you."

"Oh, when I talked with Shay, I thought I could reassure her that I am in good physical shape, a retired insurance salesman with a nice little nest egg . . ."

She saw the disappointment on his face. "I'm sorry, honey. They weren't impressed. They just have a real problem with our ages. As if it's any of their business," her voice started to rise again. "They were so condescending! They are *not* invited to the wedding!"

He stood up straight. "Is that a yes?"

She smiled up at him. "That's a yes. No, you can't kiss me until I've gone to the bathroom," she warned.

He chuckled. He pulled out something long and slender from his back pocket and held it out to her. "Oh! My grandmother's hatpin! You wonderful man! You found it! Thank you!" She took it from him. He stepped aside and held the front door open.

She started to push against the screen door and then stopped. Pressed up against the door were balloons. Everywhere, balloons. She turned back to him.

"Good thing you have a hatpin that fits through the screen. I will let you hit the bathroom first, since it's so close, but after that you have to pop all of the balloons in the hallway to find a little box. So, pop away."

⸻ ⸻ ⸻

"—and I'm going to personally strangle each and every one of my sisters. Do you know what they did . . . Gloria hands me the checks I wrote all over town." DeMaris pursed her lips. They were lying in bed facing each other. Greg was still listening to DeMaris bemoan her sisters. "Seems she knew about my divorce and everybody thought that I had no money and since Gloria knows all the business owners, Viva had her round up all of the checks I had written so that my sisters could divide them up and pay them because *obviously* I couldn't!"

"What do you mean, you have no money?" asked Greg.

"*That's* what my sisters told everybody in town! That I have no money! That I lost what little I had in the divorce!"

Greg lay there, perplexed. "Is that what you told them?"

"No, that's not what I told them. I have no idea where they got that information. In fact, I haven't told anyone the terms of my divorce. It's nobody's business except Kirk's and mine." She looked at him and then added, "You don't have to worry. I can support myself."

He chuckled. "I'm not worried. Let's remember, I do have a little bit of money coming in."

"God, they were so condescending! And worried that Viva would be embarrassed having a friend bouncing checks all over town. Have I ever embarrassed my friends? Have I ever embarrassed my friends by bouncing checks, I mean. Well . . . *knowingly*, bounce checks? To think I would purposely write bad checks because I didn't live there. Is that what they think of me? I want you to know, I have *never* bounced a check . . . I have never *consciously* bounced a check." DeMaris lay there for a moment. "I am so mad at them. That after all these years they would think I would stoop that low."

"I love you—and I don't think you would ever do anything like that."

She gave Greg a smile and once again admired the gold band with a large oval diamond surrounded by a cluster of smaller diamonds. "I am so *mad* at them! How could they do that to me? They treated me like a child the whole time. What did Gloria tell the store owners to get my checks back? She's not in her right mind? Poor thing, she thinks she has money but she doesn't or worse, since she's not from around here she figured she

218

wouldn't get caught bouncing checks? I have half a mind to never reimburse anybody *and* to not invite them to our wedding."

"DeMaris," Greg leaned up on one elbow, "they didn't know who you really were."

"So? They've known me for thirty years! They should know whether I'm an honest person or not."

"Hey," he waited until she brought her eyes up to meet his, "who's having the last laugh now?"

Jacyne sat in the back of the taxi headed for the Atlanta airport. 'Pick up a magazine, read a book.' Hmm.

She paid the taxi and found she had plenty of time to kill before boarding her flight. *Maybe . . . maybe DeMaris is right. Okay, a compromise. Just one or two drinks and a magazine or a book. Sure, it's a short flight back to D.C. I can do this.* Jacyne found the bookstand and was thumbing through magazines when a handsome face caught her eye. Even though she wasn't into celebrity tabloids, she smiled and reached for it when she recognized the face of DeMaris's dream man, Greg Delray. ACTOR TO WED. *Oh, won't De be disappointed.* Sitting behind other magazines she pulled it out of the rack to finish reading the rest of the caption: RECLUSE AUTHOR. Her jaw dropped as a very familiar face smiled back at her. What? *What? WWWHHHAAATTT?*

Jacyne whipped out her cell phone. She hit speed dial for Viva. She ripped through the magazine and started to read.

"Viva!" she screamed as soon as the phone picked up. "Have you seen the front page of—"

"Jacy—? Is— you? When is the gov— ment— get— you a new pho—? I can't un— stand—"

"I *am* on a new phone!" screamed Jacyne. A woman grabbed her daughter and hurried past her. "It says here that DeMaris—*our* DeMaris—is marrying that hunky TV guy! Hello? Viva? Damn it." Reception was poor, obviously. She glanced at more magazines and a few newspapers with pretty much the same headlines; she pulled them off the rack, hurried outside of the building and punched speed dial again. "Viva? Can you hear me now? Have you seen the paper? I can't believe this—"

"Excuse me, ma'am. You'll have to follow us back inside the store." Jacyne looked up, startled to see a man on either side of her.

"What?"

"Possession of stolen property." He tapped the magazines and newspapers in her hand.

"Don't be stupid. I have no intentions of paying for this tabloid crap."

"Yes, we can see that."

"No, no, what I meant was—listen, I didn't steal these—I can afford this —I was going to return them." They each put a hand under an elbow and turned Jacyne back toward the magazine stand.

She shook them off. "I don't have time for this. I have a plane to catch! I'll have you know I'm a general in the United States Army!"

"Yeah, sure you are lady."

"Wait a minute! Wait a minute! I can explain! My phone wasn't working inside—"

"You can explain it to the police."

She turned to the man on her right who hadn't spoken but had an elbow. "I'm doing research on a book."

———

Greg started to holler but caught himself. The music was much too loud, DeMaris would never hear him. He smiled because he knew when she had it playing that loudly . . . As he suspected, she was lip-syncing to Petula Clark. Her eyes were tightly closed as she sang and grooved to the music. Unlike some of the women who had been in his life, he knew she would not be embarrassed when caught. It was simply who she was.

". . . tell your friends that I'm your one and only . . ." She smiled broadly and chuckled, lost in her memories. Greg put a leg on either side of hers, making sure he didn't touch her.

". . . so kiss me now as if you really mean it . . ."

He brought his mouth down on hers and she let out a startled screech.

He pulled her off the sofa and they wrapped their arms around each other. "Don't ever ask me again why I love you," Greg said. "You're gonna be the one who keeps me young."

"Do you think we have a trashy-romance, cheap-novel crap kind of love?"

He smiled, ran a finger down her cheek and kissed her softly. "Well, I don't think we have a crap kind of love but, yes."

"What? No!" She stepped back from him.

"Sure. It means we'll live happily ever after."

"That's a fairy tale."

"Oh. I think of those awful romance novels I used to tease my sister about. Why are you pouting? You see us falling apart?"

"No," she quickly reassured him. "I just think of a tawdry novel as . . . cheap. I think of us as . . . *Pride and Prejudice*, classic."

He drew her into him and she wrapped her arms around his waist lying her head on his chest. "That's what I said: happily ever after."

Viva stared at the newspaper. It was true? It was ALL true? She'd kill DeMaris when she saw her. But only if she got there first imagining their other sisters were plotting to do the same.

She made us look like fools! And she's not inviting us to the wedding? She read the paragraph again. "My friends who have been supportive of this May/December romance will be invited. I have other close friends who scoffed at the idea; they will not be invited.' *Maybe I'll just crash it!*

Viva slammed down the paper.

"Wipe fingerprints."

"Sophocles, shut up!" Another reason to ring DeMaris's neck.

And to think I had her stenciling my house! I paid her! How am I ever going to explain that to people? Yes, I'm friends with international best-selling author DeMaris Azaygo but I had her stencil my house that wouldn't sell because I didn't think she could actually make any money writing; so I paid her. No, I'm not invited to the wedding; but yes, I am a very close friend. Have known her for years. Shit!

"Hide dead body."

"Sophocles!"

Wait a minute, the thought slowly dawned on her. *DeMaris Azaygo stenciled my house. DeMaris Azaygo, famous, world renowned author and personal friend, stenciled my house.*

This advertisement ran in the newspaper the following day:

House For Sale. Modern 4 bedroom, 2½ bath, porch with pool. Right on the water. Rooms decorated by best-selling author DeMaris Azaygo.

It sold in no time.

Chapter Twenty-Nine

While they were having dinner, DeMaris spoke once again about her sisters and how they didn't understand her. Clearly she was still bothered.

"Well," said Greg, "you can't exactly blame them for thinking that way. They said you've always been frugal with your money, always looking for a discount, which you still do; and you and Kirk did most of the maintenance and upkeep on your house instead of contracting it out. None of them realized how much land you owned—"

"Yes, I'm the Beatrix Potter of Michigan."

"—and then there are Kirk's cars." He paused. "Saying things like, 'Kirk bought another clunker,' and 'Kirk is at the junkyard trying to find a piece to get his car started,' tends to make one think he's fixing up cars to sell to teenagers for a couple of hundred bucks not vintage cars that sell for thousands."

"They jumped to that conclusion."

"I'm sorry, but when you talked about Kirk's cars, I jumped to the same conclusion. You may describe well in books but you don't in real life."

She gave a slight snort. "Sabrina used to say the same thing."

Greg saw the distant look on her face. "You miss her."

"Yeah," DeMaris agreed. "Talk to me about . . . your day." She ate a mouthful of potatoes and realized he hadn't said anything. She looked at him to see him studying his plate. "Greg?"

"I . . . actually have big news to tell you."

She felt her face grow warm. For the last half hour at least she had done nothing except talk about herself. *The phone call.* She vaguely remembered the phone ringing and Greg being very quiet afterward. She'd been too caught up in her own thoughts to think about him; let alone ask him. "Another movie offer?" she smiled.

"No, something better."

"Better?" She couldn't imagine anything and shook her head.

"Something more personal."

"Tell me!"

"I received a phone call from—" he paused for effect, "Allison."

DeMaris sat up straight. "My daughter called you?"

"Uh-huh. I don't know if it was all the calls and e-mails we sent her or her Aunt Jacyne strong-arming her, but she called. I also got to talk with your sorority sister. She's really a general?"

"Yeah, as it turns out. So, how did it go with Al— Wait a minute. When was this?"

"Today."

"Allison was in D.C. or Jacyne was in Michigan?"

Greg sat for a moment and decided the best idea was to say, "I don't know."

"Well, I'll be calling Jacyne after dinner to find out . . . if only I was speaking to her. Sorry. Go on. I'm very glad she called. Wait! How did it go?"

"It was okay. She just wanted to make it perfectly clear that I was not going to be any kind of a dad to her. I will simply be the guy her mother lives with.

"I told her that was fine with me but for her mother's sake I'd like it if the two of us were at least civil to each other. She thought about that for a minute and decided she could do that. I told her that I'd like to meet her. She was agreeable albeit reluctant."

DeMaris digested this. "Well, it's a start. And I'm very glad she called, but she better have been doing it from Michigan. Although, why Jacyne would be visiting Allison at college . . ."

"Well, if you were speaking to your sisters . . ."

She glared at him. "I'm still speaking to my ex-husband. I'll call him."

"Yes, well, honey, you kind of brought it on yourself . . ." he said quietly and stopped. If he didn't watch it she wouldn't be speaking to him either.

"Let's talk about something else," she said tersely.

"Okay. I went jogging today without my favorite partner along." She made a face at him. "Read some more of book number six and fielded phone calls. And then, I cooked dinner."

"Dinner was very good. Thank you."

"Why don't we talk about the wedding?"

"Book mode's going back up," she warned.

He hated book mode. Book mode was her polite way of saying she was tuning him out. "Why? Why can't we set a date?"

"I'm thinking of you."

"You're sparing my feelings by saying you want to put our wedding off indefinitely?"

"No! I'm not saying that . . . I just . . ."

"It better not be the age thing again," he warned.

She shook her head. "I've got one failed marriage behind me, I don't think you should be marrying a divorcee. You should marry someone . . . better suited to you." She couldn't look at him as she heard the clang of his fork hit the plate.

"I don't think that being married for twenty-five years can really be called *failed*."

"Actually twenty-seven."

"I still think that being together for twenty-seven years is a long time and who is better suited for me than you? I've dated a lot of women. It's not like I don't have any experience."

"Okay, fine," she said. "I think you're getting a raw deal. I'm baggage. I'm older, I've had two kids; I'm not giving you any—"

"I don't *want* kids! If I did, I'd already have them."

"—and I have nothing to offer you! You will eventually realize that and dump me which will break my heart. AND my friends will look on me with pity and millions of your fans will say, 'What was she thinking anyway? Like she could hang onto him.'"

It was quiet for a long moment. Greg reached over and took her hand in his. He tugged on it. "Look at me." She barely raised her eyes to meet his. "You are a wonderful person. You constantly keep me guessing, on my toes, I never know what you're going to say or do next. You make me laugh. You're kind, you're generous. You're the only person I know who leaves my mother speechless."

"Oh, no. You're marrying me to get back at your mother!"

He rolled his eyes and briefly set his head down on the table. He brought his head back up. Her mouth was still open. "See, this is when your imagination is NOT a good thing. I love you. I adore you. I hate when you're away from me. I want you in this house. I want you to redecorate it to your liking because I want you to be happy."

"Why do you want an old lady? You could have yourself a twenty-year-old."

"I told you, I don't like kids. If we were the same age, would you feel this way?" The silence stretched. "De, tell me the truth. Why don't you want to get—"

"Why *do* you want to?"

"Because I am crazy about you. I finally understand how someone can be in a monogamous relationship. While you were in Idaho I had plenty of chances to be with other women and I wasn't the least bit interested. I just wanted you home. I checked my cell phone repeatedly to see if you had called. You don't feel the same way, do you?" He removed his hand and sat back.

"You're not going to understand this," she said quietly.

"Sure I do. You're not in love with me."

"I am *crazy* about you." She looked up at him.

"Then you're right, I don't understand."

"I have spent . . . a good part of my life . . . dreaming about the day when I would be a recluse."

"You've *been* a recluse!" he pointed out.

"Yes, well, not exactly. I mean, I associated with my neighbors, volunteered at the schools, did stuff with my friends . . . I just don't see the rush."

"Well, for me the rush is I don't want you to find out you really like being a recluse and you cut me out of your life completely."

She smiled. "That's not gonna happen."

"Why not?"

"Because as much as I enjoyed being with my sisters, I really missed you. I don't want to spend my life feeling like that."

"Here's my question," Greg said.

"What?"

"With Liz Brown announcing who you are, how are you going to be a recluse—with or without me in your life?"

"Yes, that is a problem," DeMaris conceded. "I am already beginning to regret being talked into that. I mean . . . I've been writing for years and there have been times when people have requested I do book signings or do a TV interview and . . . I have *wanted* to do those things but I knew that would change my entire life. I wouldn't be able to be *me* anymore. Now, at this point in my life, I decided I wanted to see what it was like; so I told Liz to go ahead and set things up while I went on this last vacation. I didn't think I'd be writing any more so now would be a good time and *then* I'd go off and be a recluse having tried everything. I never saw you coming."

Greg sat and digested this. "When do you— Do you ever see yourself marrying again?"

"Before I met you, I'd have given you a definite no. However, I do think about it. And Sara said something that made me think maybe I just want to be a recluse at times and then other times, not."

"You want to be alone, have your space?"

"Yes."

He sat quietly for a moment. "Are you planning on cutting out your kids? Your sisters?"

"Well . . . no." She sat for a long moment. "I'm not going to be a recluse, am I?"

He took both her hands in his. "How about if you were a recluse for a day? Or two? Maybe a week. Ya know, a couple of times a year. Could you be married then?"

She smiled. "You'd let me do that? Seriously?"

"If I was sure you weren't with some other guy, yeah. If it means that much to you."

She chuckled. "Okay, if I want to be alone, I am not sneaking off to be with someone else." She leaned across the table and gave him a long kiss. "You are a wonderful man."

"I have my moments."

Chapter Thirty

They rode Amtrak from California to Michigan and were staying in DeMaris's house while Kirk visited his parents. Between DeMaris letting the world know who she was and their engagement both of their cell phones had rung non-stop. For the three days that it took to travel across the country they had their phones turned off. Anyone calling them at that point was told to leave a message on DeMaris's house phone. Relatives and friends had this number. Anybody else who didn't have access they didn't need to hear from. Greg sighed as he stopped in front of the phone. "Boy, now that word is out about your identity and us, people are calling." He could see there were a slew of messages on the answering machine. Mostly well-wishers and one from Greg's mom not well-wishing.

"Sorry," Greg made a face.

"You see your mother twice a year. What do I care? Now I can report that I have mother-in-law problems. Something Kirk's mom robbed me of. She's a great lady whom I love dearly."

He pressed the button again. "Next message."

"DeMaris!" a man barked. "What did you do *this* time?"

"Is that Kirk?" asked Greg.

"No, Frank."

"Once again I'm involved with the police AND the FBI because of *you!*"

"Frank?"

"Yeah, Frank Sumnerfeld, Liset's husband."

"—because of that stupid purse you gave Liset. What were you doing with a bagful of questionable money?"

Greg chuckled. "Yeah, right. Like I've got the Chairman of the Federal Reserve here."

"Yeah, that's him."

"What?" Greg pressed the 'pause' button. "Your friend Liset is the wife of the Chairman of the Federal Reserve? Are you joking?"

"No. Of course, she doesn't carry any ID on her that says that. She never took his name, don't ya know. For the number of times that it would come in handy for me to prove that she's his wife . . . do you think that's the reason she doesn't carry ID?" this was the first that this idea had hit her. DeMaris shook her head. "There wasn't any money in that purse when I gave it to her. What's he talking about?"

Greg shook his head and hit the 'play' button.

"Why is there never a quiet moment around you?" continued Frank. "I told Liset—" the machine cut him off.

"You tell her that every year," DeMaris spoke to the machine. Then her eyes went wide. "Oh my gosh! The purse!" She softly beat her head on the desk numerous times.

"Next message."

"—when I get my hands on you—" It was Frank calling back.

"What is going on?" Greg did his own yelling.

"The Gucci purse I sold Liset! No, Coach, no, Prada—whatever. It is a main clue in my book." She pounded on the ten loose-leaf binders she had used to handwrite her manuscript. "I forgot about it! Completely forgot!"

"—I gave the FBI, the CIA, and anybody I could think of, all of your addresses and phone numbers!"

"Oh, not them again," sighed DeMaris.

"They groaned when I said your name! You can explain about the money."

"I told her not to buy it from me," yelled back DeMaris.

"That's just like you to stuff a purse with old dirty bills that caught the attention of the FBI and then let Liset be your scapegoat."

"What?" said both Greg and DeMaris.

They continued to listen to Frank's tirade. "Liset spent the money that was stuffed between the lining and cover. You've gone too far this time, DeMaris!" The phone slammed down.

DeMaris looked at Greg in shock. "I have no idea what he's talking about. That purse had money in it? Well, what can I tell the FBI, the CIA, whoever, Frank?" She glared at the answering machine. "Liset demanded and paid me big bucks for that purse. I don't know anything about any money." She started to page through the first loose-leaf binder to find what she'd written about meeting the bag lady.

"Maybe I could delete it," she sat and pondered this for a moment. "If I do that, then what to do with the clothes? Well, I could dump them— No, I borrowed them. And that sweater I knit for Jacyne was a bitch."

"DeMaris!"

Slowly she looked up. "What?"

"What is going on?" Greg kneeled so that his face was across from hers.

"I sold a purse to Liset that I got from a bag lady in town. Apparently it had money in it, which I knew nothing about. Liset was really eager to get her hands on it and paid me handsomely—although depending on how much money was in the purse, maybe not. Which is what I'll tell the FBI when they get here and it'll be back in Sumnerfeld's court. Don't worry. Like you've never had the FBI come to your house before," she snickered.

"No, I haven't."

"Oh."

"Have you— No, don't answer." He got up and listened to Frank's message again. Greg turned to DeMaris and saw her sitting with her head firmly on the table. She was mumbling into the binders. Was this how she wrote? As he drew closer, he finally heard her.

"No steak, lobster, or shrimp for me tonight."

"We're having steak," declared Greg. "My mouth has been watering all day."

Her head came up. "We were going to celebrate me finishing my book. I'm not done. I left out a key element! What do I do now? Take it all out, which really throws in a curve or two? I'll have to come up with a new storyline about where I stuffed the clothes I took off, a new storyline about how I met the bag lady, or do I act like the purse wasn't anything in the end? Maybe . . . she just gives me the purse to put my clothes in and that's that . . . No, then why stuff her in the trash compactor? Do I add a teaser for the next book?"

"I don't know. DeMaris, we're having steak," Greg said as he watched her stand up and tap her lips softly as she walked the length of the room and back.

"I still want to use the police throwing me out of the Pentagon. Have to be for my next book though. Hmm, some bad guys break into Frank's house," she chuckled. "He gets cracked over the head but not before he and Liset, sees that they've stolen her Gucci, Prada, Walmart, Sears, whatever purse. No, it'd have to be an expensive purse. Liset would never hunt down a cheap one."

"DeMaris!"

"Okay, but no shrimp or lobster. Yes, I haven't forgotten about the purse; I've saved it for the next adventure." She snapped her fingers in delight.

"Fine." He pointed to the answering machine. "Frank seems to have, what can I say, a familiarity with you. How do you know him?"

"I dated him in college."

"And?"

"And he's a fraternity brother."

"And?"

She sighed. "Frank was a great guy in college. Well, he still is when he's not yelling at me. We did a lot of stupid, *really* stupid stuff together. It's best that the world not know what the man did during his college career."

"Like what?"

She wagged a finger at him. "I gave him my solemn promise to never tell although he has given me some great ideas that went into my books over the years," she smiled. "Whenever he really starts screaming—what you heard there was nothing—I just remind him of what fun we had in college. That always shuts him up." She chuckled and then Greg watched as her face slowly changed, she sat up straight and let out a line of swear words he'd never heard so tightly packed together. "And now with me coming out so to speak he's got that same power over me! I've lost that edge over him! Oh, why oh why, did I let people talk me into not being a recluse! I was happy! This is not going to be any fun at all!" She screamed the last word out and then set her head down on the table. "Oh, God, that time that we—and then once when—" her head shot up, "our senior year, oh no, no, no."

Greg rolled his eyes and shook his head. "Can you tell me anything—"

"No."

"I just didn't realize what a wild and crazy person you were back then."

"Yes, I've really mellowed."

He couldn't tell if she was being sarcastic or honest.

"Honey," she sat up and looked at him, "do you really think a sane person is going to jump out of a plane at several thousand feet above the ground with you next week?"

"Right." He stood up. "I am going to throw the shrimp and lobster back in the fridge but I'm throwing the steaks on the grill. We eat in an hour."

"I need to work on my book." She started to write.

"I will get everything ready and call you to sit down. Eat and you can return to your writing but you are eating with me."

He heard a soft sigh as he turned to leave the room. "I am through with you."

"What?" he held his breath. *She can't be serious. Just because I want her to eat dinner with me?*

"I am through with you," she raised her voice this time to make sure he heard her. "How do you spell that through? T-H-R-E-W? That's not the right *through*. T-H-O-R-O— No, that's not right. How do you spell *through*?"

"T-H-R-O-U-G-H."

"Yes, of course. Thank you." She went back to scribbling furiously.

"You're in book mode, right?"

"Yes," she said in a warning tone.

He turned around and punched the answering machine for—

"Next Message."

"Well, I don't know if you heard—" the female voice sounded none too pleased.

"Jacyne," DeMaris nodded to Greg.

"—but I was arrested for stealing magazines and newspapers with your face on them. Thanks for giving me the idea to read a book or magazine on the plane instead of drinking and passing out!" Click.

"Two of your friends were involved with the police? Honey, you've got to run with a different crowd," said Greg.

"Next Message."

"I sold my house!"

"Viva," said DeMaris.

"I sold my house! I sold my house!" Viva continued to sing. "Thank you! Oh, I'm crashing the wedding, so let me know when and where so I can get a good seat."

Greg leaned toward the machine. "I swear there was somebody in the background talking about a dead body."

DeMaris shrugged. "What can I say? She's a realtor."

"Next Message."

"I was on your side the whole time!"

"Sara," said DeMaris.

"Even before you told us, I thought to myself why can't DeMaris be DeMaris Azaygo? You certainly can write—we all know that! Oh, I went right out and bought one of your books after I got home . . . the first one. I mean, I should start at the beginning, right?"

"Oh. She came that close to getting an invitation."

"Next Message."

"I found your boyfriend's address too and gave that out!"

"Frank," they both said.

Greg stopped the machine and looked at her. "I'm beginning to see why a few of your sisters have told me I need to make you come to your senses."

"I rarely come to my senses. It's much more fun living in the imaginary world."

He turned back to the answering machine.

"Next Message."

"DeMaris. This is Chuck. Engaged? How could you? I really thought we shared something at my place. Remember what you told me? Call me."

"I can explain," she said quickly as she felt Greg's eyes on her. "Ya know, I've gotta admit," she started to laugh, "for all my imagination, I never dreamed, not even in my *wildest* dreams, that at fifty I'd have two men fighting over me. Three, if you want to count Denny Caldwell." She slapped a hand over her mouth.

"*Who*?" yelled Greg.

"God, trust me! He is nothing! He's this loser I met while I was looking at an apartment."

"An apartment? Where?"

"In Spokane—*not* to live in!" she added hurriedly. "For my book."

"Your book comes in handy for a lot of answers, doesn't it?"

"I can explain."

"Oh, God. The girls warned me about that expression," he whined. Greg saw the expression on her face and asked, "Are you thinking about Chuck?"

DeMaris rolled her eyes and looked at him. "I'm not thinking about Chuck. I'm not even thinking about you!" She banged her finger into her temple. "I'm thinking about my book—and you keep talking."

"The girls warned me—" He stopped as he saw the seething look.

"Next Message."

"What were you thinking using my name at some bank in Spokane?"

"Melissa," said DeMaris.

"The police grilled me for over an hour! And then Joe Shaver called for a follow-up!"

"Again with the police?" asked Greg.

DeMaris nodded. "This always seems to happen when we get together. I have no idea why."

Chapter Thirty-One

Calling from coast-to-coast, they got Liset out of bed and Melissa as she was sitting down to dinner. "We shouldn't be having this conversation without DeMaris," said Sara.

"Hey," Jacyne shouted into the speakerphone Shay and her were sharing, "I did try calling—"

"Yes, she did," said Shay.

"—but I got Liz Brown, who told us DeMaris was at some awards banquet and would call us 'when she found the time.'" Jacyne was obviously miffed.

"Stop yawning, Liset."

"Sorry."

"Hey, Liset," said Caroline, "how was jail?"

"I wasn't in jail. I was simply held for questioning and released on my own recognizance."

"It said in the paper it was D. B. Cooper's money. What were you doing with it?"

"No, the better question," said Liset, "is what was DeMaris doing with it?"

"What'd she say?"

"She's avoiding me at the moment. Of course, she *said* she didn't know anything about it the first time Frank got a hold of her. Ha!"

"Well, in all fairness," said Shay, "I think if she'd known about the money she wouldn't have sold you the purse at any price."

"You're probably right. I just wish she'd tell me the truth about where the purse originally came from."

"Melissa, did DeMaris go back with you to your house?"

"No, she ditched me. She got on the train saying Greg was meeting her."

"What I don't get is how did they start dating after the train wreck? He went to the hospital and Melissa, I thought you and Ron took De back with you to your place."

"Haven't you been reading the magazines and newspapers? Watched any TV? One of her books was being made into a movie and she went down to watch the production. Greg had her phone number, he called and met her there. They started dating."

"Do you think DeMaris got any counseling for the train wreck?"

"Has she gotten counseling for any of the things she's gotten herself involved in over the years?"

"And think about it—that's just the stuff we know about. I'm re-reading her books," this from Liset, "and I wonder now how much was true and how much she made up."

"Yeah," said Jacyne thoughtfully, "a couple of times when I went and stayed with them, Kirk was bruised, had a broken arm . . . he was always vague about what happened. We know the trouble she gets into with us. Poor Kirk. Maybe they got divorced because he realized she was killing him."

"Poor Greg."

"Should we warn him?"

"Have you listened to him gush about her? He'll just tell DeMaris."

"He needs to find out for himself."

There was silence; then, "What I wouldn't give to be sleeping with a thirty-seven-year-old again."

"Melissa!" several shouted in unison.

"I'm only saying what you're all thinking."

There were several sighs.

"Does anyone know where DeMaris is right now?"

"Yeah, Philadelphia," Shay said. "She's doing a national tour. She's very disappointed that we haven't supported her."

"Maybe if she'd told us all these years, we'd have been reading her books."

"No, she understands that not all of us are readers. She means that when she's been close by, none of us have showed up for a book signing."

"Not true," said Liset. "I made a special trip to New York City last week to have her sign two of my books. People were lined up out the door. No way was I waiting through that when we wouldn't even be able to talk; and we planned on getting together here in another few months. She can sign them then."

"I know. That's why I told her I didn't show," said Shay.

"Wish I'd thought of that," said Sara.

"It was true! It was packed down here in St. Louis when she came a month ago."

"Oh."

"Is anybody else crashing the wedding with me?" asked Viva.

"She is going to invite us."

"Not if we don't start showing up at her book signings."

"What does she need us for? She's got plenty of fans."

"I think it's the principle of the thing."

"The principle? What about her keeping it a secret all these years?"

"She says," said Shay, "that it kept us *natural*. I mean, really, if we knew she was writing about us . . . would we have done or said the things we did?"

"But when I think about the things I *did* say," verbalized Viva, "like 'get a job,' 'you have no money.' And think about it, we were all so quick to jump to the conclusion that she was living on the streets because she was broke."

"Well, I think that was a logical conclusion to draw."

"Yes, but why? I just can't imagine that Kirk would have literally thrown her out. Wouldn't it have been logical to wonder why Kirk wasn't the one to leave? He has parents and siblings he could move in with. DeMaris has plenty of friends in the neighborhood—and she has us. I guess what I'm saying is we should have wondered *why* she went to live on the streets instead of immediately jumping to the conclusion she was thrown out." They were all quiet.

"Remember, we weren't supposed to find out."

"How were we supposed to know she was working on her next book? She should have told us, so that we didn't jump to that conclusion."

"Well, De's always been a private person," Sara reminisced.

"She could have told *us*."

"So, you're not going to the wedding if you get an invitation, Caroline?"

"I didn't say that. I just feel really duped."

"We all do," said Jacyne.

——— —·— ———

"Honestly, Frank. Can you stop shouting?" Greg could hear DeMaris in the other room. "I *did* talk to the police . . . I was not trying to avoid them

. . . I can explain. I was in California; Greg and I went to Michigan to see Kirk and the kids, and ya know what? The state is getting really serious about my community service," she said indignantly, "so that took up some hours. We went to New York to check out the apartment I bought; then I went to D.C., and then came back here to my fiancée's house in California . . . I stopped in D.C. to try to help Jacyne with her five-finger-discount on the magazines, but she didn't want my help . . . *I have no idea* how the money got in the lining of the Coach purse! All I can tell you is that Liset was determined to pay me for it. Although, the more I think about it, she still owes me two hundred dollars—if I was seriously going to make her pay, which I'm not . . . If I'd known almost a thousand dollars was sewn inside the lining I wouldn't have let her have it so cheaply . . . Yes, that's what I told the police . . . Because it's true! She did insist on paying— hello?"

Greg was sitting on the sofa when she came into the living room. He saw the look on her face. "Worried about what Frank's going to do?"

She ran two fingers along her chin and stared off into space. "Why would somebody hide the money? Who? I mean, why would Blanche's mother smuggle her own money out?"

"Why don't you let the police worry about that?"

"I'm not worried about the police," she gave him a disgusted look. "I want to know how it works into my book; and somehow I've got to work that bird in, cuz I forgot him too. God, am I losing my writing ability?" For the first time since Greg had met DeMaris, she looked worried.

———

"Do you realize that if she's using us as characters in her books that I'm probably Lucille— Lucky— Snodgrass!" yelled Caroline on the second conference call with her sisters.

"What are you complaining about?" asked Jacyne. "I'm Sergeant Diphard."

"Now, now. In every one of her books, the sergeant is always correcting people: the 'ph' is an 'f.' It's pronounced Dew-fard." A couple of them echoed Liset.

"Well, at least you're rough and tough," said Sara. "I think I'm the meek, wringing-my-hands, can't-make-a-decision *Miss* Pringle. I'm closing in on thirty, been engaged for six years, and still a virgin?"

"You guys," said Shay calmly, "these are *characters* in a book. These people are not you. These are not real people."

"Let's see," said Viva. "This coming from the main character's—DeMaris—best friend. Now, who would that be? Besides, you always come out looking good—some of us don't."

"Don't forget, Shay's character takes a fall. DeMaris's heroine has to save you from your drug addiction—"

"*What?*"

"Yeah, I think its book six or seven."

"She actually described what the two of you—all of us—went through pretty well."

"And that time she caught you doing a striptease on stage and she hauled you off and the bar brawl that followed—"

"There was no bar brawl!"

"There is in her book."

"It was really hilarious."

"Which book— No, never mind. The brawl never happened. That's what I mean. They are works of *fiction.*" *And when I get my hands on her I'll kill her*, thought Shay. *My daughter and her friends are starting to read her books.*

"Liset, are you still there?"

There was a hesitant, "Yeah."

"You're the most avid reader among us. How many DeMaris Azaygo books have you read?" asked Jacyne.

"Um, all of them."

"And you never suspected?"

"Of course, I suspected, but I could never get her to admit anything. Look at the house she lived in and the cars they drove. Did any of you think they had money? And the fact that every Christmas Liz sends me a very expensive present with a thank-you attached. I ask her every year what she is thanking me for and she just giggles. The closest I have ever gotten is when DeMaris told me to stop sending literary agents her way; that she didn't want one. I asked her why and she told me . . . No, I can't tell you."

"What?" a collective yell.

"Well— she, oh, God . . . she, ooohhh, she said she'd already written three books but she could never publish them because . . . her friends . . . might think it was about them. That they wouldn't understand they were fictional characters."

There was silence for a moment.

"So, that's why DeMaris Azaygo has always been a recluse?" asked Sara. "That's why she's never told us?"

"In a way, she's protected us," said Viva. "I mean, all these years . . . none of us thought anything about these books."

"I guess, in a way," offered Caroline, "we're internationally famous."

"She embellished a lot," said Melissa. "Some of it—a lot of it—didn't happen at all."

"That's why they're called novels, and she has that disclaimer about the characters in her books not resembling anybody. You know what I'm talking about."

"Do any of you buy that?"

"No."

"No."

"No."

"Come on, you guys," said Shay. "Sara, although I do agree with you that by process of elimination you are probably Miss Pringle, the fact is, you lost your virginity long before thirty, you were married with two kids before thirty, and you were only engaged for two years. So, Miss Pringle really isn't you, is she?"

"Well, when you put it that way . . ."

"And think about this: you/we are played by some very A-List actresses in the movies," said Melissa.

"Oh, my gosh! You're right," said Viva.

"I don't go to the movies," said Caroline, "Who plays me?"

This line of conversation took several minutes and ended with Shay voicing the opinion that they should meet their alter egos. After all, shouldn't being DeMaris's friends have some perks? Look at what they'd all been through!

"Has anybody talked to DeMaris?"

There was a slight laugh. "Yeah, Frank has."

More laughter. "DeMaris's favorite person."

"She did fly, mind you, to D.C. to try and help me out," offered Jacyne.

"How did that go?"

"I don't really want to talk about it."

"Oh, God, what did DeMaris do this time?" groaned Melissa.

"So, you did tell her that you accidentally walked out of a store with unpaid magazines?" asked Caroline.

"Yeah. I kinda told her about that. I mean, who knew she'd fly? Particularly to come to my rescue."

"What happened?"

"Well . . . I, no, I don't, you . . . ohh, I didn't tell her everything. Like the fact I convinced the store owner I really was a general and that I really was startled to see a close friend's face on the cover of several magazines and newspapers because she is going to marry a TV star. That my cell phone wouldn't work. That the owner dropped the charges against me because his wife is a huge fan of DeMaris's."

"Boy, you lucked out."

"Tell me about it."

"So, why'd she come to D.C.?" asked Sara.

"Because I forgot to mention to DeMaris that the incident actually happened in Atlanta. I guess she thought she needed to vouch for me or something. She arrived in D.C. and I couldn't have anybody find out what had happened. God, do you know what that would do to my career?"

"So, what did you do?"

There was silence for a few moments. "Don't forget," Jacyne finally said, "she said publicly that some of her closest friends weren't going to be invited to the wedding. I did it for all of us. I mean, look at the hell she's put us through for years. I had to stop her."

"What did you do?" asked Shay.

"I was away from the office when she showed up. What could I do? You know how she loves to talk to everybody. I had to quickly get her out of there. Plus, now she's recognizable . . . at least to those people who are big readers. I couldn't chance her telling somebody why she was there."

"And?"

"I told my secretary that other than being a well-known author, I didn't know who DeMaris was or why she was there, and to get rid of her."

Everyone except Jacyne laughed.

"De must have loved that, especially after flying in to save your ass," said Melissa.

"Yeah, well, in the end . . . she didn't go quietly. The Pentagon police had to . . . forcibly remove her from the building."

More laughter.

"And then," Jacyne sadly continued, "I had to text De's cell phone to apologize and to tell her there was a store owner in Atlanta who was expecting all of her books, signed to his wife for a birthday present."

"That's twenty-six books now that the new one has come out!" yelled Liset.

"You're kidding! And they're all about us?" asked Sara.

"Oh," Liset said with disgust, "you people have to start reading. No, they aren't all about us. DeMaris writes in a couple different genres: romance, mystery, even fantasy."

"Oh, crap. Who knew she was so prolific?"

After the laughter died down Shay said, "You do realize, Jacyne, that little incident at the Pentagon will be in her next book."

"Yeah. Sergeant Diphard strikes again."

Chapter Thirty-Two

"Ruth has dug herself into a terrible hole," said DeMaris. Sitting on the set of his TV show, Greg didn't bother to look up. He was used to this kind of talk and knew DeMaris did not require or expect an answer. He also knew, after listening to Ruth's life story—abusive upbringing, pregnant by her cousin at fifteen, and addiction to crack cocaine—that she was a character in DeMaris's next book. It was fortunate that he figured this out *before* he started talking to other people about his makeup artist, also named Ruth, who was thrilled to be in a DeMaris Azaygo book.

If she only knew how DeMaris was using her, Greg had sighed to himself and thought about the first time he met Kirk, and the firm handshake as they said good-bye. Kirk had placed his left hand on Greg's shoulder, smiled, and said, "Good luck."

DeMaris's cell phone rang. She screwed up her face reading the name. "Hey, Allison. What's up, honey? What?" Greg watched her eyes narrow and heard her voice harden. "What?" Long silence. "Allison, tell me why I would be buying you a prom dress . . . But you're in college . . . I think it's great you volunteered for the Big Sister/Big Brother program, but how old is this boy? . . . No . . . No, it's not about the money. . . How much? . . . You know very well I would never spend that kind of money on a dress you're only going to wear once for a few hours. In fact, I'm not buying you a prom dress, period. You're in college! . . . If you're that determined to go, then wear one you wore in high school . . . Yes, I kept them . . . No . . . No . . . I'm done with this conversation, Allison."

DeMaris hung up the phone muttering under her breath.

241

"I always thought," said Greg, "that Big Brothers were paired up with boys and Big Sisters were paired up with girls."

DeMaris looked at him. "You're right. Holy shit! She's dating a high school kid. What the hell's the matter with her? I mean, dating some guy who is what two, three years younger than her?"

Greg stared at her. Obviously she wasn't getting the audacity of her statement.

"I wonder if I need to go home," said DeMaris.

"I thought you said your parents were watching over her."

"Yeah, well, they're doing a lousy job. Wait 'til I catch up with the two of them." She gazed at the ceiling. "I don't really see them, you understand. It's more a feeling. I am not totally crazy."

He stood up and walked over, smiled softly, and kissed her forehead. "No, of course you're not. You just act it, is all. What about Kirk?"

"The man is two hours away from her and who does she decide to call? Oh, God," she suddenly grabbed his arm and dug her nails in.

"What? What's the matter?" he was alarmed by the look on her face.

"The Big Brother/Big Sister Organization!"

"Yeah?"

"And who they're paired up with!"

"Yeah, yeah, what?"

"I think I can use that! I think *that's* my missing link! Ruth told everybody that it was her cousin who knocked her up—when in reality, it was his Big Brother. Which is why the cousin has always said he was innocent. I wanted to believe him but I just couldn't. Too much evidence stacked against him. I can give the Big Brother an African gray. I can finally tie it all in and use that bird! Where's my paper? PAPER!"

"You're holding it."

"Pen. PEN!"

"Behind your ear."

"Right. Honey, I'm sorry. I'm not going to be able to watch you perform." She gave Greg a quick kiss. "You go do that acting thing you do." She was already looking beyond him. "I've got to write, right now." She took off looking for a quiet spot.

He folded his arms across his chest and watched her leave. "Well," he muttered, "I guess you're not interested in knowing I have the rest of the day off."

DeMaris had sighed so many times, that Greg finally gave in. "What?"

"I was thinking . . . those couple of days that you have off . . . might be nice for us to . . . go on a little . . . vacation."

"That calls for several deep sighs?"

"We could go to a lake."

"Okay." He was agreeable until it hit him. "What lake?"

"They have a couple in Idaho."

"Why would we want to go to Idaho?"

"Because . . . I need to go to the bank."

"I have money," offered Greg. "And, why do you have a bank account in Idaho?"

"For my book," she said wearily.

"No. You can call the bank from here and talk to them."

"Fine," she stood up. "I'll go by myself. Have Chuck pick me up at the airport—"

Greg suddenly remembered Kirk's words of wisdom: When she's writing, there is no talking her out of *anything*. Save yourself the agony and either go with the flow or stay home.

"Hang on," Greg said. "I understand Idaho is beautiful this time of year."

They rented an SUV at the Spokane Airport and drove to the bank. As they started to get out, she put her hand on Greg's arm. "Please stay here. I just need to get a feel for the place. This is where my character comes. I want to look around; I need it quiet so that I can concentrate. I'll only be gone two minutes." *Somehow I need to find out if Brian has managed to get into the box. What story can I give Abigail to get the box open again to check it?*

"We flew all the way up here for a two-minute walk through—" Greg stopped when he saw the look he was getting.

"You had the choice of staying home."

He sighed and slumped back in the seat while she gathered up her purse. "You know," she said as she got out of the car, "Kirk found it handy to have a book to read while he waited."

"Thanks for that advice."

DeMaris made her way into the bank and slowly looked around. What had she failed to describe in her book? Oh, there was a table with coffee and popcorn on it. She didn't remember that being there before. What was the scent she was picking up?

Slowly she turned herself all the way around and saw only a teller who was busy counting money. From the look on her face and the long sigh she was having a bad day. DeMaris studied the door that led to the basement and the vault where the safe deposit boxes were. She made her way over to the door, checked the lobby again, and when the teller turned and headed away from her, DeMaris opened the door and slipped in. The door shut silently and she listened to hear if anybody was downstairs. Quiet. Softly she made her way downstairs and pulled open the box that held the signature cards. *Foxx, Foxx. Here we go. M. Bloomgarde. Huh. She came here for years. And she was the only one. Did Blanche and Owen not know about this until I brought Blanche here, even though they were listed as people who could access the box? She did seem surprised.*

DeMaris slipped the card back in place and put the box away. Out of habit, she got out her notepad and pen and started describing the old wooden desk that held all the safe deposit holders, the layout of the basement and the number of private rooms—three. She suddenly wondered if there were any security cameras down here because she looked oddly suspicious. She put everything back in her purse. *I wonder if one key fits all and you only need the second key to open the box?* Pulling the chain that held the key out from under her blouse, *(Thank God Viva bought my story that I gave the key to Blanche as it belonged to her and that Blanche, being in a hurry to get to the carnival, never asked for it. I probably need to send this to Blanche though . . . when I'm done with it)* she tried inserting it in the key holes of several boxes. Some it didn't fit into at all and a few the key went in but didn't turn. Of course, she had to go for one more. The key stuck. *I don't believe this!* She twisted, yanked, and pulled. The key was stuck in the hole. *I do not believe this! Why do I always do what my imagination tells me to do? As many stupid things as I've done, why do I never learn?* She laid both hands on the wall and tried to center her mind. *Okay, the key went in, the key has to come out. Oh. Look at my hands. Fingerprints. Aaaaahhh!!!*

Fortunately she had long ago learned to almost exclusively wear long sleeves. She pulled the sleeves down over her hands and wiped the places where her fingers had just been. With a light touch—rather than the frantic yanking she had previously employed—she pulled the key out of the hole. *Thank God!*

Suddenly she heard a slam and a chair being slid across the floor. *No!*

There is somebody down here in one of the rooms! As she heard a door being opened, she quickly shoved the chain back down her blouse and propped herself up against the wall, folding her arms across her chest and one leg crossed over the other.

A man came around the corner, carrying a safe deposit box and whistling. He stopped upon seeing her.

DeMaris nonchalantly examined her watch. "Still waiting for someone to come with the key."

He smiled, hesitated, and then walked over to the wall and slid his box into the cubicle. DeMaris stared at the door leading upstairs but out of the corner of her eye she could see him trying to keep his eye on her while putting his box away. Deciding that she wasn't a threat, he headed toward the stairs. "I'll let someone know you're waiting," he called.

"Oh! Well . . . that's very nice but . . . not necessary. Please. I don't like to cause trouble."

"No problem. The customer service here has really gone downhill in the last year. They probably forgot. I mean, these people are paid to take care of us, the customer, right? Don't worry. I'll get somebody down here."

"No! Really, that's not necessary. I—" she heard the door open and then shut. *I need to get out of here! Shit.*

Taking the steps two at a time, DeMaris was at the top in seconds. *Okay, you people have left me waiting for ten minutes. No make it twenty. Customer service around here stinks! I am taking my business elsewhere! Yeah, that sounds good.* She took a couple deep breaths and opened the door.

"Missy?"

DeMaris turned. "Abigail."

"What are you doing down in the basement without an employee?"

"I needed to check box sizes."

"Box sizes?"

"Yeah. Uncle Owen has a really big one and I'm thinking he doesn't need one that large. I wondered what other sizes there were. No reason for anybody to escort me down there for that."

"You are not supposed to be downstairs for any reason without an employee." Abigail pointed to the sign taking up most of the door: NO ENTRANCE WITHOUT EMPLOYEE.

"I'm sorry. I couldn't find anyone and I'm in a hurry."

"Step into my office. I can look to see if we have any smaller boxes available."

"I really need to get going. But, thank you for the offer."

She found herself being propelled through the hallway as Abigail wrapped her hand firmly around DeMaris's elbow. "How is your uncle doing?"

"He's doing okay. Thank you for asking, but I really need to get going."

"Oh, this will only take a minute." DeMaris didn't like the look on her face or the way she pointed to her office. DeMaris was equally not happy when she heard the office door shut behind her. Abigail went around her desk and arms crossed stared at her. "Your uncle's doing okay, huh? Cuz I read in the paper he was dead."

"Oh. Really? Gosh, who told the papers that?"

"Well, not their niece. Who *are* you?" Abigail demanded.

"Oh, don't get excited. *I* knew he was dead. I just didn't know it was common knowledge." DeMaris suddenly stopped and tried to work up some tears. "I found my poor uncle still sitting in his rocker. I was gone for such a short time. He seemed fine when I left—"

"He was decomposing!"

"Oh, wow. The newspapers got information, huh? It wasn't just an obituary notice?"

"No!" Abigail casually picked up a pair of scissors and played with them. "Seems the police suspect foul play."

"Well, I'd have to agree with that. Look, I've already spoken to the police. If you really need to know I'm a guardian for Owen and Blanche—"

"You?"

"Yes."

"Who appointed you guardian?"

"Their mother," DeMaris looked her squarely in the eye.

"And her name is?" asked Abigail.

"Maureen Bloomgarde."

"And she worked where?"

Really, you still think I'm making this stuff up? "Zimmer Real Estate agency—in Sandy Bottom Cove."

Abigail set the scissors down and took a deep breath. "Okay, okay." She seemed to be thinking to herself; for once DeMaris decided to keep quiet. "Just bring me the guardianship papers and that should do it."

"Do it?"

"Yes," Abigail's voice shook slightly. "I've been in a lot of hot water because I let you in to see their safe deposit box without authorization. I could lose my job. I need those guardianship papers. And the key."

"The key? Why do you need it?"

"You are someone who is unauthorized to have it. This bank issued it and it wasn't issued to you. I demand you give it back to me at once." She held out her hand.

DeMaris stood straighter. "No. It's none of your business who Maureen gave her key to. I don't have to give it to you. And if you're not nice to me, I won't give you the guardianship papers either." *Who do I know who can make me some that look authentic? I'm certainly not going to use that last guy. Look at the trouble I got into there.*

"All right, fine, I'm sorry. I'm just— you don't know what Bri— what I've been going through. What *he* has put me through. Would you be willing to give me the key for say, a day?"

"So you and Brian can see what's in there?"

"Brian who?"

"Brian Fox. The bank manager in Sandy Bottom Cove. He's been after the key for quite some time."

"Please, my job is at stake. I was nice to you and let you in. You need to return the favor. Just for a day." Abigail came around the desk to stand in front of DeMaris. "You don't know what he's like. You—" She stopped suddenly and DeMaris realized Abigail was staring at her throat. DeMaris slammed her hand up around her breastbone. "You— you've got the key on you."

"No, this is my personal key to my box in Michigan."

"No, it's not. All right, listen." Abigail ran around to the front of her desk, opened up a drawer, and hauled out a ring of keys. "You and I will go down together. We'll both look in the box and I can report to . . . we'll just look."

"No."

"Come on! With Blanche and Owen both dead, who's going to come after you?"

DeMaris's jaw dropped. *Blanche is dead? Nobody told me! Oh, wait. She thinks Blanche is dead because that's what I told her. I have to keep my own stories straight!*

"I was given a responsibility and I am not going to let you in," said DeMaris.

"Well, you'd better." Abigail picked up the scissors and held them menacingly.

"You are not seriously threatening me!" DeMaris could feel her blood start to boil; then she stopped. "Why are you acting like this?"

Abigail dropped the scissors, put her hands to her head, and slowly brought them down. "Look, I am in so much trouble for letting you see inside the box. What if you stole something and the owners found out?

I mean, if they weren't both dead. I don't know what I was thinking that day. But . . . the bottom line is . . . Brian's just been using me. All this time we've been dating . . . He works for the same bank I do but he manages the Sandy Bottom Cove branch. He's been interested in an account here for some time. Never told me which one, he just always asked me about the customers I came into contact with. The other day, he finally told me who he's been interested in so I told him about you coming in. How you had a key to the box. I thought he'd be happy. No! He was furious that I'd let you into the box and that I hadn't told him before about your visit. He said he is related to your aunt and uncle and that he didn't know who you were."

"Yes, well . . . I'm a long-lost cousin."

"Cut the crap. I've got bigger problems."

"What does Brian have on you?"

"My job! Give me the key! I'm begging you!"

"Why does he feel entitled to it?"

"How did you know Maureen?" asked Abigail.

"I'm assuming Brian has read in the paper about Owen. How did he react?"

"What was in the box when you looked?"

"I don't have to give that key to Brian just because he's the bank manager. Do I?"

"Are you related to the Foxxes at all or just a friend of the family?" countered Abigail.

"Do you really think Brian is related to Blanche and Owen?" asked DeMaris. Silence. "Your turn to ask a question," she said as Abigail stood there.

"Okay," Abigail said slowly, "we're not going to get anywhere like this. We need to join forces."

"Why should I trust you? And why would I join forces?"

"What was inside the box?"

"Actually there wasn't anything unusual or of interest." *You work in a bank, you see money every day.*

"Like what, exactly?" asked Abigail.

DeMaris shook her head.

"Okay, Brian said he was their nephew—but I don't believe him."

"Why not?"

"Well, for starters he spells his name with one x, they spell it with two."

"I know family members who don't spell their last names the same."

Abigail shook her head. "I had a conversation with Owen after his mother passed away. I asked him who else we should contact. He said it was only Blanche and him. Which didn't hit me until about a week after you were here. So," Abigail stared at DeMaris for a long moment. "How did you become their guardian?"

"I was a close friend of their mother's," DeMaris said. "She left the key with me."

Slowly Abigail nodded. "That makes sense." She turned to DeMaris and sighed. "Will you at least tell me what's in the box, please? And bring me the guardianship papers?"

"I'll bring you the guardianship papers," *whenever I find someone who can make up decent ones,* "but as far as what's inside . . . that's none of your business." *It's not even my business.*

Abigail stood lost in thought for a moment and then picked up the scissors again. "No, I *cannot* go back home. Certainly not in disgrace. I've worked too hard to have you ruin my career. I really need that key around your neck."

"Why would you have told Brian that you let an unauthorized person look at someone's box in the first place?"

Abigail shook her head. "Apparently my assistant has had a crush on him for quite some time. I just told him you had a key. She was more than happy to tell Brian I let you open the box. Now that he knows I didn't follow protocol, he's blackmailing me into getting the key away from you."

"Just because you let me look in a safe deposit box?"

Abigail nodded.

"I can probably fix that."

"*I know!* Hello, the guardianship papers!"

"No. I mean yes, but," said DeMaris, "I happen to know where Blanche Foxx is and could maybe get her to add my name to the signature card so that I did have permission—or at least it looks like I have permission."

Abigail stared at her. "Are you going to tell me what's in there?"

DeMaris shook her head. "No, that's confidential."

"Wait a minute. You said your Aunt Blanche was dead."

"No, I said Uncle Owen was."

"No. I distinctly remember you saying Blanche. You were helping out your Uncle Owen."

"Uncle Owen's dead."

"Yes, we've established that! Are you saying that Blanche is alive or is this another story you're pawning off on me?"

"No, this is real. Blanche is alive; I promise you."

Abigail stared at her. "You would really help me?"

"Yeah. I can ask Blanche to sign the form putting me on her safe deposit box. Might save your job. Do you really think Brian's going to try to get you fired?"

"Yes. If I don't have a job, I'll have to go back to Iowa to live with my parents. He'll make sure I don't work anywhere in this town, probably the state. He just wants me gone and out of his life." The tears welled up. "How could I have been so wrong about him?"

Boy, I sure wasn't. I thought he was scum from the beginning. But then again, for my book, he was the bad guy anyway. "We see what we want to see," DeMaris mused out loud.

"Like I haven't heard that before," Abigail snapped.

"Sorry. I was thinking . . . Here take my card." DeMaris fished one out. "Do you have a pen?"

Abigail looked at her quizzically but handed her one. DeMaris wrote on the card and handed it to her. "You have to write your own name on your business card?"

"Yeah. My name changes but the phone number stays the same."

Abigail took the card and slowly read it out loud, "DeMaris Pala. I thought you said your name was Missy—no! Melinda something—certainly not Pala. I'll ask Beth. She remembers your name. She told the police when they were here."

Oh, wow, why didn't I stick with Melissa's name? I am really getting rusty at this. "No, I said it was— That's what I mean, my name changes."

Abigail stared at DeMaris, then back at the card. She flipped it over and then back. "That's it? Your phone number? What kind of business card is this?"

"What do you mean?"

"Maybe it should have the name of a business? Or an occupation? An address? E-mail? Website? *Your real name?*"

"Naw. I had these printed up so I could drop them in places for a free lunch. And for times like this. A phone number is all anybody needs."

"You're kidding, right?"

"Why should business people be the only ones to get a free lunch? My money's good too. What am I going to put on a card? Housewife? Roving writer? Kirk's ex-wife? Mother of two? Trust me, when it comes to my kids, I'm all business."

Abby snapped her fingers. "It was Melanie."

"No, it was—" *Melissa.* "Maris. I sometimes go by that."

"Why wouldn't you put your own name on here?"

Because I'm a best-selling author and you haven't even recognized me so why bother? You probably wouldn't know my pen name either. DeMaris stood there and then leaned close to Abigail and whispered, "I'm in the witness protection program. I can't be giving out my real name, for obvious reasons."

"For obvious reasons, you shouldn't be telling me that!"

Hmm, she's got a point there. "No, I'm the person who puts people in the witness protection program. For different people, I use a different name. It was just easier to have a card made up like this." *Come on lady, work with me here.*

"You're lying! I want that key *now!*" With the tip of the scissors pointed at DeMaris, Abigail started forward.

"I'm going to see to it that Blanche empties that box to make sure neither one of you ever gets its contents. And, I'm turning your name in to the Witness Protection Program as someone not to relocate! So, don't ever ask! And while I'm at it," DeMaris started backing away from her, "I think I'll go to the top brass here at the bank and tell them about how unscrupulous you and Brian both are. How do you like them apples, honey?" She was riled up now.

Abigail advanced and DeMaris looked around for something to defend herself with when there was a sudden commotion of people screaming outside the door. *I don't believe this! A bank robbery? NOW?* Dropping the scissors, Abigail ran to the door, flung it open, and stopped.

There was a mob of women packed in the hallway, yelling and shoving. DeMaris made her escape, pushing Abigail into the crowd and squeezing herself around a very large woman.

She passed Greg signing autographs.

Chapter Thirty-Three

Greg found DeMaris sitting in the SUV. Of course, he had to search for it since she had moved it. He was grateful, once again, for Kirk's advice: "If you're ever in a jam and DeMaris deserts you AND you find the car gone, just walk in the direction it was facing."

"But DeMaris doesn't drive," Greg had said.

"Yeah," Kirk had nodded. "She says that a lot."

"That was fun," said Greg as he climbed into the driver's seat. He found a coffee waiting for him.

"I distinctly remember telling you to wait in the car; however, I do appreciate you showing up when you did. That's why I bought you the coffee."

"Thanks."

Since a portion of DeMaris's story took place in the courtroom, she had Greg drive to the courthouse next. She went inside and drew a diagram labeling all the rooms, until one of the guards started to get suspicious. She smiled, knew from past experience that an explanation would do her no good, and beat a hasty retreat back to the SUV.

"Can we go home yet?" asked Greg.

"Sure."

He was surprised and suspicious at how quickly she agreed.

"I thought you'd like to see where Viva and Harlan lived. The house sold; but they might be packing and you could meet them. You're right, though. We don't have to spend the night here. Let's go to the airport."

"You know very well I want to meet your sorority sisters. Where to?"

She directed him and soon they pulled up to a house where a moving van was parked out front. Greg was not surprised when DeMaris simply opened the door and let herself in.

"Well, it's about time this house sold!" DeMaris hollered.

They heard a screech from the back bedroom and a man's voice saying, "Oh, no!" Viva and Harlan walked into view.

"I heard that, Harlan," said DeMaris as she and Viva hugged.

"We won't get the house packed up with you— Oh, God! It's the TV star! I watch your show all the time," Harlan said as he pumped Greg's hand.

DeMaris made introductions, as did Harlan when the movers came out of the rooms to have a look at the commotion. Viva quickly steered the four of them outside to the deck by the pool. "We need a break and this is just what we needed! Let's have a drink!"

She and DeMaris took off for the kitchen to whip up drinks and appetizers; fortunately it hadn't yet been packed up.

Harlan and Greg talked amicably. "So," said Greg when there was a lull, "tell me something about DeMaris that I don't know but should."

Harlan sat back in his chair thinking.

"What about Frank?" said Greg.

"What about Frank?" Harlan screwed his face up.

"He's called DeMaris several times—something about a purse De sold his wife. He seems to have a . . . familiarity with her."

Harlan chuckled. "They dated in college and . . ." He leaned in close and Greg did the same. "rumored —"

"Harlan!" there was a sharp tone to DeMaris's voice as she came out with shrimp and sauce. Viva followed close behind with a tray of drinks.

"The kid should know what he's getting himself into," Harlan said as he sat back.

"The kid is thirty-seven." She saw the look on Greg's face. "I told you, Frank and I are old friends. That's all there is to it. Don't go making anything more out of it."

"That's probably wise advice," said Harlan.

After setting down the tray, Viva took a book out from under her arm. "I read three of your books before I knew it was really you, and now I'm starting this one. However, if I'd known . . ."

"I did it for you girls. I thought you'd be upset. I mean, not everything I write is complimentary and I didn't want you guys reading it and thinking *that's what she thinks of me?* It's not—it's fiction, it's made up. It may be based on some things that have happened but my characters are not you girls . . . are not *exactly* you girls. I hope everyone understands that."

"Well, my character is a little bitchy," said Viva.

"And see, now you're upset! I don't think of you as a bitch. She's made up. I'm going to be saying that for the rest of my life," DeMaris said looking at Greg.

"And I can tell you that Sara is really not happy being Miss Pringle."

"Who said she was? Who said you were the bitchy one? I didn't."

"Well . . . it just stands to reason . . . I mean, Jacyne is obviously the one in the military; Liset is the one with the prominent husband; Caroline is the one—"

"You girls have decided these things. How much of the stuff that's in my books has really happened? Wouldn't you agree that the majority of things *never* happened? It's made up," DeMaris spoke the last two words slowly.

"Well, I just think—"

"Oh, for God's sake," Harlan cut in, "the newspaper did a write-up on Viva being your friend and how you stenciled—actually I think *redecorated* was the word Viva used—this house. It sold the day after the newspaper came out—for our asking price. Thank you, DeMaris."

The two clinked glasses.

"You're welcome."

At Viva's insistence, Greg and DeMaris spent the night. "There is no earthly reason for the two of you to stay at a hotel. Honestly, I have the air mattresses already pumped up and I think I know which box has towels in it. Oh, wait, you don't shower any way."

"I do!" said Greg. "And I can talk DeMaris into taking one."

Viva stepped out of the bedroom to find towels; Greg plopped himself down on one of the two air mattresses Viva had inflated. It was not nearly as full as it looked and he sunk almost to the floor. "Is she bringing sheets?"

"I wouldn't count on it. She didn't mention it, anyway," said DeMaris as she opened her suitcase.

"Don't you think Viva would realize that we can afford to go to a hotel and it would be a whole lot more comfortable for us," whispered Greg.

"Of course, she does. You'll note, she didn't say she was the stupid one; she's the bitchy one."

"She's getting back at you."

"Exactly." De lay down next to him. "Did she leave the pump?"

"Nope." Greg stared at the ceiling.

They were quiet for a moment. "Maybe we could pretend these are waterbeds and have some fun."

He slowly turned and looked at her. "Darling, air and water do not move the same. This is nothing like a waterbed."

"You have to use your imagination." She suddenly shot up and Greg saw the look on her face: her wheels were moving. "Let's actually fill one with water."

"No!"

"I've never done it before and maybe I can use it in one of my books! I wonder if I set it in the bathtub if— Oh, drop it in the pool! Or the lake!"

"DeMaris, it needs to be forced in. It's not simply going to swell up on its own. Besides, you'll never get all the water out. It'll eventually get moldy."

"So? You throw it out. Maybe she pumped them up all the way and they've got a leak. We'll find out exactly where it is." She grabbed a mattress and started for the bathroom.

"No," Greg grabbed the other end. "This is not a wise idea."

"We're doing research."

"No. No, we are not."

"Okay, here are towels and sheets," said Viva coming back through the door. She stopped and looked at them.

DeMaris had wedged the mattress through the bathroom door and was getting ready to pull the plug to let the air out while Greg held onto the other end.

"I can explain," said DeMaris.

"And so it begins," said Viva looking at Greg.

"She wants to fill your air mattress with water."

The two women stared at each other. "I'm doing research."

Viva jerked a thumb. "Take it outside. There's a hose on this side of the house." She threw the sheets and towels on the floor and left the room. "Harlan!" Viva yelled. "De's buying us *another* new air mattress!"

⌐ ⸗ ⌐

"I can't leave. I got an epiphany last night while I was freezing my ass off lying on top of that waterbed outside," said DeMaris as she grabbed her notepad and pen.

Harlan, Viva, and Greg left to eat breakfast in town. "I'll bring you something back," promised Greg as he walked out the door.

DeMaris wrote for a solid hour. Greg brought her a Styrofoam box with pancakes, sausage, and an egg. "Thank you," she said taking it from him. "Where's Viva and Harlan?"

"They dropped me off. They have a bunch of stuff to do, including looking at a couple of houses. I told them we were catching a plane this evening. Whether we do it or not," he hurried to say, "is up to you. I just am not sleeping on a 'water' or air mattress another night."

"I'd like to at least take them out to dinner," she said.

He nodded.

They moved outside to the deck to enjoy the warm weather. Greg read while DeMaris wrote. A deep sigh escaped her; Greg put down the book and looked at her.

"The ending doesn't work if I stick with what I know. I'm getting confused about what are the actual facts and what I've made up. I can write an ending—but how do I solve the real mystery?"

"Leave that to the police." That was the wrong thing for Greg to say.

"I can't tell my readers that I got so far and then quit," she glared at him.

"I thought it was just a *story*, like the others."

"It started out that way—but then things happened. Now I, DeMaris Azaygo, am solving a real mystery—not one I made up."

"I've read six of your books and am finishing up number seven. From what you've told me, and from what I've read, you're in all of them. How many of the incidences that you wrote about really happened?"

"Well, lots of things happened. I mean, things happen every day. I did embellish some—I am a writer. This book has an African grey, two missing people, a bag lady, a purse that's more expensive than when the company made it, a safe deposit box that has loads of money in it, and a bank manager who chased me."

"Why would he want to chase you?"

"I mean, my character." She sighed again and then said, "Because I have a key that he wants."

Greg sat up. "Wait a minute. 'I'm solving a real mystery—not one I made up.' When you told me about how your character was going to get inside a safe deposit box without authorization— That was true? Did you actually manage to get in someone's safe deposit box the way you described to me?"

"I don't recall saying . . ." *Think! What did I tell him?*

"When you said your character found a treasure map in the box, I thought that was your storyline. Are you telling me—"

She realized her mistake. "No, I can explain. In my book—"

"Don't lie to me, DeMaris. You told me once you used to tell Kirk everything."

"Yes, and eventually he didn't want to hear anymore."

"Well, I'm not there yet—and I don't ever want to get to the point where you lie to me and then I don't trust you."

"Sometimes the truth lands me in trouble. If I can spare you from that, I think I should. I mean, I learned my lesson with Kirk."

"No, I'm an adult. Let me decide. It feels like you don't trust me."

"I trust you, Greg. I just want to protect you."

"I think I can take care of myself."

She stared at him. "You saw how big Kirk is. He thought the same thing. I just seem to have a propensity for being where I'm not supposed to be. Ya know, maybe I was supposed to kill myself all those years ago."

"Don't ever talk like that," he said sternly. "Where would Kirk have been all these years? And your kids?"

"Happier."

He rolled his eyes and shook his head. "Your sisters?"

"Much happier."

He stared at her. "You don't really believe that, do you? I've talked to a lot of these people and yes, Allison is mad at you, but I don't think she wishes you dead. Your son doesn't. Your sisters certainly don't. I don't even think Kirk does. And where would I be today?"

"I'm thinking you'd have some lovely young thing on your arm."

"I've had that, DeMaris," he stated. "I find they're superficial. They're not interested in any long-term commitment. And, most of them wanted to know what I could do for them. Give them money, buy them a car, help them with their career, something. You are young. You're fun, exciting, and you want to go places and do things."

"Just as long as I don't have to fly."

"You're getting over that. You made it here, didn't ya?"

"Yeah, but now I'm thinking I don't want to fly home. The train would —"

"I think you and I make a great team." He decided to ignore her last remark. She had to start flying with all the places he wanted to visit in mind.

She smiled. "Yeah, we do, don't we?"

Chapter Thirty-Four

They took Viva and Harlan to dinner at Bugzys, where they were treated like royalty. Afterward, they drove past a few houses that the two of them were considering to buy, and then Greg and DeMaris dropped off Viva and Harlan at their house. They'd drive back to Nevada the following day.

"Are you driving straight through?" asked Greg, wanting to make sure they really meant to drive so that he and DeMaris didn't run into them at the airport the next day.

"No, we'll stop to see friends along the way. We plan on not getting home until the end of the week," said Harlan. "You two have a safe flight tonight."

The men shook hands, Viva and DeMaris hugged.

"Do you think we can actually fly out tonight?" asked Greg as they drove out the driveway.

DeMaris sat for a moment. "Sure, drive to the airport."

He was surprised at the answer. Several minutes later he said, "Are you coming home with me?" He was never sure what DeMaris was thinking. He wondered if this would ever improve.

"Yeah, I saw what I needed to see. We can go home."

"Oh. Good." Still he was not entirely convinced she didn't have something up her sleeve. After all, this had been too easy.

Checking in at the airport, they discovered they had a three-hour wait before the plane departed; so instead of returning the SUV, DeMaris had Greg drive to Blanche's apartment. It still had a vacant look about it.

"Hang on," said DeMaris and whipped out her cell phone. "Hey, Viva!

Do you know anything about Blanche's apartment? The one here in Spokane? . . . Like, is anybody living in it? . . . Uh-huh . . . No, I was just
wondering . . . No. I wasn't planning on going in it. God, you're so suspicious! How would I get in, anyway? . . . Yes, we're flying out tonight. We
have plenty of time to spare . . . Okay, see ya." She hung up and turned to
Greg. "I thought while we were here, I'd go in one more time."

She unbuckled herself but Greg grabbed her arm.

"You just told Viva— how are you going to get in?"

"Huh? I, um, I was . . . going to ask the neighbor. He has a key."

"Why would he let you in?"

"Because he knows me."

"How does he know you?"

She stared at him. "Ya know, Kirk eventually learned to stop asking
questions. I suggest you move there. Kirk said it was a lot easier not knowing things. That way, he could honestly tell the police or whoever that he
had no idea I was planning to do . . . whatever."

"Ya know, Kirk and I did talk and he gave me some advice."

DeMaris rolled her eyes, crossed her arms, and set her jaw tight.

"He told me that when he was young and stupid he used to come to
your rescue—which he eventually realized you never needed. He told
me to not always follow blindly wherever you lead and that sitting back
and watching was sometimes the better idea. He told me to not ask questions because that only led to disaster and confusion; especially since you
change your story frequently. It made it look like he—or me, in this case
—appeared to be the one lying. And that you always land on your feet and
have pretty much talked your way out of *everything*. Hmph, I guess that
explains his scars," Greg mumbled.

"Hey, Kirk and I had some good times, good memories. We had excitement while other people were going off to their nine-to-five jobs."

"You've been writing best-sellers for a number of years, DeMaris,
which makes me wonder why did the two of you never buy new cars or
fix up your home?"

She sighed. "Kirk and I were never into the material stuff. We were
basically hippies. Once the kids came along, though, we had to act respon-
sibly. At the time, all we could afford was that old farmhouse. We made
it a home and we loved it there. Kirk worked, and I raised the kids and
wrote. I never wanted the fame or publicity; so I never provided personal
or revealing information in my books. Plus, as our kids got older, I didn't
want them reading my books and knowing how my mind works. And
when I started to make a lot of money, we realized we couldn't spend it

because people would wonder how we were paying for stuff with Kirk's meager salary.

"When we had the indoor swimming pool installed, Shay's first question was, 'Your parents approved that?' Obviously everybody thought my parents were paying for any expensive purchases. Kirk and I worked when I needed research done." DeMaris saw the puzzled look on Greg's face. "For instance, I worked at a retail store to get the feel of it and what went on behind the scenes. Trust me, I got some great ideas there. Kirk worked at the dump site because I needed to know how hard it was to hide a body there. Stuff like that."

"You didn't even tell your kids who you were?"

"Honey, we didn't even tell our parents. Kids can't keep their mouths shut about anything."

"Your own parents?"

"Look, Kirk told his parents just before my real identity was given to the press. My father died suddenly; so I never got to tell him—but I did tell my mom when she was in hospice. She was crying and upset because she was afraid Kirk and I didn't know how to handle the money we'd inherit from her. She thought we'd just blow through it; so I told her the truth." DeMaris sat there for a moment and sighed. "Kirk maintains that's what killed her seeing as how she died minutes after hearing I was a success, however I like to think she died happy knowing we really could take care of ourselves.

"Okay, I'm going in," said DeMaris. She got out, slammed her door shut, and heard the same sound on the other side of the SUV. She looked up to see Greg across from her.

"I'd really rather you didn't come in with me. I'll only be a minute."

"That's what you said the last time. Why can't I come?"

"It would just be easier—"

"Why?"

She walked over to Greg and said quietly, "I am protecting you. You may need plausible deniability because I am . . . going where I don't belong. Look, on one hand, if I happen to run into Blanche's neighbor, then I would like your protection. On the other hand, I would really like to ask him some questions and he's not gonna answer if you're standing next to me. Honestly, I'm not expecting him to be there, he should be in jail. But if he is there—he's very, shall I say—possessive."

"Of you? Oh, I don't think so!"

"Oh, for God's sake, there is no reason for you to be jealous! I just do so much better on my own. It's a lot easier to fly by the seat of my pants when I'm alone than to be dragging somebody else along who can't keep up with my storyline or worse yet tries to help me with one. Trust me on this."

"Okay, fine. In exchange for me staying put, tell me how Kirk got so many scars." He saw her getting madder by the second.

"Well," she bit off each word, "he obviously survived." Her voice rose. "And, you're obviously not reading my books."

"I am too reading your books! Which leads me to ask, which one of you jumped out of a moving car? I think it was you. True or false?"

"I am not about to jump out of a moving vehicle, okay?"

He gave a slight laugh. "I have read enough to know that your character jumps out of things that move: cars, trains, a plane."

"That is a *character* in a book! That is not me! When are you people going to realize the difference?"

"Ah, Sara told me you were once in a full-body cast. To date, the only explanation they've gotten is that you were doing research. What did you jump out of that time?" He glanced over to see her with her mouth hung open.

"How many of my sisters have you talked to?" she exploded.

He started to back-pedal. "Well, obviously Viva—"

"What did you do? Go through my address book?"

"No! They called looking for you . . . okay," he sighed. "That time that I called you and Shay picked up your cell phone, we had a very nice chat and I gave her my cell phone number. I told her I would love to meet all of them and if they wanted to call me I would be happy to talk with them; and they've called."

"So, you've talked to all my sisters behind my back," she stated.

"Not all. They're concerned about you."

"They wanted to talk to a TV star."

He shrugged. "So? They're your sisters, your closest friends. I would really like to meet all of them. Plus, Jacyne would really like me to explain to you why she turned the Pentagon police on you."

"And yet, you haven't."

"You got mad when I told you Allison called from Jacyne's place. But then you got that epiphany and how getting dragged out of the Pentagon fit right into your storyline—"

"You didn't tell her *that*, did you?"

"No. I also didn't relieve her any by telling her that you did send the signed books to the store owner."

"What stopped you from telling her?"

"It wasn't my place. That's up to you to tell her. I'm on your side."

DeMaris stood with her arms sternly folded across her chest. "Who have you talked to?" she finally asked, calmly.

"Ah, let's see. Shay, Liset . . . Viva . . . Jacyne, and Sara. So that leaves . . ." He looked at her for help. "Um, Caroline, who I haven't talked to and . . . okay, who am I missing?"

She looked straight ahead. "I'm not missing anybody."

"Don't be like that. Your sisters are relieved that you are not living out on the streets. They were very worried."

DeMaris chuckled slightly. "They are relieved that I'm not going to be living with any of them."

"Well, I don't know about that." He sighed, put an arm up on top of the roof and said, "DeMaris, I am crazy about you but . . ."

Slowly she turned and looked at him. "What?" she said as he just stood there staring at her.

"Oh, I finally have your attention."

"Of course you have my attention! You always have—"

"No, DeMaris, I don't. Do you remember when we met up again on the movie set for your book?" She nodded. "You spent time doing what you needed to do and I understood that. But when we were together, we were *together*. Things were fine and then you went off for a vacation with your sisters and came back with a new story to write. I had no idea how consuming writing was for you. I can tell when we're together, like now, that you are not really here. You are off on some voyage that I'm not a part of. I guess, when I ask about Kirk's scars, what I'm really asking is was he involved in your books . . . and I'm not?"

He watched her face soften. "Yes, I guess you could say he was involved. More involved than I've allowed you to be. Nobody knew who I was. I never allowed any information to be given out about me. Kirk and I were free to do whatever. Now, things are different. People know who I am, I'm going to be on television, my face is starting to be recognized, and you're famous in your own right. If I do something now it's going to be all over the news, the Internet, whatever. God, I miss the good old days when nobody knew me. And, if something should happen to you because of my crazy ideas, well, there goes your career."

They were both silent; finally Greg nodded. "Okay. I get what you're saying—but understand this: I don't want to be left out in the cold. I don't want to be the last person who knows anything about your books. If you want our relationship to continue, you have to let me in. You have to tell me stuff. You have to be up front and honest with me."

"I am honest with you!"

"No, you are evasive. Like right now, when people ask me what your new book is about I say I'm sorry, I'm not at liberty to talk."

"And you're not! You *know* that and you know why! I can't let anybody know my storyline!"

"Yes, I do know that. But the fact is, *I don't know the story*! Your sisters do! I'm betting even Chuck knows."

"Oh," she stood there for a moment. "You're right. He does." She saw the startled look on Greg's face. Obviously he had been shooting in the dark. She put up a hand, "He only knows because I needed information which he had access to being a newspaper guy. But, I see your point. That's not fair to you." He waited. "You know some of the reasons for my getting a divorce, but one of them was that Kirk, at some point, started thinking about all the stupid and crazy things we had done and he just got to thinking that . . . well, he didn't want to spend his golden years in jail. That's why I don't tell you stuff. You are better off not knowing, trust me."

"I don't want a fiancée or wife who shuts me out. I'm a big boy. I can decide things for myself—you need to trust me."

"Kirk felt that our luck was running out. Sooner or later we'd get nailed for something because we got caught or I couldn't talk our way out of it. We had a lot of great times but . . . Kirk was also getting older. Physically he couldn't do the things he'd been able to do as a young man. He said he thought I'd mellow with age."

"I'm kinda hoping that too," said Greg. "And that's only after reading six of your books."

"Yeah, well, since I haven't slowed down, Kirk got to calling me sempiternal."

Greg shook his head. "Guess I'll have to look up that word when we get home."

"It means never-ending duration."

"Ah."

"I thought maybe I was mellowing out, but then . . ." She stopped for a moment to gather her thoughts. "I keep a journal of story ideas. I've obviously had several over the years; and I did eventually get them all written. When I met you, I'd run out of ideas. I thought of it as my retirement. I would be there for your career. But then I went on vacation and things started coming to me. Suddenly I had a story and I fell into book mode."

"How did Kirk handle your book mode? Or the kids? I mean, I don't like that you are so totally consumed that we can't do much. I end up being by myself when you should be by my side."

"Well, Kirk used it as his recovery period."

"Maybe I don't want to know about his scars."

"And the kids . . . I don't know. They grew up with it. I guess they were used to it. I don't know. I never thought about it. I mean, I was a stay-at-home mom. I was there for them." She stared up at the apartment. "I understand what you're saying, and you're right. I don't have another story idea; so, after this, I'll be yours until something hits me. And who knows when that's going to be? I'm almost done with this book.

"But one thing you are going to have to understand is that my stories have a way of taking over. I am quite passionate about what I do when I am in book mode. I'm sorry; you are just going to have to play second fiddle during that time. Kirk consoled himself with the fact that I wasn't out with another man.

"You put a lot into your work. I respect that. You're just going to have to do the same for me if we're going to be a couple."

Slowly, he nodded.

"I was planning on getting inside Blanche's apartment because I have a key."

"Why couldn't you tell me that before?" he asked puzzled.

"Because in a court of law I might be found guilty—"

"Stop! Okay, now I understand this is where I could become an accomplice."

"Well, I don't know. You weren't there when I broke in and stole— took— borrowed—"

"Stop." Greg took a deep breath and slowly let it out. "Why don't you just tell me what your *story* is about?"

"Okay," she thought for a moment. "I'm interested in the D. B. Cooper case—which I had nothing to do with! I find it difficult to keep the facts and my story line separate but here goes: I found a key—my character found a key—to a safe deposit box belonging to a brother and sister by way of a bird."

"Okay, that's got to be your book. D. B. Cooper was a guy who jumped out of a plane with a bag of money."

"No! The bird told me it was there."

"You're scaring me, De."

"Listen! It's an African gray. He talks. Okay, I—my character—tracked down the box to a bank in Spokane. It had dirty money in it."

"How do you know it's dirty?"

"No, it really is dirty—caked with dirt. Like actual buried treasure. And that's also where I—okay, for all intents and purposes, I am the main character in my books, so let's just go with that. It's easier for me to say I. If the police or anybody ever questions you just say 'character from her book.'"

"Agreed."

"I found a treasure map that the girls and I followed and we unburied an old toy chest. Viva actually knows the people that I'm patterning my characters after. In fact, Viva has their bird."

"You mean, one of the characters in your book has the bird."

"No. Oh, do you want to go with that?"

"This is getting confusing. Look, honey, as kindly as I can say this, let the police handle it."

"What police? This is my story! Besides, they don't know what I know."

"Meaning?"

"You want me to tell the police I stole a key from a bird and lied my way into someone's safe deposit box? Oh, and that I 'borrowed' a map and . . . maybe some money?"

"Maybe? DeMaris!"

"Not to spend. Look where that landed Liset. Wait a minute. Liset spent the money and it got the attention of— What'd Frank say? The FBI? IRS?"

"FBI."

"I've gotta call Joe Shaver."

"Who?"

"My contact at the FBI. Actually, I'm surprised he hasn't called me. But then again, maybe what Frank was talking about turned out not to be important. I mean, if it was important, Joe would have called. Or, when it's really important, he bangs on my door. Not that he can find me at the moment . . ."

Greg sighed. "Please, be quick in the apartment."

"Naw, I've changed my mind. Let's go see Chuck. I need to ask him some questions." She jumped back into the SUV.

"Just the person I want to meet," Greg muttered under his breath as he got in.

Chapter Thirty-Five

At the appointed time, the girls turned on their TVs. Scattered across the nation, none of them wanted to miss DeMaris's interview. Not being able to get past agent Liz Brown the girls wondered what DeMaris would have to say—about them. A few sat holding their breath; a few paced. All had a bottle of wine on hand.

"Thank you," the commentator started, "for allowing me to be the first to interview you on TV. It's great to have you here in the studio."

"I'm happy to be here," DeMaris smiled.

"I think the first question on everybody's mind is: Why? Why have you kept your identity a secret all these years and why have you decided to tell the world who you are now?"

"I guess fear is a big reason. What if nobody liked what I wrote? What if I got terrible reviews constantly? And, I didn't want my children reading these books and thinking that's how I really think or feel. Then when my books were hitting number one on the bestseller list, I didn't want my friends or family to treat me differently. I could go off and be myself because nobody knew who I was. My first husband Kirk and I flew under the radar so nobody would get suspicious about us. Honestly, I didn't want anybody to know who I was until I was dead. Then my family, my agent, or whoever could tell the world. That was always my plan. But, at this point in my life, I've changed my mind. And I think," DeMaris smiled and leaned back in her chair, "I'm entitled to do that."

"Well, I know your fans are quite excited that you are doing book signings. Now, this is your latest book which just came out last week." The female commentator held up a hardcover copy of *Pride on a Prejudiced Street*.

"Yes."

"And you actually lived on the streets to get the feel of it."

"Yes, it was really something to experience how street people live. Some of the things in the book actually happened."

"How did your family take this?"

"Well, I picked a bad time to go live on the streets. My husband and I had just decided to get a divorce after twenty-seven years of marriage and my kids and friends thought he'd thrown me out."

"But, surely as a famous writer—"

"Remember, nobody knew that. Only my husband at the time, my neighbor who was my editor, and my agent knew who I was. It never dawned on me that people would think I was on the streets because I was poor. I mean, my friends actually thought I had no money and was too proud to ask them for help. Really, it was a shock when I found out that people viewed me as completely broke with no future in sight.

"But then again, I think people see what they want to see. Take my sorority sisters for instance. The eight of us have known each other for over thirty years. We all get together at least once a year and a few of us meet periodically throughout the year. So, we know each other very well. Now, one sister has been in the Army for over twenty-five years. When she told us she had made General, we all accepted that.

"But they could not believe that a thirty-seven-year-old actor would be interested in me. It was, however, plausible that a seventy-three-year-old man was. That's what Greg told them and again that's what they could comprehend. I had told Greg my plan to have all of us switch our identities while we were together on our last vacation—and apart from the fact that my friends think I'm losing it it has turned out to be such a great idea that it's my next book I'm working on. So when my sister Shay answered my cell phone it suddenly hit him that he could do the same thing. He became a seventy-three-year-old retired businessman on the spot and again, we told them what they wanted to hear—what they could comprehend. What they *wanted* to believe.

"So when I told my sisters I was DeMaris Azaygo, they thought I was making it up. Yes, they knew I wrote, they enjoyed my stories, they told me they thought I was great—but apparently not that great. DeMaris Azaygo is a worldwide bestselling author. Let's be realistic. That's not me. I needed to come down to Earth. There was even talk about having me committed," DeMaris laughed.

"Even though there were similarities to what we'd done, what they'd witnessed, and what some of them had read, they still didn't believe me.

However, they could accept the story that my crippled neighbor who never left her house was the author. I told them what I knew they could believe."

"She's gonna crucify us," muttered Melissa to no one.

——— ——— ———

Having received DeMaris's e-mail stating she was going to be on the cooking channel Liset clicked on the small TV in her kitchen. *DeMaris knows I love this show. Shouldn't one of my perks of being a close friend and all that I have put up with be that she took me with her?* she thought miserably. *What does De know about cooking anyway? Kirk did all of it and, from what I can tell, now Greg does.*

There was huge studio applause for the chef, and DeMaris Azaygo. Liset clapped quietly in her kitchen and then folded her arms across her chest. After a short conversation, the chef said, "Let's cook! Today, DeMaris, you said you'd give us your mother's quick, easy, and delicious recipe for fettuccine done in the microwave." *Oh, of course she'd do it in the microwave . . . that really is a good recipe her Mom gave me.*

DeMaris and the chef made the audience laugh with their light banter.

"The strangest food I've ever had?" DeMaris wrinkled up her nose having been asked the question from the audience. "I don't vary much from meat and potatoes, although I did dodge a bullet this last summer with my sorority sisters."

"No!" yelled Liset out loud.

"Oh, what's that?" asked the chef.

"I almost had snake."

"Snake can be good," said the chef.

"My sisters seemed to enjoy it—not that they knew what they were eating."

"What do you mean?"

"One of my sisters is an excellent cook. She's taken some classes on exotic cooking and talked about eating snake. We were all kind of grossed out; so I guess she thought she'd serve it to us and then tell us later. I always sleep in late, but on this vacation I was asked to be on a rowing team, so I had to get up near the crack of dawn to be out on the lake. I found my sister in the kitchen paying a guy for a dead snake. I never ate meat in the house the rest of the time I was there. Fortunately the other girls never figured out why."

"Wait. You're saying neither one of you ever told them?"

"I didn't. I have to think she didn't either. At any rate, nobody's said anything. But then again, what was the point of serving it and not telling us?" DeMaris mused on this for a moment. "I need to work that into my next book."

"Oh, but telling it on national television is just fine!" screamed Liset. *I will kill her. Kill her with my bare hands! Now I know why I didn't get an invite to the show—she'd be dead right now! I'd be out on the stage with my nails digging into her throat. Work that into your next book! The girls were having a hard enough time getting food down just watching Blanche with her awful manners. I didn't find a real good time to have a chuckle with them about snake! . . . wait, DeMaris only sent that e-mail to me. It wasn't addressed to the others because they're not into cooking. She knew I'd watch and the others wouldn't. Maybe, just maybe they'll never find out. Yeah. They don't watch this. Why would they?*

If only Liset could have seen Jacyne's frozen face in D.C. or Shay with her head bent over the toilet.

———

The girls were once again glued to their TV sets as Greg was being interviewed.

"I met her on a train. She doesn't like to fly, although she's getting better at it. And the gal that I was with, well, we were on the train . . . for recreational purposes, shall we say?

"They seat you in the dining car and its four people to a booth. DeMaris was traveling by herself to California. Nice-looking, intelligent, funny, interesting. I had a great time talking to her. We went our separate ways and then later that night we were involved in the train wreck."

"That had to be something to go through," said the talk show host.

"You can't imagine. Even now, one of us will wake up with a start. As you know, it happened about five in the morning," Greg motioned with his hands. "That tumbling over and over going down the mountain . . . people screaming . . . nothing I ever want to experience again. When the car finally came to a rest, I busted out the window. We were upside down. I helped my companion out and I looked over and recognized DeMaris. She had a flashlight and she was calming people, helping them, holding children. She was this calming presence among all the chaos and death. And the gal that I was with would not stop screaming. She was bruised—but alive. Nothing I or anyone else did could shut her up. I finally determined she was okay and went off to help others although I had a broken arm.

"DeMaris was just this tower of strength. I decided she was someone I wanted to get to know better when all of this was over. Hours later, the medics wanted to transport me to a hospital. I argued with them and started hollering to get DeMaris's attention. I was *not* leaving without getting this woman's phone number. Finally she heard me and walked over. I said, 'I would like your phone number before I leave.'

"She stared at me, looked around like I must be talking to somebody else, and then said, 'Whatever for?'

"I flat out told her I wanted to get to know her. She laughed and said, 'Yeah, sure.'

"I told her I wasn't leaving until I got her number. So she pulls a business card out of her laptop. Which, even at the time, I found a little strange. Everybody was pretty dazed and had nothing with them except what they slept in, but she never let that laptop out of her sight. Not knowing who she was I didn't realize she had her latest novel with new revisions in it. Here I thought she was clutching this thing because she was a real techie. Nothing could be further from the truth. She'd still be using a typewriter if her first husband hadn't forced a computer on her. DeMaris hand writes everything out and then puts it in her laptop.

"Anyway, she pulls out a business card, asks for a pen, writes on it, and hands it to me. Then she says to the EMT who's taking me away, 'You need to check him for a concussion. He's obviously not right in the head.'

"I look at the card. All it has is a phone number printed on it and she's handwritten Sabrina D'azayga. I distinctly remember her name being DeMaris when we ate dinner. She just smiles and says, 'Call it. Leave a message. You'll get me. Think of Sabrina as my personal secretary.'

"I asked her, 'Are you somebody famous I should recognize?'

"'You never know who you're going to run into, do you?'

"'Who's Sabrina D'azayga? Really?'

"'Call me and I'll explain,' she said."

"And that's how you met?" said the host. "What a fascinating story."

Greg smiled. "Yes. And we're going to live happily ever after in a cheap, trashy, classic- romance kind of way."

Chapter Thirty-Six

Greg and DeMaris sat across the bed from each other in the honeymoon suite. DeMaris held a small box in her hand. She smiled and handed it to him. "Your wedding present. And let me tell you, it's not easy buying for you."

He chuckled and accepted the gift. Slowly he unwrapped it and then stared. He pulled out one of the cards, flipped it over, flipped it back, stared, and then looked at her. "They're business cards."

"Not any business cards that I've ever seen—except yours of course."

"Yes, but this way they only have your phone number. If you don't want people to know it's you—I mean if somebody doesn't recognize you—you write down a fake name. Then when they call asking for that person, you know it's somebody you don't want to talk to. I do it all the time."

"How about if I don't want to hear from them, I just don't give them a card?" he asked.

"That would be impolite." DeMaris shook her head. "Besides, you're missing the point. It works and it's great for dropping in fishbowls for free meals and other drawings. I knew you didn't have anything like this," she said proudly. She had found him the perfect gift.

"You are right about that," he agreed. He too held a small box in his hand, which he handed to her. "You are not exactly easy to buy for either."

"Not true! I love jewelry."

"Since when?"

"Expensive perfume."

"We haven't agreed on a scent yet."

"A car would be nice."

"You hate to drive."

"Oh . . . that's right."

"Just open it," he said.

She did and, like him, stared at the contents. "A tape recorder?"

"Yes. A handheld tape recorder. I am tired of hearing 'Paper! Where's some paper? A pen! I need a pen!' Whenever an idea suddenly strikes you, you can press the button and speak. Take it with you wherever you go. It's small enough. You can copy it all down later."

"I am not a computer literate—"

"It's not a computer. It's small, it fits in your hand, and I got one that had no gizmos or gadgets attached. It's plain. It's just like your cassette deck. This will catch all your ideas instead of you writing along and then saying, what was that other idea that just came to me? Where is that piece of paper that I wrote an idea on last month? Just like the computer has helped you as much as you cuss and hammer on it this will help you too. This is easy to use."

"Just like my cassette deck, huh?" DeMaris pressed the button, spoke into it, pressed review, and then listened to her voice. She smiled. "Ya know what, you might be on to something. I *think* I can use this."

"I know you can," he said confidently, "and after that, you are going to learn how to work an MP3 player."

"Oh, don't be a mean husband."

——— —— ——

"*Beggar and the Borrower*? *Beggar and the Coach Purse*? *Beggar* . . . hmm."

"Beg her to come to bed? Beg her as in I had to beg her to marry me?" offered Greg, standing behind her.

"Oh, no, honey. *Beggar*, one word. As in I met a beggar on the street. But, what could I do with what you're saying?"

"Come to bed?" he whispered hoping that repetition might penetrate her brain.

She laughed. "No, that doesn't go together. Beg her . . . to stay. Probably been done before. Beg her . . . to die. Oh, I like that one." She scribbled it down. "*The Beggar and the Banker*. I like that one too but does it sound like a best-selling title? Probably not. *Beg Her To Die* does. *The Beggar, The Dumpster and the Coach Purse*, yuk. *The Coach Purse Beggar*. Better but still . . ."

"I'm begging you to come to bed." He ran his hands along her back and nibbled on her neck as she sat at the writing table.

"It's the middle of the afternoon."

"So? Love has no timetable."

"Oh, you sweet man," she gazed lovingly up at him. He knew he had her. "I like that. I think I can use that some place." DeMaris started pawing through her papers.

"No!" Greg slammed his hands down on top of them. "Later. Bed is calling," he whispered in her ear.

"I thought lunch was calling."

"I ate. You never came."

"Book mode."

"I do not like book mode. We—you need to switch to bed mode."

"Honestly," she shook her head and tried prying his fingers off her manuscript.

He blew in her ear and whispered, "I'll bring you lunch in bed afterwards."

"Awww." Her face softened. Yes, he had her this time; still he kept his hands in place. "It will cost you one title."

"*The Beggar and the Dirty Toy Chest.*"

"Not funny!"

"*The Beggar and Her Horny Husband.*"

"Greg."

He placed his hands on her front.

"Would you stop?"

Too late. He saw the smile on her face. He ran his tongue around her ear.

She wrote something, threw down her pen and wrapped her arms around his neck. He gave her a long kiss and glanced down to see what she'd written: BEG (GH) ER. She sighed heavily in his ear.

"Why do you have it spelled like that?" he asked in between kisses.

"I don't know which word I want to use. This way I'll remember where I was at."

"*Beggar* is spelled wrong." He kissed her again and tried to get her out of the chair.

"I don't think so," she moaned.

"You're trying to decide between *beg her* and *beggar*, right? *Beggar* is with an 'a' not an 'e'."

"Who in their right mind spells it that way?" She stood up to face him.

They playfully bit each other's lips. "I have a college degree, my dear. It's b-e-g-g-a-r."

"I have one too, and you're wrong. It's b-e-g-g-e-r."

He stopped and pulled away. "Let's make a little wager, Ms. Writer."

Oh no, if he was that sure . . . She whipped around and typed begger on the computer. A red line ran under the word. "No!" she screamed, clicking on it to see beggar. "That messes up everything." She started to write various ways to have the two words become one.

"What are you doing?" He looked to see: Beggar, Begher, Beggher, Begg(h)er, Beg(ghe/a)r, Beg(gar)(her) on the paper.

"My manuscript is done. I just need a title. Sometimes when I write by free-thought association something comes to me." She looked at what she'd written. "Well, that looks terrible."

"I'll give you a title after we have some fun."

"I want it done now. Not out of book mode until I do."

He made a guttural noise in his throat, took the pen from her hand and wrote: Beggar/Beg Her.

"That doesn't look good either," she protested.

"That's how a *normal* person would do it. We'll think of something— later! This way you can remember what you were thinking about."

"What book of mine are you reading?"

"The ninth," he said hesitantly remembering the girls warning him about when DeMaris changed subjects in the middle of a conversation.

"And you haven't realized yet that I do nothing normal? I want to send this to my editor this afternoon."

"No," he groaned.

"After," she smiled, "I get a title. And I had one until you messed up the spelling."

"I messed up—" He stared at her, picked up the paper she'd scribbled on and wrote: B-e-g-g-a (h-e) r.

DeMaris studied it for a moment. "I guess that goes together. I'll let my editor decide on whether the title should be *Beggar* or *Beg Her* and we'll go from there. I mean it's not a one-word title. It will be something like *The Beggar in the Dumpster* or *Beg Her to Leave*. But first we'll have to decide which word to use."

She picked up the manuscript and dropped it in the box she had prepared several days ago. She laid the sheet of paper with the different titles on top of that and wrote **Other Ideas** across it. "Oh, I know!" she said and next wrote out, 'Beg(ga)(he)r' on a sticky note, ripped it off and slapped it on the cover.

"Where is the CD I burned for you to send her?"

"I have it," she said defensively. "And I agree with you that I should be sending it out on a disk but this gal wants a hard copy; so I'm going to try her out and see how it goes. However, I'm not happy that she's not in the modern world. I mean, really, I should be sending it to her on a disk. I agree."

"She's not with it?" Greg nearly laughed. "This from a person who still walks around with a Walkman; who still records songs off the radio onto a cassette!"

"It works! I'm happy. And at least I have my manuscript on a CD."

He snorted. "You had Allison or Ryan put it on for you—and now me. You don't know how to do it yourself."

"It's how I bonded with my children . . . and now my husband." DeMaris taped the box and slapped a mailing label on it.

"Okay. But you're not mailing it out like that, are you? I mean, we can come up with a real title in a couple hours."

"No, she can figure out what I mean."

"You don't think she'll think that's your title?"

"No! The woman's not stupid. I mean, does that look like a title? That's why I wrote down all those options in the front. She'll know to pick one and elaborate on it or come up with something different. At the very least, she'll call me."

"And all the epilogues you have numbered?"

"You only have one Epilogue. Everybody knows there is only one ending. I couldn't decide on which one I liked best. Where I should cut the story off. And, you were no help. She'll pick one. She's certainly not going to leave seven epilogues in my novel," she laughed.

"I thought she was new. That you've never worked with her before."

"That's true, but she's had seventeen years of experience and came highly recommended. The woman knows how to put a book together. She's not sending it to the publishing house like this. We'll go over everything first."

"Okay." He picked her up and she wrapped her legs around him. "Now, where were we?" he whispered and then kissed her.

She moaned and gave him a dreamy look. "On the way to the post office, darling."

He groaned but continued to nibble on her neck hoping to distract her.

And DeMaris was distracted—although not in the way Greg hoped. "Maybe I need to do more research . . ."

A few of the girls met in Chicago and were shopping.
"Viva," asked Jacyne, "have you ever seen Blanche again?"

Viva shook her head. "No, however, she has communicated with me through a lawyer, if you can believe. I'm to sell her apartment in Spokane and to check on the wooded property from time to time. Did you guys ever hear the full story as to why Denny Caldwell killed Owen?"

"I thought it was for money, which they didn't have."

Viva nodded. "Denny said that Owen kept telling him that his dad always hinted they had a lot of money hidden in a box and they had to be careful about spending it. I don't know . . . Maureen worked for me for years and always insinuated they didn't have much money. She said her husband was disabled, which was why he never left the house. That he was a recluse—De could have taken lessons from him.

"Anyway, Denny was given a key to their apartment, apparently they thought him trustworthy," Viva rolled her eyes. "So, whenever Owen and Blanche went out, Denny let himself in and searched the apartment. He never found the box. Eventually, he ran into Brian Fox; the two decided that Owen and Blanche wouldn't be smart enough to know Brian wasn't related, so Brian tried pawning himself off as a distant cousin. He did check out their bank statements and told Denny they had very little money.

"One day, Denny bumped into Maureen as she was going into the bank. He noticed she was carrying a big purse that was flat. When he observed her coming out of the bank, her purse was bulging. He suddenly thought of Sophocles always saying, 'Never lose this key' and realized that if Brian was telling the truth, then they must have money in a safe deposit box.

Denny had Brian check into it and they discovered at one time the Foxxes actually had five safe deposit boxes but were now down to only one."

"So, Denny decided to go after it, huh?" asked Shay.

"Yeah, he said he tried nicely to persuade Owen to tell him, but Owen always said he didn't know anything about a safe deposit box. I don't know if he lied to Denny or if he really didn't know. Remember, Maureen died unexpectedly. Who knows if she told her kids or not?

"Anyway, Denny and Owen got into an argument and he threatened Owen, which is when Blanche hit him in the stomach with a baseball bat. From there things got out of hand. Blanche left, Denny lost it, and Owen ended up dead. Of course, now Denny claims it was self-dense. The attorney told me that Blanche would be coming back to testify. That will be something, seeing her on the stand!"

"I can't imagine that anything she says will hold up in court—if she'll even talk," said Liset.

"Have you told DeMaris this?" asked Jacyne. "I can see her writing a book about it."

Viva shrugged her shoulders and then said hesitantly, "I think DeMaris knows where Blanche is."

"Why do you say that?" asked Shay.

"Just some of the things she's said. 'Oh, Blanche is fine. Don't worry about her. She's happy, let her be.' Stuff like that."

"Well, did you ask her to elaborate?"

"She just gives me a smile."

"What can Blanche possibly be living on?"

"According to De, she has a very nice person taking care of her. I am not to worry. Yeah, like hearing that from DeMaris is a comfort to me. Did DeMaris say how the honeymoon went?" asked Viva hoping to change the subject.

"Yeah, she loved Ireland," answered Shay. "Did she tell you why she eloped?"

"Yes. Research," said Liset.

Shay shook her head. "Sara will be glad to know that her character, Miss Pringle, is finally getting married."

"What?" asked Viva.

"Yeah, DeMaris has decided after talking to so many fans and not being able to come up with a logical explanation about why she's left her one character engaged for so long that Miss Pringle needs to get married. None of her wedding scenes were working so she mentioned to Greg that maybe she needed to find somebody who had eloped and ask them questions. Greg jumped on that! 'Why don't we elope and then you'll know firsthand?' So, for research for her book, she eloped."

"And now they are planning on spending a week at the circus," added Jacyne.

"Carnival," corrected Shay.

"She keeps going back and forth between calling it a carnival and a circus, I've noticed," volunteered Liset.

"Why would they go there?" asked Viva.

"For her new book. DeMaris said she knows the owners."

Epilogue 2 of 7

Hey, Kirk, how's it going?"

"Hey, Shay! I'm fine. How are things your way?"

"Oh, just like it always is. Listen, we've all been talking and . . . we have some questions."

She heard a disagreeable sound. "Not real sure I can help you girls. Depends on what it is," he said.

"Just questions about DeMaris." She couldn't imagine the problem.

"If they are about DeMaris Pala, I can probably answer but if they are about DeMaris Azaygo I can't."

"What do you mean you can't?"

"Divorce agreement."

Shay stood there for a second with the phone to her ear. "Okay. Do you have a neighbor named Sabrina D'azayga or something like that?"

"Yeah," he admitted, "well, she recently passed away."

"Oh, I'm sorry to hear that. Is she the lady I met one time? She was in a wheelchair?"

"Yeah, that's her. Had cancer."

"Were she and DeMaris close?"

"Yeah. DeMaris and I looked after Sabrina for the twenty some years we lived here. She was paralyzed from a car accident. Got a huge settlement. Plus she worked at home. Very independent but at the same time hated leaving the house. I think DeMaris related to her, since she always wanted to be a recluse. We'd get Sabrina her groceries, take her to appointments, stuff like that."

"Ya know, De told us that Sabrina was really DeMaris Azaygo." She waited. Nothing. "Is that true?"

"See, this is where I can't talk, Shay."

"We're not talking about DeMaris. We're talking about your neighbor, Sabrina."

"No dice. I lose everything by answering a question like that."

"What do you mean?" asked Shay.

"I don't know what DeMaris told you about our divorce settlement but I'll tell you. DeMaris was always the main breadwinner. She told me you all thought she'd lost out in the divorce and was destitute. We got a good laugh out of that. De loves this house and has, over the years, bought up any land near us that has become available on the market. She's not giving this place up. I am only here as the caretaker until she decides to move back. I settled for a very nice sum of money which is in a trust. If at any time the truth comes out about her, I will lose it all because I am the only one who knows the whole truth. And what I really won't give up are my vintage cars. They are in DeMaris's name since she bought them. I have nothing to gain by ever telling anyone what I know. Sorry, Shay."

"Well, hmm," Shay sighed. "What exactly did Sabrina do for a living?"

"She proofread and edited manuscripts and short stories."

Shay thought about this for a moment. "So, she either did that for DeMaris's books, wrote them herself from the stories De told her, or the two of them collaborated and used a combination of their names, right?" Silence. "Well, De got the idea for the last name from Sabrina, right?"

"Couldn't say," answered Kirk. Trying to change the subject, he said, "Hey, I've just read DeMaris's latest manuscript. Said she sent you each a copy. Have you girls read it yet? The Traveling Sorority Sisters taking a trip to Idaho. How much of that stuff actually happened? She told me it was pretty boring sitting out on the lake all day, shopping, eating out – she gained 5 pounds. She sat and wrote most days. Said she got the idea when Viva was showing off her parrot, African gray, whatever bird she has and how the papers were running an anniversary article about D.B. Cooper. How much of that book actually happened?"

"Oh, Kirk," Shay smiled. "You know sisters never tell."

Epilogue 3 of 7

"Excuse me, sir," DeMaris stopped the man in the studio hallway. "I'm DeMaris Azaygo and I understand you're high up in the FBI?"

The man stared down at her. Not a reader, her name meant nothing to him. "I am the deputy director."

"Great. Ah, mainly I just wanted to ask you a question about espionage."

He sighed. People thought what he did was glamorous. How many times had he sat on stakeouts for nothing? Sat behind a desk. "You know, we have a website. You could go there and probably find your answer." He tried to walk around her. He was to be interviewed on TV in an hour and needed to get ready.

"I tried that. It wasn't there and quite frankly, I didn't expect it to be. You're a spy or have been a spy, right? Well, you at least know spies—"

"Ma'am, I really can't help you. I need to get going."

"Well, I just need to know—can you tell me any good stories about having to use the bathroom when you're spying on people? Like in the middle of a shootout or a stakeout, just when something is going down? Something of that nature?"

He stopped. "I beg your pardon?"

"Beg your—oh, I haven't thought of that one! I need to add that to the list. Where's my voice recorder? Voice recorder? Ah, here it is." She pulled it out of her purse and spoke into it. "Beg your pardon. Okay, back to our bathroom problem—"

"I don't know what you're talking about."

"Have you or anybody you know suddenly had diarrhea just when you were handcuffing a terrorist? In a chase down the street? Anything like that? Any bathroom problem will do. Funny, sad, hair-raising . . . I can probably use it."

"You're not the person who will be interviewing me, are you?"

Epilogue 4 of 7

The two steadily made their way upstairs. The expensive, thick, carpeting masked their footfalls. Not finding the one thing they were looking for in the huge house they determined it would just be simpler to go to the source.

They entered the bedroom and finding the couple sleeping, gently woke the woman. She came to with a start, sensing someone standing over her. A gloved finger touched her lips, "Shhh, Mrs. Sumnerfeld. I'm sure you don't want to wake your husband. No need to really. We just want to talk to you." Liset glanced over to see another masked individual standing over Frank.

"She prefers her maiden name, Graysen," this one said. *Was that a woman's voice?* Liset couldn't be sure.

"We understand you have a purse—a Coach purse. We'd like it."

Liset's mind raced. How could they possibly get in here? She had set the alarm system herself.

"Just hand over the purse, Ms. Graysen," the person by Frank said quietly.

Only her sorority sisters thought she went by her maiden name. When Frank had gone into politics, they realized that having DeMaris as a friend was not an asset. Telling the police that she was Liset Graysen (when questioned) did not ring any bells. Liset Sumnerfeld did. Of course, by now the FBI and CIA knew both her names, but they were usually sympathetic.

How did these people get passed the security system? Only Frank, their children, and she knew the code. Even her mother-in-law who lived on the property didn't have access to it.

Oh, and her sisters knew.

"DeMarrrrrrrrrisssssss!"

Epilogue 6 of 7

"Honey, remember me telling you about the FBI guy, Joe Shaver? This is him. Hey, why didn't I think to ask you about bathroom problems? I bet you've got a couple of doozies! . . .

Joe? . . . Umm . . . I can explain."

Epilogue 7 of 7

"I'm doing research–"

THE END

"Please, Greg, she'll listen to you! Beg her to stop doing these stupid things that she always does!"

"Honestly, Liset, that's too long of a title. Hm, *Beg Her To Stop*? That's one I haven't written down . . . Where's my voice recorder?"